WHAT WE REMEMBER

what we remember

A NOVEL

MARIANNE DOUGHERTY

LUMINARE PRESS
WWW.LUMINAREPRESS.COM

Printed in the United States of America

Cover Photo: Tommy Kwak, Unsplash.com

Luminare Press
442 Charnelton St.
Eugene, OR 97401
www.luminarepress.com

LCCN: 2023909061
ISBN: 979-8-88679-281-2

In memory of Valerie, Ryan, Matthew and Cale

Come back. Even as a shadow, even as a dream.

—EURIPEDES

Chapter 1

———— • ————

1986

When her daughter Lily was only three, Alice nearly lost her. They had just eaten Sunday dinner with her parents and were on their way home. Alice's Plymouth Valiant was on its last legs, but there were leftovers in the backseat and Elton John on the radio: *Hold me closer tiny dancer.*

Slowing down as she approached a red light, Alice glanced over just before her daughter was sucked into the gathering darkness: airborne for a moment, fingers gripping the door handle, then gone. How long it took to come to a complete stop was anyone's guess. Later Alice remembered the car drifting listlessly, sluggish as sap oozing from a sugar maple. By the time Alice was out of the car, Lily was already running toward her.

A teenage boy watched them from the sidewalk where he was eating a slice of pizza. "Is she alright?"

"Yes," Alice assured him after a brief examination that revealed nothing, not even a scratch.

Lily looked up at her mother, eyes wide and blue as marbles.

"You're lucky there was no one behind you," he said, wiping his hands on his T-shirt.

Alice lifted Lily into her arms. "Yes, lucky."

Some years later when she read a story in *Redbook* about a woman whose toddler died after falling out of a car, Alice couldn't shake the feeling that life was a total crapshoot.

"I keep asking myself why my daughter lived and hers didn't," she told her friend Charlotte, who'd read the same story, and Charlotte had replied, cryptically, "The mystery of selection is tragic."

Now it was happening again. That phrase—*the mystery of selection is tragic*—ran through Alice's head on a loop after the hospital called. There had been an accident. Lily had been thrown clear of her boyfriend Frankie's Ford Maverick and was in serious condition. Frankie had been driving, but Charlotte's daughter Fern may also have been in the car. There was some confusion about that.

Alice's husband Bill had taken their son Noah to his first Phillies game and would not be back until late. So, she left him a note.

———•———

ALICE LEFT HER Mercedes under a no parking sign in front of the emergency room entrance. Let them tow it, she thought. Who cares?

Frankie's mother was slumped in a metal chair that was bolted to the floor, a string of rosary beads wrapped around her wrist like a bracelet.

"What happened?" asked Alice, who had known Theresa since their children were small. "Are they alright?"

She seemed baffled. "I don't know."

"Well, somebody has to," said Alice, pinballing off a row of chairs on her way to the front desk.

The admissions clerk was on the phone. "I'll be right with you," she said, placing one hand over the receiver.

"This is an emergency," said Alice, raising her voice just enough that people looked up from their magazines to stare at her.

A sliding glass door opened with a pneumatic whoosh. "Mrs. Lombardi?" called a doctor in scrubs and a white lab coat.

Theresa rushed over. "I'm Mrs. Lombardi," she said, though technically she hadn't been Mrs. Lombardi for some time since Frank left her when Frankie was twelve years old. "How's my son?"

"He has a broken leg and some contusions, but he'll be fine."

"Oh, thank God." Theresa fished a Kleenex out of her purse and pressed it to her eyes. "Can I see him?"

"I'll send someone out to get you when he's back from radiology. We may have to wait a day or two until the swelling goes down before we can set his leg."

Alice stepped forward. "My daughter, Lily Callahan. How is she?"

The doctor—his nametag said Gerald Meyer—smiled weakly. "You need to come with me."

Alice followed him into the treatment area where a policeman drinking coffee from a paper cup leaned against the wall. Dr. Meyer pulled him aside and glanced over at Alice. The officer nodded solemnly.

"Why don't we sit down," said Dr. Meyer, but Alice shook her head. "Just tell me what's going on."

He took a moment before answering. "I'm afraid your daughter has suffered a traumatic brain injury."

Alice's knees buckled slightly, and she braced herself against the wall. "Can I see her?"

"You may not recognize her," he said with a worried expression.

"Of course, I will."

"Your daughter was thrown through the windshield." He gave Alice a minute to absorb the news. "There are deep lacerations, some bone fractures."

"Just tell me where she is."

He nodded, and Alice followed him to the end of the hall. "We've put her on a respirator to assist breathing, but the next twenty-four to seventy-two hours are crucial," he said, placing a hand on her shoulder. "Right now, we're doing everything we can to make sure that she has enough oxygen and an adequate blood supply and that there is no further injury to the head or neck."

Alice took a few tentative steps toward the gurney. Stealing a glance at her daughter's face, she quickly turned away and let the ambient noise wash over her. Yards of plastic tubing snaked from a ventilator, its rhythmic thrum a mechanical whisper: *breathe in, breathe out.*

There was a chair in the corner, and Alice dragged it across the floor to sit at Lily's bedside. "Mommy's here," she whispered, squeezing her fingers. Chipped pink polish. A razor-thin scar on her thumb from three stitches administered in an emergency room much like this one when Lily was in fourth grade.

Later when a nurse came in to check Lily's vitals, Alice stepped into the hallway. Smoking was a bad habit she'd picked up in college where she had learned to French inhale. Like most of the English majors she knew, Alice left a cigarette smoldering in an ashtray near her typewriter while she worked. At the time it felt faintly bohemian. All her favorite female writers smoked: Virginia Wolff with a cigarette holder; Dorothy Parker, who favored Chesterfields; and Carson McCullers who, it was rumored, smoked three packs a day. Alice had quit smoking cold turkey three years ago, but now the familiar craving came back in a rush. There was something comforting about holding a cigarette between your fingers, striking a match and bringing it to the tip of the cigarette, drawing the smoke deep into your lungs before letting it slowly escape. She missed it sometimes: the spike in her heart rate, a brief hit of dopamine.

At the far end of the hall someone was shouting frantically, and Alice recognized that voice. It was Frankie calling for Lily. When Alice found him, he fixed her with a mournful look. At nineteen, Frankie had become almost brutally handsome. Alice had always thought that he'd lucked out, inheriting the best features of each of his parents: his mother's angular nose and his father's sleepy dark eyes and full lips. Now his right eye was nearly swollen shut. Alice imagined that he must be in a lot of pain.

He made a feeble attempt to sit up. "They won't tell me anything. Is she alright?" He began to cry before collapsing back onto the pillow.

Alice shook her head. "What happened, Frankie? You weren't drinking, were you?"

"No!"

"Don't lie to me."

"I'm not."

Alice was inclined to take him at his word, partly because Frankie was the antithesis of his father: straight as an arrow, thoughtful and kind, singular in his devotion to those he loved.

"It was that stupid dog."

"What dog?"

Frankie closed his eyes, remembering the collie charging into the street, Lily calling out, "Frankie, don't hit it," swerving sharply to the left before losing control of the car, the ringing sound on impact as he struck a utility pole. He figured that he must have blacked out for a while because the next thing he knew he was in an ambulance and an EMT was examining his right leg, which throbbed like a toothache, and he could taste blood in his mouth. A few other people—a doctor, a couple of policemen—asked if he'd been drinking, and he told them the same thing he just told Alice, but they drew blood anyway.

"Was Fern with you?"

Frankie nodded.

"Where is she?"

"I don't know." He swiped at his eyes with the back of his hand.

"I'll find out."

The admissions clerk was talking to one of the nurses, and Alice had to raise her voice to get her attention. "Fern Horvath. Where is she?"

"She's being questioned by two police officers," she said.

"So, she's not hurt?"

"No."

The news came as an affront to Alice, though she couldn't have explained why. "Has anyone called her parents?"

"I believe one of the officers did, but no one answered."

Theresa got to her feet. "Wait, Fern was with them?"

"Apparently," said Alice. "You call Charlotte. Keep trying until you get her."

Theresa seemed happy to have something to do and took off toward a bank of pay phones, while Alice went back inside to look for Fern.

A police officer emerged from a bay at the far end of the hallway, and Alice approached him. "I'm Alice Callahan. My daughter was in the car accident you're investigating, but her friend Fern Horvath was with her. Do you know where she is?"

The officer rubbed his chin with its day-old stubble. "We've been trying to reach her parents. Do you know where they are?"

"Not really. Is she okay?"

"She's fine, but that's probably because she was wearing a seatbelt."

"Are you saying that no one else was?"

The officer pulled Alice aside. "The driver was, but your daughter, Lily?" He shook his head. "We see this all the time. Kids think they're invincible."

Alice bristled at the suggestion that Lily was somehow responsible for what happened to her, that she was careless or irresponsible because she wasn't, or at least Alice had never seen that side of her. "So, can I see Fern?"

"She's pretty shook up." He shifted a wad of gum from one cheek to the other. "Okay, come with me."

Fern sat on an examining table, her slender legs dangling over the side, her narrow shoulders drawn together like the wings of a baby bird. There was blood on her sneakers. Whose, Alice wondered.

Fern hopped down and threw herself into Alice's arms when she saw her in the doorway.

Alice stroked her hair, which was fine as silk. "What happened?"

Fern used her sleeve to wipe her face, which was wet with tears. "This dog came out of nowhere—you know how Lily is about animals—and she's screaming at Frankie not to hit it. He must have panicked because all of a sudden, we were in the wrong lane and then he hit this pole by the side of the road. It all happened so fast, this horrible crunching noise and then Frankie was slumped over the steering wheel and I didn't know where Lily was." She wiped her face again. "I couldn't get my seatbelt off, and then someone was banging on the window, some man who saw everything from his front porch. He kept telling me to hang on, that I'd be alright. And then the ambulance came, and they took Frankie away, and I kept asking where Lily was, but no one would tell me anything." She took a few shallow breaths. "When they finally got me out of the car, I could see Lily just lying in the street, not moving or anything. This policeman tried to stop me, but I had to see if she was okay." Her expression was one of such despair that Alice turned away. "There was so much blood, blood everywhere."

When Fern glanced down at her feet, Alice knew whose blood was on her shoes.

She heard Kip's voice in the hallway. Fern heard it, too.

"Daddy," she cried in a small voice that reminded Alice of the little girl who had gone to grade school with Lily. There was a picture somewhere of the two of them in matching jumpers and knee socks, clutching their Partridge Family lunchboxes as they boarded the school bus.

Alice stepped into the hallway and motioned to Kip. "In here."

Charlotte, frightened and apprehensive, was right behind him.

Alice had always envied Charlotte, who had a charmed life as far as she was concerned: all that long blonde hair and perfect skin, happily married to her high school sweetheart, the two of them as handsome as the bride and groom on top of a wedding cake.

She had known a few girls like Charlotte when she was in high school, girls who got by on their good looks, while she had to work harder to get boys like Kip to notice her. When they didn't, she went after a different kind of boy, the ones who smoked Marlboros and let their hair grow long.

Her mother (everyone called her Babe) favored the classics: Chanel No. 5, a little black dress with a string of very good pearls and twinsets. With her miniskirts and textured tights, Alice had been a disappointment in that regard. By the time she went to college, Alice no longer cared what her mother liked. She dressed for herself, and when she'd saved enough money, she went to Vidal Sassoon and asked for a cropped helmet she could style with a simple shake of her head.

Babe had a different assessment when she met Charlotte for the first time. "That girl has secrets," she said. "Take it from me, still waters run deep."

Now Alice watched while Charlotte took her daughter into her arms, begrudging her that moment and wishing, spitefully, that they could exchange places.

Chapter 2

The Mercedes was exactly where Alice left it, a lucky break that might have registered on any other day, but this wasn't any other day. Both Charlotte and Theresa had offered to stay until they moved Lily to the ICU, but Alice had insisted that everyone go home. The truth was, Alice couldn't bear to look at them wearing their good fortune like a cloak of invisibility. *The mystery of selection is tragic.* Shut up, shut up, shut up, she wanted to scream.

There was a bar a few blocks away from the hospital, the kind of blue-collar dive with a pool table in back, beer on tap and a TV mounted to the wall in the corner. Alice parked in the gravel lot and went inside. She found an empty seat at the bar and ordered a Jack and Coke.

Someone was feeding quarters into the jukebox. *Now look at them yo-yo's that's the way you do it, you play the guitar on MTV.* The bartender pushed a rocks glass toward her with a head nod. The Jack, choked by the sugary cola, burned only slightly on the way down. Alice threw back the rest of her drink like an extra in a cheap western, held up her glass with a nod to the bartender and went to the bathroom.

Marianne Dougherty

A guy playing darts in a dark corner gave her the once-over. The stalls were covered with graffiti. *Gloria + Tony Forever. Brad Eats Pussy. Love Doesn't Last, Herpes Does.* Under the circumstances, Alice decided that the prudent thing would be to pee standing up.

Her drink was waiting when she got back. There was a pack of Marlboros on the bar that she assumed belonged to the guy sitting next to her, a Gregg Allman lookalike: same round face, long blonde hair, full lips. A pretty boy.

"Can I bum a cigarette?" she asked him.

He shook one out of the pack. "Need a light?"

Alice nodded and leaned in when he struck a match.

"What's your name?"

"Alice."

"Leon."

She smiled politely and looked around the room at the sad tableau: a few grizzled old men who had most likely worked in the mines when they were young, a middle-aged barfly flirting unsuccessfully with the bartender, a few rowdy regulars in Philadelphia Phillies T-shirts. What was she doing here? Oh, right, she reminded herself: trying to get as drunk as the rest of them.

When the nurses assured her that Lily was in good hands and that she should go home and get some rest, she almost laughed in their faces. *Seriously? Get some rest?* Alice doubted that she'd be able to fall asleep at all tonight unless she was knocked out cold. She might have ordered a white zinfandel if she were out to dinner with Bill, but tonight Alice wanted to get shit-faced as fast as possible, and that required the hard stuff.

She quickly gulped down half of her drink and took another drag on her cigarette, enjoying the familiar buzz as the nicotine coursed through her bloodstream and delivered a rush of dopamine to her brain.

The bartender emptied a metal ashtray and made a pass over the dinged-up wooden bar top with a dirty rag. "You lose much on today's game?" he asked Leon.

"Fucking Pirates." He shook his head in disgust.

"I keep forgetting that you grew up in Pittsburgh."

Alice drained her glass and asked for another.

Leon raised a cautionary eyebrow. "Maybe you should slow down."

She put her cigarette out and lit another one. "I'm a big girl."

"Have it your way," he said, raising his hands in surrender.

The bartender produced a fresh drink, and Leon ordered another Iron City.

Alice hunched over her glass and wished she could pray with the same fervor that Theresa demonstrated while saying the rosary. Maybe if she could, Lily wouldn't be in the ICU. Taking a gulp of her drink, she hoped that Theresa had enough faith for both of them.

Leon glanced at Alice. "You live around here?"

"No."

"Slumming it?"

She let an ash fall to the floor.

"You're not like most chicks, talking nonstop about yourself, are you?" He withdrew the cigarette from her fingers and took a few puffs before handing it back.

Two guys in trucker caps sang along with Bruce Springsteen. *Working on the highway, laying down the blacktop.*

"So, what's your story, Alice?" Leon asked.

"You don't want to hear my story."

"Maybe I do."

"No. You don't."

He took a swig of beer. "If you say so."

The bartender turned up the volume on the TV. Footage shot earlier that day flickered across the screen: Frankie's Ford Maverick, the front end crushed like an empty can in a giant's fist. The local newscaster, a minor celebrity, provided the few details he had. "Three teens," Alice heard him say before looking away.

She drained her glass and pushed a twenty toward the bartender.

"I'll get you some change."

"Keep it," Alice told him, sliding off the barstool.

"You leaving?" asked Leon.

"Thanks for the cigarettes," she told him.

"Maybe I should walk you out to your car."

"Like I said—"

"Yeah, yeah, I know. You're a big girl." He tossed a few crumpled bills on the bar and followed Alice outside anyway.

She stood on the sidewalk trying to remember where she parked.

"Are you okay?" he asked her.

"Uh-huh."

"Where's your car?"

Alice had grown very quiet.

"You in the parking lot?"

She slapped her forehead with the palm of her hand. "Oh, right."

"Nice ride," he said when he saw the Mercedes, a cream-colored 380 SEL with leather seats. "It looks like you got lost and ended up in the wrong neighborhood."

Alice dropped her car keys, and Leon stooped to retrieve them.

"So, are you lost, Little Red Riding Hood?" His voice was low and husky.

Alice made a swipe at the keys.

"You lost?" he repeated, backing her up against the car door.

"No," said Alice, lifting her chin defiantly.

He pocketed Alice's keys, and when he kissed her, she let him. Then she was kissing him back, greedily, ravenous in a way that she had never been with her own husband. Now he was cupping her breasts under her thin T-shirt, and when he walked his fingers up her ribcage and slipped his thumb inside her lacy bra, she arched her back, closing her eyes and letting herself drift. *Go on, do whatever you want to me. I could care less.*

The die-hard Phillies fans staggered into the parking lot, pushing and shoving each other. One of them tripped and nearly fell, which made the other two double over with laughter.

"I live in the neighborhood," Leon whispered. "Why don't you follow me. My car's right over there." He handed Alice her keys.

She watched him get into a beat-up Chevelle with rusted-out rocker panels and followed him out of the parking lot. When he made a rolling stop at the corner and turned right, Alice lingered at the stop sign longer than necessary. He slowed down, waiting for her to catch up, but on impulse she made a sharp left turn and took the first exit onto the highway.

When she got home, she locked herself in the powder room. Holding a hand towel under the faucet until the water got good and hot, she dragged it across her face, over her breasts, up and down her arms like a mad Lady Macbeth.

Then she removed her clothes, every last stitch, and tossed them into the washer, pouring enough Tide into the tub to wash three loads of laundry before closing the lid.

In Lily's chest of drawers, she found a T-shirt and a pair of bikini briefs and put them on. Light from a streetlamp bathed the room in a warm glow. The unmade bed was a nest of tangled sheets and clothes tossed carelessly aside. Alice pressed her face into Lily's pillow with its lingering scent of Love's Baby Soft.

On the nightstand, a tube of Dr Pepper Lip Smacker, a stack of brightly colored jelly bracelets and a dog-eared paperback by Judy Blume. Alice picked it up: *Tiger Eyes*. She had given this book to Lily when she was struggling to comprehend a friend's senseless death two years ago. The girl in the book, Davey Wexler, had lost her father, but Alice had decided that death was indiscriminate. Father, friend, daughter, husband: mere details; grief was universal.

When she finally climbed into bed, Bill rolled over. She knew he'd be awake in that kind of half-sleep that she often slipped into whenever Lily was out past her curfew.

"Why didn't you call me?" he said in a tone that was less angry than hurt. "I've been worried sick."

"Sorry."

Neither of them said anything for a few moments, corpses laid out for a viewing except that both of them were taking slow, steady breaths. Finally, he asked, "What happened? Is she okay?"

Alice didn't feel like rehashing the details. She just wanted to go to sleep before she sobered up and wouldn't be able to close her eyes without seeing Lily's mangled face.

"Well?" said Bill, sitting up and leaning against the headboard.

"It's bad."

"How bad?"

Alice glanced at her husband, whose features swam into focus in the moonlight pouring in through the sheer curtains at the window: the strong jaw and hooded eyes, a day's worth of stubble on his chin, the kind of looks that relegated an actor to the role of best friend, not leading man. "She's on life support."

He reached for the lamp on the bedside table.

"Don't," she cried sharply.

He shifted his weight and lay back on the pillow. "Who was driving?"

"Frankie."

"Was he drinking?"

"No. It was an accident."

When he slipped one arm around her waist, Alice felt herself stiffen, but she wasn't heartless enough to push him away.

"Your hair smells like an ashtray," he said. "Have you been smoking?"

"So what?" The words were a kind of dare.

He turned away from her, taking half the sheet with him. "I don't know what you want from me, Alice. I love her, too."

"I know," she whispered, wishing she could bridge the gap between them, this deep ravine of dissatisfaction and resentment she had been nursing for years. Now she suspected that Lily's death, if it came to that, was the dark abyss that would swallow up what was left of their marriage.

Chapter 3

A lice met Bill in 1973 at the brokerage firm in Chicago where she worked as a secretary. When he proposed, they had been dating for less than six months, but he had been offered a job in his hometown and wanted Alice and Lily to come with him. Promising a bigger house in a better neighborhood than anything they could afford in Chicago, he finally won Alice over. After a brief honeymoon in the Bahamas, Alice flew to Chicago for Lily, who was staying with her parents.

Babe insisted on driving them to the airport the day they left. Reluctantly, Lily had agreed to wear a plaid cotton dress that Babe picked out at Marshall Field's, but she was complaining that her new Mary Janes were giving her blisters.

Babe kept a stash of Necco Wafers in her handbag. Hoping to distract her granddaughter, she offered one to Lily, who carefully examined the roll before making her selection. "Chocolate."

When it came time to board, Babe's eyes welled with tears, which she brushed away.

"Don't mind me," she told Alice, pulling her into a warm embrace.

Lily asked for another Necco Wafer, "but not that yukky licorice one," and Babe gave her the whole pack before leaning down to squeeze each of Lily's plump cheeks. "Be a good girl now, promise?"

Lily wrapped her arms around Babe's waist. "I'll miss you, Grandma," she whimpered, and Alice worried that she had made a huge mistake agreeing to move so far away from everyone she loved.

Now Babe held Lily at arm's length. "It's going to be alright, sweetheart. You're going to live in a great big house and make lots of new friends, and Grandpa and I will come visit."

"Okay," said Lily with a deep, shuddery breath.

Alice showed her tickets to the gate agent. Excited yet also apprehensive, she glanced over her shoulder before disappearing down the jet way.

The flight took less than two hours, but when they landed Alice felt as if she'd crossed a great ocean and, like Gulliver, been blown off course. The flight attendant lowered a set of steps, which had been built into the side of the plane, and Alice lifted Lily into her arms and carried her down the stairs and across the tarmac to enter the terminal where Bill was waiting for them. At least O'Hare had a jet way, she thought, staring glumly out the window as Bill drove them to the hotel that Merrill Lynch was paying for while they looked for a place of their own.

When Bill told her that he'd grown up near the Poconos, she had imagined lush greenery and rolling mountains, dense forests that burst into color each fall. What she had not envisioned was a place that had been mining anthracite coal for centuries and had never recovered after production declined. The sky was overcast that day, saturating everything with an ashen hue. Decapitated by strip-mining, the surrounding mountain ranges resembled a barren moonscape. Experiencing something close to regret, Alice wondered how she could have agreed to leave Chicago with its iconic skyline, the Navy Pier overlooking Lake Michigan, the collection of bonsais at the Botanic Garden.

When she was a child there had been excursions with her father to see the Cubs play at Wrigley Field and stops for thin slices of greasy pizza on the way home. As a teenager she had seen the Joffrey Ballet dance *Swan Lake* and Sir Georg Solti conduct Mahler at Orchestra Hall. Then, while in college, she'd spent long afternoons at the Art Institute of Chicago with its impressive collection of late nineteenth-century French art. Claude Monet's light-filled Impressionist masterpieces were her favorites, especially one of the Gare Saint-Lazare Train Station in Paris. Staring at that painting, she had imagined stepping inside and boarding a train for Calais where she might see the White Cliffs of Dover from the shore. Now she was married to a man who had no desire to travel any farther than Atlantic City.

Alice could probably pinpoint the exact moment of Noah's conception: a Sunday morning in late August. They'd been married less than a year, but Bill was eager to start a family. Lily had stayed with Bill's parents the night before, and it would be a few more hours before they'd bring her home.

Alice could tell by the way the box fan in the window was laboring to move the sticky air around that it was going to be another scorcher. Sometime during the night they'd become tangled in the top sheet. When Alice kicked it to the bottom of the bed, Bill reached for her, and she moved into the curve of his arm. Despite the oppressive heat, they took their time. Finally, he straddled her, his breath warm against her neck. "Let's make a baby."

———◦———

THAT SEPTEMBER WHEN Lily started first grade, Alice found a job as a copywriter at a local radio station. When she met Colin Maguire, a deejay who played soft rock hits like "Please Come to Boston" and "The Air That I Breathe" from 10 a.m. to 2 p.m., she knew that she'd made a mess of things, marrying the wrong man and then meeting the right one at the wrong time.

Alice's job required her to write ad copy for their sponsors, like Gable's Department Store and Littman's Jewelers, and she spent part of each afternoon in the recording booth with Colin, who did the voiceovers. Trapped in marriages that, if not exactly loveless, were at least unsatisfying, their attraction was immediate and mutual.

Colin and his wife were seeing a marriage counselor. "Okay, it's actually our priest, but we couldn't afford a real therapist," he told Alice over a late lunch in the break room.

"Is it helping?" she asked, carefully unwrapping a turkey sandwich she'd made that morning.

"I don't think so." He gazed longingly in her direction.

Alice swallowed hard and scooted her chair over, closing the space between them.

"I've got two kids," he told her. "That's the problem."

Alice nodded knowingly, taking a bite of her sandwich.

For the next couple of months, she and Colin did nothing more than exchange heartsick looks in the studio or as they passed in the hallway. Then one afternoon he asked Alice to meet him in the van the station used for live remote broadcasts. There was a thin layer of frost on the windshield, but Alice could see Colin sitting behind the steering wheel. He cracked the window. "Get in, it's freezing out there." Alice climbed into the van and pulled the heavy door shut behind her.

Colin had the heat on full blast, and his sandy hair fluttered in a stream of warm air. When he glanced over at her, shy and unsure of himself, a range of conflicting emotions washed over Alice, who had missed her period the month before. She knew that even being there in that van with Colin was playing with fire, but now that her feelings were out in the open, she couldn't just take them back like shoving a genie into the bottle once it popped out, looked around and decided that it wanted to stay.

When he leaned across the seat to kiss her, Alice brought her hands up to cover her face. "I think I might be pregnant."

"Oh."

Alice didn't think she'd ever heard a sound so woeful or filled with regret. "I wish I'd met you first," she said through splayed fingers.

Now he was covering her mouth with kisses so desperate, so frantic that she was certain they'd leave bruises. When he snaked one hand under her sweater, his fingers cold as ice against her warm skin, she didn't push him away, but she knew they'd crossed some line and that now she had a secret she'd have to keep from Bill.

Telling Colin about the baby seemed to heighten the sense of impending doom, rendering them star-crossed lovers: Vronsky and Anna, Heathcliff and Catherine, Orpheus and Eurydice. Thanksgiving was nearly unbearable for Alice:

four whole days without seeing Colin. Bill's mother made turkey with all the trimmings, but Alice was distracted all day and picked at her food.

"Is something wrong, dear?" asked her mother-in-law while they were washing dishes.

Alice shook her head and carried a stack of Betty's good china to the dining room. Bill and his father were watching football, and every now and then they'd raise their voices, shouting at the TV after someone fumbled the ball or missed a field goal. Alice wondered why she couldn't be happy with the life she had. Bill was a good person, and his parents were fond of Lily.

When she brought Bill home to meet her parents, she could almost hear their collective sigh of relief. Finally, their daughter had made a sensible decision and found someone who would be a good provider and not shirk his responsibilities the way Lily's father had done, and they had been right. What more did she want?

That Monday she walked purposefully toward Colin's studio, having decided to put a stop to whatever this was before it was too late. She and Bill were having a baby, which meant that she and Colin had no future together.

"That was 'Walk on By' by Dionne Warwick," said Colin in his deep and seductive radio voice, and Alice wondered if it was an omen: *I just can't get over losing you.* She watched him spin his chair around and drop the needle on another record. When he saw Alice through the plate glass window, he waved her in.

"Hey, girl," he said, removing his headphones. "I missed you." When he kissed the back of her neck, her steely resolve to do the right thing began to crumble, and she lost her nerve.

Colin selected another album from the rolling cart and slipped it out of its protective sleeve. Replacing his headphones, he cued up the track he wanted and leaned into the microphone. "We've got a little Bill Withers for you this morning."

"I played that one for you," he told Alice, who closed her eyes and let the words wash over her: *Ain't no sunshine when you're gone.*

That afternoon she went home and made dinner like she always did, but she felt disconnected as if she was hovering near the ceiling, watching with indifference as she set the table, passed a plate of fried chicken to Lily, exchanged small talk with Bill. After loading the dishwasher, she climbed the stairs to draw a bath for her daughter. That night Lily asked for two stories, and Alice complied before going downstairs to sit on the couch next to Bill like a good wife while he watched *The Rockford Files.*

Impulsively, she pushed herself up from the sofa. "I just remembered that we're out of milk." That was a lie, though not the first she'd told him.

"Okay."

She grabbed her coat from the closet. "Be right back."

He glanced up from the television. "Pick up some Doritos while you're out."

Alice called Colin from a pay phone in front of the 7-Eleven. She decided that if his wife answered she'd hang up, but it was Colin who picked up on the first ring.

Her sense of relief was palpable. "Thank God," she said. "I wasn't sure you'd answer, but I've been thinking about what we should do, and it's so obvious that I can't believe we didn't think of it before."

"Whoa, slow down."

"We should run away together. Why not? We can make it work. We'll take Lily with us and raise this baby together." Listening to herself, her words colliding at breakneck speed like cars in a freeway pileup, she knew how ridiculous she sounded.

"Alice, what's going on?"

"I can't be with him anymore," she said, her voice barely a whisper.

There was background noise—children squabbling over something, then someone (his wife?) calling, "Who's on the phone?"

"No one," he hollered, and Alice felt deflated, like this had been a bad idea. She could tell that he'd placed his hand over the receiver to muffle the sound. "Can we talk about this tomorrow?"

Alice knew she'd lose her nerve once she hung up. "Tomorrow will be too late," she said, hesitating for a few moments before gently replacing the receiver in its metal cradle.

Colin was on a remote at the opening of a new Ford dealership the next morning when Alice turned in her resignation, making some excuse about her doctor recommending complete bed rest for the next couple of months. By lunchtime she'd cleaned out her desk and gone home. Noah was born in June and Alice resigned herself, for better or worse, to the life she'd chosen.

Chapter 4

The phone was ringing from somewhere deep within the house. *Lily.* Heart pounding, Alice sat stock-still on the edge of the mattress, holding her breath. Someone picked up on the third ring. Her head was throbbing, but when she closed her eyes images of Lily's shattered face bloomed behind her eyelids like bloodroot, foxglove, larkspur, each poisonous enough to induce seizures.

Bill hovered in the doorway. "You're awake?" He looked surprised.

Alice seemed puzzled at first, but then she remembered drinking too much and chain-smoking cigarettes that belonged to some guy with long hair sitting next to her. Letting him kiss her in the parking lot. His hands all over her.

Lily had an Etch A Sketch when she was little. One twist of the knobs on front of the red plastic frame and the pictures on the screen disappeared. Now Alice wished that the unpleasant memories taking root inside her head were so easily erased.

Bill crossed the room to sit next to her. "The hospital just called. She's stable."

"Thank God," said Alice.

"Noah wants to go to the hospital with us."

"He's too young. They're not going to let him in the ICU."

"We can't leave him here, and I'm going with you," he said in a tone of voice that told her to leave it alone. "I'll sit with him in the waiting room while you're in with Lily, and then we'll switch places."

"I have to get a shower," said Alice, who went into the bathroom and closed the door behind her.

When she came downstairs, Bill was in the kitchen with Noah, who was eating a bowl of soup. "Did Daddy dress you today?" she asked him.

He gave his head a wet-dog shake.

"Where'd you find this?" She tugged at the hem of his T-shirt. "It's way too small for you."

Noah recoiled reflexively, crossing his slender arms over his chest where a happy dolphin leaped over the words *Cape May New Jersey*.

Of course, thought Alice. Lily bought him that shirt on the last day of their vacation three years ago. She put her arm around Noah's shoulder, the bones as delicate as a baby wren's. "Finish your lunch," she said, "and then we'll go."

At the hospital Noah slipped his hand into Alice's as the elevator made its slow ascent, and she was struck by the impact that Lily's death, if it came to that, would have on her family.

A nurse wearing scrubs, her hair in a French braid, escorted Alice to the ICU. When she was in high school, Alice had been in awe of the nurses who worked at the hospital where she volunteered as a candy striper. In their starched white uniforms and sensible shoes, hair tucked under crisp white caps, they took care of business with practiced efficiency, locating a pulse on a patient's wrist and counting the beats per minute, shaking a thermometer to lower the mercury level after taking a temperature. Alice knew that it had been a long time since nurses were subjected to such rigid dress codes, but she hoped that this nurse was as serious about her job as those nurses had been about theirs.

Lying in repose as it were, Lily reminded Alice of a princess who had been put under a spell in some ancient fairytale. "I'm right here, sweetie," she said, leaning over the bedrail and forcing herself to look at her daughter's disfigured face. Dragging a chair closer to Lily's bed, she remembered something her father used to say: *There are no atheists in fox holes.* Apparently, there were no atheists in the ICU either, she thought, praying for a miracle even if it felt like she was just going through the motions.

The nurse poked her head into the room. "Your husband wants to know if he can see your daughter now?"

Alice nodded and followed her into the waiting room where Bill was reading *Highlights* magazine to Noah. Watching them for a few moments, she willed her heart to open like a rusty gate after someone gave it a good shove.

"Your turn," she said with a slight shake of her head. "Don't expect—" Her voice trailed off.

"I just want her to know I'm here," said Bill, setting the magazine aside.

Alice sat next to her son, who leaned against her shoulder. "I asked God to make Lily better," he said. "Grandma says that if we pray hard enough, God answers our prayers."

Alice sighed. She knew Bill's mother meant no harm, but she wished she wouldn't fill Noah's head with faith-based nonsense that was bound to induce crippling guilt if it didn't work. Years ago, Theresa had explained prayer like this to Alice: "You know that praying isn't like placing an order at a restaurant and expecting the waiter to deliver exactly what you asked for?"

"Then why pray at all?" Alice had asked, and Theresa, clearly frustrated, had replied, "Because it allows us to establish a deeper relationship with God."

Now Alice wondered if God, as she had often assumed, simply did not exist, and again she heard Theresa's voice, clear and resolute: "Just because God is silent doesn't mean he's absent."

Frankie hobbled into the waiting area on crutches, Theresa following close behind. Alice knew none of this was Theresa's fault, but she also resented her because her son was going home while Lily remained here in a state of perpetual limbo.

Bill emerged from the ICU with a doctor Alice didn't recognize. "May I?" asked the doctor, indicating a vacant chair, and Alice nodded.

"Come on, buddy, let's get something to drink," said Bill.

Dr. Greenfield introduced himself as Lily's neurologist and took a seat. "So, your daughter is in a coma, which means that her brain is functioning at the lowest level of alertness. Right now, we're doing everything we can to relieve pressure on the brain." He placed a hand on her shoulder in a kindly gesture. "What you've got to understand is that in cases like this, the brain can swell or bleed, pushing fluid up against the skull. The swelling can actually cause the brain to push down on the brain stem, which can damage the part of the brain responsible for arousal and awareness."

"She'll wake up though, won't she?" asked Alice.

"There's no way to know for sure," he said. "Typically, a coma doesn't last more than a few days, a couple of weeks at the most." He removed his glasses. "I'll be honest with you," he said, massaging the deep crease between his eyes. "If we haven't seen any signs of improvement in the next couple of days, Lily's chances of making a moderate or good recovery are slim."

"How slim?"

"Less than ten percent." He gave her a minute. "I know this is a lot to take in."

"I can't lose her," said Alice.

"I understand."

"Do you?" It was a fair question.

"The young man who was driving—" He gestured toward Frankie, who was sitting next to Theresa. "He'd like to see your daughter if that's alright with you."

A slight nod from Alice and Dr. Greenfield motioned for Frankie to join them. In the unforgiving fluorescent lighting, he looked a sight, his beautiful face battered and bruised.

Alice felt obligated to tell him that he might not recognize Lily, but he told her he didn't care and followed her down the hall. Frankie let his crutches clatter to the floor and hopped on one foot to the bed where Lily lay sleeping, Princess Aurora awaiting true love's kiss. He looked at Alice as if asking for permission before leaning over the bedrail, but she turned away when he began to weep. The sound, so raw and filled with anguish, was unsettling.

"What did I do?" he moaned, wiping his face with his T-shirt.

"It's not your fault," Alice said because she knew that Lily would tell him the same thing if she could.

He turned toward Alice and took one of her hands in his as if grateful for her show of support. His fingers were surprisingly warm despite the fact that the ICU was as cold as a meat locker. His left eye was still swollen shut, and Alice wondered if it hurt when he cried, all those bottled-up tears with nowhere to go.

Over the PA, a voice announced that visiting hours were over.

Frankie wiped his face again and leaned over Lily's bed. "You are the only girl I'll ever love," he whispered, bringing her hand up to rest against his cheek.

If either of them had expected a fairytale ending, Lily's eyelids fluttering in response to Frankie's outpouring of emotion, they were disappointed. There was only the ventilator's jarring cacophony, the intermittent beep-beep of the heart monitor.

Alice retrieved Frankie's crutches. "We should probably go."

Reluctantly, Frankie placed a crutch under each arm and took a few halting steps before glancing over his shoulder with a despondent expression.

"Here, let me," said Alice when he struggled to open the door. "Can you imagine what Lily would say if she could see you now?"

"She'd probably tell me I look like Quasimodo," he said, white-knuckling the grips on each crutch as he dragged himself down the hallway.

"Frankie," called Alice, and he turned around, nearly losing his balance in the process. He narrowed his one good eye as if to bring her into focus.

She wanted to tell him how grateful she was that he was the first boy to love her daughter because he'd provided a blueprint for every other relationship she'd ever have, but the words caught in her throat so all she said was, "Never mind."

In the waiting room, Noah was stuffing himself with junk food from the vending machine.

Exhausted, Frankie collapsed into a chair. Theresa closed the magazine she was reading. "Are you in pain?"

Frankie shrugged, and Alice could tell that he was somewhere else.

"We should all go home," Bill suggested, gathering up empty soda cans and candy wrappers and depositing them in the trash.

Noah was rhythmically kicking the back of his chair, and when Bill told him to stop, he shook his head. Alice had been watching them dispassionately as if sensing a disturbance in the Force. Lily loved *Star Wars* and had spent hours discussing its mythology with Alice, who had asked if the Force was God.

"It's bigger than that," she said. "Think of it as a vast energy field that connects every living thing, and when some catastrophe or other traumatic event occurs, the Jedi sense a weakness in the fabric of the Force."

They rode home in complete silence, Bill's hands in a death grip on the steering wheel. Alice stared out the window, worried that Lily's accident was the traumatic event that was already shifting the energy between her and Bill and that what she'd done outside that bar last night was a distress flair fired from a ship lost at sea.

Chapter 5

Alice was reading to Lily. *The Wind in the Willows* had been her favorite book when she was a little girl, and the chapter she liked best was *The Piper at the Gates of Dawn*. Alice remembered how astonished Lily had been to discover a Pink Floyd album with the same name in a box of records that had been boxed up and stored in the garage.

"You know that God is the piper, don't you?" she'd asked Alice. "At the very least, he's some divine force."

Now, since that chapter with its range of emotions had resonated with her daughter, that's where Alice began. "The Willow-Wren was twittering his thin little song, hidden himself in the dark selvedge of the river bank."

A young nurse came in to check Lily's catheter. "I'll get out of your way," said Alice, marking her page.

When she stepped into the hall, Dr. Greenfield took her aside. "We need to talk."

From his grave expression, Alice was certain that nothing good was going to come of their conversation.

"So, we conducted an assessment of brain stem reflexes on your daughter this morning," he said, "and I'm afraid that the results have not been promising."

The words floated in the ether like a bad omen. "What does that mean exactly?" said Alice, who felt like she did in algebra class when asked to prove a difficult equation.

"We're looking for some response to external stimuli that tells us that Lily's brain is functioning," he explained, "but her pupils aren't responding to light and her eyes don't blink when the surface is touched." Sensing her confusion, he told her, "Let's not make any assumptions about Lily's condition just yet. We'll repeat the tests in the morning, and then I'll confer with my colleagues."

Now he was being paged. "Wait," said Alice, who was hesitant to let him go before she got some answers. "I want to know what you think."

"Let's see how things are tomorrow," he said with a benign smile.

Alice watched him walk to the end of the hall before letting herself into Lily's room. Seeing her daughter like this was discomfiting. Lily had been born with a kind of nervous energy, refusing to nap for fear of missing something, tapping her foot in church until Alice threw her a warning look, racing through the neighborhood on her banana bike with its ape-hanger handlebars. This relentless stillness seemed out of character.

When Lily was a little girl, Alice had insisted that she hold her hand while they walked to the playground, but she always raced ahead when she saw the jungle gym. Scaling the metal structure, she'd hang upside down from the top bar, pigtails airborne. Frankie called her fearless, and maybe he was right. Lily had signed up for trapeze classes at summer camp when she was twelve, and she and Frankie had gone skydiving last summer, though Alice only found out about that after the fact. Now she wondered if Lily would remember any of it when she woke up. Alice refused to use the word *if* when discussing Lily's condition. There was no *if*, only when.

The book was on the nightstand where she'd left it, and Alice removed the bookmark (a thoroughbred in full gallop) to read a few more pages. Mole and Rat had been rowing all night in search of the baby otter, and now Mole felt a great awe descending upon him. Trembling, he dared to look into the kindly eyes of the great god Pan. Alice glanced at Lily as if expecting her to clap her hands like she used to when the baby otter was discovered sleeping peacefully between Pan's hooves.

Finding her place again, she continued. "All this he saw, for one moment breathless and intense, vivid on the morning sky, and still, as he looked, he lived, and still, as he lived, he wondered."

Alice had hoped that the passage, which had always brought Lily to tears, might elicit some reaction, but there was only the mechanical heartbeat of the ventilator.

It was nearly five o'clock. "I'm going to call Daddy," she told Lily out of habit more than anything.

There was a pay phone at the end of the hall, and Bill answered just as she was about to hang up. "You sound out of breath."

"I just finished mowing the lawn."

"Jesus, Bill, who cares about the grass when our daughter is on life support?"

"It keeps me busy," he said. "Otherwise, all I'll do is worry."

"I know, I'm sorry." She softened her voice. "Can you put Noah on?"

"Theresa said he's been in the pool all afternoon with Tina and he's having a good time. I'll pick him up in a little while. I think he wants spaghetti for dinner. I'm no Chef Boyardee, but I can—"

She cut him off. "Don't wait for me. I'll get something to eat here."

"Alice, what's going on?" His voice was gentle now.

"The doctor doesn't think Lily's going to come out of her coma," she said, her voice breaking.

"Is that what he told you?"

"He said she isn't responding to any of their tests."

"I doubt that he knows anything for sure right now. It's only been a couple of days," he said, and Alice felt the knot in her stomach begin to unravel. Her father had always been able to assuage her deepest fears—of the dark, of losing one or both of her parents, of raising Lily by herself—and she was happy to allow Bill to assume that role now.

She took the elevator downstairs to the cafeteria and had a bowl of tomato soup. Her mother used to doctor it up with noodles that had been cut into the letters of the alphabet, challenging Alice to find her name when she was just starting to read. She'd done the same thing with Lily when she came to visit every summer.

Pocketing a few packets of oyster crackers for later, Alice took the elevator up to the fifth floor where she saw Nina at the nurse's station. They hadn't seen each other since Nina moved to Virginia a year ago, and now here she was as if Alice had conjured her up just when she needed her.

Alice had just moved to Canterbury Commons when she met Nina for the first time at Cookie Shapiro's house. The streets were named for characters in *The Canterbury Tales* and Cookie, who lived on Franklin Street, was a member of Welcome Wagon. When she dropped off a book of coupons for discounts at local businesses, she asked Alice if she played bridge.

"I haven't played for a while, but I think I remember how." Alice had learned the game from her mother, who found it more intellectually stimulating than pinochle or hearts because players could finesse a trick, essentially outfoxing their opponent and gaining the advantage with low-ranking cards.

"You're a life saver," said Cookie, who was hosting bridge club at her house that month and needed a fourth for one of her tables.

Before the game got underway, Cookie pointed out the refreshments: cheese balls rolled in walnuts and bowls of Chex Party Mix. Showing Alice to a table where three other women were already seated, she shooed her purebred Himalayan off the chair, releasing puffs of white fur into the atmosphere.

"This is Alice," she said. "She just moved here from Chicago so let's make her feel at home."

Theresa, who was shuffling a deck of cards with the agility of a Vegas blackjack dealer, said a quick hello. Alice was fascinated by her eyebrows, which were heavily penciled in as if she'd plucked them to within an inch of their life and immediately regretted her decision. Nina reminded her of one of the Breck girls whose cocoa-colored pageboys and expressive brown eyes represented the prevailing notion of feminine beauty and purity when she was growing up.

"You'll be my partner," said Charlotte, who appeared to wear no makeup at all except for mascara and lip-gloss, radiating a kind of effortless beauty that Alice presumed she took for granted.

Now Cookie was passing a plate of stuffed mushrooms.

Just to be polite, Alice took one, which she placed on a cocktail napkin.

"Anyone else?" Cookie glanced at Theresa, who seemed conflicted. "Going once, going twice."

"Still trying to lose the baby weight?" asked Charlotte with a sympathetic glance in Theresa's direction.

"The last ten pounds are taking forever."

"Theresa had a baby girl about six months ago," said Charlotte, selecting a cashew from a cut-glass bowl.

"I have a little boy, too," said Theresa. "He's six."

"Theresa calls Frankie her miracle child," said Nina, glancing at Alice over the fan of cards in her hand.

"Well, he is," said Theresa defensively. "How else do you explain the fact that I only got pregnant after Frank and I went to Rome and received a blessing from the Pope?"

Alice could think of a lot of reasons why that might happen, coincidence the most obvious, but she decided to keep them to herself.

After they'd played a couple of rounds, Cookie announced that dessert was being served. Alice lifted a glass dome and helped herself to a piece of red velvet cake, which she carried to the dining room table.

Nina gestured to an empty chair next to hers. "Do you miss Chicago?" she asked, dropping a sugar cube into her coffee and waiting for it to dissolve.

"Sometimes," said Alice, hedging her bets. After all, she had to live here.

"I'm from Virginia so—" They exchanged knowing looks.

"Cookie mentioned that you have twins," said Alice. "They must be a handful."

"Harper and Hayley are a year old," said Nina, "but I have a daughter Grace from my first marriage."

"We have something in common then."

Nina gave her a quizzical look.

"I was married before, too. Big mistake, but I had Lily so—" Alice shrugged. "I guess it all works out." She took a bite of cake. "Lily's father left us when she was a year old so she has no memory of him."

"Ethan never even got to meet his daughter," said Nina. "He was killed in Vietnam when Grace was only a few months old."

"I'm so sorry," said Alice. "That must have been awful for you."

"It was," said Nina with a rueful smile.

Cookie placed a tray of Mexican wedding cookies on the table. "You two look thick as thieves."

"Hmm," said Nina, her smile elusive now.

Alice took a cookie, leaving a trail of powdered sugar in her wake. "So, does Charlotte have any children?"

"A daughter, Fern."

"Like the little girl in *Charlotte's Web*?"

"It was her favorite book growing up."

"There you are," said Theresa, who had been looking for Alice. "I have something for you." She removed a dog-eared paperback from her handbag: *The Flame and the Flower*. "I borrowed this from Cookie, but I'm sure she wouldn't mind if you read it."

Alice examined the lush, glossy cover art, a woman in a state of near *déshabillé* about to be ravished, and thought it best not to mention that Truman Capote's *The Grass Harp* was on her nightstand.

"I just love romance novels, don't you?" said Theresa. "This one's pretty steamy."

Alice forced a smile and glanced at Nina, who met her gaze with an almost imperceptible roll of the eyes.

That's when Alice knew that they'd become best friends, and they had.

So much had happened since then, so much that neither of them had anticipated.

"I can't believe you're here," said Alice, dumbstruck. "Who told you?"

"Theresa." A gold bangle bracelet swam on Nina's slender wrist. She had always been slim, but now she seemed as fragile as a crystal wine glass so delicate the stem could snap in your hands. "I'm sorry that I've been out of touch for so long."

"You're here now. That's all that matters." Alice gave Nina a hug. "How long can you stay?"

"A couple of days."

"God, I've missed you," said Alice, who wondered how she'd gone an entire year without seeing the one person who made life bearable in this godforsaken town. "You weren't planning on staying at Theresa's, were you?"

Nina followed Alice down the hall to the ICU. "I was hoping I could stay with you."

"Of course, you can."

It was irrational, she knew, but Alice was always disappointed when she returned to Lily's room and did not find her sitting up in bed, miraculously herself again.

"Oh, sweetheart," said Nina, stroking Lily's hand. She glanced at Alice with a downcast expression.

Lily seemed lost amidst so much equipment trying to stave off the unthinkable: IV pumps and central lines, monitors to measure heart rate and rhythm, blood pressure and respirations, a machine moving air in and out of her lungs, and always the whisper of the exhalation valve.

"Let's go home," said Alice. "I've been here all day, and you've had a long drive."

"Okay," said Nina. "I'll meet you there."

Alice lived on Bath Street, but Nina took a slight detour, driving past the house she had lived in with Paul in what seemed like another lifetime now though it had only been a year. A young cardiologist and his wife had bought the house, and Nina wondered if they were any happier there than she had been.

Bill was in the kitchen boiling spaghetti. "Hi, stranger," he said, dumping a jar of Ragu into a saucepan and wiping his hands on a dishtowel so he could give Nina a hug.

"She's going to stay with us for a couple of days," Alice told him.

"That's great." Crouching down to look through one of the cabinets under the island, he asked Alice where she kept the colander, but she had already gone to look for Noah, who was in the family room watching cartoons. Shaggy and Scooby had just transformed into babies.

"We've got company for dinner," Alice told him. "You remember Nina, don't you?"

"Harper and Hayley's mom."

"She's going to stay with us for a few days. Won't that be nice?"

"Uh-huh."

"Why don't you get out of that wet bathing suit and put on some clothes?"

"It's not wet anymore," said Noah, arching his back to show Alice his swimming trunks. "See."

"Well, change anyway."

He slithered off the La-Z-Boy. "When's Lily coming home?"

Alice shrugged. "We're not sure." A bald-faced lie but one she hoped would buy her a little time.

Noah drew a pirate sword from its plastic scabbard and held it aloft. "She's never coming home, is she?" he said, swinging the blade from side to side like a drunken buccaneer.

"We don't know that yet," said Alice gently.

He brought the sword down hard on a modular castle with towers and a dungeon that he and his father had built of LEGO. Colored bricks went soaring across the room.

"Noah, stop," said Alice when he began hurling knights and archers like missiles at the television.

She looked up when she saw Bill in the doorway.

"What's going on?" he asked.

"Our family is falling apart," she said without a hint of irony.

AFTER DINNER ALICE made coffee, and she and Nina sat at the kitchen table like they used to when their problems could be solved with a long talk or a good cry.

"It looks like Bill's been a big help," said Nina.

"I guess so," said Alice with a dismissive shrug, and Nina gave her a worried look. "Sorry, I'm just angry at everyone."

"Who's everyone?"

"I haven't talked to Theresa or Charlotte since that night."

"Why not?"

"Frankie got off with a broken leg, and Fern got off scot-free." Alice scowled. "Not a scratch on her. Not even a hangnail."

"I don't think Fern got off scot-free, do you? She's been through a traumatic experience, and Lily is her best friend," said Nina. "There are a lot of people who care about you and Lily. Don't shut them out."

Alice pushed herself up from the table and squeezed Nina's shoulder before going into the dining room. "I thought we had something stronger, but I guess not," she said when she returned with a bottle of Frangelico.

"Did you hear me?"

"Yes, I heard you." Alice doctored her coffee with a generous pour and handed the bottle to Nina. "So, I did something really stupid the other night."

"How stupid?"

"I went to a bar and got really drunk and made out with some guy in the parking lot." Alice stole a glance at Nina to see if she had any reaction, but there was none. "It was the night of Lily's accident."

"You must have been in shock or something."

"Or something."

Nina looked concerned. "What's going on with you?"

"I don't think I want to be married anymore," said Alice, who felt like she'd been slogging through the past couple of years in a trance.

"You don't mean that." Nina reached for Alice's hand and gave her fingers a comforting squeeze. "Let's just get through the next couple of days."

Alice removed a pack of Marlboro Lights from her handbag.

"When did you start smoking again?"

"Don't judge me."

"I don't want you to die of lung cancer."

Alice laughed, a short, clipped burst, like gunfire. "Lung cancer is the least of my worries." She lit her cigarette and tossed the match into a saucer. "If I lose my daughter, I'm not sure I'll want to live either."

"You have a son, and he needs you," Nina reminded her. "I don't want to hear any more of this kind of talk."

Alice's expression was wistful now. "Do you ever wish we could go back in time and spend one afternoon in Theresa's family room again watching soap operas? I miss those days." She closed her eyes, remembering. "Our kids were so young." She glanced at Nina, who had grown pensive. "It all went so fast."

"What were our kids doing while we were downstairs," said Nina. "Were we even paying attention?"

"They were probably getting into trouble," said Alice, smoke circling lazily from her cigarette. "Remember the time Theresa found Fern in the kitchen teaching Frankie and Lily how to turn salt into glue? She had a fit."

"What was that game that Grace and Lily used to play?" asked Nina. "Mystery Date?"

Alice nodded. "You lost if you got the dud, remember?"

"Just like in real life."

"I think he had a beard or something. That's how you knew he was a dud," said Alice, exchanging looks with Nina, who burst out laughing. "I miss us: The Fab Four. Isn't that what Theresa used to call us?"

"The diehard Beatles fan," said Nina with a thoughtful expression. "We thought our lives were so boring then. It's like we were waiting for something to happen."

Alice took a long drag on her cigarette. "And then it did."

Chapter 6

In high school, Theresa was a real knockout with an hourglass figure. She was also a devout Catholic, who was determined to walk down the aisle on her wedding day with her virginity intact. In that respect Theresa wasn't that different from a lot of girls in her class at Holy Rosary Catholic School in the Little Italy section of Cleveland. She was simply more adept at fending off a boy's advances with the alacrity of a boxer, who learns early on not to drop his hands, not to let his opponent pin him into a corner.

Then, in her senior year, she met Frank Lombardi, the very definition of tall, dark and handsome. Frank Lombardi tested her resolve, stirring up feelings she had only permitted herself to explore while gazing at photos of Paul McCartney in the fan magazines she bought with her allowance. Theresa had very nearly fainted when she saw the Beatles at the Public Auditorium in downtown Cleveland that fall, had actually twisted the hem of her skirt into knots when Paul's dreamy brown eyes went soft as he leaned into the microphone: *If I fell in love with you, would you promise to be true?* Oh, yes, yes, a thousand times yes, she thought, her mascara pooling beneath her lashes.

That winter she and Frank went out two or three times a week. Sometimes they'd go ice-skating with other couples at Erieview Plaza. Or, if they went to the movies at the Lake Theater, they'd sit in the back row, close to the wall, and kiss for hours, Frank working his fingers inside her coat and under her sweater until a little moan escaped from Theresa's lips. Frank always brought Theresa home early, parking a few blocks away so they could make out until Theresa's curfew: 10 o'clock on school nights, midnight on weekends. When she finally permitted him to guide her hand to the erection that strained against his Levi's, Frank decided that he was making progress.

Still, Theresa being Theresa, progress was slow. Finally, that summer, she allowed him to unhook her bra at the drive-in and touch her breasts with one of his big hands, rough from the construction job he'd taken right after graduation. Images flickered on the enormous movie screen: Cat Ballou being escorted to the gallows in a white lace dress.

"That's enough," she said when Frank's fingers roamed a bit further south. Moving away from him on the bench seat, she expertly refastened her Playtex Cross Your Heart bra.

Frank lowered his head onto the steering wheel. "Jesus Christ, Theresa, what do you want from me?"

"Seriously?"

He looked up. "Yeah."

Theresa fluffed up her bangs and smoothed down her hair. "Marry me."

So, on a warm day in September, Frank Lombardi pledged his troth to Theresa Moretti, his arm circling her tiny waist as he lifted her white tulle veil to kiss his bride.

Frank's uncle Tony owned a company in Scranton that manufactured glass doors, and when he offered his nephew a job as plant manager, they started their new life in a town Theresa had never heard of nearly four hundred miles away from where she grew up.

Early in their marriage, she and Frank had gone back to Cleveland for all the major holidays, but those visits had gradually tapered off. Theresa missed her family, especially the boisterous Sunday dinners at her maternal grandmother's house after mass when extra leaves were added to the table to accommodate the entire family: her brother Matteo and his wife Connie, her younger sisters Giulia and Sofia, and assorted aunts, uncles and cousins.

Every year in late August, Theresa's maternal grandfather played the accordion in the annual Feast of the Assumption parade, which kicked off four days of festivities celebrating the gospel of life, faith and family. After a solemn mass at Holy Rosary Church, the statue of the Virgin Mary was carried in procession throughout the neighborhood, and on the final night there was a candlelight prayer service to honor the Blessed Mother followed by fireworks.

It had been an idyllic childhood as far as Theresa was concerned, and she had wanted her children to have the same experience, though that seemed unlikely since they lived so far away from any extended family. On the other hand, she was so in love with her husband that she would have moved to Alaska and lived in an igloo with him if he'd asked.

All that chemistry they'd had in high school had paid off in spades, and Theresa, who believed in monogamy as fiercely as she had believed in virginity, was smart enough to know that things could have gone the other way. Frank could have been a lousy lover and then what? Theresa shuddered just thinking about it. For a chaste Catholic girl, she had hit the jackpot by marrying a man who made her feel naughty in bed, letting things unfold slowly until she was practically begging for it. Pure, wanton, unbridled sex without the guilt: every Catholic schoolgirl's dream.

When they were newlyweds, Frank came home to hearty platters of Tuscan chicken, rigatoni or lamb ragù. Theresa loved to eat, but she also loved to cook, and she was good at it.

"Julia Child has nothing on you," Frank told her, patting his mid-section as he pushed himself away from the table.

Later, after Theresa had washed the dishes, she'd join him in the living room, feigning interest in some show he liked while he absently stroked her hair. There was a lot of sex that first year: sex on the sofa as episodes of *Batman* flickered on the console television, sex in their king-size bed with its massive carved wood headboard, sex at cheap motels in the Poconos or at the Jersey Shore. One night after dinner, Frank swept their dirty plates and cutlery out of the way and took Theresa right there on the reclaimed pine trestle table.

Yet even with all that frenzied copulation, Theresa was unable to get pregnant. So, on their first anniversary they went to Rome where they received a papal blessing. Nine months later their son, Francesco Gianni Lombardi, Jr. made his way into the world after a record twenty-two hours of labor.

Pregnancy had been like a Get Out of Jail Free card, a one-way ticket to an all-you-can-eat buffet for Theresa who reasoned that if her waistline was going to go anyway, why not enjoy the ride? Those nine months seemed to fly by in a blur of tiramisu and pasta puttanesca, and by the time Frankie was born Theresa had packed on sixty pounds, less than nine of which were actual baby.

She thought about the women in her family, who had looked like Italian film stars (Claudia Cardinale or Anna Magnani) in their wedding photos yet were almost unrecognizable now. At fifty-four, her own mother's once voluptuous figure had become sturdy and thickset, her enormous bosom the prow of a ship cutting through placid waters each time she entered a room.

"It's in the genes," her mother proclaimed with an air of finality, as if corpulence was a *fait accompli*, a done deal for Moretti women.

Undeterred, Theresa swore off pasta and gagged down meal replacement drinks that had the consistency of pancake batter for breakfast and lunch. Three times a week she wriggled into a pink leotard to do floor exercises at Elaine Powers or use one of the vibrating belt machines that promised to "jiggle you like Jell-o."

When some of the girls chanted, "Whiskey, vodka, bourbon, gin, this is why we're fat not thin," Theresa laughed along with them, though she knew full well that food, not alcohol, was her drug of choice. She was back to her fighting weight and feeling pretty good about herself when she found out she was pregnant with Tina, and it was all downhill from there.

Chapter 7

Frank had started his own business with seed money provided by his uncle, and within five years Carpet Warehouse was doing so well that he and Theresa built a swimming pool in their backyard. It wasn't one of those glorified wading pools that sit above ground but an in-ground pool with a vinyl liner in a tempting shade of aquamarine that enticed you to dive right in. To celebrate they hired a caterer and threw a theme party.

Theresa had asked everyone to dress like a character in a Beatles song, though it seemed like only a handful of people thought she was serious. "Rita the Meter Maid," she had to explain to just about everyone who had no idea who she was in her sharp black skirt and jacket, though she presumed that her military-style cap was a clear giveaway.

Charlotte was easier to identify. "Lucy in the Sky with Diamonds," squealed Theresa when Charlotte arrived in a pink tulle skirt, twirling so the sun caught the Swarovski crystals scattered throughout her long blonde hair.

"Why aren't you wearing a costume," she asked Kip, who removed a bottle of Tanqueray from a brown paper bag.

"The doctor came in stinking of gin," he said, meandering toward the pool where "Norwegian Wood" blared from jerry-rigged speakers.

"Don't take it personally, Theresa," said Charlotte. "He won't even dress up for Halloween."

Inside, Frank was mixing cocktails in a pith helmet at a fully stocked wet bar. "What'll it be, Lady Madonna?" he asked when Alice deposited Lily's Baby Tender Love doll and a Chatty Cathy on a barstool.

"A pina colada."

"Coming right up."

"So, who are you supposed to be?"

"Bungalow Bill." He tipped a can of Coco Lopez into an Oster 10-speed blender in the latest color, avocado green. Adding two shots of Bacardi and some pineapple juice, he set the speed to high and flipped the switch. "State-of-the-art," he said over the whine of the blender. "I'll bet this thing could pulverize a T-bone steak."

Alice was tempted to ask him why anyone would want to, but she thought better of it. Pouring the contents into a red Solo cup, Frank poked around in a drawer until he found a cocktail umbrella.

"Nice touch," said Alice, taking a sip.

"So, how is it?" He raised one eyebrow suggestively.

Was he flirting with her? It was hard to tell, though he was emitting bad vibes the way the bug zapper on her deck discharged ultraviolet light. Platinum blonde curls sprouted from Baby Tender Love's vinyl skull, and Alice gave her a pat on the head. "Watch the kids for me," she told Frank.

Chatty Cathy was slumped against Tender Love's shoulder, and Alice pulled her string before heading outside. "Take me with you," implored the mechanical voice.

Theresa had kept the renovations a secret, and now Alice could see why she wanted the big reveal to be a surprise. The centerpiece was the swimming pool that could be accessed from the patio by wide stone steps. Dense shrubs and broadleaf evergreens were chosen for shady areas, and there were herbaceous borders of native perennials—black-eyed Susan, brilliant orange butterfly weed and garden phlox in varying shades of purple. Red maple and white pine with clusters of blue-green needles flourished in the bright sunshine.

Alice didn't recognize half the people splashing in the pool or playing horseshoes on a stretch of loose dirt that ran alongside the white-cedar fence. On the diving board, Kip was dancing with a woman wearing half-glasses and a cotton housedress. Eleanor Rigby? Charlotte was watching them from an Adirondack chair.

"What's going on?" Alice asked her.

"Who's that woman with Kip?"

"Never saw her before," said Alice. "Maybe she works for Frank."

"She's been following him around all day. Should I introduce myself? I am the little woman after all." She glanced at Alice with a sardonic smile.

"You jealous?" said Alice.

Charlotte pulled a face. "Of her? Hardly."

"Then what's the problem?"

"I don't know," she said with an exasperated sigh. "Do you ever feel like your whole life has been pointless?"

"Where did that come from?"

She shrugged. "Aren't you sick of folding laundry and scrubbing bathrooms and making the five same things for dinner week in and week out?"

Alice hadn't given it much thought. She was just happy that Bill made enough money so she didn't have to work and could stay home with Noah and Lily, who had been in daycare until she was four.

"Sometimes I wish I could go back and start over," said Charlotte, whose voice had taken on a plaintive quality. "Do something else with my life."

"Like what?"

She closed her eyes, remembering. "It doesn't matter anymore."

Now Kip was using the bottle of gin as a microphone to sing along to "Back in the USSR."

Charlotte looked up, shielding her eyes against the sun. "He's making a fool of himself," she said, getting to her feet and wandering over to the deep end of the pool.

"Get down from there right now."

Kip, who was perched precariously close to the edge of the diving board, momentarily lost his balance. While he was struggling to regain his footing, Eleanor Rigby inched her way toward the ladder and climbed down in a hurry.

Alice finished her pina colada and tossed the empty cup into a trash can. Mean Mr. Mustard—he told her his name was Tony and that he installed carpet for Frank—had taken up residence under an oak tree where he was mixing up a batch of grain alcohol and Hi-C in a plastic jug.

He wiped his forehead with the sleeve of his yellow T-shirt. "Want to try some?"

Alice shook her head, remembering the time she drank grain alcohol at a fraternity party in college and had no idea how she got home.

Charlotte gave Alice a playful shove. "I wondered where you went."

"I thought you and Kip's girlfriend were going to duke it out."

"Did you see how fast she took off when I showed up?"

"Maybe you'd like to sample the wares," said Tony, offering a glass of jungle juice to Charlotte.

"I'd think twice before drinking that," Alice warned her, but she had already taken a gulp.

"Don't tell the boss where you got this," he whispered, and Charlotte drew her finger across her lips and pretended to throw away the key.

At a redwood picnic table with an outdoor umbrella, some of their neighbors were playing cards. A couple whose HELLO MY NAME IS nametags said Desmond and Molly Jones scooted over to make room.

"You're not playing?" Charlotte asked Desmond, who told her that his real name was Dave.

"I've got a regular poker game on Friday nights," he said. "We play for serious money. This is just penny ante, but my wife's cleaning up."

"We play bridge," Charlotte announced, casting an inclusive glance at Alice.

"Way too complicated for me." He took a swig of beer.

Charlotte leaned in and whispered, "I think bridge is just an excuse for us to get together without our kids and drink way too much rosé."

"I'm going to get another drink," said Alice. "Be right back."

Now Queen was pouring from the speakers: *Is this real life, is this just fantasy?* Alice saw Theresa hurrying toward the house as if it was on fire.

Waitstaff in uniform were setting up on the patio where a metal table was draped in white linen, and Alice stepped aside until they finished. It was so bright outside that it took a minute for her eyes to adjust when she went indoors.

Frank, who had ditched the pith helmet, was singing along with Freddie Mercury: *Any way the wind blows doesn't really matter to me.*

Theresa gave him a hard stare. "This is a Beatles party."

"You've been playing that crap all afternoon. I'm the deejay now." Casually pouring himself a jigger of whiskey, he threw back the shot with a hearty, "Damn the torpedoes."

Theresa glowered at him and stormed off.

"Refill?" he asked Alice, who sent a weak smile in his direction.

The Osterizer roared to life, and Frank ducked down behind the bar to insert a new tape into the 8-track player, cranking the volume way up as the first menacing notes of "Kashmir's" hypnotic opening riff poured out of the speakers.

"You like Zeppelin?" he asked, handing Alice a fresh drink.

She had pegged him for more of a doo-wop kind of guy. "I was hoping you had some Billy Joel back there."

"The fucking piano man? He's as bad as Barry Manilow. You broads are all the same. It's either Joni Mitchell or Carole King or some other sappy shit like that."

He poured himself another shot.

"I think I'll get something to eat," Alice told him and carried her drink outside.

Father Phil helped himself to the wagon wheel pasta salad, and Alice wondered what he was doing here. The youngest priest at Mother of Sorrows, Father Phil was so good looking that teenage girls nearly swooned when he placed the communion wafer on their quivering tongues.

"Great costume," someone said in passing. "Father McKenzie, right?"

Father Phil smiled. *Why not?*

Theresa charted a course for the buffet table. "Father, I'm so glad you decided to come."

"It's a lovely party," he said. "Thank you for inviting me."

Alice popped a cocktail weenie wrapped in puff pastry into her mouth. "These are really good," she told Theresa, who was gazing at Father Phil with something bordering on adoration.

When it became clear that she was being ignored, Alice nabbed a deviled egg and went to look for Bill, who was reclining on a lounge chair near the deep end of the pool.

"They're serving dinner," she said. "You hungry?"

He leaned back against the cushioned headrest. "You know what they say? Move your feet, lose your seat."

"Seriously?"

"This is prime real estate," he said. "How about if you bring something back for me?"

"Do I look like your mother?" she said, a familiar refrain of late, though they both knew she'd cave.

"Thank you, honey," he called after her.

A kid wearing a concert T-shirt that reeked of reed (*Johnny Cash at San Quentin*) got in line behind her. Surprisingly chatty for a stoner, he told her he was a loader at Carpet Warehouse. "It's a lot of manual labor. Loading and unloading trucks, lifting and stacking boxes."

"You like it?"

"It's okay," he said, taking a set of plastic cutlery snug in its napkin fold and shoving it into his back pocket.

Alice wondered if he'd conduct a life review one day and conclude, as Charlotte had, that his existence had been pointless. Or was getting stoned his way of avoiding life's thornier philosophical issues?

As the line inched forward, he loaded up on barbequed ribs and potato salad. Grabbing a piece of garlic bread, he gave Alice a head nod. "See ya."

She made a plate to share with Bill that included two pieces of fried chicken, his favorite. There was a tiered dessert stand with fancy dipped strawberries, and she wrapped two of those in a cocktail napkin.

Bill took the plate from her and made room on the chaise lounge. "Frank must have spent a fortune on this shindig," he said. "I don't think we had half this much food at our wedding reception."

Alice smiled, remembering the simple fare served in the banquet hall at the church that day: stuffed cabbage, baked chicken, whipped potatoes, brown sugar-glazed carrots and a garden salad. She took a few bites of pasta and watched a couple tossing a frisbee on the lawn.

"I saw a cooler around here somewhere," said Bill. "Want to get us something cold to drink?" He threw her a sheepish smile.

"I'd be happy to, but how about if you do something for me in return?"

He tore off a chunk of chicken. "Sure."

"Let me sleep in tomorrow and you pick up the kids at your mother's house," she said, and he nodded agreeably.

The cooler was on the patio, and she fished out a warm Pepsi (the ice had turned to soup). At the far end of the manicured lawn, Charlotte and Kip sat deep in conversation, foreheads nearly touching. She nodded in agreement with something he said, and then he helped her to her feet. Standing on tiptoe, she wound her arms around his neck, and instinctively he placed one hand on the small of her back in a gesture that seemed surprisingly intimate. Alice, who had often wondered what it would be like to be as madly in love with her husband as Charlotte was with hers, looked away.

She handed the can of Pepsi to Bill, who made a face. "Yeah, I know, it's warm as bathwater, but at least it's wet," she said, taking a bite of a chocolate-covered strawberry.

"How much longer do we have to stay?" He pretended to hang himself.

"Why? You bored?"

He hauled himself to his feet. "Maybe I'll go inside and get something a little stronger to help me make it through the night."

Now someone jumped feet-first into the deep end of the pool, shouting "Cannonball!" Like lemmings rushing into the sea in droves, a dozen other people followed suit, displacing enough water to soak anyone standing near the edge. Startled screams and then this from the outdoor speakers: *Here come old flat top, he come grooving up slowly.* Game, set and match for Theresa, thought Alice.

Nina crossed the patio, nearly colliding with Desmond/ Dave, and Alice waved her over. "I wondered when you'd show up," she said. "Where's Paul?"

"He's not coming." Her expression was hard to read behind her dark sunglasses. "Theresa told me she invited Father Phil. Have you seen him?"

"He's here somewhere," said Alice. "Maybe he's upstairs."

"Boo!" said Charlotte, who had crept up on both of them. "Hey, where've you been hiding?" she asked Nina, draining what was left in her cup.

Nina turned to go, and when Alice took hold of her wrist, she flinched.

"What's going on?" she asked, but Nina shook her off. "Nothing."

Charlotte stared into the empty cup, a gypsy reading tea leaves. "I don't know what's in this stuff, but it sure packs a punch," she said, erupting into a fit of giggles.

"It's 95 proof," said Alice, who watched Nina disappear into the house.

"Compliments of the host," said Bill, handing Alice a pina colada. He took a sip of his drink. "I made him break out the good stuff. Johnny Walker Black."

Now Nina emerged from the house with Father Phil, who helped her navigate the paving stones that wound through a thicket of silver maple. She settled herself on an outdoor garden bench, and Father Phil let her talk, nodding every so often.

"What's going on with her?" Alice asked Charlotte, who shrugged.

"Her husband's an asshole," said Bill as if that explained things, but Alice wasn't paying attention. She was watching Nina, who seemed to be crying. Now Father Phil sat next to her, patting her knee every so often. More nodding, more patting, and then Nina looked at the handsome priest with an expression so tender Alice didn't know what to make of it. Seconds later, she kissed him. It was hard to tell which of them was more astonished, but now Nina was crying in earnest.

"Jesus Christ, Nina!" shouted Theresa, who had also been watching the events unfold. "What the fuck!"

Father Phil struggled to his feet. Alice couldn't tell if he was more upset that one of his parishioners had just made a pass at him or that Theresa had not only taken the Lord's name in vain but had also used the F-word.

Alice stared at him, slack-jawed.

"I should be going," he said, and Alice followed him into the house. He adjusted his collar, which seemed to have him in a stranglehold. "Please don't make too much out of what you saw out there."

"Seriously?"

"Obviously she's distraught."

"Obviously."

Father Phil shook his head. "I've said too much already."

"You haven't said anything," Alice told him.

There was some kind of commotion going on outside. Charlotte had taken a garden hose and was using it like a flamethrower. Bill tried to wrestle it away from her, and in the ensuing scuffle Charlotte blasted meatballs out of their chafing dish and soaked a tray of bacon and cheese pinwheels.

"Oh, my," said Father Phil.

With a renewed sense of purpose, Charlotte turned the hose on her intended target, blowing the wig off Eleanor Rigby's head and into the pool. "Stay away from my husband," she shouted before dropping her weapon.

The hose flopped around like a fish on a hook until Kip turned the water off at the source. "Nothing to see here," he said to a crowd of onlookers watching in disbelief from the patio. Then, lifting his wife into his arms, he carried her across the lawn and through the self-closing pool gate.

Alice suggested that Father Phil might want to leave through the front door, which was upstairs, to avoid the mayhem on the patio. "I'll walk you to your car."

They passed through the kitchen where the crew was cleaning up. In Theresa's formal living room with its pristine white carpet, someone was picking out *Für Elise* on the piano.

"I don't think you'll see any of us at mass tomorrow," said Alice, holding the door for Father Phil and following him to his car.

"It's a mortal sin not to observe the Sabbath," he said, sliding into the front seat of his baby blue Ford LTD, "but I'll give you all a pass just this once."

Alice watched him drive away before going back inside. When she passed the powder room, she thought she heard someone crying and rapped softly on the door. "Is everything okay in there?"

"Go away."

She recognized Theresa's voice. "It's Alice. Let me in."

There were a few muffled sobs, but then Theresa opened the door and pulled Alice inside. "I am never talking to Charlotte again. Everyone's leaving because of her." She jerked a tissue from a crocheted box on the lid of the toilet and blew her nose. "And what about Nina? She kissed Father Phil."

Alice tried to contain a smile because if you really thought about it the whole thing was kind of funny. The look on Father Phil's face was priceless: shocked, yes, but not entirely displeased.

Catching her reflection in the mirror over the sink, Theresa looked crestfallen. "Frank has ignored me all day, and no wonder. Just look at me."

"Don't be so hard on yourself."

"Ever since I had Tina, I've had a hard time losing weight. It's a constant struggle." Theresa slumped against the sink. "Oh, God, I said fuck in front of Father Phil." She buried her face in her hands. "He's never going to talk to me again."

"That's not true," said Alice. "He's a priest. That's his job. This will all blow over, you'll see."

Theresa fixed Alice with a pitiable look. "I think Frank is having an affair."

Alice was inclined to believe her since Frank had always come across as something of a sleazeball.

"He's been eating yogurt for breakfast," she said, a prosecutor revealing the smoking gun during a murder trial, "and he goes to the gym to lift weights three times a week."

"That doesn't prove anything. Maybe he's trying to get in shape."

"For who?" asked Theresa. "He's not doing it for me."

"You don't know that for sure."

"We haven't had sex in six months." She burst into a fresh round of tears. "I can't believe I just told you that."

"Your secret is safe with me," said Alice, who coaxed her into going back downstairs.

There were a few stragglers, mostly people who worked for Frank, floating on rubber rafts and singing along with Queen: *We will rock you.*

Fucking Frank, thought Alice.

Bill was stuffing paper plates and plastic cutlery that Charlotte had hosed onto the patio into a trash bag. Plastic cups and napkins and all manner of garbage were floating in the pool.

"Have you seen Frank," asked Theresa, taking in the carnage.

"Not really." Bill tossed a wad of sodden napkins into the garbage bag. "Want me to go look for him?"

"Don't bother." Her doleful expression suggested that she suspected Frank Lombardi was long gone and that he did not want to be found.

Chapter 8

All four of them were watching *Days of Our Lives* in Theresa's remodeled family room (fake wood paneling, orange shag carpet and a Zenith Space Command color television against one wall).

"Cookie saw Frank coming out of Fitness World with a girl last week," said Theresa during a commercial break.

Charlotte was flipping through the pages of *Ladies Home Journal*. She had been reading "Can This Marriage Be Saved?" for years and was fascinated by the juicy details that real-life couples were willing to share about their marital issues.

"Maybe it's a coincidence," she said, marking her page. "They could have been leaving at the same time and Cookie jumped to conclusions."

Theresa shook her head, a firm no. "She was sure about what she saw."

"Which was?"

"She said they looked pretty lovey-dovey."

"So, do we know who she is?" asked Alice, who had been trying to follow the conversation while stealing glances at the television to see if Mike was finally going to tell Margo that he knew she was dying.

"Cookie said she looked like one of the cashiers who works at Montgomery Ward."

"Well, that's insulting," said Alice, miffed enough for both of them. "At least he could replace you with better material."

"Not helping," said Nina, and Alice pulled a face.

"Have you confronted Frank yet?" asked Charlotte.

"No."

"Why not?"

"Ann Landers says not to ask a question if you don't want to know the answer."

"I'd want to know," Alice said.

"I can't get a divorce," said Theresa. "I wouldn't be able to take the sacraments."

"Let's not get ahead of ourselves," said Nina diplomatically. "Lots of couples work these things out."

Charlotte, who had read a number of promising stories in *Ladies Home Journal,* nodded enthusiastically.

Alice turned off the television. No one was watching *Days of Our Lives* anyway since a real-life soap opera was unfolding right in Theresa's family room.

"I wish we'd never joined that stupid gym," said Theresa, pushing herself out of the La-Z-Boy recliner and snapping at Tina, who was grinding Play-Doh into the carpet.

"I don't think Fitness World is the problem," said Alice. "Frank could have met someone at Carpet Warehouse or Burger King. You said he eats there every day."

Nina shot Alice a warning look.

"Pfft," said Alice, who gathered up her things.

Nina pulled Theresa into an awkward hug. "Sorry I can't stay," she said. "Grace has a piano lesson in an hour."

Theresa had encouraged Grace to use the baby grand piano in her living room since no one else played it, and she had been upstairs all afternoon practicing Chopin's *Fantaisie-Impromptu*. It was a difficult piece, especially for a ten-year-old but one that she was determined to master.

"Time to go," Nina said to the twins, who were playing with Tina's Weebles treehouse.

"We don't want to leave," they said in unison.

A stern look from Nina and Harper got to her feet. Hayley, who was inclined to test the limits of her mother's patience, pushed a dog with a red cap down the slide, and he shot out the front door.

"Okay," she huffed when Nina narrowed her eyes.

Fern and Lily were playing Hearts. "Time to go," said Charlotte, and Fern gathered up the cards.

Theresa scowled. "You're like a bunch of rats deserting a sinking ship."

"Don't be so dramatic," said Alice, handing Noah to Lily, who hoisted him onto her hip.

Noah closed his fist around a handful of Lily's T-shirt as she carried him up the stairs. "Bye, Frankie," she called over her shoulder.

"Bye," said Frankie, who was organizing his collection of Matchbox cars and seemed perplexed that he was sorry to see her go.

WHEN THERESA DIDN'T bring up the subject of Frank's infidelity again, they all assumed that things had gone back to normal. Then Alice and Charlotte ran into her in the parking lot at Fitness World that summer. Frank's cardinal-red Pontiac GTO sat in the blistering sun with the top down. Reaching into a plastic shopping bag, Theresa removed a carton of Dannon strawberry yogurt and tore off the lid. Winding up for the pitch, she let it rip. When the gooey pink contents hit the windshield, she did a little dance: the star quarterback in the end zone after a touchdown.

"What are you doing?" asked Alice, squinting against the glare.

"What does it look like I'm doing?" Grabbing another container, she lobbed it into the front seat. Then another: Dannon again, this time with fruit on the bottom. The cartons whizzed past like grenades, exploding on impact.

"Looks like you're out of ammo," said Alice when Theresa fished around in the flimsy bag and came up empty.

"What's going on?" asked Charlotte.

"He's in there with her." Theresa cocked her head toward the massive concrete structure Alice called Club Fed. "He hardly ever takes a Saturday off, but he promised the kids we'd have a cookout this afternoon, and then he made up some excuse about having to be somewhere for a few hours, some problem at the warehouse, but I knew he was lying. So, I followed him. Does this look like a warehouse to you?"

"It kind of does," said Alice just to lighten things up.

A piece of banana clung momentarily to the rearview mirror before sliding into the muck that was oozing onto the floor-mounted shifter.

"I saw them with my own two eyes," said Theresa. "She was wearing these tiny little shorts that barely covered her ass. He's not even trying to keep it a secret."

Alice gave her a minute and then asked, "And how is this helping?"

"I thought I'd teach him a lesson. He wants to eat yogurt, let him eat it off the seats of his precious car." Theresa let the plastic bag flutter into the back seat and wiped her hands on her shorts.

Alice peered into the GTO where clots of yogurt were starting to congeal on the bucket seats. "I'd love to see the expression on Frank's face when he gets here," she said, eliciting a small smile from Theresa.

When Frank came home that afternoon, he called Frankie outside. Theresa was dying to find out how he was handling the fact that someone had vandalized his car, but she was afraid to show her face for fear of tipping her hand. A few minutes later when she heard someone come in through the front door and go upstairs, she assumed it was Frankie, but now he was calling to her from the hallway, breathless and excited.

"Dad gave me five bucks to clean his car," he said. "You should see it, Mom. Some nut smeared yogurt over everything."

"Oh, no," said Theresa with fake concern, though she wondered what Frankie would think if he knew that his mother was the nut in question.

By the look on his face, Theresa could tell that he was already deciding how to spend his windfall. "I need paper towels and Windex and maybe some kind of soap." He stood on tiptoe to reach the bucket on the top shelf of the broom closet. "Do we have clean rags or something?"

Theresa handed him a bottle of Pine-Sol and a sponge.

"Thanks, Mom," he said and rushed back outside.

Leave it to Frank to get his own son to do his dirty work, thought Theresa, who suspected that Frank would always be one step ahead of her. What she wanted was for this nonsense to end, for Frank to come to his senses, and she went on a crusade to find an explanation for his aberrant behavior.

"Charlotte thinks he's having a mid-life crisis," she told Alice one afternoon when they were working out at Fitness World.

"He's too young for a mid-life crisis," she pointed out.

"My mother thinks he has a chemical imbalance," she said, and again Alice poked a hole in her trial balloon.

"She watches too much *Donahue*." Alice believed that a lot of theories, including this one, were just a way of excusing bad behavior that people used to be ashamed of, like falling down drunk at your sister's wedding, or murder. "You need to give him an ultimatum. It's either you or Wendy." Thanks to Alice, who had done some sleuthing, the bimbo had a name.

"I think this whole thing will blow over if I just give it time," said Theresa, whose M.O. was to let sleeping dogs lie.

"If I were in your place, I'd be mad as hell," said Alice, who had never sugar-coated her advice and wasn't about to start now. "Face the facts, Theresa, you married an asshole."

Theresa's face fell, and Alice quickly apologized.

As it turned out, it was Wendy who forced the issue, and Frank didn't waste any time packing his things.

Theresa followed him from room to room, watching him empty out drawers, shove clothes into a duffel bag and box up the trophies he'd won as a running back at Cleveland Central Catholic High School. In the garage, he jammed everything into the trunk of his car, thus managing to condense their entire history into a space the size of an outdoor pizza oven.

Tossing his leather jacket onto the front seat, he slid behind the wheel of the GTO.

"Don't think I'm giving you a divorce," said Theresa, playing what she thought was her trump card.

"Want to play hardball? See if I care," he said, inching his way out of the garage. "We'll just live in sin."

Numb, she walked from room to room, the silence nearly deafening with Frank gone. Tina's miniature ironing board was in the living room. Her pink plastic iron rested on its heel as if she had been called away to answer the phone or check on a pot roast she was making for dinner. Theresa had been president of Future Homemakers of America when she was in high school. In home economics, she'd learned how to set a proper table, hem a dress, starch and iron a shirt, roll out a piecrust and serve budget-friendly canned fish in an attractive way. Now she worried that Tina was following in her footsteps for all the good it would do her.

Chapter 9

O n a bitterly cold day in February, Theresa pulled her station wagon into a vacant spot in front of Shop 'a Lot Supermarket. She could already feel a headache beginning at the base of her skull. In the back seat, her children were squabbling over a pack of Bubble Yum, and Theresa told Frankie to give his sister a piece so she'd quit yammering.

"She'll just swallow it," Frankie said.

"So, let her swallow it." She cut the engine and rummaged around in her purse for a bottle of Excedrin.

Frankie tossed the entire pack of gum at his sister, who let out a yelp. "Big baby," he said, giving her a shove.

In exasperation, Theresa dumped the contents of her hobo bag onto the front seat: a checkbook, a hairbrush, a tube of lip-gloss in some ill-advised shade of plum, a Bic pen and a Nine West wallet bulging with maxed-out credit cards. No Excedrin. There was a box of Milk Duds though, and she popped one into her mouth where she let it dissolve slowly on her tongue like a tab of nitroglycerin.

"Come on, I've got to get stuff for dinner," she said.

Her son hunkered down inside his parka. "I'm staying."

"You're coming with me. Now let's go."

"Come on, Mom. I'm twelve years old. No one's gonna kidnap me."

But Theresa had been watching *20/20,* and she knew better. "I said let's go."

The parking lot was so icy that Tina slipped and fell not once but twice. Theresa wrestled with a tangle of shopping carts until one broke free, and her children followed her like ducklings as she pushed the cart into the store.

A display of Valentine's Day cards assaulted her: an onslaught of hearts being pierced by Cupid's arrow or pictures of love-struck couples holding hands, and Theresa turned away, remembering the heart-shaped Whitman's Sampler Frank had given her for Valentine's Day when they were still in high school. Now, one too many chocolate buttercreams later, she barely remembered the girl with the wasp-waist who could drive Frank Lombardi to distraction.

Taking a deep breath to clear her head of memories she'd rather forget, Theresa headed toward the dairy case. "Get down," she admonished Tina, who tried to mount the cart from the side as it wobbled down the aisle.

Frankie grabbed his sister roughly by the shoulder. "Mom said to get off."

Tina collapsed into a heap on the cracked linoleum and screwed up her face. Her small features seemed to close in on one another, the petals of a flower blooming in reverse.

"Enough with the waterworks," said Theresa tersely, tossing a package of Blue Bonnet margarine into the cart. "And wipe that smirk off your face, Frankie, before I do it for you."

Tina placed her thumb in her mouth and rhythmically stroked the bridge of her nose with her index finger as she followed her mother around the corner into the snack aisle. Theresa realized her mistake at once and backed up, but not before Frankie tossed a bag of Lays Barbeque Potato Chips into the cart.

"No junk food," said Theresa, placing the bag back on the shelf. "I'm on a diet."

"Then why are you so fat?" He laughed at his own joke and added a bag of Cheez-Its and a box of Oreos to his haul.

"I said no junk food," said Theresa, who resisted the temptation to slap Frankie right there in the middle of the aisle for his insolence. She might have, too, if she wasn't worried that someone would report her to Child Protective Services. Already an elderly woman who had been examining the fine print on the back of a box of macaroons was eyeing her suspiciously.

Sometimes Theresa worried that Frankie was becoming just like his father, who never missed an opportunity to insult her. Most of those insults were about her weight, which had become more of a problem since Frank moved out. The fact was, Theresa just couldn't stop eating: Ruffles potato chips with French onion dip, slabs of cheese on Ritz crackers, peanut butter straight from the jar.

She'd finally joined Weight Watchers and was determined to lose twenty pounds by Easter, though her team leader had suggested that this might be an unrealistic goal. Steering her cart into the produce section, she loaded up on baby carrots, celery and iceberg lettuce. She was checking a grapefruit for freshness when she saw Frank's girlfriend, who was wearing a cropped sweater under her faux fur jacket. When Wendy stood on tiptoe to tear a plastic bag off the roll, Theresa caught a glimpse of her bare midriff: flat as a stretch of repaved interstate.

Her own flesh was literally spilling out over the elastic waistband on her baggy sweatpants, and there was a stain on her sweatshirt that could have been special sauce from the Big Mac she gobbled down for lunch that day. Before she could stop herself, her cart was picking up speed.

"Slut!" she screamed, throwing all her weight into the cart as she raced down the aisle. "Whore!"

Wendy placed a bag of bell peppers into her buggy alongside a quart of skim milk and a box of Wheat Thins. Seconds before the collision, their eyes met. Her lips parted slightly, but no sound escaped.

Backing up to retrench, Theresa attempted a flanking maneuver, using her cart like a battering ram.

Wendy was making plenty of noise now, abandoning her cart, which had careened into a display of golden delicious apples. Theresa chased her as she ran screaming past the bulbous purple eggplant.

A boy wearing an Aerosmith T-shirt was mopping the floor. Wendy slipped on a wet spot and skidded off toward the bakery department.

"Come back here, you little shit," said Theresa, picking up a tomato and letting it fly. Tomatoes weren't in season so they were hard as rocks. The sound was not quite the satisfying *splat* she anticipated but rather a kind of *boink*.

Like a pitcher on the first day of spring training, Theresa's aim was less than true, but she soon got the hang of it, firing three, four, a half dozen tomatoes at Wendy, who streaked past the racks of cinnamon rolls and freshly baked pumpernickel.

"Watch your sister," Theresa barked to Frankie, grabbing a baguette and going after Wendy, who was hightailing it into the meat department. There was a sale that day, and Theresa backed Wendy into a display case brimming with ground round.

"Do you know who I am?" Theresa asked, wielding the baguette like a machete.

Wendy blinked, and her feathered bangs quivered.

"I'm Frank's wife, you little homewrecker," said Theresa, beating Wendy about the head and neck with the baguette.

Wendy called for help, and a butcher in a bloodstained apron came running toward them.

"Do something," wailed Wendy, who brought her hands up to ward off Theresa's blows. She peeked out from behind her acrylic nails, which were at least four inches long. Someone had airbrushed x's and o's on each of them.

The butcher tried to subdue Theresa in a voice airline personnel reserve for irate passengers who have just been bumped. "Okay, okay, let's just calm down now, alright."

Theresa shot him a look that suggested he mind his own business.

Frankie was tugging on her arm. "Mom, stop!" She shook him off and went after Wendy, who had been inching her way toward aisle five and freedom.

"Why don't you get a husband of your own and leave mine alone," screamed Theresa, waving the baguette, which had been badly damaged in the scuffle.

Dean Martin's smooth baritone blared over the PA system: *When the moon hits your eye like a big pizza pie, that's amore.*

Wendy had armed herself with a can of Dinty Moore Beef Stew, which she brandished like a weapon. "Look lady, I didn't steal your husband. Your marriage was already over by the time I came along."

"Oh, yeah. Tell that to my two kids. Does he look familiar?" Theresa shoved Frankie in front of her. "He should since he looks just like his father."

"Leave me alone," said Frankie, wriggling to get free. "Man, you're crazy just like Dad says."

Theresa dropped the baguette.

"Come on lady, let's go," said the butcher, taking her by the elbow. Then to Wendy: "You want me to call the police?"

"What for? I mean, look at her, she's got enough problems," said Wendy smugly, fluffing her hair over the collar of her coat.

Tina came running over and wrapped her arms around one of Theresa's enormous thighs. "Are we going to jail?" she sobbed.

"No, stupid," said Frankie. "They don't put kids in jail. We're going home."

Chapter 10

———————

After the incident in the grocery store, which Alice called "The Attack of the Killer Tomatoes," Frank told Theresa that he'd get a restraining order if she ever came near his girlfriend again.

"I think she got off easy," said Charlotte. "Wendy could have pressed charges."

"For what? A broken fingernail?" Alice had gained newfound respect for Theresa now that she was showing some backbone.

What Theresa needed, she decided, was to get back in the game, and that would require a complete makeover. Fernando's Hideaway was the only beauty salon in town that had happy hour on Tuesday, or any other day for that matter.

"All the other salons in town are dead, dead, dead on Tuesday," Fernando explained, "but we're busier than ever."

His boyfriend, Marco, swanned around with glasses of complimentary red and white table wine from Gallo to the delight of the customers.

Fortunately, Fernando had a cancellation that day and was able to squeeze Theresa in for a new cut and color.

Charlotte, who had come along for moral support, took him aside when they arrived. "Her husband left her for some bimbo," she said, and Fernando nodded gravely.

Fingering a gold rope chain that nestled in the dark pelt of hair on his chest, Fernando appraised Theresa's current hairstyle, a cross between Marla Thomas in *That Girl* and Emma Peel in *The Avengers*. A few pumps of the hydraulic foot pedal and their eyes met in the oversize mirror.

"You're not married to this hairstyle, are you?"

"I know, I'm stuck in a rut," said Theresa with a downcast expression.

"What I see before me is a beautiful woman who just needs a little self-confidence." He placed one hand on each of her shoulders and gave them a little squeeze. Her head drooped slightly as she yielded to the gentle pressure of his practiced fingertips. She knew that Fernando was what her father called light in the loafers and that the church frowned on his lifestyle, but it hardly mattered. What he was doing was close to intimacy, and she willingly surrendered.

Fernando snapped his fingers, and the shampoo girl appeared like a magician's assistant. "Luciana will take care of you," he said, "and then we go to work."

Now Marco made a pass with a tray of canapés: wedges of Gouda and cheddar cheese impaled on toothpicks wearing festive cellophane frills.

"That was his idea," said Fernando with obvious pride.

Alice nabbed a chunk of Gouda. "He's a keeper," she said, and Fernando sighed. "Don't I know it."

When Theresa was comfortably seated, Fernando took her gently by the shoulders and explained what he had in mind. "I'm thinking Gina Lollobrigida in the early sixties.

Remember her Italian cut, those all-over waves and fluffy kiss curls?"

Theresa had no idea what a kiss curl was, but Fernando's voice was so seductive, so reassuring, that she nodded amiably.

Charlotte showed Alice a story in *Cosmopolitan* about dating again after an ego-shattering divorce. "I'm going to give this to Theresa," she said, tearing out the pages and stuffing them into her purse.

"Don't bother," said Alice, who had been trying, unsuccessfully, to get Theresa to even consider the idea. Draining her glass of mediocre red wine, she suggested that they find the nearest State Store for something stronger.

"We close in ten minutes," said the lone employee who was manning the register.

"We'll hurry," said Charlotte.

Alice grabbed a bottle of Captain Morgan Black Spiced Rum: 70 proof. "This should do the trick," she said. "What do you think?"

Charlotte examined the label. "He looks like Errol Flynn in *Captain Blood*?"

"Who?"

"Captain Morgan."

"I guess," said Alice, carrying her purchase to the register and settling up with the cashier, who slipped the bottle into a paper bag.

Fernando was standing on the sidewalk in front of the salon smoking a cigarette when they pulled up. He hurried over to the car and motioned for Alice to roll down the window.

"Wait until you see how she looks," he said, grinding his cigarette out under the heel of his glam-rock platform boot.

Luciana had coaxed Theresa's hair into soft waves. Removing the cutting cape, she motioned for Theresa to do a little twirl.

"She did my makeup, too," said Theresa, whose eyes were rimmed in winged-out kohl eyeliner. "What do you think?"

Alice seemed spellbound by the transformation. "You look like a completely different person."

"This calls for a toast," said Charlotte, uncapping the bottle of rum. Marco went to the break room and returned with a sleeve of plastic cups and a six-pack of Coca-Cola.

Using the tail end of a tint brush to mix drinks for each of them, Fernando handed one to Theresa. "I would love to see the look on Frank's face the next time he sees you."

Marco raised his glass. "Honey, he's going to be sorry he let you get away."

"Now all I have to do is lose another twenty pounds," said Theresa, who had already lost weight under Alice's tutelage on the Atkins diet.

Fernando draped his arm around Theresa's shoulder. "In Italy, we like our woman to have a few curves. The English can have their Twiggy. We've got Sophia Loren."

Charlotte drained her glass and asked Marco for a refill.

"So, what's the plan?" asked Fernando, removing his smock to reveal a form-fitting blue polyester shirt with huge lapels. "It's disco night at the Best Western. Anyone want to go?"

Charlotte pulled a face. "I hate disco."

"Blasphemy," said Fernando in mock horror.

"Let's do something else."

"Like what?" asked Theresa, who seemed game for anything.

"Let's go slash Frank's tires," said Charlotte with a wicked grin.

"I have a better idea," said Fernando. "Wait here."

He disappeared into his office, returning with a bumper sticker. "Let's put this on his car."

Charlotte examined the pink triangle. "I don't get it."

"The Nazis made fags like me wear pink triangles like this one on their clothing," he explained. "So, we've adopted them as a symbol of our fight against oppression. We're here and we're queer, baby."

A slow smile played across Alice's face. "You're a genius, Fernando. Come on, I'll drive."

"It's still early," said Theresa, climbing into the backseat of Alice's Mercedes. "He's probably at Fitness World. He practically lives there now."

Fernando called shotgun and turned on the radio. Flipping through the channels, he zoomed right past a snippet of *All Things Considered* and rejected "Nobody Likes Sad Songs" by Ronny Milsap with an emphatic, "Hell, no."

When he finally settled on a station, they all sang along to 'My Sharona.'"

"If I ever have another baby, I'm calling her Sharona," called Charlotte from the back seat.

"No, you won't," said Alice.

"I might have another baby," said Charlotte. "You don't know."

"But you won't name her Sharona."

Fernando cranked up the volume when he recognized the opening chords of "Hot Stuff." Alice rolled down the windows, allowing a rush of warm air to wash over them, and they were all shout-singing when she pulled up in front of Fitness World where Frank's Pontiac sat all by its lonesome under a streetlamp.

"Shit," said Alice when she saw Frank and Wendy emerge from the gym.

"That can't be the woman he left her for," said Fernando in disbelief. "Who the hell did her hair color?"

"Just go," Alice told him. "I'll come get you."

Weaving serpentine through rows of parked cars, Fernando plastered the pink triangle on Frank's bumper. He was just getting to his feet when Frank saw him.

"What the fuck are you doing?" he shouted, leaving Wendy behind and charging down the stairs.

Alice stepped on the gas and pulled up alongside Frank's car. Reaching across the front seat, she pushed the door on the passenger side open and Fernando dove in.

Alice floored it, and the Mercedes picked up speed.

"That should ruin lover boy's reputation," said Fernando, howling with laughter as Alice hightailed it out of the parking lot.

Chapter 11

The morning Theresa heard that John Lennon had been murdered, she was in the kitchen doing dishes. Shot three times in front of the Dakota just two weeks before Christmas. A suspect that authorities were calling a local screwball was in custody. Theresa had to sit down to absorb the shock of what she'd just heard.

The last time she'd felt like this was when JFK was assassinated. The principal had canceled classes for the rest of the day, and like everyone else she knew, Theresa watched the funeral on television: Jackie stoic in her filmy black veil, John-John saluting his father's casket as it passed by, the rider-less horse following the caisson, an empty saddle, saber and boots reversed in the stirrups. It seemed like the whole country was in mourning.

Then in February Theresa heard "I Want to Hold Your Hand" for the first time, and it felt like the country had turned a page and that everything was going to be okay. Now someone had rewritten the script, replacing all of her happy memories with something dark and foreboding.

She spent the rest of the day listening to the radio, which

played one Beatles song after another. When Theresa was in high school, their music had made her feel happy just to be alive. So many songs about falling in and out of love. Such longing and passion. *And when I touch you, I feel happy inside.* When Frankie was a baby, she had played "Blackbird" as if it were a lullaby, cradling him in her lap and rocking him to sleep.

By the time she heard the pneumatic hiss of the school bus coming to a stop outside, Theresa was all cried out. She opened the front door and watched her children trudge up the walk, their backs sharply curved under the weight of their heavy book bags. Tina dropped her lunchbox, and in a rare display of affection Frankie stooped to pick it up. It was a gesture so without guile that Theresa caught a glimpse of that little boy she had held in her lap so long ago.

It was Frank's night with the kids, but instead of taking them out to dinner, which he did every week, he brought a pizza and suggested that they all eat together.

"I thought you could use some company," he told her. "I was watching *Monday Night Football* when I heard about it."

"I didn't find out until this morning," said Theresa, removing dinner plates from the cupboard. "Why didn't you call me?"

Frank shrugged. "I thought you knew."

Theresa handed him a stack of dishes.

He seemed perplexed. "What do you want me to do with these?"

"I don't know, play frisbee with them?" said Theresa, who was becoming exasperated. "Just set the table."

"I can't believe that Howard Cosell actually interrupted the game to break the news last night," called Frank from the dining room.

Theresa turned off the radio, which was playing "Imagine" again. All that wistful yearning with no practical solution felt depressing to her now. There was something so innocent about their music, and to have it end with cold-blooded murder just felt wrong.

"Tell the kids that dinner's ready," she told Frank, who went into the hallway to holler up the stairs.

Theresa lifted the lid on the box from Bella Notte: thick squares of pizza oozing with extra cheese. It had been their favorite place when they were newlyweds, and the gesture felt like an olive branch.

Frank squeezed her shoulder. "It's going to be okay, Tess." It had been his nickname for her when they were in high school.

"You haven't called me that in years," she reminded him.

"I guess hearing all that Beatles music on the radio today took me back."

"What happened to us, Frank?"

"I don't know. Life?"

Theresa took a good look at her husband. His dark hair was longer than usual, and he was growing a mustache. Technically, they were still married, but Frank had started divorce proceedings now that Pennsylvania had become a no-fault divorce jurisdiction, which galled Theresa, who knew exactly who was at fault in this scenario. There was a time when Frank could make her weak in the knees, but she had learned how to suppress those feelings over the past year or so in order to keep her sanity.

"I'm sorry for the way things ended with us," said Frank, following Theresa into the dining room.

"Sometimes I wish we'd never moved here," she said. "We left everyone, Frank, and for what? Maybe our families were the glue that might have held our marriage together."

Frank had often wondered the same thing. He knew that his mother would never have tolerated the kind of bad behavior he had engaged in, but what was the point of dwelling in the past?

"Things have a way of turning out like they should," he said, which sounded glib to Theresa.

"For you maybe," she said. "You've got Wendy."

"You'll find someone," he told her, but Theresa wasn't so sure she wanted anyone else. That was the conundrum.

Tina waltzed into the dining room in the pink tutu she'd worn at her ballet recital last spring. "Ooh, pizza," she said when Theresa placed a slice on her plate.

Frankie was listening to Van Halen on his new Walkman. Theresa did not think that David Lee Roth was a proper role model for a thirteen-year-old boy. She'd heard stories about all the groupies he'd slept with while on the road, but she knew better than to press the issue. She had enough problems handling Frankie's mood swings, his preoccupation with his weight, the constant door-slamming and dirty looks, the unwashed cereal bowls she discovered under his bed, on his dresser, on top of his stereo.

"At least take your headphones off while we're having dinner," she told him.

Frankie glanced at his father.

"Listen to your mother," said Frank, which was a first, and Theresa wished it could be like this every night: all four of them at the table together, an even number that made sense to her.

But Frank was gone and it was just the three of them now: a fragile, wobbly, rickety cart that had lost one wheel.

Chapter 12

Nina had suffered from mild depression for years, but it always got worse after Christmas when cashiers who had been quick with a "Merry Christmas" just a week ago sullenly bagged her groceries. She understood that they'd grown tired of hearing the same old Christmas carols ringing from speakers at every store in town, but she missed them: the classics by Percy Faith, "The Christmas Song" by Nat King Cole.

Even now when she heard "Blue Christmas" on the radio, she thought of Ethan, who had shipped out to Vietnam on Christmas Eve. On the advice of her mother, Nina had shared very few details with Grace about her father. Eleanor had reasoned that if Paul had to compete with a martyred father who loomed larger than life in the child's memory, Grace would never bond with him. It made sense at the time, but Nina had begun to regret the deception.

The Fraser Fir, its boughs drooping with ornaments she had collected for years, was dropping needles onto the hardwood floor. The room would look naked and forlorn when it was gone, but Paul would drag it to the curb on New Year's Day like he did every year.

Her mother had called Nina's bouts of depression the blues, but this year it seemed different, a kind of pervasive sadness she just couldn't shake. She and Alice had made a habit of spending the day after Christmas shopping the sales at the mall and having dinner someplace nice, which had been a distraction, but Nina wasn't sure she wanted to go anywhere today.

"Why aren't you dressed? It's almost one o'clock," said Alice when she showed up. "You look terrible by the way."

"I've had trouble sleeping,"

Harper and Hayley thundered down the stairs, nearly colliding with their mother in the foyer. "We're hungry."

Nina covered her face with her hands. "I can't," she said, and Alice offered to make lunch for them.

The twins followed her into the kitchen, which was a wreck: the table sticky with syrup, Cheerios floating in a puddle at the bottom of a bowl, a glass of orange juice that had been overturned, scrambled eggs left in a pan on the stove, a sink full of dirty dishes.

"Tell you what," she told the girls. "I'm going to clean up this mess, and then why don't we all go out to lunch? Ask Grace if she wants to come, too."

"Yay," said Harper, chasing Hayley up the stairs.

Alice loaded the dishwasher and wiped down the counters. Then she called Lily to see if she wanted to come along. Maybe they could all go bowling. Or ice skating at the rink in the mall.

She found Nina on the sofa. "I'm going to take everyone out for the afternoon," she said with a worried look. "Why don't you take a nap while we're gone. We'll be back before dinner."

"You going to be okay here by yourself?" asked Grace, who seemed concerned.

"Don't worry about me."

Alice herded everyone to the front door. "Get some rest," she called from the hallway.

After they left, the house felt preternaturally still as if all the energy had been used up. There was a handknit throw on the sofa, and Nina drew it around her shoulders. I'll just close my eyes for a little while, she thought before dozing off.

Now someone was shouting. Paul? He snapped on the overhead light, startling Nina awake.

"It's like a tomb in here. Where is everyone?"

"What time is it?" she asked, slightly disoriented.

"Almost six-thirty. Why isn't dinner ready?"

"I must have fallen asleep."

"You're still in your pajamas," he said with a dismissive expression.

"I've been depressed," she said. "You know how I get after the holidays."

"What do you have to be depressed about? I know plenty of women who would trade places with you in a heartbeat."

Nina drew her knees toward her chest. She knew better than to argue with Paul.

He crossed the room and riffled through the bar cart. "I had a bottle of Macallan here last week. What happened to it?"

"I don't know."

"It's your job to keep this thing stocked," he said, inspecting a bottle of Dewar's with less than a finger of whiskey left before jamming it back into the trolley with such force that the barware rattled on the glass shelf. He pushed aside a bottle of gin and another of vodka to reach a handle of Jameson Irish Whiskey.

Nina watched while he poured himself a drink. The harsh overhead light cast shadows across his face, enhancing every imperfection so he looked older than his years. He might have been a stranger to her, his eyes dark as pitch in the unflattering light.

She turned on a lamp that cast a circle of warm light over a group of photographs in silver frames on the console table, all but one of them of their children. There was a formal portrait taken on their wedding day, and she picked it up. Her ivory satin gown had an empire waist, and she wore a Juliet cap with a fingertip-length veil as light as gossamer. Paul chose a black double-breasted tuxedo with a red rose, long believed to symbolize love and passion, tucked into the lapel.

"Till death do us part," he said, draining the last of his scotch.

The phone in the kitchen rang sharply, and Paul went to answer it. After a few moments, he grabbed his car keys from a bowl on the credenza and told her he was going out. "Don't wait up."

"Who was that on the phone?" she asked.

"Wrong number," he said, slamming the door behind him.

The Westport clock on the mantle chimed on the hour: 7 o'clock. The girls should have been home long ago. She called Alice's house, but no one answered. It would probably be a good idea to start dinner, she thought, since the girls would be starving when they got home. Putting on a pot of water for spaghetti, she looked for a jar of sauce in the pantry.

An hour went by, then two. It wasn't like Alice to be this irresponsible, and she was worried now, imagining the worst: a horrible car accident or a psychopath on a rampage.

The idea wasn't that far-fetched. Just last year a teenage girl had opened fire at an elementary school in San Diego, killing the principal, the custodian and eight children. When the police asked why she did it, she told them that she didn't like Mondays. The story had made the news, and some new wave band Grace liked wrote a song about it. Their name escaped her at the moment, not that it was important.

She was about to call Alice again when she heard a car pull into the driveway. Thank God, she thought, rushing into the foyer. Harper and Hayley charged through the front door.

"Take off your boots," said Grace, closing the door behind them.

"Where have you been?" said Nina, her voice thick with emotion. "I've been worried sick."

Grace looked puzzled. "We went to the movies. I called to tell you we'd be late."

Harper tugged at Nina's sleeve. "We saw *Popeye!*"

Hayley was yammering for Grace to help her out of her moon boots. "In a minute." She looked at her mother. "Didn't Paul tell you?"

Nina lowered her eyes. *Wrong number.* That's what he'd told her.

"Jesus, Mom, that's just cruel."

"What's cruel?" asked Harper, and Grace told her to go upstairs and get her pajamas on if she wanted a story tonight. "Both of you, go," she said, and they scampered up the stairs.

Grace fixed her mother with a look that bordered on pity. "Why do you stay with him? He's a horrible person."

Now Nina wondered how much Grace knew about what went on between her and Paul. She had tried to shield her children from the truth, but maybe she hadn't done a very good job.

WHILE SHE HAD no intention of sharing her marital problems with her teenage daughter, Nina suspected that it might be time to confide in someone else. So, she called Alice the next morning and asked her to come over.

"Now?"

"I have something I need to tell you, and I'm afraid I'll lose my nerve if I don't do it right away."

She went to wait in the living room. Even though the sky was overcast, soft light poured in through the picture window, casting gentle shadows on the Aubusson rug.

Alice let herself in. "So, what's the emergency?" she called from the hallway.

Now Nina felt like maybe this had been a mistake. She'd seen the look on Grace's face last night, and she couldn't bear it if Alice looked at her that way, too.

"Come on, spill your guts," said Alice, shrugging out of her heavy coat.

"I shouldn't have called you," said Nina. "I'm sorry to drag you over here for nothing."

They had been friends long enough for Alice to know that Nina was hiding something. Crouching down so they were on eye-level, she asked, "What happened?"

"It's a long story."

"I'm not going anywhere."

Nina took a few shallows breaths before going all the way back to the beginning when Paul threw a tantrum on Christmas Eve. At first it was verbal abuse more than anything, she told Alice, but she had learned to live with the threats and intimidation, the slights and put-downs. Then he began pushing her around, twisting her arm hard enough to leave bruises. Quick to lose his temper, Paul had also punched a hole in the wall more than once, but Nina decided to keep that information to herself for now.

Alice stared at her, incredulous. "I'm going to kill the son of a bitch."

"It's not like he does it all the time," said Nina, defensive now. "It's usually when he's had too much to drink."

"Are you listening to yourself? You sound like one of those women we met at the shelter last year."

"It's not like that," she said. "He's not some low life."

"Abuse is abuse, Nina," said Alice. "You don't have to wear a wife-beater to be a wife-beater."

Now Alice was pacing, which she did when she wanted to clear her head. "You know, emotional abuse is just as damaging as physical violence or sexual assault. It's all about power and control."

"There's not much I can do about it."

"Press charges," said Alice. "File for divorce."

"I can't," said Nina with a quick shake of her head.

"Why not?"

"He said he'll get custody of the girls if I ask for a divorce."

"That's ridiculous. You're their mother."

"He knows every judge in town," Nina explained. "He said none of them will give custody of his kids to an unfit mother."

"You're not unfit."

"He says my depression makes me unfit."

Alice looked exhausted, like someone who had gone a few punishing rounds with Muhammad Ali. "You can't live like this. I don't care who Paul knows."

"Let's face it, he holds all the cards," said Nina with a sigh of resignation. "Besides, how would I support myself if I left?"

"Maybe you could get back into nursing."

"That was my mother's idea," said Nina. "I wanted to to study art."

"Really?" said Alice. "How come you never told me?"

"That was a long time ago," said Nina with a shrug.

"So, why didn't you go to art school?"

"My parents wouldn't let me. They said I needed to find a job that would pay the bills."

"So, take some classes now," said Alice. "You could go to community college."

"I haven't picked up a brush in years."

"It will be like riding a bicycle. The new semester probably hasn't even started yet."

Nina frowned. "I'll be the oldest student in the class."

"Tell that to Grandma Moses," said Alice. "She started painting when she was seventy-seven."

Chapter 13

There are those watershed moments we recognize only in hindsight. The two weeks they spent in Cape May with their children in the summer of 1983 was one of them. Nina had found a lovely Victorian house for rent on a corner lot with a wide front porch where baskets of morning glories and tuberous begonias were suspended from hooks beneath the eaves. They arrived late in the day, the sun casting long shadows on the lawn.

"Isn't it beautiful?" said Nina, pushing against the wrought-iron gate until it swung open onto a cobblestone walkway.

Alice dragged her heavy suitcase down the brick walk and lugged it, one step at a time, up to the porch where an American flag mounted on a cast iron pole flapped in the breeze. "This reminds me of my grandmother's house in Evanston," she told Nina. "She had a porch swing that my sister and I used to pretend was a stagecoach. We'd get it going so fast that it scraped the wood off the clapboard siding."

The house had eight bedrooms, one in a turret that Fern and Lily claimed for themselves. Noah ran upstairs to join Harper and Hayley, who told him he could stay in their room.

Arranging her toiletries on a small oak dresser with a tilting mirror, Alice heard Lily calling her from the hallway. "In here," she shouted.

There were two single beds with hobnail chenille coverlets, and Lily flopped down on one of them. Downstairs, a screen door slammed, and the sound of Charlotte's laughter floated up the steps.

Alice removed a stack of books, including a tattered copy of *War and Peace* from a canvas tote. "Want to go outside and look around?" she asked Lily, who hopped off the bed and ran down the stairs ahead of her mother.

The backyard was redolent with the scent of roses, and there were vine-filled urns in every corner. Wisteria, with its hanging clusters of fragrant, lilac flowers, climbed a trellis.

Lily examined an iridescent glass sphere on a pedestal near a stone bench. "What is this?" she asked, catching her reflection in the mirrored surface.

"It's a gazing ball," said Alice. "The Victorians thought they warded off evil spirits."

"We should get one for our backyard."

Alice threw her a bemused look.

"Better safe than sorry," said Lily, reclining on the bench and stretching her long legs out in front of her. A rubber flip-flop dangled from one foot.

Noah darted into the yard. "I'm hiding from Harper," he whispered before disappearing around the corner of the house.

"Scoot over," said Alice.

Lily sat up to make room for her mother and drew her knees toward her chest.

"Your hair's getting really long," said Alice, stroking her daughter's toffee-colored hair, which fell in loose waves past her shoulders.

"I know." Lily gave Alice a beseeching, sidelong glance. "Can I get blonde streaks this summer?"

"Put some lemon juice in your hair when you go to the beach."

"I mean real streaks like the ones you get."

"Maybe when you're sixteen."

"That's a whole year from now," Lily said, watching a bee in a bed of purple lavender. "I can't wait that long."

"Don't be in such a hurry to grow up. You've got your whole life ahead of you."

Theresa leaned out of an upstairs window. "Oh, there you are," she said when Alice looked up. "Grace is going to stay here with the kids so we can all go to the supermarket. You want to drive?"

"Sure," said Alice, who went to look for Noah. She found him crouching behind a crape myrtle. Alice always seemed surprised by how much Noah resembled his father. When he was a boy, Bill had been a towhead just like Noah, but even now they had the same eyes, a shade her mother-in-law called periwinkle blue. She kissed the top of her son's head with its loamy, summer scent. "Let's go inside."

"There's nothing to do there," said Noah, sulking.

Lily scooped him up. "I brought Uno, and I think I saw some checkers upstairs. We'll play later." She threw her brother over her shoulder and carried him, shrieking, into the house, his heavy, flaxen hair swinging from side to side.

Alice and Nina were at the carved mahogany table making a grocery list when Grace wandered into the kitchen. "Look what I found in the bookcase." She handed the slim volume to her mother.

"What's it about?"

"Vietnam," said Grace. "The author was a war correspondent for *Esquire* magazine."

Nina placed the book on the table.

"My father died in Vietnam," Grace reminded her mother. "I want to know what it was like."

"No, you don't," said Nina, her voice barely audible.

Grace, clearly exasperated, sighed deeply. "I have the right to know what he went through before he was killed."

Killed. The word sounded so harsh, so unnecessary to Nina, who preferred not to think about the way Ethan had died. Now Grace was dredging it all up again.

"You never talk about him," said Grace, who had nothing but a faded photograph of her father in uniform. He was holding a rifle, his gold wedding band glinting in the sunlight, but that told her nothing, just that he looked like a kid, no different from the boys who went to school with her. She wasn't sure if she could learn anything about her father from a book, but she hoped she'd find something in these pages that would help her understand what he must have experienced when he was a soldier. So, she carried the book out to the front porch and began reading. *Chapter One: Breathing In.*

After lunch the next day they took blankets, beach towels, folding chairs and a cooler filled with soft drinks and juice boxes with bendable straws to the beach. The teenagers set up camp as far away from their mothers as possible, spreading two of Nina's old quilts out on the sand. Fern brought a cassette player with a built-in radio, and the girls sang along with the Go-Go's: *Vacation, had to get away.*

Frankie kept to himself, sitting at the far edge of one of the blankets where he stole furtive glances at Lily when he knew she wasn't looking. His sister wore a pink inner tube like a bloated hula-hoop around her waist.

"Go away," he said when she coaxed him into the water. He tried to keep his voice low, but Lily must have heard because she looked over, a quizzical expression on her face. "I'll go in with you," she said, taking Tina's hand.

A seagull squawked overhead and dive-bombed a cone of french fries someone had dropped in the sand. Frankie shooed it away. Backlit against the sun, Lily and Tina jumped the foamy waves that broke along the shoreline, and Frankie wanted to kick himself for being such a jerk.

"Where are you going?" asked Theresa when Frankie yanked his T-shirt over his head and stomped off, kicking up sand behind him.

"Nowhere."

"That boy is going to be the death of me," said Theresa.

Alice removed her black Jackie O sunglasses to apply sunscreen to her face and arms before reclining in a beach chair where she intended to make a serious dent in Tolstoy's masterpiece.

"Only you would bring a Russian novel that's over a thousand pages long to the beach," said Theresa, shaking her head. She removed a paperback from her tote. "This is what you read on vacation." She held up a copy of *The Thorn Birds*. "You want junk food, not a heavy, five-course meal when you're working on your tan."

"At least you're not reading those awful bodice-rippers you used to love," Alice observed.

"I'm through with romance," said Theresa, oiling her arms and legs with Hawaiian Tropic. Unlike Alice, Theresa tanned easily and already looked like an Italian film star.

One sharp blast of the lifeguard's whistle and every mother within earshot began a frantic search for their missing children.

"Have you seen Noah?" Alice asked Charlotte, who had just returned from gathering seashells and pieces of colored glass with Fern.

"He's making sandcastles with Nina and the twins."

"Look what we found," said Fern, flopping down on a beach towel and dumping out the contents of two plastic buckets. "I can make jewelry out of these."

Charlotte removed her floppy hat and knelt down next to Fern to sift through an assortment of round, paper-thin jingle shells in translucent shades of yellow, silver and white.

Alice held up a larger, fan-shaped shell with fluted edges. "This one's pretty."

"That's a bay scallop. I can make you a necklace out of that one," said Fern. "It's much rarer to find ocean scallops around here. Did you know that bay scallops spend their entire lives in and around sea grass beds?"

Alice shook her head.

"I want to be a marine biologist when I grow up," said Fern, appraising a pear-shaped shell with raised spires.

"You must be pretty good at science."

"It's not just science. You also need to understand chemistry, calculus and physics."

"She gets A's in everything," said Charlotte, smiling at Fern, who smiled back.

"Lily's a bookworm, just like me," said Alice. "Math and science make our eyes glaze over."

Charlotte glanced at the book that lay unopened in Alice's lap. "So, have you made much progress?"

"I think I got as far as page three."

"Told you so," said Theresa. "We're going to Atlantic Books tomorrow, and I'm going to buy you a copy of *The Word* by Irving Wallace. You won't be able to put it down."

Nina had been taking painting classes for a couple of years and had become fairly adept at capturing people's likenesses. Her instructor, Mr. Graves, had been a commercial artist, but he'd told the class that advertising merely paid the rent. Portraiture was his passion, and it had become Nina's as well. For Christmas, she gave Alice a portrait of Lily, and Alice gave her a book about the Impressionist painter Mary Cassatt, who had been born in Western Pennsylvania, Pittsburgh actually, though she had lived in Paris most of her adult life.

"Her portraits of mothers and their children were very unconventional, but so was she," Alice told Nina. "I don't think she ever married."

It had been raining for two days straight so Nina set up her easel in the solarium. She preferred to work from photographs, and each of the children had reluctantly agreed to pose for her that week. That morning she had picked up two rolls of film from the one-hour photo lab in town. Now she fanned the pictures out on the dining room table.

There was one of Grace that she set aside. Her face was flushed, her gaze direct: fierce, dark brows, all that precocious beauty deferred before bursting into full bloom. She lifted the corner of another photograph, this one of Tina, who at ten radiated an aching vulnerability that made Nina fearful for her. Nina had played with depth of field to photograph Fern, whose lovely face with its sprinkling of freckles across the bridge of her nose filled the frame. Under a fringe of pale lashes, her eyes were disarmingly blue. Now, Nina examined a photograph of Frankie, whose brooding good looks would spell trouble for some young girl one day; she was sure of it.

Gathering up the rest of the photographs, she slipped them into an envelope. She would paint Frankie, remembering what Mr. Graves had taught her about capturing the personality and even the mood of your subject when painting someone's portrait.

Thunder, deep and resonant, rumbled in the distance. Nina went to the window and watched low, dark clouds move swiftly across the lilac sky.

Alice appeared in the doorway. "The natives are restless."

"We've been cooped up in here for days," said Nina, putting her things away. "Let's go out on the porch."

Alice grabbed a cotton sweater from a coat rack in the foyer and followed Nina outside. The air had a sweet, pungent scent. "I love thunderstorms."

"When I was a little girl, I'd hide under my bed when it started to thunder. My mother told me not to be afraid, that it was just God bowling."

"You must miss your mother," said Alice.

"All the time. I can't believe it's been two years."

"Do you ever wish you were a kid again?"

Nina nodded. "I had the best childhood."

"Me too," said Alice, remembering summers sprawled across the glider on the screened-in porch reading Jane Austin or Charles Dickens, the Sunday drives to Peterson's in Oak Park for ice cream.

Drops of rain bounced off the porch steps and splattered against the lavender hydrangea. "It's so peaceful here," Nina said. "It's going to be hard to go home."

Alice extended her hand, and Nina took it.

They kept company in silence for a few minutes, the

silver bracelets on Nina's slim wrist clattering as she squeezed Alice's fingers. "You're a good friend."

<hr/>

EACH NIGHT AFTER everyone else was asleep, Grace carried the book she'd found between copies of *Catch-22* and *From Here to Eternity* into the living room. Right away certain words and phrases leapt off the page: *bagged and tagged, killed by a grenade, boots of the dead men.* Other passages made her uneasy, like the description of a blindfolded prisoner whose elbows were bound behind his back, but she read every single word, including these: *You could fly apart so your pieces would never be gathered, you could take one neat round in the lung and go out hearing only the bubble of the last few breaths.*

Grace was fairly certain that her father had been killed in the Ia Drang Valley. She knew very little about what happened, just that his body had been recovered and sent home. Now she wondered if he knew he was dying and if he was afraid. Did he call out for his mother, or for her mother when he took his last breath? When she finally closed the book, Grace thought that maybe her mother had been right. Perhaps there were some things she didn't need to know. She got up from the sofa, and with a mixture of sorrow and regret put *Dispatches* back in the bookcase where she found it.

The sky was overcast for the next three days. Grace had hoped to spend that time at the beach reading drivel (Theresa had brought plenty of paperbacks that fit the bill) that she hoped would distract her from the dark and eerie images that had taken up residence inside her head ever since she finished Michael Herr's memoir. So, when she found a stack of board games in a closet in the front hall, she carried a couple of them into the living room.

"Monopoly or Game of Life?" she asked Lily, who was absorbed in a book as usual.

Lily turned the page, deep in concentration.

Frankie sat down on the sofa. "Earth to Lily," he said, nudging her foot. "Monopoly or The Game of Life?"

"What?" Lily looked up as if startled. "Oh, Life, I guess."

"Me, too," said Frankie, whose fingers lingered on Lily's toes. Each small nail was painted a shade of pink that reminded him of the inside of a seashell.

Fern came in from the kitchen with a can of Dr Pepper. "What's going on?"

"We're taking a vote," Grace explained. "Monopoly or The Game of Life?"

Fern popped the ring tab and took a sip. "I hate Monopoly."

"So, I guess we're playing Game of Life," said Grace definitively, removing pieces from the box: the green spinner wheel, plastic mountains and bridges, pink and blue people pegs.

Fern sat in one of the wing chairs that flanked the coffee table. "Can I be the banker?"

"Be my guest." Grace handed a stack of play money to Fern and opened the game board.

Lily, who had been shuffling the Life tiles, placed them Life-side-up in the draw pile. Frankie separated the cards into four decks: Career, Salary, House Deeds and Stocks and placed them near the game board along with insurance policies and bank loans.

Lily placed a pink people peg in a red plastic car and moved it onto the starting space.

"First, we all have decide if we're going to college or starting a career," said Grace, who parked her green car next to Lily's.

"You'll make more money if you go to college," said Fern, moving her car onto the game board.

Frankie jammed a blue people peg into a blue car. "I'm going to work for my dad."

"It's a game, Frankie, not real life," Fern reminded him. "The *game* of life, remember?"

"So, then I'll start my own business."

Fern sighed, but Lily cast a shy, sidelong glance at Frankie, who suppressed a smile.

They all spun the wheel to see who would go first.

"Looks like you're up, Frankie," said Grace.

Frankie chose a Career Card and moved his car onto the Start Career path. When it was her turn, Lily hesitated, then followed suit.

Fern decided to start college instead.

"Big surprise," said Frankie.

"Delayed gratification has its advantages," Fern told him.

"I'm not going through life playing it safe," said Frankie. "Bet I end up in Millionaires Estate before you do."

"Life is a crapshoot," said Grace, giving the wheel a good spin. "You're either lucky or you're not." She moved her car ahead and landed on an orange space: *Win marathon! Collect $10,000.* "What did I tell you?"

Lily advanced five spaces and groaned.

"Ski accident, pay $5,000," said Fern, clearly relishing her role as banker.

The game continued apace. Grace landed on Mid-Life Crisis and had to trade her salary and career cards for new ones. Frankie took out a bank loan and bought a house.

Lily had just landed on the Get Married space when Grace stood up and stretched. "Who wants popcorn?"

"I'll help," said Fern, who called "no cheating" to Frankie on her way out of the room.

Frankie leaned back against the sofa cushions. "Don't worry, I'm not going to rob your bank."

Fern liked teasing Frankie, but she saw the way he looked at Lily. Sometimes she wondered if anyone would ever look at her like that. The expression on Frankie's face when Lily walked into the room reminded her of the song that Sandy sang to Danny Zuko in *Grease*: "Hopelessly Devoted to You." Fern had been obsessed with that movie and had begged her mother for the soundtrack, which she played so often that Kip begged her to listen to something else.

Lily sat primly on the edge of the sofa, the heels of her hands resting on the cushion, unsure of what to do next. She stole a glance at Frankie, who was watching her. The air between them felt heavy and substantial, the way clouds seeded with silver iodide swell with moisture before a downpour. Frankie reached for Lily's hand, lacing his fingers through hers, but Lily let go when she heard Grace coming down the hallway

"Hope you like butter because Fern used a whole stick of it," said Grace, placing a speckled enamelware bowl of popcorn on the coffee table.

Fern swept up a handful of popcorn. "I think it's still your turn," she said to Lily, whose car was parked on the Get Married Space. Lily drew a Life Tile and added a blue people peg to her car. Wow, she thought, getting married, at least in The Game of Life, was a real letdown.

Frankie spun the wheel and moved ahead to the Pay Day space where he collected his salary. Fern had a run of bad luck and lost her shirt when the stock market tanked. After a few more rounds of play, Frankie did exactly what he'd told Fern he'd do and retired with more money than all of them.

⁂

WHEN THE RAIN finally stopped that weekend, Frankie discovered two old Schwinn bicycles in the detached garage and went looking for Lily. "Want to take a ride to Higbee Beach with me this afternoon?" he asked her.

Lily nodded. She had never been tongue-tied around Frankie before, but now the girl who was the first to raise her hand in class felt shy and unsure of herself.

"It's about six miles from here," he told her. "Think you can handle that?"

"Uh-huh," she said. Apparently speaking in complete sentences was out of the question.

At lunch, Lily ate a few bites of her grilled cheese and shoveled the rest into the trash when no one was watching. She simply felt too nervous to eat with Frankie sitting across the table from her. Like the way you're told not to look directly into the sun during an eclipse, Lily had been afraid to make eye contact with Frankie ever since that afternoon when he held her hand in the living room.

Noah marched one of his action figures across the table, tipping over a glass of ginger ale. Lily was mopping up the mess when Frankie announced, "Lily and I are going for a bike ride."

Alice, who was leafing through an issue of *People*, looked up briefly. "Wear sunscreen."

"Can I come along?" asked Fern.

Lily glanced at Frankie, who scraped back his chair. "There are only two bikes."

"Okay, forget it."

Lily could tell that Fern felt left out, but the truth was, she didn't want Fern tagging along, and that made her feel guilty. "Maybe we can take a bike ride tomorrow," she suggested.

Fern shrugged.

Noah examined his peanut butter and jelly sandwich before offering it to Lily. "It's all wet," he said, wiping his sticky fingers on his T-shirt with its photo of E.T. tucked in a basket on Elliott's BMX bike.

Lily sighed. "I'll make you a new one."

Frankie went outside. From the window over the farmhouse sink where Lily was spreading Jif on slices of white bread, she could see him striding toward the garage. It felt like her heart was literally pounding beneath her thin T-shirt. Cutting Noah's sandwich into quarters, she placed them on a paper plate and carried it to the table. "See you later, pal," she told her brother, who used his new G.I. Joe with its swivel-arm battle grip to grasp one of the bite-size pieces.

The garage smelled of grease and fertilizer and rotting wood. "There's a trail behind Higbee Beach we can walk if you want," Frankie said, pushing one of the bikes toward Lily. "Or we could sit on the rocks and watch the ferry come in."

Lily wheeled her bike out of the garage. "Whatever you want to do."

Frankie straddled the seat and pedaled to the corner where he waited for Lily to catch up. Every now and then he'd glance over his shoulder, throwing her a crooked grin. When they came to a dead end on New England Road, they ditched their bikes, and Frankie motioned for Lily to follow him on foot. The dirt road diverged into trees whose branches hung heavy with wild white roses and pale-yellow honeysuckle.

Frankie took Lily's hand and pulled her along through the thick woods. When they emerged, the beach stretched out before them shrouded in a dense tangle of vegetation. The dunes soared more than thirty-five feet in some places, while the sand cliffs dropped sharply to the shoreline.

He squeezed Lily's fingers. "It's beautiful, isn't it?" A foghorn sounded in the distance.

"Look, you can see the ferry from here," said Frankie with a nod toward the horizon. He tugged on her hand. "Come on, I want to show you something."

At the water's edge, an elderly man with a metal detector was dowsing for buried treasure. He tipped his khaki fishing hat in their direction. "Good day."

"Any luck?" asked Frankie.

"Depends on what you're lookin' for."

"Seen any Cape May diamonds today?"

"Lots of 'em. Just have to know where to look."

Frankie walked ahead a few feet and crouched down to sift through the sand.

"What's a Cape May diamond?" Lily wanted to know.

"Pieces of quartz washed down and worn smooth from the upper Delaware River," he told her. "They say the trip takes thousands of years."

"What's so special about them?" Lily asked the old man, who explained that most quartz turns into sand. "The fact that these have made it this far and are still big enough for us to see and to appreciate is pretty special, don't you think?"

"I guess so," said Lily, who was watching Frankie, whose long hair whipped his face. When she glanced over, the old man was walking slowly away, swiping his machine from side to side.

"These are for you," said Frankie, depositing three translucent pebbles in Lily's hand. "Put them in your pocket so you don't lose them."

Lily gave him a shy smile, and Frankie, tasting of the clove gun he was always chewing, leaned in to brush his lips against hers. "I've wanted to do that for a long time," he said, stuffing his hands into his pockets to keep them from shaking.

"How long?"

"How long what?"

"How long have you wanted to kiss me?"

He laughed. "You don't want to know."

"So, do it again," she said, lifting her chin and feeling her pulse quicken when he wrapped his arm around her waist and pulled her close.

They stood there for a long while, watching the water lap against the shoreline, Lily taking in Frankie's scent, a combination of sweat and soap and something she couldn't identify.

"I never want to forget this day," she said.

"Me either."

A gull squawked overhead. Frankie raked his fingers through his hair and narrowed his eyes against the sun, which loomed large on the horizon. "I guess we should start heading back."

Lily took Frankie's hand. "I hope no one stole our bicycles."

"Then we'll have to hitchhike," said Frankie, affectionately ruffling Lily's hair. "You worry too much."

———— • ————

ON THEIR LAST night in Cape May, Nina persuaded Grace to play something for them on the Baldwin piano in the parlor. The instrument was horribly out of tune, at least to Grace's trained ear, but she agreed in part because she understood on some level that their lives were about to change and that these two weeks were not likely to be repeated.

Grace had been accepted at the Curtis Institute of Music in Philadelphia to study piano. Classes started in a couple of months. After that it was only a matter of time before Lily and Fern would go off to college somewhere, too. Lily wanted to study literature at Oberlin, a liberal arts college in Ohio, while Fern had her heart set on Boston University, which offered a rigorous program in marine sciences. As for Frankie, Grace had no idea what he'd end up doing with his life, but for some reason she couldn't imagine him working for his father at Carpet Warehouse.

Grace's audition at Curtis, which required twice the repertoire as Julliard, was grueling. "Everyone just stares at you while you're waiting for your turn," she told her mother. "It felt like we were waiting to be executed."

Still, she knew how lucky she was to have been accepted, and she planned to work hard in order to live up to the standards of the school's most distinguished graduates, notably Leonard Bernstein.

Grace riffled through the sheet music in the piano bench, an assortment of popular show tunes, before deciding that the occasion called for something appropriately wistful and melancholy. Her long, slender fingers hovered over the keyboard for a few seconds. Then she closed her eyes and began to play a study for solo piano that Chopin had called his most beautiful melody.

Alice recognized the opening chords of *Etude Op. 10 No. 3* from a film she saw as a young girl. Cornel Wilde played Chopin, who died of consumption when he was only thirty-nine years old. Alice's mother had never understood why her daughter was moved by such blatant sentimentality, but Alice had always been drawn to stories about lives cut short by catastrophe, all that promise and potential unfulfilled.

Alice had loved all the romantic poets: Lord Byron, who died in Missolonghi at thirty-six; Keats, dead like Chopin of tuberculosis at twenty-five. Shelley's boat capsized in a sudden storm off the coast of Italy when he was twenty-nine, but his body was not recovered until ten days later. His wife Mary kept his heart in a silken shroud, and after her death, the heart was discovered in her desk drawer wrapped in the pages of her husband's last poem, an elegy for Keats. Only one of their five children, Percy Florence Shelley, survived into adulthood. How, Alice wondered, did someone bear such tragedy?

Alice had been so lost in thought that she didn't realize that Grace had struck the last few notes until she heard Theresa, Nina and Charlotte clapping enthusiastically. Grace bowed at the waist, and Fern and Lily tossed rose petals at her from an arrangement of cut flowers Nina had placed on a walnut table next to the sofa.

It would be years before one of them would wonder why no one had taken a photograph that night of all four of them, their children safe and sound, their families intact.

Chapter 14

G race moved to Philadelphia that September to start classes at Curtis, and Nina went along to help her get settled in an apartment she'd be sharing near Rittenhouse Square with two other girls. Fen Hua (her name, Grace learned, meant beautiful flower) had been playing the violin since she was three. Her parents owned a dry-cleaning business in Grand Rapids that did well enough to pay for private lessons and music camp at Interlochen Center for the Arts each summer. Julia grew up in Rochester, the only child of anthropology professors at Ithaca College, and played the cello with eyes closed, head thrown back, her dark hair falling to her waist.

During orientation week Grace and her roommates attended a welcome party where she saw Gary Graffman, a member of the piano faculty, moving through the crowd. Grace knew that he had been accepted to Curtis when he was only seven years old and had studied with the Russian pianist Isabelle Vengerova, who helped found the school.

"I heard he injured his right hand and can't play anymore," Julia whispered, drawing her finger across her throat with a grimace. "That's why he's here."

They watched the famed pianist move through the crowd, placing a hand on an incoming freshman's shoulder or nodding appreciatively when another student gushed effusively about what an honor it was to meet the man who had studied with Rudolph Serkin *and* Vladimir Horowitz.

"Did you ever see the Woody Allen movie *Manhattan*?" asked Julia, handing Grace a plastic cup quivering with some kind of fruit punch. "He played *Rhapsody in Blue* on the soundtrack."

Grace took a sip of her punch. "I want you as a partner if we ever play Trivial Pursuit."

Julia smiled. "I'm a wealth of useless information on a variety of subjects." She tossed her empty cup into the trash. "Let's get out of here, okay? I'm starving, and these finger sandwiches aren't cutting it."

"Should we look for Fen Hua?" asked Grace.

"I saw her leave with a couple of string players about a half hour ago. You like Chinese food?"

Grace nodded. "Sure."

"Good. Let's go to Chinatown. I've got enough money on me for a cab."

At Julia's request the cabbie dropped them off at 10th and Arch Street near the Friendship Gate, which was still under construction. Even in the waning light it was possible to make out a procession of mythical animals on the brightly colored tiles. Julia pulled Grace into a Cantonese restaurant on the corner where they ordered tea and wonton soup at a sticky table along the wall and shared an order of roast pork over steamed rice, the meat slightly pink and honey-sweet.

"We don't have anything like this back home," said Grace.

"I'm not even sure if we have any Asian people in Rochester," said Julia, expertly pinching a slice of pork with her chopsticks. "I'm kidding," she added when Grace looked perplexed.

"How did you learn to do that?" Grace was struggling to move even one piece of meat from her plate to her mouth.

"Years of cello practice make for nimble fingers." Julia flagged down their waiter and asked him to bring a fork for Grace. "I heard that some boat people from Vietnam opened a restaurant down here somewhere. You interested? The food's supposed to be really good."

"My father died in Vietnam," said Grace.

Julia looked up mid-bite. "Oh, God, I'm really sorry."

Grace shrugged. "I was just a baby when it happened. I never even got to meet him."

"My parents marched in anti-war demonstrations in college," said Julia. "They said we had no business being there in the first place."

Grace poked at her rice. "Well, in hindsight, I guess they were right."

Julia nodded. "So, here's another piece of trivia for you. In 1970 a group of Curtis students and some kids from other music schools in Philadelphia staged an outdoor concert of Mahler's First Symphony to protest the war."

Grace put her fork down. "Well, my father was already dead by 1970 so I guess their protest didn't do him much good."

———— · ————

GRACE TOOK THE bus home for Christmas, and by the time she arrived, Nina had already decorated the tree and added eucalyptus to the floral arrangements in every room.

When Grace was young, she and Nina had dyed bottle brush trees in shades of turquoise, silver and hot pink and placed them in Mason jars on a bed of cotton batting.

"Maybe it's time to throw these things away?" Grace suggested when Nina brought them out.

"Are you kidding? I plan to pass them down to the grandchildren you're going to give me someday."

"What if I don't want to have kids?" asked Grace, who was already imagining a career as a concert pianist.

"Don't say that. You and your sisters were the best thing that ever happened to me."

"Now that's just sad." Grace placed one of the Mason jars on a side table. "Didn't you ever want to do something else with your life?"

"Like what?"

"I don't know. I've seen your paintings. You're really good. You could have been Georgia O'Keeffe." Grace narrowed her eyes as if considering the possibilities. "Or Frida Kahlo." She picked up one of the snow globes and shook it until a storm of silver glitter descended upon an angel playing a mandolin. "Why didn't you go to art school?"

"Long story," said Nina. "Did you know that neither of them ever had children?"

"Who?" asked Grace.

"Georgia O'Keeffe and Frida Kahlo."

Grace placed the snow globe back on the coffee table. "Maybe their art was enough for them."

"Well, it wouldn't have been enough for me."

CHARLOTTE, WHO HAD been hosting a New Year's Eve party for years, enlisted Fern to keep the younger children entertained. Lily was useless now that she and Frankie were "going steady," and Grace was at a party with a boy she had a crush on in high school, though he seemed woefully immature compared to the boys she met at Curtis who were as serious about music as she was.

Noah found a copy of *Tales of a Fourth Grade Nothing* in Fern's bookshelf and coaxed her into reading to him. After climbing into bed with her, he settled back against Fern's shoulder.

"I won Dribble at Jimmy Fargo's birthday party," she began.

His head popped up. "Who's Dribble?"

"A pet turtle," Fern explained, and Noah, who seemed satisfied, lay back down.

Fern read a few more pages, but Noah kept interrupting her. "What kind of name is Farley Drexel Hatcher? Is Juicy-O a real drink?" Finally, Fern closed the book and let him talk for a while.

"I'm glad I don't have a little brother like Fudge," he told her. "I have a big sister."

"I know."

Noah shifted his weight and sighed deeply. "Does your mom ever yell at your dad?"

"Where'd that come from?" asked Fern, turning on her side to face Noah.

"Sometimes when I'm trying to go to sleep, I can hear them."

Noah's expression was so unguarded that Fern's heart went out to him. "All parents fight. It's nothing to worry about."

"Okay." Noah's eyelids fluttered once or twice.

Fern reached over to turn off the lamp on the nightstand, throwing the room into total darkness except for the dozens of glow-in-the-dark stars Kip had affixed to the ceiling when she was Noah's age. When Noah's breathing became slow and rhythmic, she slipped out of bed and went downstairs where she saw Frankie kissing Lily under the mistletoe in the foyer. Quickly turning away, she rushed down the stairs to the family room where Tina was playing Pac-Man with Harper and Hayley, who screeched when she wiped out three rows of dots and gobbled up a power pellet to earn bonus points.

Bored, Fern went back upstairs to join the grownups in the living room who were waiting for the ball drop in Time's Square. Kip motioned her in and handed her a party horn, its paper tube coiled tightly inside. At the stroke of midnight, Old Man Decker who lived next door walked out on the patio in his Woolrich field coat and fired his rifle into the air just like he did every year.

"Someday he's going to kill someone," said Charlotte, shaking her head, but Kip just laughed.

That night none of them knew what 1984 held in store: that Indira Gandhi would be assassinated, that over a million people would die from widespread famine in Ethiopia, or that a man would walk into a McDonald's Restaurant in San Ysidro, California, and open fire on the customers, killing twenty-one people and wounding nineteen others before being shot to death by police. They knew nothing really, which was probably a blessing.

Chapter 15

Later, Nina would remember the gunmetal-gray sky, the birch trees stripped bare in the front yard, how bitterly cold it was that day as if the natural world had been appropriately aggrieved on her behalf. The call from Hahnemann University Hospital came in while Nina was loading the dishwasher. That she should have been occupied with such a mundane task when her life was about to change irrevocably seemed ludicrous in retrospect.

On the kitchen counter was a Valentine's Day card Nina planned to mail to her daughter later that afternoon. Now someone was telling her that Grace had been brought in by ambulance early that morning with symptoms that included double vision, vomiting and a pounding headache. The rest of the conversation was so disturbing that Nina seemed to hear it in fragments: *we regret to inform you, cerebral aneurysm, nothing the doctors could do.* Nina dropped the receiver, tethered to the wall phone by its yellow plastic cord, and sank to the floor. Her instinct was to hang up as if on a prank caller. What she said was, "I have to call you back." Then she dialed Alice's number.

"Grace is dead," she said when Alice picked up.

"What?"

"Grace is dead."

Alice seemed indignant, as if Nina had insulted her. "What are you talking about?"

"I don't know what to do," Nina whimpered.

"I'll be right over."

The front door was unlocked, and Alice found Nina upstairs in Grace's room where she was stroking the sleeves of a gray cashmere sweater. "She forgot to take this with her," she said. "It was her favorite sweater." The vacant look in Nina's eyes reminded Alice of Jackie Kennedy in her bloody pink suit standing next to Lyndon Johnson on Air Force One.

At Kearney Funeral Home, Paul stood dutifully next to his wife near the casket. The rosary Grace carried at her confirmation was laced through her fingers, and her dark hair spilled onto the white satin pillow under her head. A strand of amethyst beads that had belonged to Nina's mother was knotted at Grace's throat and would be interred with her. Nina wore the matching choker, a metaphysical thread between this world and the one to come.

Inside the visitation room where people sat stiffly on folding chairs after paying their respects, Alice was nearly overpowered by the cloying odor of lilies. Hundreds of them had been fashioned into standing sprays, crosses and other elaborate arrangements. A hinge spray of white roses and long-stemmed myrtle rested in the lid of the coffin, the word *Daughter* written in glitter on the satin funeral ribbon.

The receiving line stretched all the way into the vestibule. "I don't know half of these people, do you?" said Bill, signing the guest book.

Alice shrugged, though she imagined that many of them were business acquaintances of Paul's. Still, she wasn't surprised by the turnout. A gifted pianist with a promising future whose life was tragically cut short was bound to attract a crowd. Alice recognized Nina's father, who looked lost, a child stranded in a bus station in an unfamiliar town.

"I can't go up there," Lily whispered to Alice.

"You have to for Nina's sake."

Her eyes brimmed with tears. "Then I'll wait for Fern."

Alice handed Lily a funeral card. Jesus, blonde and blue-eyed, gestured toward his Sacred Heart crowned in flames. "You should keep one of these."

Now Nina embraced a young woman wearing a knit hat trimmed in fur, and Bill asked who she was. "One of Grace's roommates from Curtis," Alice told him. "She's going to play the cello at her service tomorrow."

Theresa motioned for them to sit with her in the front row, nudging Tina, who moved down a few seats. Frankie tugged at his tie, craning his neck to scan the back of the room, and Alice knew he was looking for Lily. His long legs in their black dress pants jiggled nervously until Theresa told him to stop it.

Alice lowered her voice to a whisper. "It makes me sick watching Paul up there acting like the doting husband when we know that he will not give Nina one ounce of support when they get home."

Frankie leapt to his feet when he saw Lily approaching the casket with Fern, who discreetly stepped aside. Lily threw her arms around Frankie's neck and dissolved into tears.

"This is torture," said Theresa. "I don't know how we're going to get through the actual funeral."

"Where are the twins?" asked Alice, who just realized that she hadn't seen them all evening.

"Paul's mother took them home with her earlier today. Apparently, Harper had some kind of breakdown this afternoon when she saw Grace for the first time." Theresa removed a Kleenex from her pocket and pressed it against her face. "How does a family get over something like this?"

"I don't know," said Alice. "Maybe they don't."

Later while everyone else was praying the Rosary, Lily excused herself to use the restroom. Frankie followed her downstairs and caught her wrist when she came out of the bathroom. There was a sofa in a faded floral pattern in the hallway, and he pulled her onto his lap.

Lily smoothed her black taffeta skirt down over her knees and placed her hand against his chest. "I can feel your heart beating."

Frankie wrapped both arms around Lily's waist, surprised by how fragile she seemed and how protective he felt toward her. Frankie knew that his parents had met when they were in high school, but he had trouble imagining his father having the same kinds of feelings for his mother that he had for Lily, a kind of desperate longing coupled with the fear of losing her.

Lily disentangled herself and looked earnestly at Frankie. "Do you believe in God?"

He frowned. "Why?"

"I keep thinking about Grace."

"What about her?"

"Do you think she's in heaven?"

"My mother does, that's for sure."

Lily looked at Frankie as if he was an oracle. "But what do you think?"

"I don't know. I stopped going to church after my parents got divorced."

Lily sighed. "Part of me knows that Grace's body is upstairs in that room, but another part of me wonders where she is, where all that energy went. We don't just disappear after we die, do we? I don't think I could live with that."

"In catechism they taught us that when we die, our bodies separate from our souls and our souls go to meet God," said Frankie, who was not sure if he believed much of what he learned in Catholic school, but Lily was looking for answers and he wanted to provide them. "I don't know if that helps or not." His voice trailed off.

Lily produced the funeral card from her pocket and handed it to Frankie. "Did you get one of these?"

He shook his head. "We used to swap them like baseball cards when we were kids." His favorite had been Saint George mounted on a white horse slaying a dragon, and he'd traded two Saint Judes and a Saint Patrick for one. Now, remembering a boy who thought Francis of Assisi was Francis the Sissy, he stifled a laugh.

Lily made a face. "Be serious," she said, turning the card over. "Look, there's something on the back."

"Let me guess. You're going to read it to me."

She jabbed him in the arm.

"Okay, I'm listening."

Lily took a deep breath. "Do not stand at my grave and weep, I am not there, I do not sleep." She glanced briefly at Frankie, then back at the card, her brow furrowed in concentration. "I am a thousand winds that blow, I am the diamond glints on snow."

"What's wrong?" asked Frankie when she grew quiet.

"Nothing."

"Want me to read it?"

"Yes, please." She offered the card to him.

"I am the sunlight on ripened grain, I am the gentle autumn rain." Frankie tried not to stumble over the words like he usually did. "When you awaken in the morning's hush, I am the swift uplifting rush of quiet birds in circled flight. I am the soft stars that shine at night."

"Let's go outside," said Lily, taking Frankie by the hand.

Alice was standing on the sidewalk with Charlotte when they pushed through the front door.

"Your father went to get the car," she told Lily.

"We'll be right back," she said, pulling Frankie around the side of the funeral home, which had once been a private residence for a family of eight. "Look." She pointed at the night sky with its bright array of stars and constellations.

Frankie seemed to understand right away. "Good night, Grace," he hollered.

Lily gripped his arm. The air was so frigid that it hurt to breathe. "My hands are freezing."

Frankie blew on Lily's fingers as if stoking embers in a fireplace, and she stood on tiptoe to kiss him. Just as quickly she whirled around to take it all in—the stars that flickered above the steeply sloping roofs, the moonlight glinting off the snowdrifts in the vast expanse of frozen grass behind them. Grace, she realized with startling clarity, was not gone; she was everywhere, in everything.

Lily closed her eyes, listening carefully to the murmur of wind rushing through the broad, bare branches of Live Oak and White Ash, their bark a mosaic of cracks and fissures, and when her scarf fluttered at her neck she took it as a sign, an invocation, a promise. *I am not here. I do not sleep.*

Chapter 16

For the first few weeks after Grace's funeral, Alice came over after breakfast and tidied up the kitchen or threw in a load of wash. Charlotte usually arrived by lunchtime to coax Nina into eating something—a bowl of tomato soup or a piece of toast. Never one to take no for an answer, Theresa ignored Nina when she insisted that she had no appetite and made huge pans of lasagna or chicken parmesan, which she covered in foil and warmed up when she got to Nina's house in time for dinner.

Paul had all but abandoned ship, but Harper and Hayley were happy to let Theresa fill in for their mother, who had stopped doing motherly things for them since Grace died, like making pancakes for breakfast on Saturday morning or asking about their day when they came home from school or starching and ironing their Gap button-down shirts.

One afternoon Theresa offered to teach the girls how to make acquacotta, an Italian peasant soup her grandmother taught her how to make when she was their age.

"What's in it?" asked Harper suspiciously.

"Well, you need water, onion, tomatoes, stale bread, olive oil and vegetables," Theresa said, placing Nina's All-Clad stockpot on the stove. "My grandmother threw in anything she had left at the end of the week. Nothing went to waste in those days."

Harper hopped up on one of the bar stools at the island and watched Theresa chop onion and celery. "So how long does it have to cook?"

"Not long. Half an hour or so." She handed Harper a couple of potatoes. "Peel these." She placed the pot on the stove and began heating the olive oil. "You want to fry the celery and onion until they're soft. Then you add some water and the tomatoes and cook for about ten minutes."

Hayley wandered into the kitchen. "Something smells good."

"We're making soup," said Harper.

Hayley removed a banana from a ceramic bowl on the counter and peeled back the skin. "It looks like Theresa's doing all the work. You aren't doing anything."

"I'm peeling potatoes."

Hayley bit into the banana's soft flesh and chewed thoughtfully. "Mom's sleeping."

"Your mother is depressed," said Theresa, pouring a can of tomatoes into the saucepan. "She just lost her daughter."

"Is she going to be okay?"

Theresa wiped her hands on a terrycloth towel. "It's going to take time."

Harper fingered the delicate gold chain at her throat. A few days ago she'd gone into her sister's room when her mother was downstairs and opened Grace's jewelry box, the one that played *Clair de Lune* when you lifted the lid. Inside was a pale jade ring that Nina had given Grace for her sixteenth birthday, a gold scarab bracelet with a broken clasp, a pair of sterling silver hoop earrings, a brown hemp necklace with cowrie shells and the necklace Harper was wearing now. She didn't want to take anything that would be missed. She just wanted something that Grace had admired and worn, something tangible to remind her of the sister who went back to college after Christmas break and never came home.

Harper remembered that day in vivid detail: a veil of thick gray clouds seemed to hover, a portent of snow. Their mother had tried to talk them into driving to the bus station with her, but she and Hayley had come up with some excuse, she can't even remember what it was now, and had barely looked up when Grace said goodbye. Now Harper wished that she had known that she would never see Grace again. She might have behaved differently, might have thrown her arms around her sister's waist and pulled her close, breathed in the scent of lily of the valley that clung to her clothing even now when Harper went through her closet.

"Here, let me," said Hayley, removing the potato peeler from her sister's hand.

Theresa handed Harper a loaf of day-old Italian bread. "Why don't you tear this into chunks," she suggested, squeezing Harper's shoulder. "We'll pour the soup over them when we serve it."

"Does Mom even care about us anymore?" asked Hayley, who was skinning a potato with such ferocity that the peelings went sailing across the Corian countertop.

"Of course, she does," said Theresa, tapping her wooden spoon against the lip of the saucepan.

"What if she never gets better?" asked Harper. This question took a lot of effort to formulate, but it had been on her mind for weeks.

"She will," said Theresa though without much conviction. At the funeral Father Phil had read from Philippians 4:7: *The peace of God, which passes all understanding, will guard your hearts and your minds in Christ Jesus.* Theresa wasn't so sure that she believed anything Father Phil had to say anymore. None of it gave her much comfort in light of Grace's senseless death.

"This peace will transcend our ability to understand it," she overheard Father Phil tell Nina after Grace was lowered into the ground, but peace seemed to have eluded her friend, who seemed more distant with each passing day.

"Does your father ever come home for dinner anymore?" asked Theresa.

The girls shook their heads.

Hayley braided and unbraided a lock of dark hair and stole a glance at Harper. "We heard them fighting the other night."

"About what?"

Harper shot her a look, but Hayley ignored her. "He told her to snap out of it."

Theresa slammed the spoon down. "Snap out of it? Her daughter is dead."

Harper winced.

"Oh, honey, I'm sorry," said Theresa. "I need to learn when to keep my big mouth shut."

Tears pooled in Harper's eyes.

"Mommy yelled at me for playing the piano last week," said Hayley, who had been in the middle of Debussy's *Arabesque No. 1* when Nina stormed into the living room, pushed Hayley aside and brought the lid on the Steinway down hard.

Hayley knew that the piece reminded her mother of Grace, who used to play it when she was anxious or upset because it helped her relax, but she didn't care because the familiar notes seemed to conjure up Grace's spirit. Grace had taught Hayley how to play the arabesque before she went away to college, and she had practiced every day until she mastered the series of triads that cascaded like waterfalls so she could surprise her sister when she came home for Christmas. She still remembered how Grace seemed to hold her breath in astonishment until Hayley struck the last chord.

Theresa carried three soup bowls to the table and told the girls to wash up for dinner. "I'm going to see if your mother wants to join us."

She climbed the stairs and found Nina in Grace's bed. The room was illuminated only by the faint glow of the Bulova alarm clock on the nightstand.

"Go away," said Nina, rolling over to face the wall.

Theresa sat on the edge of the bed. "I'm not going anywhere."

"I'm not hungry."

"We're just having soup." She placed her palm on the small of Nina's back.

"I said I'm not hungry."

"You don't have to eat anything. Just come downstairs and spend some time with the girls."

Nina pulled the quilt up around her shoulders.

"Okay, I'll be downstairs if you need me," said Theresa when it became clear that Nina was not going anywhere.

"We started without you," said Harper, slurping soup from her spoon. "You were up there for a long time."

Theresa pulled out a chair and sat down.

"Is Mommy coming down?" asked Hayley.

"I don't think so."

She carried her bowl to the sink. "Thanks for dinner."

"Why don't you stay here with us for a little while," said Theresa, but Hayley shook her head.

Harper was smashing the potatoes at the bottom of her bowl into pulp. "Let her go."

"You don't have to finish that," said Theresa, who was beginning to wonder if she should be more concerned about the twins than about their mother.

Theresa didn't recognize the first few notes of *Arabesque No. 1*, which wafted in from the living room, but Harper did. "Shit."

Neither of them heard Paul come in.

The delicate melody with its sweeping arpeggios gave way to a faster tempo, which became more frantic before dissolving into a clash of dissonant chords struck at random, a jarring progression of notes that begged for resolution, but there was none. Then, just as quickly, the cacophony came to an end.

"What the hell's wrong with you?" her father shouted as Hayley rushed up the stairs. "That's a goddamn Steinway. Do you know how much I paid for that thing?"

Harper pretended to load the dishwasher, and Theresa stepped aside when Paul walked into the kitchen.

"What a surprise," he said, pouring himself a glass of scotch. "Why don't you just move in."

"She came over to make dinner for us," said Harper, who felt protective of Theresa, the only adult who had provided any stability in her life since Grace died.

Paul screwed the top back on the bottle of Glenlivit. "Where's your mother? Still in her pajamas?"

Theresa shook her head. "What's wrong with you anyway?"

Paul ignored her. "Don't you have homework?" he asked Harper, who looked at Theresa as if it was a trick question.

"Don't look at her. I'm your father."

"There's no need to talk to her like that," said Theresa. "She's just a child."

"Don't tell me what to do in my own house," he said, shoving Theresa out of the way and taking the bottle of scotch with him when he went upstairs.

"Go to your room and lock the door," Theresa told Harper. "You know my number. Call me if you need anything."

Harper wrapped her arms around Theresa's waist. "I hate it here."

"It's going to be alright. I promise."

Harper looked unconvinced.

"Want me to stay a little while longer?" asked Theresa, and Harper nodded. "Let's go sit in the living room."

In the foyer, Theresa looked up and saw Nina on the landing. When she held out her hand, Harper vaulted up the stairs and threw herself into her mother's arms.

"It's late," called Nina. "You can go home."

"You sure?"

Nina turned, and Harper followed her down the hallway.

Theresa let herself out. The walk hadn't been shoveled since it snowed earlier in the week, and she was careful to avoid the icy patches. Before getting into her car, she turned to look back at the house, worried for the first time about what went on behind closed doors, but her own children were at home waiting for her so Theresa put the car in reverse and backed out of the driveway.

Chapter 17

When Nina met her husband in the parking lot at George Mason University School of Law in Arlington, Virginia, the first thing she noticed was his eyes, which were a striking shade of green. Coming to her rescue that day, Paul had seemed like a knight in shining armor, and their courtship felt like something right out of a fairytale. Things didn't fall apart right away, but then they usually don't. Instead, they tend to unravel, a skein of yarn left unattended until the cat happens upon it. A mystery that reveals itself in fits and starts.

One of the perks of her job (Nina worked in the Office of Admissions) was free tuition at the university, which had a School of Nursing. Two nights a week while Nina was in class, Eleanor watched Grace. During the day while she was at work, Nina left Grace with Mrs. Healey, who subsidized her meager income by watching other people's children plus two of her own. One Friday afternoon just as Nina was getting ready to go home, the Dean called her into his office, so she was already running late when she got to her car: Ethan's old Ford Falcon with a three-speed manual column shift. Late one night before he left for Vietnam, he'd taken her to the parking lot at the A&P and taught her how to drive a stick.

When the car wouldn't start no matter how many times she tried, her first thought was that the battery was dead. Her second thought was that if Ethan were here, he'd know what to do.

Nina rolled down the window when Paul rapped on the glass, and she was struck by how handsome he was: hair like honey that curled over his ears, a wicked grin and those eyes the color of jade with an amber starburst circling each iris.

"I think the engine's flooded," he said.

"Can you fix it?"

"You've got to wait for a while until the fuel evaporates."

Nina glanced at the clock on the dashboard. If she didn't leave right now, she'd be late again, and Mrs. Healey would not be pleased. "How long will that take?"

"About twenty minutes." He stood back to get a better look at Nina. "You work in Admissions, don't you?"

She nodded.

"I'm Paul."

"Nina," she told him. "If you're not busy, I could really use your help. My daughter is at day care and I can't be late picking her up."

"You've got a kid?"

"She's three."

"Come on, I'll give you a lift. We can come back for your car later."

Nina locked up and followed Paul to his car. He held the door open for her while she slid into one of the bucket seats before getting in on the driver's side.

"Nice car," she said when the engine roared to life.

"You know much about cars?"

"Not really."

He laughed.

"Okay, I know that this is some kind of muscle car," she said. "That's what you call them, right?"

"It's a Dodge Charger so yeah, I guess it is," he said, shifting into reverse. "Kind of looks like a Mach 2 jet on wheels, don't you think?"

Nina, who was forced back in her seat when Paul accelerated, had no idea what a Mach 2 jet was supposed to look like but she smiled amiably.

"You know that movie *Bullitt* with Steve McQueen?"

"Sure."

"He out-drove the bad guys in a Ford Mustang GT, which is a complete joke. They were in a Charger R/T with a 440, which is faster and more powerful than the Mustang."

Nina glanced over at Paul and nodded to suggest that she knew exactly what he was talking about. She'd done the same thing when watching football with Ethan. All that talk about yards down and sacking the quarterback and wishbone plays made her head spin.

"Where to?" Paul asked when they approached the exit.

"Make a left."

Mrs. Healey lived in an iffy neighborhood, but there weren't a lot of options in those days, and Mrs. Healey was the best Nina could do. Paul waited in the car while Nina pounded on the front door. She could hear the TV blaring inside. Finally, the door swung open.

"Mommy!" squealed Grace.

"Where's Mrs. Healey?" asked Nina, stepping inside.

"Upstairs."

A toddler with a runny nose wailed from a playpen in the middle of the living room. A small boy with scabs on both knees sat on the shabby couch eating pudding from a plastic container. Nina lowered the volume on the TV and hollered for Mrs. Healey. When she appeared at the top of the stairs, her hair askew as if she'd just woken up, she glared at Nina. "You're late."

"Were you sleeping?" Nina asked, incredulous.

"You're late," Mrs. Healey repeated.

"My car broke down."

"If you're late again, I'll have to charge you extra," she said. Then she disappeared into the dimly lit hallway.

"Where's the cereal we brought this morning?" Nina asked Grace.

"Mrs. Healey put it in the cupboard."

The boy on the sofa sat up straight as if on high alert. His watery eyes followed Nina as she went into the kitchen. Dirty dishes were piled in the sink. One scuffed Buster Brown lay on its side in the middle of the floor. Nina picked it up and turned the gas off underneath a pot that had boiled over on the stove.

She poked around in the cupboard until she located the box of Cheerios and marched back into the living room where Grace was perched at the edge of the sofa. The baby in the playpen clung to the bars, blubbering wordlessly. Nina picked her up, and she wound her chubby arms around Nina's neck.

Grace wandered over and looked up at her mother. "She cries a lot."

Nina sighed and lowered the baby back into the playpen. Her eyes were still watching Nina in wonder when she closed the front door softly behind her.

"Where's our car?" asked Grace as Nina hurried her down the sidewalk.

"It broke down," she said. "We're getting a ride from a friend of mine."

Paul held the door on the passenger side open, and Grace scrambled into the front seat, crawled over the console and planted herself behind the wood-grain steering wheel.

"I want to drive," she said, yanking the wheel sharply in one direction and then the other.

Nina smiled weakly at Paul.

"I have an idea," he said. "How about if you sit on your mommy's lap and be my co-pilot?" He opened the glove box and removed a map of Virginia. "Come on, you can be my navigator."

Grace seemed dubious, but to Nina's relief she scrambled over to sit on her lap. Paul unfolded the map and asked Grace if she'd ever been to the ocean, which he pointed out to her.

"Grandma and Pap-Pap take me there every summer," she said, extending her legs and flexing her toes inside her canvas sneakers.

"Want to listen to the radio?" Paul asked her, and she nodded, pigtails bobbing. He fiddled with the dial, and Grace turned up the volume so loud that the dashboard vibrated with low base booms. *GET IT ON, BANG A GONG.* "This is my favorite song," she told him.

Paul backed the car down the driveway and flashed Nina a smile, reaching over to ruffle her hair before moving effortlessly onto the street.

They were married a year later after Paul graduated from law school, and when he accepted a position at a prestigious law firm near his hometown, Nina and Grace went with him. Eleanor was subdued the day they left, though she put on a brave face. As Paul pulled away from the curb, Nina leaned out the window for one last hug from her mother, while Grace sat primly in the back seat, her bottom lip trembling. She'd already said goodbye to her grandfather before he left for work that morning, and now she watched as her grandmother receded in the distance.

The twins were a surprise coming so soon after their marriage, and Eleanor stayed for a month to help out after they were born. When she went home, Nina was on her own. It had been decided early on that they would spend Thanksgiving in Virginia with Nina's parents and Christmas in Pennsylvania. Paul's mother, Carmella, came from a large Italian family, and Christmas Eve was a big event that included the Feast of the Seven Fishes. There was shrimp, salmon fillets and lobster tails stuffed with crabmeat, dried salt cod called baccalà, mussels, smelts, spaghetti with clams simmered in olive oil and garlic, and for dessert, homemade cannoli. After dinner the extended family convened in the living room to exchange gifts, a laborious process that went on until it was time to leave for midnight mass.

Paul expected Nina to do the Christmas shopping for everyone on his list, which included his father and mother, her four sisters and assorted aunts, uncles and cousins. The twins, who were still babies, had been fussy all day, and Nina was still upstairs wrapping presents when Paul came home from work on Christmas Eve.

"We have to be there in an hour," he told her, stepping over a stack of boxes wrapped in gold metallic paper and red satin ribbon. He worked his tie loose and went into the bathroom.

"Harper has a poopy diaper," announced Grace from the doorway, "and I'm not changing it this time."

"Fine, don't," said Nina, tearing a piece of scotch tape from the dispenser.

"You're not even dressed," said Paul, tossing his shirt into the hamper in the walk-in closet.

"You could help, you know."

"I work all day," he reminded her.

"So do I," said Nina, but they both knew it wasn't the same thing. What she did was woman's work, and she was never going to get any respect from him for that.

"Did you remember to get the oranges?"

That morning he'd asked her to pick up a bag of oranges at the grocery store so they could put one in the toe of each stocking that hung from the mantel. That was another of his mother's Depression-era traditions left over from a time when finding a piece of fresh fruit in your stocking on Christmas morning must have been a rare treat.

Nina's hand flew to her mouth. "Shit."

What happened next was as surprising to her as if Santa had literally come down the chimney. First, Paul kicked the boxes she had wrapped so fastidiously and sent them sailing across the bedroom. Then he grabbed a roll of wrapping paper and began tearing it into pieces, which he tossed at her like confetti.

On the stereo downstairs, Bing Crosby was dreaming of a white Christmas.

Nina stared at her husband in disbelief as if he had grown claws and his eyes had turned blood red.

"What's wrong with you?" she said. Then she went downstairs to call her mother.

"What did you do?" asked Eleanor when Nina explained

how Paul had flown into a rage.

"I forgot to buy oranges. What does it matter?"

"It's Christmas Eve, Nina," said Eleanor. "Find a way to make things right. You've got a family."

So, Nina made things right and kept Paul's abuse, their dirty little secret, to herself until the day Alice came over and the sordid details came tumbling out like dice from a leather cup.

Chapter 18

There wasn't much Nina remembered about Grace's funeral except for the mournful sound of Julia's cello. Sitting next to her daughters in a Xanax-induced stupor, she had zoned out until Julia drew her bow across the strings and the first languid notes of *Nimrod*, one of Elgar's *Enigma Variations*, washed over her: an ablution, a balm.

Julia had offered to box up Grace's things so Nina didn't have to do it herself. The carton had been sitting in Nina's foyer for a week, but she was too afraid to open it. So, she called Alice, who came right over.

The fragile items were wrapped in newsprint. There was a mug with a ram, Grace's astrological sign, on the side. Alice handed it to Nina, who remembered that when Grace arrived on a Tuesday in late March, she still hadn't decided on a name. After taking one look at her granddaughter, Eleanor had turned to Nina and declared, "Tuesday's child is full of grace." After that, nothing else would do.

Nina popped the lid on Grace's CD player, expecting to find Vladimir Horowitz or Glenn Gould on the spindle and surprised to find *War* by U2 instead. "I didn't know she liked this band, did you?" she asked Alice.

"Don't you remember telling me that Grace's father was Irish on his mother's side?" said Alice. "I thought she needed to hear 'Sunday Bloody Sunday' if she wanted to understand Irish history so I gave her that album for Christmas last year."

"You were like the cool aunt she always wanted."

"I actually had an aunt like that, but it was books, not music that we bonded over."

"What kinds of books?"

"The Russians—Dostoyevsky, Tolstoy, Nabakov. I read *Lolita* with a flashlight under the covers when I was thirteen, hoping my mother wouldn't catch me."

"I wonder how much Grace kept from me," said Nina, leafing through the pages of a weekly planner crammed with notations: recital at 8, dinner with Julia at McGillin's, *Amadeus* at 7:30.

"All girls keep secrets from their mothers."

"Do you think Lily keeps secrets from you?"

Alice shrugged. "I wonder if she and Frankie have done the deed yet, but I'm not sure she'd tell me even if they had."

"I wouldn't worry about that if I were you."

"Why not? They're teenagers." Alice sighed. "Raging hormones."

"Frankie's just a kid," said Nina, removing a silk scarf from the box and pressing it to her face. Musical notes were scattered against the white background like dice tossed onto a game board: base clefs and treble clefs, round hollow whole notes, sixteenth notes, flags fluttering from their stems.

Alice lifted a stack of sheet music from the box and placed it on the piano bench. "He's seventeen, and if he's anything like his dad he's been pressuring her."

"I think Frankie is the complete opposite of his father."

"Do you?"

"I know he thought the sun rose and set on Frank's head when he was a kid, but I think he knows the score by now."

"What, that Frank's a prick?" said Alice with a smirk.

"That's one way of putting it," said Nina, who had discovered Grace's leather journal.

"You aren't going to read that, are you?" said Alice, removing a few more items from the carton.

"Maybe." Nina flipped through a few pages, pausing at an entry written just before Thanksgiving: *Julia and I had dinner at this restaurant near Chinatown today. I met the owners, Nhu Lai and Thuyen Luu, who left Vietnam in 1978 with their eight children. Julia thinks they're from Saigon. I told them that my father died over there, but I'm not sure if they understood me. There is so much I'd like to ask them about their country.*

"Well?" said Alice.

"It looks like she went to a Vietnamese restaurant and met the owners," said Nina with a slight lift of her shoulders.

"She must have had a lot of questions about the war. Didn't she read *Dispatches* when we were in Cape May last summer?"

Nina nodded, and Alice opened another CD: *Rachmaninoff's Piano Concerto Number 3 in D Minor.* Grace had told her that it was incredibly difficult to play and that she intended to master it one day, a feat she compared to climbing K2.

Alice put the jewel case aside. "How much did you tell her about what happened to Ethan over there?"

"Not enough apparently, and now it's too late." Nina thumbed through the pages until she found another entry in Grace's spidery handwriting: *Kind of dreading the holidays.*

I swear if Paul gets drunk on Christmas Eve like he usually does and ruins it for my mother, I'm going to kill him. I just don't understand why she lets him push her around.

She let the journal slip from her fingers.

Alice cocked one eyebrow. "What's wrong?"

"I set the worst possible example for Grace."

"That's ridiculous."

"She was ashamed of me." Nina handed the journal to Alice.

"She was worried about you, not ashamed," she said after reading the brief passage. "Anyway, she didn't know the whole story."

———— ◦ ————

FOR HER BIRTHDAY that August, Alice gave Nina a book of drawings by Edgar Degas that included sketches of his best-known paintings as well as items from his notebooks and letters. Nina brought a pitcher of iced tea outside, and they sat in her back yard where a red oak threw shade on the patio.

"Do you think he and Mary Cassatt were lovers?" Alice wondered.

"She destroyed all the letters he wrote to her before she died so I guess we'll never know."

Alice looked out across the swimming pool, which Paul had insisted upon once he found out that Frank Lombardi had one. The late afternoon sun danced across the water, smooth as glass and a shade of blue somewhere between azure and cyan. Alice hated to see summer come to an end, but in a few weeks the pool boy would come to shock and chlorinate the water before stretching the heavy vinyl cover over the pool, tucking it in for winter.

"So, how are things going with you and Paul these days?" said Alice, who had been afraid to ask until now. "Look, if it's none of my business, just say so."

Nina removed her sunglasses. "I've been sleeping in Grace's room so—" Her voice trailed off.

They watched a song sparrow, its brown feathers streaked with black, hop across the patio looking for seeds between the cracks in the cement.

"I don't think he loved any of us," said Nina, who had been deep in thought.

"I'm sure he did," said Alice, "at least in the beginning."

Nina's expression was one of acquiescence. "I don't think Paul is capable of loving anyone but himself."

"Not even Harper and Hayley?"

"He wanted a boy, and he ended up in a house full of women," she said, retreating behind her dark glasses again.

Next door, the whine of a lawn mower as the cord was pulled, three sharp barks a rejoinder from a neighbor's dog. Alice glanced at Nina, who had gone quiet.

THE RED OAK began dropping its leaves in late September, and in the pre-dawn hours the wind scattered them across the patio where they assembled in copper and yellow clusters along the edge of the pool. One weekend when the twins were invited to a sleepover, Nina had a rare Sunday morning to herself. She'd gone back to sleep after the light filtering in through the curtains woke her up, and now it was nearly noon.

She still had time before she had to pick up the girls so she decided to get a shower. With any luck, she thought, Paul had left hours ago. He spent so little time at home these days that she wondered if he was seeing someone, not that she cared.

How could she have been so wrong about someone? That's what Nina wanted to know. In hindsight, it seemed foolish that she had believed Paul had been heaven-sent when they met in the parking lot at George Mason University.

It was best to push those thoughts away. Closing her eyes, she let the water, good and hot just how she liked it, stream down her face and across her shoulders. She had just stepped out of the shower when she heard him rattling the doorknob.

"Why is the goddamn door locked?"

"Go away."

"I'm your husband, and this is my house. Now open up."

Nina toweled herself off and ran a comb through her hair. She had hoped he'd give up, but now he was hammering at the door.

She leaned against the doorjamb. "You're scaring me."

This time he pounded on the door so hard that Nina expected to see his fist come through the wood.

"You know what, Nina," he shouted, "Screw you."

She waited until she heard his footsteps receding down the hallway before cracking the door open. When she came downstairs, he was in the kitchen banging one cupboard door after another, and suddenly she was tired of being afraid. *I just don't understand why she lets him push her around.*

"I wondered how long it would take before you'd start acting like a proper wife again," he said when she began assembling things to make a sandwich.

"I'm making this for myself," she said in a tone of voice she barely recognized: clear and resolute. "Make your own lunch."

He narrowed his eyes, those eyes such an astonishing shade of green that they had been the first thing she noticed about him. "You're a piss-poor excuse for a wife, you know that?"

"And you've been a poor excuse for a husband," she said, undoing the twist tie on a loaf of bread.

"Look around, Nina." His expression was smug, self-satisfied. "Who do you think pays for all this?"

She took in the country kitchen: the delft blue cabinets, the Viking range and butcher block countertops, every wall papered in a floral chintz print. "I didn't marry you for this."

"So, why did you?" He lowered his throaty voice to a whisper. "Marry me."

"Because I thought you'd love us the way Ethan would have," she said, remembering how attentive Paul had been to Grace in those early days.

A range of emotions played across his face: fondness, affection perhaps, a fragment of that old tenderness he'd felt so long ago. Then just as quickly, the moment passed.

"I never could live up to your expectations," he said, digging his fingers into the soft flesh of her upper arm. "Could I?"

"That hurts." She pushed him away, but he followed her into the foyer and caught her by the wrist. She struggled to free herself, but it was like being in Chinese handcuffs.

"You're kind of sexy when you're mad," he said, backing her into the credenza.

She turned away when he tried to kiss her.

"You're my wife," he reminded her. "Start acting like one."

Now he tore at her clothing. Her thin shirt fell away from her shoulders, buttons skittering across the tile floor.

"Get off me," she said, and he grabbed a handful of her hair, yanking her head back with such force she saw stars. "I could snap your neck like a twig if I wanted to," he said, his voice low and mean. Even as his fingers closed around her throat, her mind was somewhere else entirely. She had fought back once before, and Paul had dislocated her shoulder. So, she let herself drift.

Outside, a car raced past, radio blaring, and it was like some spell had been broken. "Forget it," he said with a derisive shake of his head. "You're not worth going to jail for."

Nina backed up slowly, inching her way toward the living room. Then she broke into a run, throwing open the sliding glass door and darting outside. He was on her almost immediately, pushing her to the ground. "Where do you think you're going?" he said, angry now.

The fenced-in yard had a gate that was just a few feet away, and she crawled on her hands and knees in that direction, but he dragged her toward the pool. Peeling back a corner of the vinyl cover, he shoved her head under the water and held it there. She felt her throat contracting and her nose and mouth beginning to fill with water. Then, abruptly, he let her go.

Gasping and gulping for air, Nina watched him take long strides toward the house. Harper had left her aluminum softball bat in the grass, and with a rush of pure adrenalin Nina pushed herself into a standing position and grabbed the handle with both hands. Her entire body uncoiled like a spring as she rushed forward and swung as hard as she could, following through until Paul went down on both knees before hitting the cement face-first.

She tossed the bat across the patio and went to the house next door.

The Honorable George M. Flaherty, Court of Common Pleas, seemed surprised to find Nina dripping all over his welcome mat. "What happened to you?"

"I think I killed Paul."

Chapter 19

As it turned out, Nina had confessed to a crime she did not commit. Paul had a concussion, but he recovered, and it was Judge Flaherty who presided over their divorce proceedings a few months later. Despite his repeated threats to do so, Paul did not file for custody of his daughters. Nor did he contest Nina's decision to move back to Virginia where she hoped to take care of her ailing father. The girls were eager to start over someplace new where their grief didn't linger in the carpets and draperies and furniture like the smell of smoke after a fire.

Nina promised Alice that she'd visit as often as possible, but she'd put it off for a whole year. At Compassionate Friends, Nina had met other parents who lost children, and they all assured her that grief was not the final destination, just a stop on her long journey toward acceptance and hope. Somehow, she understood that it would be a long time before she'd complete that journey.

She had slept fitfully on the sofa bed Alice made up the night before, but it was nearly eight o'clock so she threw back the covers and got up. Her therapist had recommended meditation to relieve anxiety, and she had found it to be almost as effective as the Klonopin her doctor prescribed after Grace died. Almost.

Alice had framed a portrait of Lily that Nina had painted from a photograph: lips slightly parted, brows as sharp as knife blades. Now, under Lily's watchful gaze, Nina assumed the lotus position, closed her eyes and took a few centering breaths.

She hadn't heard Alice come downstairs. "I made coffee if you want some," she said, gone as quickly as she had appeared, an apparition.

In the kitchen Noah was poking at a stack of pancakes swimming in syrup.

"Come on, buddy, finish eating so we can get going," said Bill, who asked Nina how she'd slept.

"So-so."

"Yeah, me too."

Alice was buttering a piece of toast, and Nina gave her a hug.

"I've got to drop Noah off at Theresa's and stop by the office for a few minutes," Bill told Alice, "but I'll meet you at the hospital later." He rinsed out his coffee mug, "You should call her."

Alice frowned.

He stuffed Noah's bathing suit into his backpack. "I don't know what we would have done without Theresa this week." He gave Alice a peck on the cheek. "You can't blame her for what happened. She's as upset as we are."

"I doubt that," Alice observed dryly. "Her son's not the one in a coma."

Nina understood Alice's need to blame someone for what happened to Lily because she'd experienced similar emotions after Grace's senseless death. For a while, she blamed God, who had been an abstract concept at best even after twelve years of Catholic school. Was she being punished for something, she wondered, though that made no sense. Why would God take Grace's life for something she had done? Now she hoped that Alice wouldn't have to grapple with the mysteries of life and death that still seemed unfathomable to her.

Nina drove the two of them to the hospital. Every now and then she stole a glance at Alice, who had been staring out the window since they left the house. As they passed Wesley Methodist Church, Nina pointed out the yard sign: *Why didn't Noah swat those two mosquitoes?*

Alice smiled, though she seemed to regret the impulse almost immediately.

"It's okay to laugh," Nina told her, pulling into the parking lot reserved for visitors. "You're human."

Alice removed her sunglasses. "It just feels wrong."

Nina cut the engine. "I know."

"Let's just sit here for a few minutes before we go in," said Alice, fishing around in her handbag for her cigarettes.

They waited for Alice to finish smoking before going inside. One of the nurses told them that Dr. Greenfield was still in surgery and would be held up for a few more hours. Alice pulled a chair up to Lily's bedside and was reading another chapter from *Wind in the Willows* when Bill arrived.

"Has the doctor been in yet?" he asked Alice, who shook her head.

"Want me to find out what's going on?"

Alice nodded, and Bill left the room, happy to be of use. "She has to wake up," said Alice to no one in particular. "She just has to."

Sometimes Nina wondered if it had been easier to learn of Grace's death after the fact, the information dispatched with the efficiency of an executioner's sword. Over before you knew what happened. Was it worse for Alice? The endless days of waiting and wondering, of hoping for a miracle? She wasn't sure.

"He's on his way," said Bill when he returned, and instinctively Alice reached for Lily's hand. *I'm right here.*

"Sorry to keep you waiting," said Dr. Greenfield, removing his surgical cap. "Why don't we talk somewhere else. There's a room down the hall where we'll have more privacy."

"Do you want me to wait here?" asked Nina, and Alice shook her head.

"So, we did another EEG this morning to measure electrical activity in the brain," Dr. Greenfield explained. "We also did apnea testing where we temporarily remove all ventilator support and closely monitor the patient while we allow partial levels of carbon dioxide to rise."

"And?" said Bill, reaching for Alice's hand.

"I'm afraid the tests are rather definitive," he said. "I've conferred with another neurologist, and we've both come to the same conclusion."

Bill squeezed Alice's fingers. "Which is?"

"That Lily has suffered an irreversible loss of all functions of the brain."

Alice's shoulders sagged.

"Once we take her off the ventilator, Lily's heart will continue to beat, but she won't be able to breathe on her own."

"I'm not ready," said Alice with an obstinate shake of her head.

"I guess we can wait a day or two, but there's not going to be a change in your daughter's condition," said Dr.

Greenfield. "If there's anyone who would like to say good-bye, they should get here as soon as possible."

"You need to call your folks," Bill told Alice, whose parents had just made the trip from Chicago two weeks ago for Lily's high school graduation. They had left to go home on Sunday morning, and now Alice realized that they must have made it as far as Ohio when Frankie's car struck a pole, irrevocably altering all of their lives.

There had been a party in the backyard on Saturday for family and a few friends. Frankie gave Lily a locket with their pictures inside so she wouldn't forget him when she went to college in the fall. Alice's sister Audrey, who was living in Italy with her husband, a visiting scholar at the University of Rome, was unable to be there, and now she would never see her niece again.

The doctor explained that while normally children under twelve were not allowed on the floor, he'd make an exception for Noah if he wanted to see his sister.

"Absolutely not," said Alice. "He's too young. I don't want him to see Lily looking like this." She blinked back a few tears. "I want him to remember her the way she was."

Bill glanced at the doctor, who lifted his shoulders in a gesture of solidarity. "Her death might not seem real to him if he never sees her again," said Dr. Greenfield. "Just think about it."

Nina knew that Alice would need her support if she was going to get through the next few days, but with her own grief still raw, she hoped she had the strength to see her friend through this ordeal.

Chapter 20

B abe, who had been dreading Alice's call, promised to leave first thing in the morning. With just one stop for a late lunch at Howard Johnson's outside of Cleveland, they got to Alice's house early the next evening.

"Sam, why don't you go up to bed," Babe told her husband, who carried their bags in from the car. "You look exhausted." She glanced at Alice. "He wouldn't let me do any of the driving."

Bill took his father-in-law upstairs, and Babe followed Alice into the family room where Nina was struggling to pull out the sleeper sofa.

"Here, let me help you." Alice gave the pull tab a good yank.

Nina stepped aside to give Babe a hug. "I never thanked you for the beautiful flowers you sent for Grace's funeral."

"I didn't expect you to," said Babe with a wistful expression, glancing at Nina and then at Alice. "You two must miss each other. You were such good friends."

Casting a tender smile in Nina's direction, Alice shook out a blanket that billowed like a sail before settling on the mattress. "Are you hungry?" she asked her mother.

"Frankly, I could use a drink."

"Want to join us?" Alice asked Nina, who shook her head. "I'm going to turn in," she said. "You two probably need some time alone."

"Why don't we go into the living room?" said Alice, who didn't think she'd ever seen her mother look so old.

An antique bar cart was stocked with a variety of wine and spirits, and Alice busied herself making drinks for each of them. "We hardly ever use this room," she said, handing her mother an old fashioned glass. "Why don't you sit down." She gestured toward one of the blue toile loveseats.

"When I was a girl a room like this was called a parlor," said Babe. "Mother only used it when company called. That's where I'd go to read when I was growing up because I knew no one would disturb me there." She placed her drink on the tempered glass and gilt-iron coffee table Alice had found at an estate sale not long after she and Bill were married.

"Wait here," said Alice, who remembered a box of photographs on the top shelf of the hall closet. "I've been meaning to put these into albums for years," she told her mother, "but I just never got around to it."

She placed the box on the coffee table and sorted through dozens of black-and-white photographs taken when she and Audrey were children: celebrating birthdays, on Santa's lap, forcing smiles for the school photographer. There were others of Lily and Noah as toddlers with milky skin and hair soft as down, and later shapeshifting into creatures she barely recognized, shedding baby fat for lean angles and long limbs.

Alice showed her mother a picture of Lily in her christening gown. "I can't believe how many generations this dress has been in our family," said Babe with a slow smile of recognition. "I was the first to wear it, and then you and your sister were baptized in it, and then Lily and Noah. Audrey cried bloody murder when the priest poured water over her head. You were only three so you probably don't remember, but I thought I'd die. She just screamed and screamed." Babe glanced at the picture again. "That dress swam on Lily. Remember what a tiny little thing she was?"

Alice nodded. How could she forget?

"Oh, my, look at this." Babe examined a photo of Alice and Audrey in matching sundresses on the wide front porch at the guest house in Ocean City, New Jersey, where they stayed every summer until Alice was twelve. "I made those dresses for you two, remember?"

Babe had been an accomplished seamstress, who made all of Alice's clothes well into high school. Now Alice was sorry that she hadn't appreciated how lucky she was instead of complaining that she'd rather wear Villager or Ladybug dresses like all the other girls she knew.

"Where was this taken?" asked Alice.

Babe studied the faded photograph. Audrey was just a baby, her chubby face peeking out from the hood of her snowsuit. She and Alice were on a sled, dwarfed by snow drifts as high as a field of corn on either side of the walk that had been shoveled earlier.

"We took this at your Grandma Harvey's house in Dayton the day after Thanksgiving," she said. "They called it the storm of the century. Some parts of Ohio got thirty inches, and the wind, why it could have knocked you off your feet it was so strong." She took a closer look at the photograph. "I think that sled belonged to your uncle when he was a little boy."

Sifting through the box of photos, Alice passed each one in turn to her mother: Lily holding her baby brother on her lap the day Alice brought him home from the hospital, Lily in her Brownie uniform, Noah with a helicopter he built for his LEGO airport, Lily and Noah in front of the Cape May Lighthouse three years ago. Alice had taken lots of pictures at Lily's graduation, but the roll of film was still in her camera. Now she wondered if she'd be able to look at those pictures without wanting to scream when she finally got them developed.

"I can't look at any more of these," she said to her mother, who removed her reading glasses and slipped them back into their case.

"One way or another," she promised her daughter, "we'll get through this."

Babe had never been a demonstrative person, but now she extended her arms and Alice simply fell into them.

———•———

CONSIDERING THE CIRCUMSTANCES, the hospital made an exception to the two-visitor policy in the ICU. Bill's parents and his brother Scott, who had flown in from Boston, arrived early that morning. Frankie crutched into the waiting room, his face a mask of stoic reserve, and sat next to Fern.

Charlotte handed Theresa a cup of vending machine coffee. "First Grace and now—" Her voice trailed off.

Bill arranged a private moment with Lily for each of them, a traffic cop keeping things moving through a busy intersection.

Noah had made it clear that he wanted to see his sister one last time, and Alice had reluctantly agreed.

Now, drawing close to her bed, he scrutinized Lily's face "That's not her."

Alice knelt down and gathered Noah into her arms. "You just don't recognize her because she's been in a terrible accident." She threw Bill a look: *I told you this was a bad idea.*

Noah pulled away from Alice and gripped the bedrail, shaking it until it rattled. "Wake up, Lily," he shouted. "Stop fooling around."

Bill pried Noah's fingers from the metal bar. "Come on, buddy, it's time to go."

"That's not my sister," Noah insisted as Bill nudged him toward the door.

Father Phil arrived just before noon to administer last rites. Alice was relieved when he dispensed with the sacrament of confession since she did not believe that Lily had anything to confess and would be welcomed into heaven, if there was such a place, with open arms.

In high school Sister Mary Agnes had been very clear about the importance of last rites. "The end of life is the devil's last chance to tempt us before we face Jesus Christ as our judge."

While Alice no longer believed in ecclesiastical canon, she found it strangely comforting when Father Phil placed his fingers on Lily's forehead and eyelids, anointing them with oil.

Bill's parents took Noah home with them, but Alice wanted her parents to be with her when the end came since they had been there when Lily took her first steps, said her first word, celebrated her first birthday. Dr. Greenfield had already told them what to expect. Sometimes after the withdrawal of mechanical ventilation, he said, there was respiratory secretion that made it sound like the patient was choking. He called it post-extubation stridor, but he insisted it was nothing to worry about.

A team of experts waited outside Lily's room, but Alice asked if she could be alone with Lily for a few minutes. Ever since the night of the accident, she had been afraid to cry. What if she started and couldn't stop? Now as she approached Lily's bedside, tears seemed to be the appropriate response. *Weeping, wailing, crying your eyes out, crying your heart out.* So many ways to describe the body's natural response to pain. To the indescribable, the ineffable, the unspeakable.

Wiping her face on the sleeve of her shirt, Alice decided that Noah was right. The battered, unresponsive body connected to plastic tubing and machines was not his sister, and that made it easier to let go. Lily took her time being born. Labor was interminable, seventeen hours or more, but when Alice finally held her baby, swaddled in a fleece blanket, Lily had lifted her head on its thin stem and looked Alice right in the eyes as if staking her claim, and she had.

Leaning over the bedrail to trace Lily's eyelids with the pads of her thumb, Alice whispered, "Safe travels. Wherever you're going, I hope you're happy."

As it turned out, terminating Lily's life was decidedly anticlimactic. Dr. Greenfield simply turned off the ventilator, and they waited. After a few minutes, the nurse informed them that Lily's heart had stopped beating. Alice wasn't sure what she'd expected, but the lack of fanfare was disturbing. Shouldn't there have been some Old Testament rending of garments? Instead, a team of doctors and nurses swept into the room to prepare Lily for organ donation.

It was Nina who talked Alice into agreeing to what the organ procurement organization called the "gift of life," arguing that Lily's death would not have been in vain. So, her corneas, kidneys, heart, lung, pancreas and liver were packed into sterile containers and shipped to transplant centers all over the country, while Lily's body was delivered to Kearney Funeral Home.

Alice would never know who received the gift of life her daughter's death had made possible, but she liked to imagine that it made a difference to some of them: the grateful children not ready to lose their father to heart failure, a teenager on dialysis who could resume a normal life, or perhaps a young woman who lost her sight as a child and could finally see the faces of all the people who had loved her since the day she was born.

Chapter 21

That fall Frankie went to work for his father and learned to install carpet. Tony Pastore, who had worked for Carpet Warehouse since Frankie was in grade school, showed him the ropes: how to install gripper strips against the walls, how to use a knee-kicker to jam the carpet into the edges of the room, how to work a carpet stretcher so there were no unsightly bulges later. Tony was more than happy to let Frankie haul the heavy carpet rolls from the van to the job site, while he sat in the cab listening to classic-rock and shoveling Doritos straight from the bag into his mouth.

Frankie had heard some of the guys call him Fat Tony, but not to his face. Sometimes he opened up while they drove from one job to another, telling Frankie how his wife left him for "some Polack who didn't know his ass from a hole in the ground."

Frankie wanted to tell Fat Tony that he knew how it felt to lose someone you loved, but it wasn't the same thing so he kept his mouth shut. Tony let Frankie tear out the old carpeting, hard work that he was happy to hand off to a nineteen-year-old kid with the brute strength of a grizzly bear and knees that didn't ache every time he knelt down.

It was mindless work, which suited Frankie just fine since he hadn't been able to concentrate on much of anything lately. In his wallet was the prayer card from Lily's funeral. *Miss me a little but not too long, and not with your head hung low. Remember the love that we once shared. Miss me but let me go.* Frankie read the card at least twice a day, but he wasn't there yet.

Sometimes when he looked up at the night sky, he liked to imagine that Lily and Grace were together, their energy, infinite and unbounded, reorganizing itself in nebulae where new stars were beginning to form. Other times he worried that there was no afterlife, no kingdom come, no spiritual realm where existence simply continues to take place.

Theresa felt helpless in the face of Frankie's crippling grief, and like she did for Nina after Grace died, she cooked: ravioli, enormous pans of lasagna, spaghetti carbonara, but Frankie claimed he had no appetite. Tina tried to coax her brother into playing Nintendo with her like they used to. They had everything: Donkey Kong, The Legend of Zelda, Super Mario Bros, but when Frankie showed no interest in any of them, Tina gave up.

Frankie hadn't seen that much of his father since he remarried, but now that he was on the payroll he was expected to visit now and then and make nice to Wendy. They had a two-bedroom apartment in Dunmore, home of the largest landfill in the state of Pennsylvania. Wendy preferred to think of Dunmore as the gateway to the Poconos, which made Dunmore sound a lot more appealing than it was, but Wendy was always doing that, putting on airs.

Last winter she talked his father into buying all this expensive ski equipment so they could go to Jack Frost or Camelback and stay overnight at some chalet that cost a fortune. Frankie knew his father would rather be home watching football, but he let Wendy run the show. "She has your father's balls in her purse," was his mother's assessment.

Wendy had also talked his father into getting a dog, a Yorkshire Terrier named Biscuit that was no bigger than a loaf of bread. Frankie knew that his father would have preferred a Lab or a German Shepherd, but as usual Wendy got her way. Frankie was always worrying that he'd step on Biscuit by accident when he came over, which would only add to his burden of guilt, but he agreed to take her out twice a day when they were out of town, which was a lot lately. He couldn't remember his parents doing anything together when they were married, but his father was always going places with Wendy. They'd been to Vermont to see the fall foliage, and they stayed at Bally's when they went to Atlantic City where gambling was legal now and the drinks were free as long as they were feeding quarters into the slot machines.

The refrigerator at their apartment was always stocked with Coors or Genny Cream Ale, and Frankie found that three or four of those could numb whatever pain he was feeling, at least temporarily. Sometimes he put his feet up and watched TV in his father's recliner, which had a built-in cup holder. If he had enough to drink, he'd doze off and wake with a start hours later. Once he woke up to find Biscuit asleep in his lap, and when he stroked the soft fur behind her ears, she cocked her head and fixed him with a stare suffused with sorrow and compassion, her eyes black as obsidian. They were friends after that, and Frankie began staying over after he took Biscuit out at night, making up the pullout bed in the living room and letting Biscuit curl up next to him.

Twice Frankie had driven to Lily's house after dark and parked across the street. Her bedroom window faced the front of the house, and he liked to pretend that she was inside and might part the curtains at any moment. Occasionally he wondered how Noah was doing, but he was afraid to ask Alice if he could visit even though she'd taken him aside after the funeral and insisted that what happened was an accident and that she didn't hold him responsible.

The truth was, Frankie blamed himself, so it didn't matter what Alice or anyone else thought. No, he hadn't been drinking, he hadn't run a red light, he hadn't been driving recklessly. None of that altered the fact that he had been behind the wheel of the car when it struck a pole, ending Lily's life.

One day while he and Fat Tony were having lunch at McDonald's, Frankie saw Fern. She was by herself, and she left before she saw him, which was a relief since he didn't need Fat Tony asking a lot of questions. That night he removed the prayer card from his wallet just to see her name: Lily Marie Callahan. In the lithographed image on the front, Mary stood on a crescent moon, a crown of twelve stars, one for each of the tribes of Israel, on her head. Frankie turned the card over. There was the familiar admonishment to let go, but there was also, at the very bottom, this: *When you are lonely and sick of heart, go to the friends we know.* So, he called Fern, and that's how it began.

The first time they saw each other, they met for lunch at Friendly's. It was Saturday, and Frankie had just finished a job. It seemed like with Christmas only a few weeks away, everyone wanted new carpet in time for the holidays, but

Frankie was grateful for the overtime. It was better than being at home listening to his mother and Tina fight all the time.

"So how do you like working for your dad?" asked Fern, which was an innocuous enough question, but at least it broke the ice.

"It's okay, I guess," said Frankie. "The pay's good."

A waitress approached them, pulling out her order pad. "You two need a minute?"

"I'll have a cheeseburger, but no tomato. I hate tomatoes." It had been Frankie's experience that no one ever listened to him, so he glanced at the waitress to see if she had been paying attention.

"Got it, no tomato," she said. "Anything else?"

"Fries and a Coke."

"I'll have the same thing," said Fern, who waited for their waitress to leave before asking him, "So, how are you doing?"

There it was, thought Frankie, whose initial reaction was to lie. Now that he was sitting across from Fern, he wondered if maybe this was a mistake. "Not so good," was all he could manage.

Fern sighed deeply. "Me either." She lowered her eyes when the waitress returned with their drinks and a couple of straws.

Frankie pushed his straw aside and took a gulp of his Coke, wishing Fern would keep talking, but she seemed as ill at ease as he was. Finally, he asked her about school. "So, I guess you'll graduate in June."

Fern nodded.

"You going to college?"

"Boston University."

"You must be pretty smart."

She shrugged.

Frankie cracked his knuckles. "Sorry," he said when Fern made a face. "My sister hates when I do that, too."

Fern was looking at Frankie with a doe-eyed expression that was slightly disconcerting. It was alright when Biscuit looked at him as if she could read his mind, but he wasn't so sure he wanted Fern inside his head. He began rearranging the condiments—a bottle of Heinz Ketchup, a jar of yellow mustard, pats of butter wrapped in foil—anything to avoid making eye contact with Fern.

"Oops, bad luck," she said when he knocked over the saltshaker, scattering crystals across the Formica table. "Throw a pinch over your shoulder."

Frankie frowned. "I don't think my luck could get much worse, do you?"

"No, I guess not."

Their waitress was heading their way, a plate in each hand. "Two cheeseburgers, no tomato. Can I get you anything else?"

Frankie shook his head.

Fern dipped a french fry in ketchup and took a bite. "Have you seen Lily's mom?"

"I wouldn't know what to say to her."

"I've been over a couple of times."

Frankie wiped the corner of his mouth with his napkin. "What happened?"

"Nothing really. I helped her go through some of Lily's things. She's not sure what to do with it all, clothes mostly. She asked me if I wanted anything."

Frankie took another sip of his Coke and pushed his hair out of his eyes. "So, did you take anything?"

"Her Benetton sweater, the pink one with the really big sleeves."

Frankie smiled. "I remember that one."

"And this—" Fern was wearing Lily's charm bracelet.

"Do you know what happened to the locket I gave her for graduation?"

Fern pushed her plate aside. "I can find out."

"It doesn't matter," said Frankie with a shrug.

"It does matter, Frankie. It does. I'll ask Alice to look for it." When she reached across the table, her fingers grazed his hand.

"Do you want to come over sometime and listen to music?" he asked without thinking it through, but Fern was already saying yes, she'd love to, so it was too late to take it back.

"Maybe next weekend," he said, and Fern nodded.

<hr />

THAT FRIDAY WHEN Frankie got home from work, he called Fern. "My mom and my sister are having dinner somewhere and then going to a movie so do you want to hang out?"

"At your house?"

"Yeah. I can order a pizza if you want, and we can listen to music like I said."

"I can have my dad drop me off if you'll bring me home later."

"I can do that."

This isn't a date, he told himself when he hung up, though he could understand why Fern might think it was. He didn't want to mislead her, but he had no one else to talk to who understood what he was feeling. Fern was there when it happened.

He went upstairs to change out of his work clothes. His mother was always hounding him to take a shower when he came home from work, but most days it felt like too much trouble. All he wanted to do when he got home was put on his headphones and listen to music.

He pulled his flannel shirt over his head in one swift motion without undoing the buttons. Fat Tony had taught him to layer in the winter, so he was wearing the Van Halen T-shirt he'd found in his father's dresser over a Hanes crew-neck undershirt. He tossed them all into his hamper and wandered into the bathroom.

Hair still damp, he answered the door in a clean pair of jeans and an AC/DC concert tee with Malcolm and Angus on the front.

Kip tapped on the horn as he pulled away from the curb.

"My dad said to say hi," said Fern, wiping her feet on the doormat.

Frankie took her coat and draped it over a chair in the formal living room with its white wall-to-wall carpet and baby grand piano that was just for show as far as he could tell. When Frankie's father lived with them, he called it the inner sanctum, and even though Frankie had no idea what an inner sanctum was, he knew enough not to step one foot inside that room unless he took off his shoes.

"Why don't you just rope it off, Theresa," his father used to say, usually when he'd had a few drinks.

Fern followed Frankie into the kitchen.

"What kind of pizza do you like? I was going to call Domino's."

"Pepperoni."

"Cool." He looked the number up in the phone book. "So, you want a salad or something? Girls like salads, don't they?"

"Sure."

"It's going to take an hour," said Frankie when he hung up. "Want to play Ms. Pac-Man?"

"Lily and I played that game all the time at the arcade in the mall," said Fern. "Didn't you like the one where you rode around shooting at aliens?"

"Moon Patrol." Frankie found the Atari switchbox and hooked it up to the cable input. "You can go first," he said, handing one of the joysticks to Fern, who waited until Ms. Pac-Man appeared at center stage before deftly devouring a row of dots, turning a corner and gobbling up another row.

"You're pretty good at this," said Frankie when Fern wiped out four blue ghosts and racked up 800 points.

"You're ruining my concentration," she said, evading one ghost before two more trapped her in a corner. She frowned while the computerized sound of Ms. Pac-Man dying spiraled out.

Frankie made a sad face. "Too bad."

"I've still got four lives left," she reminded him.

"But once they're gone, they're gone."

They exchanged glances.

"I miss her, too," said Fern, who felt like all the anger she'd bottled up since the accident was going to erupt like lava from a volcano. "I know you were her boyfriend, but we were best friends."

"It's not the same."

"No, but it's not insignificant either."

"Is that one of the big words on the SAT you probably aced?" asked Frankie with a small smile.

"What?"

"Insignificant?"

"Hardly," she said, punching him in the arm, "but abrasive is, and that's what you're being right now."

"Saved by the bell," said Frankie, pushing himself off the couch to answer the door.

They ate in the kitchen at the enormous island with a four-burner Jenn-Air grill on one end and a rack of copper pots and pans overhead.

"Your mom must really like to cook," said Fern, dousing her salad with Italian dressing from a packet.

Frankie got two root beers from the refrigerator and handed one to Fern. "My dad's new wife can't boil water."

"I guess he didn't marry her for her cooking."

"Or her brains either. She's kind of a bimbo." Frankie folded a piece of pizza in half and took a bite.

"Oh, wait, I forgot," said Fern, hopping off the barstool. She removed a small box from her handbag. "This is for you."

It was Lily's locket. "Thanks," he said, slipping it into his pocket. He'd look at it later when he was alone.

"Sure." Fern took a slice of pizza and cut it into bite-sized pieces.

"Okay, that's just wrong," said Frankie. "No one eats pizza with a knife and fork."

"I do."

Frankie took another bite, and oil dripped down his chin.

"See, that's why I use a knife and fork like a civilized person."

"You've got an answer for everything, don't you?"

"I was raised to be a strong and independent young woman." Fern handed Frankie a napkin. "My mother said it's important for me to have options."

"Like what?"

"Like going to college and getting married when I want to, not because I have to."

Frankie took a fresh slice of pizza. "Like she did?"

"Like she did, and Lily's mom did," said Fern, stabbing a piece of lettuce with her fork. "She wants me to be able to make enough money to support myself so I don't have to rely on a man for anything."

"Lily used to say you were going to be the next Jacques Cousteau." He mimed a swimmer doing the breaststroke.

Fern shook her head. "He was an underwater explorer. I'm going to be a marine biologist."

"Isn't that the same thing?"

"Not really."

Frankie finished his pizza and threw the crust into the box. "Want to go upstairs and listen to some music?"

Fern had known Frankie since they were kids, but she couldn't remember ever seeing his room. On the walls, which were painted blue to match the shag carpet, was a disparate collection of posters: rock bands like Black Sabbath and AC/DC; the cover art from Pink Floyd's *Dark Side of the Moon* and Led Zeppelin's *Houses of the Holy*, which Fern found menacing and macabre; and combat aircraft from World War II: Liberators, Mustangs and Corsairs. A B-17 he'd built himself when he was twelve—"The Flying Fortress," Frankie explained when Fern admired it—was suspended over the single bed.

There was a tape deck on the nightstand. "I want you to hear this song called 'Ride On' by Bon Scott. He was the lead singer for AC/DC, but he died of alcohol poisoning or something," Frankie said. "I played it all the time after Lily died."

Fern braced herself, but this was a bluesy ballad, not at all what she expected. Leaning against the headboard, eyes closed, Frankie heard something that eluded her in the seductive melody, the mournful lyrics about another empty bed and getting back to the start and riding on. Frankie extended his hand, thinking perhaps that it was Lily sitting beside him, and Fern took it.

Chapter 22

———— ◆ ————

Carpet Warehouse closed early on Christmas Eve, and Frankie asked Fern to go the mall with him. He had no idea what to get for his mother or his sister, but Fern had a knack for that kind of thing. She said it was just because she paid attention to people. She knew, for instance, that Tina wanted an album by some British rock band called The Smiths. She also knew that Theresa's favorite perfume was Wind Song and that Noah wanted a robot superhero called Optimus Prime.

"So, can you help me wrap this stuff when we get home?" he asked her.

Fern rolled her eyes. "You're helpless, aren't you?"

"I guess I am, unless you want me to change your oil or install wall-to-wall carpet for you."

"You know I'm teasing, right?"

"I know." He liked it when Fern teased him. It meant that things were returning to normal.

It was almost fifty degrees out, so no white Christmas this year. Tina was outside decorating the bay window with a can of fake snow when Frankie pulled into the driveway.

The flowering dogwood tree in their front yard had shed its leaves, but robins, starlings and other birds were drawn to its clusters of bright red fruit, which they ate all winter long. Startled, a pileated woodpecker took flight, spreading its great black and white wings with a series of piping calls.

Frank Sinatra was on the stereo in the living room— "Have Yourself a Merry Little Christmas"—and Theresa was in the kitchen, which was fragrant with the aroma of garlic and oregano. A pot of mussels, clams and scallops in tomato broth simmered on the six-burner stove.

"Can I do anything?" asked Fern.

Theresa gestured toward the refrigerator. "I put a couple heads of lettuce in the crisper. Want to break those up for me?" She turned to Frankie. "Show Fern where I keep the salad bowl."

Frankie got the big ceramic bowl down from the top shelf of the pantry and took a seat at the island.

Fern tore the lettuce into chunks. "How many people are coming tonight?" They'd been celebrating Christmas Eve at Theresa's house for as long as Fern could remember. Last year Nina drove in from Virginia with her father and the twins, and, of course, Lily was there with Noah and her parents.

"Nina isn't coming this year," Theresa said, deftly crushing a clove of garlic with a chef's knife, "and Alice isn't celebrating Christmas, not that I blame her."

"What about Noah?" asked Frankie, who felt sorry for him. It was Christmas, and he was just a little kid.

"It's none of our business," said Theresa, though she wasn't entirely convinced that leaving Alice to her own devices was the best course of action. None of them had seen much of Alice since Lily died, and it had been more than six months.

"Frankie," said Theresa, "get the calamari in the fridge for me, will you?"

"Don't put any on Fern's salad," he told his mother, easing off the barstool. "She hates it."

Theresa lifted the lid on the Dutch oven and gave the soup a good stir. "How could anyone hate calamari?"

"It's octopus," said Fern with a shudder.

"I brown it with a little olive oil, sea salt and garlic," Theresa explained. "You'll love it."

"You're not going to change my mind," said Fern, firmly but politely.

"Nonsense. Just have one bite."

"That's what you used to say to get me to try clams," said Frankie, who still refused to eat them. "You might as well eat an eyeball."

Theresa smacked him with a dishtowel.

Frankie removed the Tupperware container of calamari from the refrigerator and briefly considered dangling one of the ivory-colored rings in front of Fern like he did with earthworms when they were kids, but the impulse felt childish somehow and he thought better of it.

"Can you and Fern set the table?" asked Theresa, who was whisking olive oil and balsamic vinegar in a bowl. She tore a sheet of Saran Wrap from the roll and placed it over the dressing. "I still have to get a shower."

Fern followed Frankie into the dining room. On the buffet were dozens of pastries arranged on two-tiered plates—anise-flavored pizzelles, fruit-filled horns sprinkled with powdered sugar and cannoli with sweetened ricotta.

"Your mother sure goes all out for Christmas," said Fern. "She should start a business."

Frankie handed her a stack of dinner plates from the china cabinet. "What kind of business?"

"Catering. She'd make a fortune."

"I don't know about that." Frankie couldn't imagine anyone wanting to pay top dollar for the kind of food he grew up with.

"I can tell the day of the week by what my mom makes for dinner: macaroni and cheese on Friday, Sloppy Joes on Saturday, roast beef and mashed potatoes on Sunday, leftovers on Monday," Fern told him. "Boring. You have no idea how lucky you are."

Frankie opened a walnut chest with his mother's good silver nestled in the plush velvet lining.

"Forks on the left, knives on the right," Fern reminded him, folding linen napkins into triangles and placing one next to each plate.

"So, can you help me wrap those presents after we finish?" asked Frankie, working his way around the table.

"Does your mom have any wrapping paper?"

"What do you think?" Frankie deadpanned, and Fern smiled.

Frankie was right. Theresa had rolls of wrapping paper in the guest bedroom, which she used for craft projects. Over the years she had hooked rugs, made refrigerator magnets out of brooches, and used paint and glitter to turn Mason jars into soap dispensers, cookie jars and terrariums.

Fern wrapped both presents in red foil paper, fashioning bows from white curling ribbon.

"Go put these under the tree," she told Frankie when she was finished.

They passed Tina on the stairs. "Mom said to change into something nice," she said to Frankie, who punched her on the arm and raced down the stairs before she could punch him back.

Fern often wondered what it would be like to have a brother or sister, and she envied Frankie and Tina, whose pinches and pokes, the knowing looks they exchanged when they were all watching a movie on VHS that Fern had never seen before, were a kind of shorthand that Fern would never understand.

"I need to go home and change, too," Fern told Frankie.

"You look fine."

"It's Christmas Eve. I'm wearing jeans and a sweatshirt."

"So?"

"Frankie!" Her tone was the vocal equivalent of a stomped foot.

"You're such a girl," he said, but then his face fell and she knew he was remembering Lily, the original girly girl. Favorite color: pink. Favorite movie: *Sixteen Candles*. Favorite song: "Time After Time."

No one could accuse Fern of being a girly girl: a bookworm maybe, but not a girly girl. Her favorite movie was *2001: A Space Odyssey*, her favorite song U2's "Pride (In the Name of Love)." The only piece of clothing she owned that was pink was that Benetton sweater that had belonged to Lily.

Frankie gave Fern a boost into the front seat of his pickup truck. After the accident, he got rid of his Ford Maverick even though the garage said they could repair the damage to the front end. There was just no way he could drive that car again without seeing Lily sitting in the front seat that day, the window down, her long hair blowing across her pretty face.

He dropped Fern off and drove past Lily's house. Last year Frankie helped Bill string hundreds of multicolor bulbs along the eaves and gutters, while Lily wrapped strands of tiny white lights around the boxwood planted in huge terracotta pots on the front porch. This year the house was dark except for a light over the kitchen sink. Frankie wasn't even sure anyone was home, and it made him sad because Christmas had been Lily's favorite holiday.

His mother was still in the kitchen when he got home, but now she was wearing a red mohair sweater with padded shoulders that Frankie thought made her look like a full-back. "I pressed your black dress pants and your good white shirt. They're hanging on the back of your closet door," she said, tossing a bowl of pasta with toasted bread crumbs. "Tell your sister to get a move on. I could use some help."

Frankie rapped on Tina's bedroom door. "Mom wants you downstairs," he said, pushing the door open.

"Get out of my room," she shouted, fanning the air at the window, which was wide open.

"Are you smoking pot?"

"None of your business." She brought the sash down hard.

Frankie shook his head. "If Mom finds out, she'll kill you."

Tina gave the room a good spritz with Air Wick 2 in 1. "So, are you and Fern a thing now?" she said, pushing him aside.

"No."

"You spend an awful lot of time together."

"We're just friends."

"Whatever you say," said Tina, who went into the bathroom, slamming and locking the door behind her.

Frankie flopped onto his bed and stared at the ceiling for a few minutes. Rolling over, he reached for his wallet on the nightstand and removed Lily's prayer card. He traced her name with his thumb, kissed the card and placed it back in his wallet. After a while, he heard his mother calling from downstairs so he put on his good shirt and pants just to make her happy and worked some gel into his hair to keep it out of his eyes.

Fern and her parents were in the living room when he came downstairs, and Tina was passing a tray of cheese and crackers around. Percy Faith was on the stereo, some record his mother played every Christmas: lush arrangements heavy on the strings with lots of brass.

"Merry Christmas, Frankie," said Charlotte, who crossed the room to kiss him on the cheek. "I know how hard this holiday must be for you."

Frankie stuffed his hands into the pockets of his pants. What did she want him to say?

Kip slapped him on the back and nabbed a piece of cheese as Tina sailed past, her tray held aloft like a waiter at an expensive restaurant. "You and Fern have been spending a lot of time together," he said, and Frankie wondered if it was an accusation or merely an observation.

Tina shot him a raised-eyebrow look, and he glared at her. "We're just friends," he told Kip, trying not to sound defensive.

"I wasn't implying anything. I'm just glad that you two have been able to help each other get through this—" Kip cast about for the right word to describe what *this* was and came up empty. "It's just that everyone's worried about you two."

From the doorway, Theresa announced that dinner was served.

Fern was on the sofa, and when she stood up Frankie noticed that she was wearing a short dress, something sparkly that caught the light when she walked toward him. Frankie didn't think he'd ever seen Fern wear makeup, but she was wearing it tonight.

"You look really pretty," he said. When she lowered her eyes, which was very un-Fern-like, Frankie wondered if he'd said something wrong.

Kip threw his arm around his daughter's shoulder and gave it a squeeze. "That's what I told her when we left the house tonight."

"Okay, now you're embarrassing me," said Fern, though Frankie thought she might be pleased.

The table was ablaze with tapered candles, and everyone waited until Theresa took her seat before finding one of their own. There was a brief toast. "To Lily and Grace," Theresa said, raising her glass of Chianti, and when everyone had taken a respectful sip, Theresa disappeared into the kitchen, returning with a terrine of soup, which she ladled into bowls.

"You don't have to eat that if you don't want to," Frankie whispered to Fern, who sipped at the broth but left the mussels and scallops dry-docked at the bottom of her bowl.

Theresa asked Charlotte to help her plate the salad, and when Fern discreetly pushed her calamari to the side, Frankie snickered.

"Shut up," Fern told him.

Platters of roasted salmon and cod were passed, and pasta in cream sauce was heaped onto plates. Kip helped himself to seconds of the casserole stuffed with rice, crabmeat and shrimp. Lemon sherbet was scooped into footed bowls to cleanse the palate.

After dinner, Charlotte made coffee, while Theresa served dessert. "Why don't you change the record," she told Kip, who took his time selecting an album from a stack near the stereo. When he dropped the needle, Karen Carpenter's clear soprano filled the room: *It came upon a midnight clear.*

As was their tradition, they all went to Midnight Mass. Theresa liked to get there early so she could sit up front. There was a time when they commandeered an entire pew, but there were less of them now. Dozens of red and white poinsettias donated in memory of some loved one or another blanketed the altar. Theresa had paid for two of them, and she scanned the insert in the bulletin until she found their names: Lily Callahan and Grace Hudson.

So much had happened in the past few years, none of it good as far as Theresa was concerned. Tomorrow her children would spend the day with their father and his new wife, which didn't seem fair. Why should she, the injured party, spend Christmas Day alone? Still, her children would come home at the end of the evening, unlike Grace and Lily.

Frankie sat on the aisle, fidgeting. Theresa had imagined him leaving this church with his bride someday, though she never expected Lily to be on his arm when that day came. Frankie put on a brave face when she was accepted to Oberlin, but Theresa knew that it was just too far away for them to make it work. Now it was a moot point, and her son was as broken-hearted as she ever hoped him to be again.

None of them saw Alice arrive late and take a seat in last row, and none of them saw her leave early either.

Chapter 23

———•———

That winter when they got tired of playing video games or listening to music, Frankie and Fern went to the movies. Fern preferred serious dramas, but she knew better than to suggest an art-house film to Frankie, whose tastes ran toward action movies like *Lethal Weapon* and *RoboCop*. Sometimes Fern wished that she and Frankie had more in common. She'd actually spent one whole day watching a Three Stooges marathon on TV with him, and while she had tried to find the humor in grown men hitting each other in the head with hammers, ultimately it had eluded her. Fern didn't think her mother and father had anything in common either, and she wondered if they would have broken up if they didn't have to get married.

Fern tried to convince Frankie to watch one episode of her favorite TV show, *Highway to Heaven*, but he'd shot her an are-you-kidding look designed to shut down any further conversation.

"Come on, Fern. *Highway to Heaven*?"

"It's not like that," she explained. "It's about this angel who wanders around on Earth helping people."

"You're digging your own grave here."

"Just listen. One time Michael Landon got these greedy businessmen to see why they should use their wealth for good."

"So, it's a fairytale."

"Oh, forget it. I don't know why I bother talking to you at all."

And she didn't, at least not for a couple of weeks, but then in March they went to see *Lethal Weapon*—Frankie's choice, though Fern liked it better than she thought she would. They were both sick of winter by then, but at least it wasn't freezing outside anymore, just overcast and cloudy as usual. After the movie, they went to Denny's where they always ordered breakfast for dinner: the Grand Slam for Frankie, an omelet with cheddar cheese for Fern.

"My dad's in Atlantic City this weekend," said Frankie, stabbing a piece of sausage with his fork. "I have to go over there and take the dog out. Want to come with me?"

"Sure," she said, tearing open a package of grape jelly.

"He's got HBO. Maybe we could watch a movie."

Fern reached across the table to steal a forkful of pancake soaking up a pool of syrup. "I'm kind of movied out for one day."

"*Airwolf*'s on at 9," he said. "Want to watch that?"

Fern shrugged. "What's it about?"

"Some guy steals a supersonic military helicopter, code named Airwolf, and uses it to fight bad guys," he said, taking a gulp of Coke and chewing on an ice cube. "It's pretty good."

Fern pushed her plate away with an enigmatic smile he was free to interpret any way he wanted. When Frankie finished off the rest of her omelet, she wondered why he didn't weigh three hundred pounds.

"See that guy over there," said Frankie, motioning to a man wearing an Army field jacket seated a few tables away from them. He'd made an effort to hide his long hair under a cap bearing the Marine Corps logo.

Fern glanced quickly in his direction. "You know him?"

"He works in Receiving," said Frankie. "My dad said he's kind of messed up, from the war I guess."

"He was in Vietnam?"

"I think so."

"Did you know that Grace's father was killed in Vietnam? She never even met him."

"That sucks," said Frankie, snatching up the check and removing a twenty from his billfold.

"Want me to chip in?"

"Don't worry about it. I got paid yesterday."

Fern worked one arm into the sleeve of her coat. "I know you don't believe in an afterlife, but I hope that Grace finally got to meet her dad."

"Maybe they're on the highway to heaven together," said Frankie, who knew by the look on Fern's face that he'd said the wrong thing, or at least said it in the wrong tone of voice.

"Not funny, Frankie."

He gave the check to the girl working the register, who seemed to take forever ringing up the bill.

Fern was waiting for him outside.

"Sorry," he told her. "I'm an idiot sometimes." His hair blew across his forehead, and Fern brushed it out of his eyes.

He grabbed her wrist and fixed her with a look so serious that she flinched. "I never said I didn't believe in an afterlife," he told her. "I just don't think it's like the nuns think it is—God sitting on some throne and all these angels flying around."

He told her about his crazy notion that Grace and Lily were reforming as stars in some distant galaxy, but Fern didn't think it was so crazy.

"Did you ever heard of Pythagoras?" she asked him.

"The triangle guy?" asked Frankie, who had barely passed algebra.

Fern gave him a plaintive look. "He was also a philosopher, who came up with this idea called the transmigration of souls. Lots of ancient civilizations believed the same thing. The Egyptians thought our souls passed into the body of some animal after we died and that after thousands of years we entered a human body again."

"Like reincarnation?"

"Yeah."

"My mother thinks we either burn in hell after we die or we're up there playing a harp with St. Peter." Frankie laughed, revealing teeth that only high-priced orthodontics could render so straight and white. "So, how do you know all this stuff?"

"I read a lot."

"I read," he said defensively, offering her a stick of gum.

"Comic books don't count," Fern told him. "Come on, let's go."

They parked on the street in front of his dad's apartment building and walked the three flights of stairs to the third floor. Biscuit began barking before they even made it down the hall where Frankie had to fidget with the lock just to get his key to work.

Frankie knelt down to let Biscuit lick his face.

"Oh, my God, she's got you wrapped around her little paw," said Fern, turning on the lamp in the living room.

"Shut up." Frankie took Biscuit's leash from the hook

by the door and clipped it to her collar. "I'll be right back."

Fern used the bathroom while he was gone. There was a bottle of Obsession on the Formica counter, and she removed the cap, inhaling the spicy amber scent. She caught her reflection in the mirror above the sink. Her eyes, which were wide and expressive, were her best feature: dark blue like her mother's. Fern had never thought of herself as beautiful, not in the way that Lily had been beautiful, but now that her hair was longer, she thought she might be pretty.

What she wondered was whether or not Frankie thought she was pretty, but that line of thinking made her feel guilty. The whole situation was so complicated. Lily was her best friend, or rather she had been, but now all she could think about was what it would be like to kiss Frankie. There was something so uncomplicated about him, so essentially masculine that it unnerved her.

She snapped off the overhead light when she heard Frankie come in and went back to the living room.

He got each of them a beer. "Want a glass?" he asked, and Fern said yes, in fact, she did, and he went to the kitchen to get one. He popped the pull-tab on a can of Pabst Blue Ribbon and waited for the foam to settle before pouring it into a beer mug that he'd bought at Epcot when he was a kid. He handed it to Fern.

She took a sip and placed the mug on the *TV Guide* so she wouldn't leave a ring on the coffee table. "So, is he?" she asked.

"Move over," said Frankie, sitting down next to her on the sofa. "Is he what?"

"World's Best Dad?" The words were engraved on the side of the glass.

"I used to think he was. I gave him that mug for Father's Day when I was twelve."

"It must be weird seeing your dad with someone else."

"What's weird is seeing the way he acts around Wendy." Frankie made googly eyes at Fern. "It's gross."

Biscuit clawed at the sofa until Frankie gave her a good scratch behind the ears. "See what's on," he said, gesturing to the remote on the end table.

After rejecting a romantic comedy on cable (no way was Frankie watching that) and some horror movie on HBO (no way was Fern watching that), they settled on a David Copperfield special. "He's in the Bermuda Triangle," she told Frankie, "but it's almost over."

"Don't change the channel. *Airwolf*'s on the same station." Frankie went into the kitchen and returned with a bag of potato chips.

"How can you be hungry?" Fern asked him.

"I'm always hungry." He shoveled a few chips into his mouth. "Do you know how many ships and planes have disappeared in the Bermuda Triangle?"

"I don't know, how many?"

"A lot. Did you ever hear of Roberto Clemente?"

"The guy who played for the Pirates?"

"Yeah. Back in the '70s his plane disappeared over the Bermuda Triangle, and they never found it or any of the crew members either." Frankie wiped his hands on the tail of his flannel shirt. "There are a lot of UFO sightings there, too. My dad thinks that all those planes and ships disappear because aliens abduct them."

Fern muted the volume. "Did you ever see *Close Encounters*?"

"I loved that movie," said Frankie, who went into the kitchen and came back with another beer. He took a few gulps and sat the can on the coffee table.

"So, if you had the chance, would you leave everyone you love to go into outer space like Richard Dreyfuss did?"

Frankie scratched his cheek. "I don't think so."

"Me either."

"Remember Simon? Don't tell me they didn't get the idea for that game from *Close Encounters*. A total rip-off."

Fern, who recalled the colored lights and the sequences of musical notes that allowed the scientists to communicate with the aliens in the movie, had to agree.

"Okay, my show's on," he said, grabbing the remote and turning up the volume. "No talking."

"Aye aye, Captain," said Fern with a mock salute.

Frankie gave her a shove. "You're asking for it." He used the remote like a pointer, aiming it at the television. "That's Stringfellow Hawke. He's this really cool daredevil pilot."

Fern feigned interest, nodding amiably, but she wasn't watching the television; she was watching Frankie, who was perched at the edge of the sofa, filling her in on characters from previous episodes.

"Want another beer?" he asked her during a commercial break.

"I haven't finished this one yet," she told him.

"Wimp," he said, giving her a playful shove again. Frankie was always doing that, punching her in the arm, slapping her knee, but now his sheer physicality made her heart race a little.

"I'm not much of a beer lover," she told him, "but you go ahead."

"You trying to get me drunk?"

"Maybe I want to have my way with you," she joked, though once she'd floated the idea, she couldn't take it back.

He gave her a look that was hard to read: confused, intrigued? She couldn't tell. "You want a Coke or something?"

She shook her head. "I'm okay."

Frankie raked his fingers through his hair, revealing a razor-thin scar near his eyebrow from a run-in with one of his mother's rose bushes when he was a kid. He got another beer from the refrigerator and drank half of it standing in the doorway before sitting down next to Fern on the sofa. Now the show was back on again, but Frankie wasn't watching it anymore. He was looking at Fern, eyes dreamy and unfocused, those long lashes slightly unsettling. Hair falling into his eyes, he kissed her, and Fern kissed him back with an urgency that surprised her. She had been kissed a few times before, but never like this. She sensed Lily's ghost hovering, and she wondered if Frankie felt it, too, but when he kissed her again, his breath ragged and uneven, she let him slip one hand inside her sweater, his fingers warm against her skin.

"I'm a virgin," she said.

"Me, too."

This was a surprise to Fern, who had always imagined that he and Lily had gone all the way, though Lily had never said as much.

Frankie pulled away and flicked his hair out of his eyes. Fern wished he'd kiss her again, wished, in fact, that they could just go on kissing, though she was fairly certain that it was too late for that.

"Be right back," he said, and Fern watched him stumble down the hallway, bracing himself against the wall with splayed fingers. After a few minutes, she heard the toilet flush.

Fern worried that Frankie might have changed his mind, but he sat back down right next to her, like that's exactly where he wanted to be.

When the show was over, Frankie turned off the television and pushed himself off the sofa. There was a stack of cassette tapes near an elaborate audio system. "I hope you like Rod Stewart."

Biscuit watched them from her dog bed, head cocked to one side.

Frankie finished his beer and burped like he used to when they were kids and he'd chug Mountain Dew like water. "Sorry," he said, fast-forwarding through "Maggie Mae." He sent Fern an apologetic look. "I hate that song."

"Is this wrong?" Fern asked him. "What we're doing."

"I think I'll always love Lily," he said, narrowing one eye into a kind of squint. When he finished his beer, he went into the kitchen for a refill.

Fern ran one finger across her mouth, tracing the path where Frankie's lips had touched hers and deciding that she was not going to feel guilty about anything that happened tonight. She remembered how jealous she'd felt in Cape May when she saw the way Frankie looked at Lily. Well, now he was looking at her that way.

Frankie let "Mandolin Wind" play out before he sat down on the arm of the sofa as far away from Fern as he could get. Taking a few swigs of beer, he placed the can on the end table where it teetered precariously near the edge.

Fern felt the distance between them like a chasm.

He looked away as if to spare her feelings. "I wanted my first time to be with her."

"I know."

"I'm really drunk," he said.

"Are you saying that you won't remember anything in the morning?"

"I don't know. Maybe."

"Maybe you will or maybe you won't?"

"Don't ask so many questions."

On the stereo Rod Stewart was looking for a reason to believe.

Frankie's hands were trembling when he lifted her sweater over her head, and when he helped her out of her jeans and touched her there, Fern caught her breath.

Now Frankie shucked off his shirt. "Are you sure?" he asked, kicking his own jeans to the floor while he waited for her answer.

"I'm sure," said Fern, winding her arms around his neck.

When he pushed inside her, hesitant and shy, neither of them was thinking about Lily.

One of them turned out the light, and later, eyes half-closed, Frankie reached for the afghan, which was draped over the back of the couch, and covered them with it before falling asleep.

Fern lay there in the dark for a long time, barely suppressing a smile as she remembered every detail of what had just happened. She knew her mother would be worried when she didn't come home tonight, but it was too late to call now, and besides, she didn't want anything to intrude on what had just taken place, which felt consequential and important. When she finally did fall asleep, it was with Frankie's arm flung across her side, his breath warm against her neck.

Chapter 24

———— ◆ ————

Frankie dropped Fern off at her house the next morning, but when she leaned across the seat to kiss him goodbye, he gave her a tight smile that told her everything she needed to know. She got out of his truck and slammed the door.

Frankie lowered his head onto the steering wheel and sat there, the engine idling, until Fern went inside. After a few minutes, he shifted into first, taking the long way home to avoid driving past Lily's house.

Fern went straight up to her room. She was pretty sure her mother bought her story about falling asleep while watching a movie with Frankie when she called home that morning. Now she was grateful her parents were still at church and she had time to pull herself together. Would her mother know just by looking at her that she wasn't the same girl who left the house yesterday?

When she woke up this morning, Frankie was still asleep, one arm thrown across his forehead, and she rolled on her side to study his handsome face.

"Good morning," he said, squinting at her in the half-light that filtered in through the vertical blinds before closing his eyes again.

A line of dark hair snaked down his bare chest, and Fern, perplexed by a range of emotions she couldn't identify, leaned up on one elbow to kiss him. Reflexively, he turned away. She hadn't known what to expect, but she was hurt and disappointed that Frankie, who had been so unguarded and affectionate last night, seemed so distant and detached this morning. Wriggling into her jeans, she found her sweater and lacy bra and carried them into the bathroom.

<hr />

THERESA WAS IN the kitchen making lunch when Frankie got home. "You hungry?" she asked without looking up.

"Not really." He found a Coke in the refrigerator and chugged the entire can. He passed Tina in the upstairs hallway.

"Where were you all night?" she asked.

"Dad's."

"What do you do over there when he's not home?"

"Nothing. Watch TV."

"Was Fern with you?"

"Why would she be?"

Tina shrugged. "I don't know. You two are like Siamese twins."

"No, we're not."

"It's okay if you like her, Frankie," Tina said just before she went into the bathroom and shut the door.

He put a Guns N' Roses tape into the cassette player and reached for his head phones, allowing Axl Rose's tremulous tenor to wash over him: *Welcome to the jungle.* Cranking up the volume, he hoped to erase the images that bloomed like nightshade behind his eyelids: Fern soft and warm beneath him, her breath quickening when he entered her. Now Axl was remembering the girl with eyes of the bluest skies, which always reminded Frankie of Lily, and he paused the tape, sorry for everything.

Frankie didn't call Fern at all that week. He wished he could get a do-over like in high school when he failed a biology quiz and the teacher let him take it again. At work, he volunteered for overtime so he'd have an excuse in case Tina or his mother wondered why Fern hadn't been around. Sometimes he'd remember things from that night, like how easily he'd responded to Fern's kisses, how quickly he'd betrayed Lily. He hadn't been to mass for years, but now he wondered if going to confession would make him feel better.

The worst part was that he missed Fern. It was nice having someone to talk to, someone to do things with instead of spending all his free time playing Final Fantasy or watching TV by himself. He picked up the phone a couple of times over the next few weeks, but then he'd remember that he wasn't in love with Fern, not the way he had been with Lily, and that calling her would just make things worse if she was in love with him.

Fern called him a month later, and he was surprised by how happy he was to hear from her. "I missed my period," she said, taking the wind out of his sails.

He was on the extension in the upstairs hallway, and he dragged the phone into his bedroom.

"Say something, Frankie."

"I thought I pulled out in time," he whispered.

"Well, you didn't."

"What do you want me to do?"

"I need you to go to the drugstore with me so we can get one of those home pregnancy tests," she said. "You have to buy it. I don't want anyone to see me doing it."

"Want me to come over now?"

"Yes, now. Jesus, Frankie."

"Okay, sorry."

Fern waited in the truck while Frankie went into the pharmacy. Two girls she recognized from school were standing near the entrance, flipping through the pages of some teen magazine. They were still standing there when Frankie came out, and Fern saw the way they looked at him. Girls always looked at Frankie like that, and for just a second she allowed herself to imagine what a baby of theirs would look like.

He slid into the driver's seat and handed her a plastic bag. "I got two of them in case you make a mistake."

"Did you see anyone we know in there?"

"Not really." He backed up and pulled out of the parking lot. "So now what?"

"I take the test, and we find out."

Fern's parents had gone out for dinner, so they drove to her house.

"So, how does this work?" Frankie asked her.

"I pee on the stick and wait to see if it turns blue."

Fern went into the powder room and closed the door. Frankie kept vigil, going to the window every few minutes to make sure her parents hadn't come home. It seemed to him that she had been in there for a really long time, but when she finally came out, he could tell that she'd been crying.

Frankie put his arms around her. "Maybe you should do another one. Just to be sure."

"I did." Now Fern was crying again. "I need to think," she said, wiping her face with the hem of Frankie's T-shirt.

"About what?"

"About everything." She looked at Frankie like he was one of the slow kids who had to take remedial reading in high school.

Frankie knew that Fern had a scholarship to Boston University. That's all she talked about when they first started spending time together. He wondered if she could still go to college if they got married. It wasn't like he was ready to be a husband and father, but he wanted to do the right thing. He could probably get a job installing carpet in Boston, and they could find someone to watch the baby while Fern was in class.

"It's going to be okay," he told her, but that was just wishful thinking on his part.

"How do you know?"

"I don't." He followed Fern into the living room. "I'm just trying to help."

"How could I be so stupid?" she said. "My mother is going to be so disappointed in me. I'm the one who's supposed to do something with my life."

Frankie watched Fern pace, smart enough to understand that this was a soliloquy, a word he learned from her, and that nothing was required of him other than to listen.

"I've ruined my life." When she slumped onto the sofa, Frankie sat down beside her, tentatively placing one arm around her shoulder.

After a few minutes, Fern told him, "You should go before my parents get home."

CHARLOTTE CONFRONTED FERN a few days later after finding the pregnancy test sticks in the wastebasket when she was cleaning the powder room.

"Shit," said Fern when she saw the blue and white boxes, which she had forgotten to take out to the trash after Frankie left that night.

"So, are you?" asked Charlotte, afraid to finish the sentence.

Fern nodded.

"Oh, my God, Fern. You're only seventeen. You have your whole life ahead of you."

"Don't you think I know that?" said Fern, adopting a defensive tone since this was one conversation she did not want to have.

"I assume it's Frankie's baby?"

"It's not a baby yet," said Fern, "but yeah, it's Frankie's. Who else's would it be?"

"So, have you told him?"

Fern nodded.

"And?"

"And nothing."

"What do you mean, nothing?" said Charlotte, taking Fern by the arm. "He's going to take responsibility, isn't he?"

"Mom, stop it," said Fern, wrenching her arm away.

"Does Theresa know?" Charlotte asked.

Fern shook her head.

"I need to call her," said Charlotte, "and we have to tell your father as soon as he gets home."

"Don't tell Daddy," said Fern, who couldn't bear to disappoint her father.

"We can't keep him out of this." Charlotte shook her head. "I thought you were smarter than me, but I guess hormones trump brains every time, don't they?"

"I've got a paper due tomorrow," Fern lied. "Can we talk about this later?"

Charlotte nodded, sensing that they both needed some time to think.

Fern went upstairs to her room, which smelled like Lemon Pledge. Her mother must have been cleaning all day.

There were fresh sheets on her bed, and her collection of glass figurines—horses rearing on their hind legs, French bulldogs, a Norman Rockwell piece called *First Dance* her mother had ordered from the Danbury Mint—had been dusted and rearranged on her dresser. All of her laundry had been washed and folded and books, which had been scattered around her bed, were placed neatly back in the bookcase.

This is how my mother spends her time, thought Fern, who had imagined a bigger life for herself. Now one mistake had put everything in jeopardy.

She reached for the pink Princess phone on her night stand and called Frankie. "My mother knows," she said when he answered.

"What did she say?"

"What do you think?"

"We could get married," he said impulsively.

"What?"

"We could get married."

Fern twisted the phone cord around her fingers. "Are you serious?"

"Do you want to?"

"Marry you?" she said, floating the idea like a cartoon thought bubble, giving into the fantasy for a moment and imagining a dress of white, the sure, slow walk down the aisle on her father's arm to the altar where Frankie would be waiting.

Alice used to say that Fern and Lily were hopeless romantics, but Fern could also be practical and focused when she needed to be, and now her inner pragmatist kicked in.

"The thing is, you don't love me," she told Frankie.

"Does it matter? I could."

"Don't do me any favors."

"I'm not, but if I said I did you'd know I was lying."

"Forget it," said Fern.

"You don't love me either," Frankie observed, throwing down a gauntlet.

Fern thought it over. She knew that she felt short of breath if his hand grazed hers when they were out somewhere, that her heart raced when he looked at her with a kind of half-smile, but was that love? For the first time in weeks, she thought of Lily, who used to say she fell for Frankie when she was thirteen and saw him wipe away tears when Elliott had to say goodbye to E.T. Lily's other favorite movie that year was *The Outsiders* because Ponyboy Curtis, a potent combination of virility and vulnerability, reminded her of Frankie.

"Maybe you should talk to your mom before my mother calls her," said Fern, feeling more confused than she did an hour ago.

"Okay, but I meant what I said, you know, about how I could love you," he said, but Fern had already hung up.

Frankie went downstairs where he found his mother in the kitchen washing dishes. He and his mother had never even talked about sex (thank God), but now she'd know what he had been doing with Fern, though it had only been that one time.

"Oh, Frankie," she said, wringing a dishtowel in her hands as if trying to strangle it. He hadn't heard his mother sound this unhappy since the day his father moved out, but it didn't take her more than a few minutes to put a positive spin on things. "Okay, so what's done is done. You're not the first person who had to get married. I'll have her parents over for dinner this weekend, and we'll work things out."

"I don't think that's a good idea," said Frankie, imagining an inquisition, he and Fern on trial for something they shared in private that should have remained that way.

Theresa, who was already calling his father, shushed him.

Frankie blew out a long breath. There was no point arguing with his mother so he went upstairs. He was listening to AC/DC when Theresa rapped on his door. "They're coming over on Friday, so make sure to come right home from work."

Frank showed up early that Friday, and he brought Wendy with him.

"Absolutely not," said Theresa when she answered the door. "This is a family matter, and she is not part of our family."

"She's my wife," said Frank, stepping across the threshold, "and she goes where I go."

"Well, she can go to hell as far as I'm concerned," said Theresa, blocking his way.

Theresa had *Gone With the Wind* on VHS and must have watched it at least a dozen times. Now, seeing Frank on her front porch smugly defending that tramp he married, she wished she had a handful of red earth she could fling in his face the way Scarlett did when Jonas Wilkerson drove up to Tara like he owned the place with Emmy Slattery, his new wife, who was nothing but poor white trash.

After a brief standoff during which Theresa summoned her inner Scarlett, Frank stalked off to talk things over with Wendy, who wisely decided to wait in the Trans Am. Frankie watched his mother's tirade with trepidation. He could only imagine what his wedding day would be like if it came to that. Would his mother and Wendy trade punches in the receiving line? He remembered the time his mother chased Wendy around the grocery store. He hated her that day and was mean to his sister, who was just a kid. Lily had helped him become a better person.

Frank leveled his gaze at his son. "You and I need to talk."

"I don't need a lecture," Frankie said, but his father gave him a shove toward the living room.

"Your mother can give me shit if she wants to, but I'm not taking my shoes off," said Frank, making a big production of stepping onto the spotless white carpet in his Reebok Hi-Tops.

"She doesn't make people do that anymore," said Frankie.

Frank glanced round the room, which Theresa had redecorated. Instead of the floral chintz sofa, two Belgian linen loveseats flanked a glass coffee table. "I gave this house to your mother free and clear when we got divorced. Did she ever tell you that?"

Frankie shrugged. "Mom never really talks about the divorce," he said, though he wasn't being entirely truthful. Theresa may not have divulged any of the details about her financial settlement, but she'd made it clear over the years that his father was a lying, cheating son of a bitch (her words).

Frank tossed a crystal paperweight from one hand to the other before placing it back on the end table. "I gave this to your mother for Christmas when you were a baby. Waterford or something. Only the best for your mother."

"What did you want to talk about?" Frankie asked.

Frank twisted a signet ring on his pinkie. "I thought you had more sense than to knock some girl up."

"Maybe I'm not as smart as you."

"Are you sure it's yours?"

"It's mine. Geez, Dad."

"You're not even old enough to drink yet, and you're going to be a father." He shook his head. "So, where'd you

Marianne Dougherty

two do the deed? Was it at my place? If I knew you and that girl were getting it on, I would have told you I keep a box of rubbers in the nightstand."

Frankie winced. "Dad, stop."

"Don't be such a pussy." Now Frank was examining a photograph in a silver frame: a studio portrait of Frankie taken before his senior year in high school. "How come I didn't get one of these?"

"I guess you'll have to ask Mom," said Frankie, who was tired of being a pawn in their death matches, which reminded him of watching hardcore wrestling with his father, who got off on the brawling, bloody style of Abdullah the Butcher and Bobo Brazil. Frankie had never understood what his father found so fascinating about the escalating violence, the fighting among spectators in the concession stands.

The doorbell rang, and Frankie went to answer it.

Kip nodded tersely, and Charlotte gave him a weak smile. Fern, solemn and contemplative, followed her parents into the house.

"Are you okay?" Frankie asked her, but she just shook her head.

Frank strolled into the foyer and clapped Kip on the back. "I don't know about you, but I'm not old enough to be a grandfather."

"You think this is funny, Frank?"

"Just trying to lighten things up," Frank said defensively, but Kip pushed past him, joining Charlotte and Fern on one of the loveseats in the living room.

"Can I get anyone a drink?" asked Theresa, moving a centerpiece of silk flowers out of the way to make room for a plate of cheese and crackers, which she placed on the coffee table as if this were one of her cocktail parties.

"We're fine," said Kip, the designated spokesperson for his entire family as far as Frankie could see.

"I could use a beer," said Frank, and Theresa told him to get one out of the refrigerator.

She sat down next to Frankie on the other loveseat.

Kip cleared his throat and nodded at Frankie. "I need to get something out of the way before we start."

Instinctively, Theresa grasped one of Frankie's hands the way she used to when he was a little boy and they were about to cross a busy street.

"Do you love my daughter?"

"Daddy," snapped Fern.

"It's a fair question." Kip looked at Frankie, who struggled to form a response that would be to Kip's liking.

"So, this was just a one-night stand?" said Kip after an uncomfortable silence.

Frank had returned with a couple of beers and handed one to Kip.

"I'm trying to figure out if your son is good enough for my daughter."

"Now wait a minute," said Frank, placing one hand on Frankie's shoulder in a sign of solidarity.

"Stop it," said Fern, cutting her eyes at her father. "This isn't Frankie's fault, and he's not the bad guy."

"So, you're not the first couple to find yourself in this situation," Theresa said brightly, looking from Charlotte to Kip and back at Fern. "You'll get married like your mother and father did. It worked out for them."

"We would have got married anyway," said Kip. "This is different."

"All I know is that my son will do the right thing," said Frank. "He made his bed, now he has to lie in it."

Kip got to his feet, and Frankie thought he was going to slug his dad, but Charlotte tugged on his shirt, and he sat back down.

Frankie stared at Fern, willing her to make eye contact, but she was staring at her hands, which were clenched in her lap.

"So, we're all agreed?" said Theresa.

Charlotte glanced at Kip, who shrugged. "I don't see what other option we have."

"Of course, we'll pay for everything," said Theresa.

"We don't need any favors from you," said Kip. "I can pay for my own daughter's wedding."

"No one's asked me what I want to do," said Fern, who had been observing these proceedings with an air of indifference until now. "Maybe I don't want to get married."

"You can't have a baby out of wedlock," said Theresa, as incredulous as if Fern had suggested going over Niagara Falls in a barrel. "It will be illegitimate."

"Jesus Christ, Theresa, it's not the 1950s. No one cares about that shit anymore," said Frank. "She just said she doesn't want to get married. Maybe she wants to raise the kid by herself."

"Maybe I don't want a baby at all," said Fern, lowering her eyes. "Frankie and I made one mistake. We shouldn't have to pay for it for the rest of our lives."

"I don't understand," said Theresa.

"Do you want her to spell it out?" said Frank. "She wants an abortion."

"But that's a mortal sin," said Theresa with a sharp intake of breath.

"Not now," said Charlotte, turning to take Fern by the shoulders. "I think we should go home and talk about this in private."

Fern pushed herself off the sofa. "I don't want to talk about it anymore."

Theresa nudged Frankie. "Say something. You're the father. You have rights."

Frankie wasn't sure how he felt, other than blindsided, but he followed Fern outside where his mother's dogwood tree was in full bloom. Frankie vaguely remembered his mother telling him some story about how the cross on which Jesus was crucified was made from a dogwood tree and how God had decreed that the tree would never grow large enough for anyone to make a cross out of it again. So much of what his mother believed was based on dogma or superstition or maybe a combination of both.

"Did you mean what you said in there?" he asked Fern. "Yes."

Part of him felt relieved, like he'd dodged a bullet, but the other part felt disappointed, though he wasn't sure why. He understood that it was important to support Fern no matter what she decided, but he wasn't sure he wanted her to have an abortion either, though that didn't seem fair since he wasn't the one having the baby. Everything was happening so fast.

"Can we talk about this?" he asked her.

She sighed deeply. "Why? We both know that you wanted to marry Lily, not me." She met his gaze for the first time, and he noticed that her irises were flecked with gold. Why hadn't he noticed that before, he wondered. "I want to go to college and do something with my life, and someday I hope to get married to someone who loves me as much as I love him, and we both know you're not that person."

He shoved his hands into the pockets of his jeans. "Can I ask you something?"

"Go ahead."

Fern was backlit in the late afternoon sun, and Frankie had to squint to see her clearly. "Do you even care what I think?"

"Please don't make this any harder for me than it is."

A pair of goldfinches took small bites of suet from a bird feeder in the front yard before taking flight. Frankie recognized the male's distinctive song, a message to other males in the area that this female was taken.

"Okay," he said.

"So, we have to talk about how we're going to pay for it," said Fern. "Since you're working and I'm not, I think it's only fair that you come up with the money."

"No, you're right," said Frankie, who didn't care about the money. It was Fern's brisk, business-like demeanor that threw him off. "How much do you need?"

"Five hundred dollars."

He'd been saving up for a new truck and had at least a thousand dollars in his account. The truck would have to wait. "Alright."

Now Fern's eyes welled with tears, and she wiped them away with the back of her hand.

This brief display of sentiment prompted him to put his arms around her. Before pulling away, Fern kissed him, but not like she did that night at his dad's apartment. This time she was kissing him goodbye.

Chapter 25

———— ◆ ————

Frankie drove Fern to the clinic where he had to shield her from protestors blocking the entrance. While they waited, Fern stole a cursory glance around the waiting room: a girl in a Marywood College sweatshirt, a woman with a tight perm pretending to read a magazine, another teenager, like Fern, picking at her nail polish. There was one girl with cracked, peeling lips who picked at the scabs on her scrawny arms and announced defiantly, "This is my third abortion," but she was the exception.

Like Fern, most of the women in that room knew exactly why they were there. They'd made a difficult decision for any number of personal reasons, and they were going to do something that could not be undone, and none of them was cavalier about it.

When the nurse called Fern's name, Frankie got to his feet and gave Fern an awkward hug. "I'll be here if you need me."

The nurse held the door open, and Fern turned to take one last look at Frankie before the door closed behind her. Fern had never been to a gynecologist and had no idea what to expect, and she felt slightly embarrassed when the nurse asked her to place her feet in the stirrups so she could give her an injection to numb the cervix.

The doctor, a kindly man with thinning hair, introduced himself, but Fern wasn't paying attention. Instead, she closed her eyes and thought about Baba who died when she was fourteen. Fern had loved her grandmother and believed that she watched over her. Now she asked Baba to take care of her baby and send it back to her when she was ready to be a mother.

The whole procedure was over in less than ten minutes, and Fern was wheeled into recovery where she and three or four other women sipped apple juice from paper cups and ate cookies, like they were all in pre-school and it was snack time.

Now each of them had a secret, which they'd either carry to the grave or share with someone else someday. A girl not much older than Fern started to cry, and Fern averted her eyes, afraid she'd start to cry, too.

The nurse gave her a sanitary napkin and a prescription. "Make sure you fill this and take all of your antibiotics no matter how good you feel," she said. "Call if you soak two maxi pads per hour for two hours or if you have a fever of 104 or higher."

It was almost noon when Fern was discharged, and when she saw Frankie waiting for her exactly where she left him, she threw herself into his arms.

Outside a knot of protestors brandished signs with graphic photographs of bloody fetuses, and without thinking Frankie grabbed one of them and tore it in half.

"Get out of the way," he shouted, supporting Fern with one arm as if they were running the gauntlet.

He helped Fern into his truck and locked the doors. "Some lady in there told me those people are from Operation Rescue. Did you ever hear of them?"

Fern shook her head. "I don't think so."

"Some bunch of crazy pro-life Christians," he said, stopping just short of lumping his mother into that category. "Guess what else she told me? The guy who started Domino's Pizza gives them a lot money." He drummed his fingers on the steering wheel. "I'm never eating Domino's again."

"You're a good person, Frankie," Fern told him with a faint smile, "but you love Domino's, remember?"

He backed the truck out of the parking lot and shifted into first. "So, I'll learn to love Pizza Hut."

<hr />

BEFORE FERN LEFT for college that fall, she and Frankie visited Lily's grave. It had been a year since the accident, a year since Lily's death, a year in which so much had happened that they felt like some sort of ceremony was in order before their paths diverged.

Frankie picked Fern up at her house. A dozen pink grocery store roses wrapped in cellophane were on the front seat. She climbed into the truck and pushed them aside. They parked on a gravel road and meandered among dozens of headstones until they found Lily's. A winged angel carved from sandstone kept watch, and Frankie reverently placed the roses at her feet.

Watching Frankie tear up, Fern thought to herself, "We did the right thing," yet she knew that even if she never saw Frankie again, they shared a bond that, for better or worse, united them as tightly as a Palomar Knot.

Chapter 26

It was a beautiful fall day when Nina took the Metro to D.C. and got off at Foggy Bottom, a fifteen-minute walk, some of it through the campus of George Washington University, to the National Mall. On one of the benches flanking the tree-lined walkways in the Quad, she saw a young couple who looked about the same age as she and Ethan were when they met. Shifting her bag to the other shoulder, she kept walking until she saw The Washington Monument in the distance. Straight as a sentinel, it would be her North Star, leading the way to Ethan's name on polished black granite that had been quarried in Bangalore, India.

Nina had been invited to a New Year's Eve party at her friend Jane's house in Georgetown where she noticed Ethan right away: a spill of dark hair that fell into his eyes and inched past his collar. He gave her a head nod when they made eye contact.

"Who's that?" she asked Jane, who was making lime-flavored daquiris in a Waring blender with rum pilfered from her father's liquor cabinet. Her parents were celebrating the holiday in Aspen; hence the lime-flavored daquiris.

"I think he goes to school with my cousin Georgie." Jane licked her finger. "Why? You like him?"

"Maybe."

Jane cocked one eyebrow and poured the contents of the blender into a row of plastic cups.

There was a stack of 45's on the record player. When the needle dropped on "Last Train to Clarksville," Ethan crossed the room and asked Nina to dance. It would be years before she learned that the Monkees' hit was about a soldier on his way to Vietnam: *And I don't know if I'm ever coming home.*

That night though, neither of them was thinking about Vietnam. Ethan had a student deferment and figured the war would be over long before he graduated. He told her that he was majoring in liberal arts and hoped to be a writer one day.

Nina had never met anyone like Ethan, who had grown up in Loveland, Colorado, about an hour north of Denver. His father worked for Hewlett-Packard, but his grandparents had been farmers: first sugar beets and then cherries, which were harvested by hand.

"When I was a kid, we used to go to the Cherry Blossom festival every summer," Ethan told her. "There was a big parade and a pie baking contest. My grandmother made a hundred pies for the festival one year. People came from all over to get a slice of cherry pie with ice cream."

"I guess I'm more of a big city girl," Nina told him. "Last year Jane got fake IDs so we could see Carolyn Hester at The Cellar Door in Georgetown."

"Never heard of her," said Ethan.

"Seriously? Bob Dylan played on her third album. That's how he got signed with Columbia Records. Her recording of 'House of the Rising Sun' is way better than Eric Burdon's."

"Maybe you can take me there sometime," he said, taking a pull from a bottle of beer he'd been nursing for the past hour.

"Really?"

"Sure, why not?"

Someone had pushed a mid-century sofa up against a bank of windows that overlooked the quiet, tree-lined street. When two girls got up to dance, Ethan took their place, pulling Nina onto his lap. Now Jane was handing out noisemakers, and someone turned the volume on the television way up so they could hear the countdown from Times Square, and then Ethan was kissing her for what seemed like a really long time and it was 1966.

Nina had never had a boyfriend. Everything she knew about romance came from movies—Natalie Wood driven to madness over Warren Beatty in *Splendor in the Grass*, Julie Harris letting James Dean kiss her on a Ferris wheel in *East of Eden* before turning away, insisting that she loved his brother, really she did. Now here was this boy, who made her heart race, and he wanted to see her again.

Ethan shared an apartment in Fairfax with a roommate, and they met in secret there all winter. Theirs felt like a sacred union, and they didn't want anyone to intrude on their privacy. Nina was certain that if she took Ethan home to meet her parents, some spell would be broken. Most likely her father would find fault with his long hair, and her mother would see right through her duplicity every time she called to say she was staying in the city with Jane.

That spring Ethan's father, who had been paying his tuition, lost his job. "I can work construction and save up some money," Ethan told Nina when he dropped out of school. "I'll go back eventually."

When he was notified that his status had changed from II-S to I-A, what he and his friends jokingly referred to as cannon fodder, Ethan knew it was just a matter of time before he'd be called up. What surprised him was how fast it happened. In June he got a letter instructing him to report to his local draft board, and two weeks later he was at an induction center where there was a physical to determine if he was fit for military service.

The decision to elope was an impulsive one, but it also seemed hopelessly romantic. They drove to Frederick, Maryland where parental consent was not required to marry as long as you were eighteen years of age, and a justice of the peace pronounced them man and wife. Nina called her mother from a pay phone to break the news. "No, I didn't have to," she told Eleanor. "I wanted to."

Ethan withdrew enough money from his savings account so that they could have a honeymoon of sorts in Savannah before he had to report for eight weeks of basic combat training. It took a whole day to get there, and the streets were choked with tourists, but they found a room at a hotel in the French Quarter where, as it turned out, Grace was conceived. A week later Ethan reported to Fort Dix where a barber shaved his head, all that feathery hair falling to the floor.

They wrote to each other, sometimes twice a week, but his letters became less frequent after he was sent to Fort Polk, Louisiana, for advanced infantry training. Then in December he called to tell Nina that he got a three-day pass and would be coming to see her before he shipped out. By then she was far enough along that he could feel the baby kick if she placed his palm on her abdomen. There each night in her childhood bed, they talked in hushed tones about the future.

Ethan left for San Francisco on Christmas Eve. Strangers, seeing him in uniform, offered to buy him dinner, and he called Nina that evening like he promised. They talked until he ran out of change and had to say goodbye. The next morning, he boarded an Air Force C-135, which made an emergency landing on Wake Island in the middle of the Pacific Ocean. On a dirt pathway, Ethan saw a battered telephone booth. The makeshift sign read: *Call the states, $6.75 per minute.* He emptied his pockets and phoned Nina, but no one answered.

Eleanor made a pork roast with sauerkraut for good luck on New Year's Eve and they watched the ball drop in Times Square. At the stroke of midnight Nina thought of Ethan, who was deep in the jungle in Southeast Asia where it had been 1967 for eleven hours already.

When Grace was born that March, Ethan was on a search and destroy mission in the Ia Drang Valley in the Central Highlands. It was weeks before he found out he was a father, and he tucked the photo that Nina sent of Grace, her hands folded under one plump cheek, her hair soft as down, into the scapular he kept in the pocket of his fatigues so he wouldn't forget that he had something to live for.

During a firefight he triggered an S-mine with the toe of his boot. The infantry called it a Bouncing Betty because it was programmed with a four second delay so it would spray 360 steel balls or even pieces of scrap metal horizontally at a very high speed. Almost impossible to outrun, it maimed as many soldiers as it killed. The officers who delivered the news assured Nina that Ethan had died immediately, but she assumed that they told everyone the same story.

By the time his last letter arrived, Ethan was already dead and buried, but he'd included a photograph. He's wearing a sun-bleached helmet with a leafy green camouflage pattern. "We call them steel pots because they're so damn heavy," he wrote. Nina thought he still looked like Ethan: same sweet smile, a bump on the bridge of his nose from a bad fall as a boy, but he'd written something on the helmet band the way someone who's been kidnapped might scrawl the words *help me* on a dusty windshield: WAR IS HELL.

It had been twenty years since Ethan's body was interred in a small cemetery in Loveland, and Nina had only visited his grave once since then. Before she married Paul, she took Grace to see her grandparents. They hadn't made much of an effort to stay in touch with Nina after the funeral, but she thought that it was what Ethan would have wanted. They were both gone now, and she had not heard from Ethan's only sister in years.

Now there was this wall with his name grit-blasted on one of the panels, each a kind of headstone on a mass grave. Nina found his name in a directory as thick as a phonebook on a podium near the entrance. Negotiating the gradually sloping terrain as if entering a tomb, she began searching for Panel 19E.

The narrow cobblestone pathway was littered with dozens of long-stemmed roses and carnations. Nina was surprised by the sheer amount of stuff that people left here, mementos to the fallen—canteens, POW/MIA flags, bullet casings soldered into a circle, a pack of Marlboros, a catcher's mitt, a Purple Heart and an ace of spades, the death card. Someone had left a pair of combat boots, their laces untied, in front of one panel next to a pocket Bible with the inscription: *I carried this every day on every mission and leave it here in memory of those who did not make it home.*

A man wearing a jacket adorned with service ribbons and combat patches knelt before one of the panels. He glanced up at Nina. "Are you looking for someone?"

"My husband."

"What's his name?"

"Ethan Hudson." Nina sighed deeply. "He's supposed to be on Panel 19E."

"I'm Henry," he said, getting to his feet. "What branch of the service was he in if you don't mind my asking?"

"Army."

"We lost a lot of guys over there," he said with a rueful smile.

"Were you in the Army?"

"Yes, Ma'am. 1st Battalion, 26th Infantry Regiment." His eyes softened. "A claymore got one of my buddies two weeks after we arrived. I was walking point that day. The VC had built these elaborate tunnels. We'd be going through an area and all of a sudden they'd show up out of nowhere and ambush us." He rubbed the back of his neck. "We didn't know the country and the people like they did. I don't think I slept at all in the jungle. You're kind of half-awake all the time, you know?"

Nina did not know, but she nodded sympathetically.

He shrugged, fixing her with a look so intense that she lowered her eyes. "So, what panel did you say he was on?"

"19E."

"This is 16E so you're not far." He looked away. "If you don't mind, I'm going to stay here a little longer."

A vet with long hair and a full beard, a yellow First Sergeant patch on the sleeve of his fatigues, nodded at Henry. "Excuse me, brother," he said, and Henry stepped aside so he could pass.

"I'll bet he has some stories to tell," Henry whispered. "I would have eaten glass for my First Sergeant. His name's on here somewhere."

"I should get going," said Nina, and Henry shook her hand.

"Hey, thanks for listening." He cleared his throat. "It's just that no one wants to hear what happened over there so I appreciate it."

She didn't have to walk very far to find Ethan's panel. Someone had left a bouquet of mixed flowers next to a framed photograph of a soldier in fatigues lying in a field of grass. A scrap of white paper affixed to the glass identified him as Lt. Edward Morrow Crowley, KIA April 29, 1967. Nina stared at the photo. A cigarette dangled from his lower lip, while one hand shielded his eyes against the relentless afternoon sun. Ethan and Lt. Crowley had died within days of one another, though by the time Lt. Crowley drew his last breath, Ethan's body had already been transported by Huey to the mortuary at Tan Son Nhut Air Base in Saigon where it was placed in a metal casket and loaded onto a plane. Nina had often thought about the young soldiers assigned to identify the bodies and prepare them for burial, none of them old enough to walk into a bar back home and legally order a beer.

Apprehensively she scanned each row until his name leapt out at her: ETHAN A. HUDSON. Ethan had never cared much for his middle name, Abbott, but it had been his mother's maiden name, and she was proud of the fact that the Abbotts could trace their lineage back several generations to Ulster, a province in Northern Ireland.

Now she crouched down in front of Ethan's panel and removed a half dozen photographs of Grace from her bag. In one she is dragging a single candle through the cake that Eleanor had iced for her first birthday. In another she is bowing deeply in yards of pink tulle after her first piano recital. There is one of her looking over her shoulder as she hurried down the sidewalk in her prom gown with the boy who would break her heart that summer and two of her at the piano at Curtis. The one Nina liked best was of her on the wide front porch in Cape May, backlit by the afternoon sun.

One by one Nina leaned each photo against the granite panel, her face reflected in its mirrored surface. "Ethan, this is your daughter, Grace. I wish you could have met her. She would have loved you." Then, pushing herself to her feet, she took one last look at his name as if committing it to memory. "Goodbye, Ethan," she said. "Take good care of our little girl."

Chapter 27

Frankly, Nina was glad to see the '80s go. The decade had begun on a sour note with John Lennon's murder and gone downhill from there. They'd lost both Grace and Lily, and then three months ago her father died. Lloyd had never really gotten over the loss of his wife, but losing his granddaughter had exacted a steeper price, and Nina believed that he'd lost the will to live.

Charlotte talked her into coming to her New Year's Eve party, which had been their tradition. Seniors in high school now, Harper and Hayley planned to ring in the new year with friends so Nina made the trip herself.

Alice was quiet all evening, sipping Campari and soda while Bill got drunk on Irish whiskey. Like he always did, Kip passed out noisemakers and they watched Dick Clark count down the minutes until the ball dropped in Times Square. Old Man Decker had passed away the year before so there was no gunfire at midnight.

Later, while she and Theresa were helping Charlotte clean up, Nina asked about Alice.

"She's been kind of distant lately" said Charlotte, jamming

a lasagna pan into the dishwasher.

There was a bottle of Lambrusco on the counter, and Theresa poured the dregs into her glass. "I'm surprised she even showed up tonight."

Now Nina was sorry that she hadn't been a better friend in the past couple of years.

"So, I have some news," said Theresa. "Frank's having a baby. Well, Wendy's actually having the baby, but yeah."

"Wow," said Charlotte. "How do you feel about it?"

"I'm fine." Theresa had allowed herself a smug smile of satisfaction when she learned that it took two rounds of IVF for Wendy to accomplish what she had managed the old-fashioned way. "My revenge will come when she puts on fifty pounds. Lombardi babies are big."

"Glad you're handling it so well."

"Life goes on," said Theresa, who had noticed a shift in her feelings ever since she found out that Frank would be a father again. It was like a circuit breaker had been tripped, shutting off the flow of electricity so individual circuits wouldn't overload by drawing more power than they could safely handle.

Nina gave her a hug. "I'm going to see if Alice is ready to leave."

Bill was asleep on the sectional sofa, and Kip was watching MTV. Madonna, in a black slip and crucifix, was dancing in front of a burning cross.

"What's this song even about?" Kip said. "I don't get it."

"I don't either," said Nina.

"I guess we're officially old."

"Speak for yourselves," said Alice from the La-Z-Boy. "I'm younger than both of you."

"Why don't we let Bill sleep it off here, and I'll take you home?" said Nina. "It's really late."

Alice glanced at her husband, who had passed out before midnight this year. "Good idea," she said, lowering the footrest.

Charlotte and Theresa waved goodbye from the front porch and waited until Nina backed out of the driveway before going inside. She took a right on Bath Street and drove through the neighborhood. Cookie was the only Jew in Canterbury Commons as far as Nina knew, but her house was lit up to beat the band every year.

Alice had some trouble finding her house keys, but once inside she flicked on the overhead light in the foyer and locked the door behind her.

Nina followed her into the kitchen. "Where's Noah?"

"At a friend's house. He'll be home in the morning," said Alice, opening and closing cupboard doors until she located a bottle of Amaretto. "How about a night cap?"

Nina pulled out a chair. "Okay."

Alice filled two aperitif glasses and handed one to Nina, inhaling the scent of her perfume, certain that the floral bouquet of hyacinth, jasmine and spicy carnation would remind her of Nina for the rest of her life. "To us," she said, downing the liqueur in one swift motion the way you would a shot of bourbon.

Nina took a sip of her drink. "What can I do?" she asked, remembering how Alice had come to her rescue all those years ago. "You seem so unhappy."

Alice drew back, her eyes glazed and unfocused, before barking out a laugh. "I don't want to be married anymore. What can you do about that?"

Nina wondered if Alice was serious or just had too much to drink. She'd said the same thing after Lily's accident, but Nina had assumed it was grief.

Alice rummaged around in her handbag until she located a pack of Newport Lights. "Lily left a gaping hole when she died, you know?" She stuck a match but let it burn until the flame licked her fingertips. "Since then, I feel like I've just been going through the motions."

"What does that mean?"

"That I don't think I can pretend anymore."

"What about Noah?"

Alice released a dense cloud of smoke. "What about him?"

"How will he feel if you break up the only family he has left?"

"He's a freshman in high school," said Alice, letting an ash fall to the floor. "In three years he'll go off to college."

"Even so," said Nina, but Alice cut her off.

"I thought you'd understand, considering."

"Considering what?"

"You left Paul after Grace died, and your girls turned out alright."

"That's different. Paul tried to kill me."

"Well, this—" Alice glanced around the kitchen, that timeworn symbol of domesticity. "This is killing me." Dragging an ashtray across the table, she let her cigarette smolder there while she looked for something stronger to drink. When she found a bottle of single malt whiskey in the pantry, she poured some into a juice glass. "I've been unhappy for a long time, but Lily's death ripped the Band-Aid off. I can't go on working out at Fitness World three times a week and making stuffed pork chops on Sunday and coming up with every excuse in the book to keep from having sex with my own husband."

"I didn't know things were that bad," said Nina, remembering that there was a time when she and Alice saw each other every day. Now they were lucky if they spoke on the phone every couple of months.

Alice took a sip of whiskey and pulled a face. "I don't know how Bill drinks this stuff," she said, pushing the glass away. She fixed Nina with a doleful expression. "I'm tired of feeling numb. Can you understand that?"

"You're still grieving," Nina said, but Alice shook her head.

"I'm forty-three years old and what have I done with my life?"

"You had two beautiful children."

"And now I have one," Alice pointed out with grim resignation. She finished her cigarette. "I never should have married Bill."

"Why not?" Compared to Paul, Bill was a saint, though Nina didn't think that's what Alice wanted to hear right now.

"I don't think I was ever really in love with him. I mean, I loved him, but I wasn't *in love* with him. There's a difference." Alice knew the difference. She had once been in love with Colin Maguire.

"So, what are you going to do?"

Alice shook her head. "I don't know."

"You've had a lot to drink," said Nina. "Why don't we talk about this in the morning?"

"Wait here," said Alice, who went into the living room and returned with a hardback book, the dust jacket missing, the spine broken. Flipping through the pages until she found what she was looking for, she held the book at arm's length and began to read: *I love thee with the passion put to use in my old griefs, and with my childhood's faith. I love thee with a love I seemed to lose with my lost saints.* " Alice closed the book and clutched it to her chest. "That's how I want to feel before I die." She let the book drop with a thud. "She ran off to get married against her father's wishes."

"Who are we talking about?" Sometimes it was hard to keep up with Alice's train of thought.

Alice frowned. "Elizabeth Barrett Browning. She fell in love with Robert Browning, but her father thought he was a fortune hunter so they eloped and went to Italy. She never saw her father again."

Nina thought that all sounded rather dramatic. "Let's talk about you and Bill," she said, redirecting the conversation.

Alice sat down with a sigh. "I don't want to talk about him." She seemed bewildered. "I'm really drunk."

"You think? Let's go to bed, okay? It's three in the morning."

Nina helped Alice up the stairs. On the landing, they paused in front of Lily's room.

"Bill wants to turn it into an office," said Alice. "What the fuck, Nina? An office?"

"Well, we won't let him."

Alice hugged her. "I love you," she said, spreading her arms wide. "I love thee with the breath, smiles, tears of all my life."

Was she quoting Browning again, Nina wondered.

Alice sighed deeply. "I don't remember the rest."

Nina nudged her down the hallway toward her bedroom and helped her out of her party dress. When she pulled back the covers, Alice crawled under them.

"I used to know that sonnet by heart," Alice said glumly. "I could recite Shakespeare word for word. I could do a lot of things."

When Nina sat on the edge of the bed, Alice leaned up against the pillow. "What happened to me?" she asked. "I have no idea who I am."

"You'll figure it out," said Nina, who wished she had better advice to offer.

"Sometimes I feel like running away. I've been a terrible mother since Lily died. Noah would be better off without me."

"You don't mean that."

Alice fixed Nina with a pitiful look. "If I disappeared, do you think anyone would notice?"

"Now you're just being ridiculous," said Nina. "We'd all notice."

Alice closed her eyes, and Nina sat with her until she fell asleep, her hands folded against one cheek as if in prayer.

Chapter 28

Harper and Hayley graduated from high school in June, and no one was more surprised than Nina that Paul showed up. The girls had seen very little of their father since the divorce except for the two weeks the court required them to spend with him each summer. Since he had no idea what to do with two adolescent girls who were nothing like him, they spent most of their time at his mother's house, which suited them just fine.

Nina would have preferred to sever all ties with Paul, but she relied on child support to make ends meet and couldn't risk crossing him. Sometimes she wondered who came up with such a half-assed system, a sword of Damocles that gave Paul all the power. One wrong move and she'd be chasing the blue light special at Kmart.

Now that the girls had turned eighteen, he was officially off the hook. They all were, she supposed. There had been some question about whether or not Paul would pay for college unless they agreed to study business, economics, or political science. The end game, he said, was a law degree or an MBA.

Nina's father had left the house to her so money would no longer be a problem. In the end, that had been important to Lloyd. Nina had been such a gift to him and Eleanor when she came after three miscarriages, and they'd imagined a big life for her. The trauma of losing her young husband and then her daughter as well had never figured into any of their plans.

Paul drove in a day early for the graduation and brought his new wife, Bethany, with him. After they checked into the Four Seasons, he called to tell Nina not to save seats for them the next afternoon; they'd find their own. Now she fanned herself with her program and looked around. He could be anywhere, she thought. The place was packed.

When the band director raised his baton and the first few notes of "Pomp and Circumstance" rang out, everyone rose to their feet, and the graduating class of 1990 began its dignified procession into the auditorium. It was impossible to deny the emotional impact of Elgar's march, and Nina found herself thinking of Grace. Both she and Ethan had died before they'd ever really lived, a cruel twist of fate for which she had no explanation.

Nina still had the 35 mm. Minolta she'd used in Cape May to photograph each of their children. Now, she adjusted the shutter speed and aperture settings and took a few photos as her daughters crossed the stage to receive their diplomas. A few inspirational words from the principal, who instructed the graduates to move their tassels to the left, and hundreds of mortarboards took flight.

Nina maneuvered her way through the crush of people blocking the aisle. When she found Harper, who broke into a wide smile, Nina squeezed her so yard she yelped. "I'm just so happy for you," she said, "and proud."

Hayley and her friends were exchanging hugs and high-fives, and Harper whistled to get her attention. It was a trick she'd learned from a boy she met at band camp when she was in junior high, and it worked.

"Is Dad here somewhere?" asked Hayley, accepting a spray of pink roses from her mother.

"He's probably out front," said Nina. "Why don't we go look for him."

"We get to meet his new wife," said Harper. "What fun."

It was Nina who noticed him first. His face was fuller, more florid than she remembered, but he was still as handsome as he had been when they first met.

"I guess congratulations are in order," said Paul, giving each of his daughters a perfunctory hug. Glancing at his wife, who had just lit a cigarette, he offered a blanket introduction.

Bethany took a long drag and allowed the smoke to escape slowly from her nostrils. Alice had always said that French-inhaling, a trick like shuffling two decks of cards, was difficult to master.

"Which one of you is which?" she said, looking from Harper to Hayley.

When they were younger, the twins grew tired of people asking them that question, which they felt diminished them as individuals and was usually accompanied by a lot of staring and other annoying questions. If they were really fed up, Hayley might pretend to be Harper, who would happily go along. Now Nina hoped they wouldn't play that trick on Bethany, which would just provoke their father.

"I'm Harper," said Harper to Nina's relief, "and she's Hayley."

Bethany had the kind of patrician good looks that suited a powerful attorney with political ambitions. According to the girls, Paul had hinted that a few local

Republican operatives wanted him to run for office. Since he hadn't bothered, Nina introduced herself to his wife.

Dropping her cigarette to the pavement, Bethany crushed it beneath the sole of her stiletto. "Nice to meet you," she said, linking her arm through Paul's like a dog marking its territory.

"I made a reservation for us at a seafood place that's known for its crabcakes," said Paul. "Why don't you follow me."

Nina asked him for the address, "just in case we lose you," and he rattled it off. There was a parking lot in back, and Nina pulled in after Paul, who was driving a new Porsche 911 Carrera convertible. Harper pretended to gag herself when she saw the vanity plate: LEGEGL.

"Let's just get through this," said Nina, unbuckling her seatbelt.

A hostess saw them to their table and doled out five leather-bound menus.

Paul flagged down a busboy who was clearing a nearby table. "I'd like a Glenlivet," he said. "On the rocks."

"Your waiter will be with you in a few minutes, sir," said the boy, who was stacking dirty plates one on top of the other.

"Forget it," he said, scowling. I'll get it myself."

"I'll come with you," said Bethany, squeezing his shoulder with one of her perfectly manicured hands. She rose from her chair like Venus, the goddess of beauty and love, emerging from the sea.

"Go ahead and order starters if you want," Paul said to his former family.

"Let's order one of everything," said Harper with an impish smile when her father was out of earshot.

Their waiter placed a basket of warm rolls on the table. "I'm Sean, and I'll be taking care of you tonight." Gesturing toward the two empty chairs, he asked, "Are we expecting anyone else?"

"They're at the bar," said Nina, "but we're going to order drinks and a few appetizers."

"I'll have a Cosmopolitan," said Hayley, who had seen photos of Madonna holding one at a Grammy Awards party.

"She'll have an iced tea, " said Nina, "and so will her sister. I'll have a glass of sauvignon blanc."

"Why don't you take a look at the menu," said Sean, "and I'll go get those drinks for you."

"So, what do we think of Dad's trophy wife?" asked Hayley.

"Cold as ice," said Harper. "They're perfect for each other."

Nina thought it best to keep her opinion to herself, which was that Bethany would take Paul to the cleaners when she finally divorced him. Sometimes Nina wished that she'd done exactly the same thing, but she had been so worn down by Paul's abuse that she had no fight left in her.

"Have we made any decisions?" Sean asked when he returned with their drinks.

"How about the spicy shrimp," said Hayley, "and the fried calamari."

Harper glanced at her mother. "They've got your favorite, mushrooms stuffed with crabmeat. Let's get those, too."

Now Paul was heading in their direction.

"Where's your wife?" asked Hayley, who was buttering a roll.

"Ladies room." He placed his drink on the table and opened his menu, which he studied as assiduously as Nina imagined he had studied for the bar exam.

Bethany (a fresh coat of lipstick had been applied) approached the table, and Paul jumped to his feet to pull out her chair. The girls exchanged can-you-believe-this-shit looks with their mother, who shook her head ever so slightly. Appetizers were served and small plates passed around for sharing.

Nina stole a glance at Paul's wife whose perfectly executed haircut fell from a center part to her jaw, the perimeter razor-sharp, and she knew with absolute certainty who was the alpha dog in this relationship.

When Sean offered to tell them about the specials, Paul groaned. Nina suppressed a smile because in all the years she'd known him, Paul had never ordered *the special*. It was a long list. Bethany had the good manners to pretend to pay attention, nodding every so often and glancing sideways at Paul when he started drumming his fingers on the tablecloth.

At last, Sean finished his spiel. "Why don't we start with the ladies, " he suggested, pivoting to take Nina's order.

"I'll have the rainbow trout with sauteed spinach," she said, "and maybe a salad to start." Determined to have a little fun at Paul's expense, she decided to prolong the conversation and asked Sean if he preferred the wedge with bacon or the Caesar salad. Paul was drumming again, and Bethany shot him a stern look. Finally, Nina ordered the house salad, but she made a big production out of deciding between the blue cheese dressing and the vinaigrette.

Hayley caught on right away and asked Sean to go over the specials again. "Actually, none of them appeals to me," she said when he was finished. "I think I'll have the surf and turf."

Bethany raised one expertly arched eyebrow to signal that she knew exactly what they were up to and fixed them with a withering look. Closing her menu with an air of finality, she asked Sean for "the swordfish, no sauce, asparagus dressed with lemon only, and a garden salad, oil and vinegar on the side."

"I'll have the crabcakes," said Harper, who avoided confrontation at all costs, "and a baked potato with sour cream."

"Guess it's my turn," said Paul with a sardonic grin. He handed his menu to Sean without making eye contact. "I'll have the ribeye. Medium rare." Rattling the ice cubes in his empty glass, he asked for a refill.

"You get two sides with that."

"Garlic mashed potatoes and green beans." Still no eye contact."

"Very good, sir," said Sean, who departed as swiftly as a victim fleeing the scene after a toxic chemical spill.

"So, why the University of Arizona when there are plenty of first-rate colleges right here on the east coast?" said Paul, glancing from Harper to Hayley and back again. "Did you even consider my alma mater?"

"Not really," Hayley said.

Nina rushed to fill the awkward silence. "They've got a good humanities department."

"Humanities," said Paul with a dour expression. He turned to Harper. "What about you?"

"Sociology."

"What do you think you're going to do with a degree like that?"

"Lots of things."

"Like what?"

"Urban planning, community development, advocacy," she said, throwing in "non-profit work" just to get under his skin.

"You girls are just like your mother," he said.

A food runner returned with their entrees and conversation, such as it was, ground to a halt. Later, after dessert had been served and Paul asked for the check, he removed two envelopes from the inside pocket of his jacket and handed one to each of the girls. "Good luck," he said. "You're going to need it."

He gave the bill a cursory glance before placing his Amex in the leather folder Sean had discreetly left on the table. "You're a smart girl," he said to Hayley. "Why didn't you go into pre-law?"

"I don't want to be a lawyer," said Hayley, resisting the impulse to add "like you" because she didn't want to be anything like him.

"Well, don't come crying to me when you can't get a job."

In the parking lot, Harper ran to catch up with her father. "Mom's going to college with us," she told him. "She's going to study art."

He shook his head.

"She's going to be a painter," said Hayley, "and a good one."

Bethany slipped into the front seat of the Porsche and put on a pair of enormous sunglasses, while Paul squeezed behind the wheel. When the engine roared to life, Nina was reminded of the afternoon he gave her a lift in his Dodge Charger and she had imagined he'd come to her rescue.

"Heads in the clouds, all three of you," he said in parting, revving the engine just to show off.

They waited until they saw his taillights recede, happy to see him go.

Chapter 29

When Frank's daughter was born, Frankie and Tina were summoned to the hospital to meet their baby sister. As soon as they got home, the first question Theresa asked was, "Does she have a name yet?"

"Buttercup," said Tina.

Frankie stifled a laugh and went upstairs to his room.

"What kind of name is that?" asked Theresa.

"It's from *The Princess Bride*," said Tina. "It's Wendy's favorite movie."

"And your dad's alright with that?"

"He lets Wendy do whatever she wants."

Now, to celebrate Buttercup's first birthday, Wendy was planning a party complete with pony rides, a juggler and a castle made entirely of pink balloons. Tina's own first birthday had been a decidedly low-key event: cake and ice cream with the grandparents.

"Dad's dressing up like Big Bird," Tina told her mother. "He already ordered the costume."

"Does that bother you?"

"What? That Dad's making a fool of himself over a kid

who can't even talk yet?" Tina raised one eyebrow, which she'd pierced recently. "I could care less."

Theresa knew better than that. In fact, she assumed that Tina's daddy issues would require a lot of therapy to resolve and that the piercings (she had one in her tongue as well), the black leather bracelets with metallic spikes snaking up her skinny arms and her obsession with some band called Nirvana, whose music gave Theresa a headache, were a cry for help.

Tina had graduated from high school, though just barely, and all she had done since then was float around on a raft in their pool or watch TV all afternoon. Most of her friends had summer jobs as lifeguards or camp counselors or cashiers at Walmart, but Tina seemed to have absolutely no ambition. On the few occasions that Theresa ignored the KEEP OUT sign on Tina's bedroom door, she'd noticed an unpleasant, faintly herbal odor, which was not exactly like running over a skunk at night but close.

Theresa knew that she and Tina were long overdue for a mother-daughter talk, but right now she had a to-do list a mile long. She was catering an anniversary party that weekend for Joan Cabot. She and her husband were the types of people whose names showed up in the society pages in the local newspaper, and Theresa hoped to make a good impression since the guest list included a lot of other attorneys and their wives, who entertained all the time.

Theresa's catering business had taken off in the last year, and she had Fernando to thank for that. He's the one who suggested that she start her own business. Alice had been telling her the same thing for years, but she had lacked the confidence to do anything about it until Fernando hired her to cater his annual Christmas party last year. Since then, he had sent a lot of business her way, and she was finally starting to make some real money.

The downside was that she sampled everything and had put on a lot of weight. Fernando was fond of telling her that she wasn't fat, just *zaftig*, but Theresa suspected that *zaftig* was just Yiddish for fat, only sexier. She imagined a ripe, succulent peach.

Theresa went over the menu again before going downstairs to get a load of towels out of the dryer. Tina was sprawled across the sofa in front of the television. Last year she had become addicted to some show called *Twin Peaks*, which Theresa found disturbing and sinister. The Black Lodge or whatever it was called seemed to be a place of pure evil, and Theresa had to sleep with a light on after Tina coerced her into watching a few episodes.

Theresa started up the stairs before thinking better of it. "When do you plan to get off the couch and actually do something with your life?"

Tina regarded her mother with a distinct lack of interest. "Haven't you ever heard of summer vacation?"

"I worked at Dairy Queen every summer when I was in high school." Theresa put the laundry basket down. "I think it's time we had a little talk."

"We never talk," said Tina. "You talk, and I listen."

"That's not true," said Theresa, though without much conviction. Had she become just like her own mother, who never listened to her? She hoped not. "I think you need a sense of purpose in your life. Isn't there anything you're passionate about?"

"No."

"Have you given up on going to beauty school?"

"I'm over that. Hair, makeup—all that stuff's just shallow and superficial."

Theresa thought of Fernando and how his makeover had done wonders for her self-esteem. "Why are you being so difficult?"

Tina shrugged.

"How would you like to work for me this summer?" said Theresa, the idea only just occurring to her. She could use the extra help now that she was catering larger events, and they'd get to spend more time together.

"Doing what?" Tina asked, looking up from the TV where the credits were rolling at the end of some sitcom.

"Food prep, set up and clean up, maybe passing *hors d'oeuvres*."

"Sounds boring." Tina was flipping through the channels now and only half paying attention.

"Turn that off for a minute," said Theresa. "I want to talk to you."

"Fine," said Tina petulantly, depressing the POWER button and tossing the remote onto the coffee table. "Happy now?"

Theresa looked at her daughter, ignoring for a moment the unwashed hair, the flannel shirt that looked like something you'd buy at Salvation Army. Who wore a flannel shirt in the middle of July anyway? Where was that little girl with the heart-shaped face, who had a collection of Care Bears: Cheer Bear with its carnation-pink fur and a rainbow belly badge; the fearless Sunshine Bear, who exuded sunny optimism; Share Bear, who considered everyone her friend? Theresa barely recognized her anymore.

"I'll pay you five bucks an hour. That's more than minimum wage," said Theresa firmly, leaving the room and taking the remote with her.

"Hey," shouted Tina, but Theresa was resolute.

"You start tomorrow."

When Tina came downstairs on Saturday morning in cut-off jeans, a Ramones T-shirt and Dr. Martens steel-toe work boots, Theresa sent her back upstairs to change. "You're not wearing that."

"Why not?"

"For one thing, it's the middle of July. Who wears shoes like that in this heat?"

"They're Docs."

"I don't care what they're called, you're not wearing them." Theresa turned back to the stove to stir a pot of meatballs. "You want to be comfortable because you'll be on your feet all day."

"My Docs are comfortable."

"They look like combat boots," said Theresa. "You must have a pair of white tennis shoes in your closet."

"How long are we going to be there?" asked Tina, who wore a sullen expression, one of three she kept in rotation, the other two being sulky and surly.

"We set up at three and start serving appetizers at five," said Theresa. "I asked one of Fernando's receptionists to help out, but she can't come until after work."

Tina put a bagel in the toaster. "I told some friends I'd meet them later."

"What's later?"

"I don't know. Eight?"

"We won't be done cleaning up until at least ten."

"Ten? Are you serious?"

"Dinner isn't served until seven, and we have to wash all the dishes and pack up the car." Theresa removed two pans of lasagna from the refrigerator and slid them into the oven. "It takes forever."

The toaster dinged. "This is bullshit," said Tina.

"Watch your mouth." Theresa set the timer for forty-five minutes and closed the oven door. "I ironed a white shirt for you. It's in the laundry room. I wear mine with a black skirt. I'm sure there's one in your closet."

Tina pulled out a bar stool and sat down at the island. "I haven't worn a skirt since middle school."

Theresa opened the refrigerator again and found a tub of cream cheese, which she handed to Tina. "That's the uniform."

Tina tore off a piece of bagel and dipped it into the cream cheese. "This sucks."

"Sometimes life sucks," said Theresa, giving the meatballs another quick stir. "Get used to it."

Theresa had traded her old car in for a Dodge Caravan with enough cargo space to transport all the serving equipment she needed, not to mention the table settings, insulated containers, tubs for ice, a fifty-cup coffee urn, grocery bags filled with ingredients for food she planned to prepare onsite, and the enormous trays of food ready to be placed into chafing dishes and kept warm with cans of Sterno.

The minivan had faux wood paneling, which reminded Theresa of the Ford Woody the Fuller Brush man drove when she was a girl. He had a glass eye that both fascinated and frightened her. Her mother said he'd lost his eye in the war and that she was not to stare, but it was hard not to. Trapped in the house with a passel of kids all day (they only had one car), Theresa's mother waited for the Fuller Brush man to show up with his satchel of household supplies like an *ingénue* expecting a suitor.

The Cabots lived in a historic old home along the river that was built in the eighteenth century. The frame house had a stone chimney in the New England style and a rear addition and wide front porch. Tina helped Theresa unload the car and carry things into the kitchen.

Hugh Cabot showed them in. "My wife will be down shortly. She's just getting dressed. You must be Theresa."

"Nice to meet you." Theresa placed a pan of lasagna on the counter near the stove and shook his hand. "This is my daughter, Tina."

"Hey," said Tina, barely making eye contact.

"So, do you two need some help? I can call my son down to lend a hand."

Tina went back out and came back in, her arms filled with boxes. "Where do you want this stuff?" she asked Theresa, who gestured toward the island.

"So, should I get Chase?" Hugh removed his wire-rimmed glasses and let them dangle from his index finger.

"That would be very kind," said Theresa.

"Who are you, the Queen of England?" said Tina when Hugh went to look for his son. She mimicked her mother, affecting a posh British accent. "That would be very kind."

"Oh, shut up. These people are old money, very important."

"They're richer than us, that's for sure," said Tina, taking in the open industrial kitchen with its wide plank floors, handcrafted cabinets and marble countertops.

"We're *nouveau riche*," said Theresa. "There's a difference."

"What does that mean?"

"It means that your father got rich by selling a shitload of carpet. These people inherited their money."

"So, when I inherit Dad's money, I'll be old money, too."

"It doesn't work that way," said Theresa, who imagined Princess Buttercup and her social-climbing mother frittering most of it away by the time Frank dropped dead. "Your father's money will never be old enough for these people."

Joan Cabot sailed into the kitchen, her highlighted hair pulled into a low chignon. She was wearing a sleeveless chemise and a string of what looked like very expensive pearls. Theresa couldn't help but notice that her underarms were as taut as the skin of a drum. Joan Cabot had to be at least sixty years old, though she didn't look a day over fifty, possibly because she had her plastic surgeon on speed dial, at least according to Fernando.

"It's so nice to meet you, Mrs. Cabot," said Theresa.

"Call me Joan," she said, extending her hand the way the Pope might offer his ring to be kissed.

Hugh was back with his son, who looked about as happy to be here as Tina did.

"This is our son, Chase," said Hugh.

"Nice to meet you," said Chase, who had a louche, rakish appeal in his pleated pants and slightly wrinkled button-down shirt, the sleeves rolled up to the elbow.

He and Tina exchanged looks like double agents talking in code.

As if laying stake to her claim, Joan placed her hand lightly on Chase's forearm. "Would you be a dear and make Mummy a drink first?"

A shock of dirty blonde hair flopped over his forehead, and he palmed it back in place. "Gin and tonic?"

Joan smiled benignly, and Chase went off to fetch her drink.

"He'll be a junior at Yale next year," said Joan, fixing Tina with a he's-out-of-your-league look as lethal as Strychnine.

"Wow," said Tina, fixing Joan right back with a who-gives-a-shit expression.

Chase returned with his mother's gin and tonic, and Theresa dragged Tina out of earshot. "I told you to be on your best behavior today. Don't mess this up for me."

"She's an asshole," said Tina under her breath.

"She's a client," Theresa reminded her.

"Whatever."

"We better finish unloading the car," Theresa said in a voice loud enough for Chase to get the hint.

Fernando's receptionist, Carla, arrived in time to help Theresa set up the buffet. Tina was passing plates of shrimp and rosemary crostini, fried dough with grape tomatoes, and croquettes stuffed with ground veal and potatoes. The guests were sipping cocktails and generally enjoying themselves from what Theresa could see. Tables had been set up in the addition with its vaulted ceiling, and everyone waited until Hugh and Joan made plates for themselves before they rushed the buffet.

"The food is delicious, Theresa," said Hugh effusively. "I'm going to have to hit the gym tomorrow to work this off." He patted his stomach.

"Yes, everything's lovely," said Joan.

Theresa noticed that Hugh's plate sagged under the weight of angel hair primavera, Tuscan chicken, lasagna, garlic parmesan potatoes, and eggplant rollatini, while Joan had helped herself to a scoop of fruit salad and three skewers of grilled shrimp with bell peppers and mushrooms.

"It's your anniversary, eat something," Theresa wanted to tell her, though she had to admire her discipline. No one would ever call Joan Cabot *zaftig*.

After dinner, a trio of musicians arrived to set up in the formal living room where guests were invited to listen to jazz while they enjoyed coffee and amaretto. Theresa hadn't seen her daughter for at least an hour, but she didn't have time to look for her. She was too busy wrapping up leftovers and hauling things out to the car.

She and Carla were washing dishes when Joan appeared in the doorway. "Look who I found upstairs in my son's room," she said, giving Tina a little shove.

Theresa felt the color drain from her face. "In bed?"

"Certainly not," said Joan as if the idea were repugnant to her.

"I'll just take out the trash," said Carla, discreetly slipping out the side door with a Hefty bag full of garbage.

"She was smoking pot," said Joan.

"Excuse me?"

"She had a joint in her hand."

"Where did she get it?"

"I presume she brought it with her. My son does not do drugs of any kind."

"Well, neither does my daughter," said Theresa, pushing aside for a moment that peculiar odor she'd detected in Tina's room and the fact that Joan had seen her holding a joint. Or did she say smoking a joint? Theresa was certain that a lawyer would make that distinction in a court of law if it came to that. "Maybe you should ask your son to come downstairs so we can get to the bottom of this."

Tina stared at Theresa with an almost imperceptible shake of her head. So now *they* were speaking in code.

"That won't be necessary," said Joan with a tight smile. "It's obvious who's at fault here. My son is at the top of his class at Yale. Your daughter is, well, just look at her."

Theresa glanced at Tina and saw exactly what Joan Cabot saw: the eyes rimmed in kohl, the tiny gold ring in her right eyebrow, the bleached-out hair with three inches of dark re-growth. She also saw that little girl with the heart-shaped face, clutching her Harmony Care Bear with both hands.

"I'd like you to pack up your things and go," said Joan curtly. "This party could have generated a lot of business for you, but under the circumstances I won't be recommending your services to any of my crowd."

Theresa considered her options before deciding that she only had one. "You and your crowd can go to hell. Come on, Tina, we're leaving."

For the first time in months, Theresa saw a smile play across her daughter's features. It was small, but it was something.

Carla was smoking a cigarette in the driveway.

"Tell Fernando I'm sorry," said Theresa. "I kind of said some things in there that Joan may hold against him."

"Joan's a bitch," said Carla. "Don't worry about it." She took a final drag from her cigarette and tossed it into the grass. "Should I go back in there and bring out the rest of your stuff?"

"What's left?"

Carla tried to remember. "The coffee urn? Maybe one of your chafing dishes."

"Leave them," said Theresa. She offered the car keys to her daughter. "You want to drive home?"

"Okay," said Tina, who stopped to retrieve Carla's cigarette from the grass on her way to the car. "We don't want to burn down the house while we're at it," she explained when Theresa gave her a puzzled look.

They were almost home before Tina said anything. "I wasn't smoking pot. I mean I have smoked pot. I think you've probably figured that out by now, but I wasn't smoking tonight. I wouldn't have done that to you." She glanced at her mother, whose expression was unreadable in the dark. "It was his. He handed it to me when his mother walked in on us."

"Why did you let her think it was yours?" asked Theresa.

Tina came to a stop at the red light and looked over at her mother. "The way he passed it to me and the look on his face, I knew that he couldn't be the one caught with it." The light turned green, but Tina wasn't paying attention. "He's actually not a bad person. He hates Yale, but his parents have his whole life mapped out. He doesn't want to be a lawyer like his dad, but try telling them that."

The driver behind them flashed his brights and laid on the horn. Tina rolled down her window and threw him the finger.

Theresa stole a look at her daughter. Somehow, she couldn't imagine Tina ever taking the kind of shit from a man that she had been willing to take from Frank.

Tina turned up the radio: more existential despair from that band that Tina loved. *I feel stupid and contagious, here we are now, entertain us.*

"Why do you like them so much?" Theresa asked, genuinely interested.

A soft rain was falling, and Tina turned on the wipers. "They changed everything. Music will never be the same because of Nirvana. I knew that the minute I heard this song."

"I felt like that about the Beatles," said Theresa, remembering how she'd held her breath when she heard *She Loves You* for the first time.

"You grew up in a totally different era," said Tina. "Things were so innocent then. I want to hold your hand. All you need is love. That's not how I grew up. Kurt Cobain's parents divorced when he was little, too, and it had a huge effect on him. He sings about what it feels like to be sad, to be lonely, to be ugly. There's this one song, *Polly*, about a girl who was raped. He sings about real life, not some sugar-coated version of it."

"I'm sorry," said Theresa.

"For what?"

"For everything."

Tina pulled into the driveway. "It's okay, Mom." She touched the remote on the visor, and the garage door lumbered open. "I'm starving. Want to heat up some leftovers?"

"I could eat," said Theresa. "So, what did you think?"

"Of what?"

"The food? Do you think they liked it?"

"You're a great cook, Mom. Everything you make is delicious."

"Joan Cabot hardly ate a bite," said Theresa. "Do you think on her deathbed she'll regret all the pasta carbonara and tiramisu she turned down to look like a Pez dispenser?"

Tina cut the engine. "Fuck Joan Cabot."

"Language," said Theresa out of habit, though what she was thinking was, "Bless your little Care Bear heart."

Chapter 30

Noah had been accepted to Carnegie Mellon University where he planned to study computer science, and Alice drove him to Pittsburgh to help him get settled. They took a slight detour and stopped for lunch at the Nittany Lion Inn in State College, a small concession to Bill, who had lobbied hard for Noah to go to Penn State, his alma mater, though Noah had no interest in football and did not believe the sun rose and set on Coach Joe Paterno. He reserved that honor for Herb Simon, who had been on the faculty at Carnegie Mellon since 1949 when it was still called Carnegie Tech and who had won the Turing Award, often called the Nobel Prize of computer science, in 1976.

It was an unseasonably warm day, and the hostess suggested that they wait outside on the flagstaff patio for a table in the dining room, which was crowded with incoming freshmen and their parents. Alice had always loved this place, which was built in the Georgian style in the middle of the Great Depression and had maintained its historic integrity over the years. When a second wing and then a third were added, they used the same masonry to provide continuity, and Alice found something comforting in the absence of disruption.

When the hostess finally seated them, Alice looked around the dining room with its inky blue walls and cream-colored woodwork, the patterned carpet plush enough to absorb the footfalls of busboys filling cobalt-blue water glasses arranged with military precision on white linen tablecloths.

A few years ago, she and Bill spent a weekend here during football season and stayed in one of the rooms upstairs. They arrived midday, and warm light filtered in through the sheer ruffled curtains at the dormer windows. There was a double bed with a white chenille bedspread and a floor lamp with a fringed shade like something out of another era. While Bill went to the bar to meet some of his fraternity brothers, Alice took a nap. When she woke with a start an hour later, the light had faded to a dusty shade of purple. Briefly disoriented, she thought she was in her bedroom in Lincoln Park where she grew up and for a few moments disremembered her adult life with its attendant grief and sorrow and unbearable loss.

That was the feeling she'd been chasing since Lily's death. Now, finding herself in the geographic center of Pennsylvania surrounded by Appalachian Mountain ranges and forests, she knew she had two choices: drop her son off in Pittsburgh, turn around and go home, or keep heading west, through Ohio into the flat plains of Indiana and Illinois, through Missouri into Texas and Arizona with its ancient saguaros, and then New Mexico, Land of Enchantment, until she reached California where its rugged coastline rose and fell alongside an ocean so boundless that it must hold the key to the secrets of the universe.

"It is a beautiful campus," said Alice after lunch as she and Noah walked back to the car.

"Now you sound like Dad," said Noah, shaking his head. "I'm excited about going to CMU."

Traffic was heavy when they got to Pittsburgh, and Alice got lost in Oakland trying to find Noah's dorm. It was after six by the time they hauled everything up to his room, but he didn't want to unpack right away.

"You're only here for one night," he said. "Let's do something special."

"Like what?"

"You're going to think it's stupid, but I really want to ride the Incline. I've done a little research, and it's supposed to be the best way to see the city, especially for the first time."

Alice looped her arm through his. "Okay."

They had to drive downtown and cross the Monongahela River to enter Pittsburgh's South Shore where they parked in a gravel lot near the lower station. Alice paid for two tickets while Noah took a brochure.

"Earlier inclines were used to hoist coal to the top of Mt. Washington," he told her. "The Germans called it Coal Hill. They're the ones who suggested that someone build inclines along the face of the hill so people could get up and down. On opening day in 1870, 944 fares were collected, but the next day over 4,000 people rode the incline. Guess how much it cost?"

Alice had been looking out the window where a red cable car was inching its way down a set of steep tracks. "How much?"

"Six cents." Noah broke into a wide grin. "That's insane."

"Come on, it's our turn," said Alice when the cable car came to a stop at their station. Making the three-minute ascent to the top of Mt. Washington, they turned around to look down the tracks where the city lay just across the Monongahela River.

The incline conductor directed them to the overlook on Grandview Avenue where they'd have a panoramic view of the Pittsburgh skyline. "That's where George Washington stood to map out the land and rivers below for the British," he told them. "You two live around here or are you just visiting?"

"I'm a freshman at CMU," Noah told him. "My mom's just dropping me off."

Alice asked the conductor if there was a good place to eat within walking distance.

"I'll tell you what," he said. "Since this is kind of a special occasion, kid going off to college and all, I'd go to Station Square." He explained that it was a riverfront complex built on the site of the former Pittsburgh & Lake Erie Railroad. "If you take the incline back down, it'll only take you a minute or so to walk there. The station itself is a restaurant now. That's where I'd eat."

Noah extended his hand. "Thanks, mister."

"Good boy you have there," the conductor said to Alice, but she already knew that.

The Grand Concourse was redolent with Edwardian ambience: vaulted ceilings, stained glass windows. "Order anything you want," she told Noah. "It might be the last good meal you'll have in a while."

It was late when Alice dropped Noah off on campus, and when he hugged her goodbye, she finally understood how her mother must have felt when she disappeared down the jetway with Lily all those years ago. Now Lily was gone, and Noah was starting a new life without her.

When she checked out of the Hilton the next morning, the valet brought her car around. "Need directions?" he asked her.

"No, I'm good," she told him.

Heading east, she picked up the Pennsylvania Turnpike. At the tollbooth, she took her ticket, but instead of taking the exit toward Harrisburg, she took I-76 West toward Ohio. She realized her mistake almost at once but simply kept on going.

She called Bill from a pay phone at a museum in St. Louis near the Gateway Arch where she learned about the westward expansion.

"What the hell, Alice," he said. "I was worried sick when you didn't come home the other night. I called Noah, but he had no idea where you were." He sounded angry, and Alice couldn't blame him, though she was at a loss to explain her sudden defection. "What's going on?"

"I don't know," she told him, which was the truth.

He wasn't buying it. "That's bullshit and you know it."

"I'm sorry," she said, though sorry for what she couldn't say. Sorry that Noah had been dragged into their domestic drama?

"When are you coming home?" asked Bill. It was a fair question after all, but she hadn't thought that far ahead.

"I don't know," she told him and hung up before she lost her resolve.

When she got back in the car, she spread out a map she found in the glove compartment. Chicago was almost five hours away, though admittedly in the wrong direction, but if she took a slight detour she could drive through the neighborhood where she grew up and see her childhood home one last time. Alice's mother had died two years ago from breast cancer, her father a year later of a heart attack. She and Audrey had spent two weeks sorting through a lifetime of accumulated possessions before putting the house up for sale.

Years before, Babe had bequeathed her service of Lenox china to Audrey and her sterling silver flatware to Alice, but they had no idea what to do with all of their mother's clothing, her collection of Hummel figurines, the boxy handbags and straw totes and shoes too small for either of them. There was a time when Babe's shoes were too big to fill. Alice remembered playing grownup in her navy and white Spectator pumps with their round toes and Cuban heels.

They kept a few pieces of their mother's jewelry: a cameo brooch, her good pearls, a silver charm bracelet with trinkets celebrating birthdays and anniversaries or places she'd visited: an Eiffel Tower from Paris, Big Ben from a trip to London, a hula dancer from a vacation in Hawaii.

Alice boxed up a few other things that had sentimental value: their father's letters to their mother from the Pacific theater during the war, family photographs in silver frames and a music box that played "Stardust," which Babe treasured because it had been a gift from Sam on their first anniversary.

Audrey and her husband had moved to Phoenix so Alice had no reason to visit Chicago anymore, but somehow it seemed imperative that she see the house on a tree-lined street in Lincoln Park one last time. Lincoln Park was home to one of the oldest zoos in the country, which was also home to the Bur Oak, a tree so old it would take three people to hug its massive trunk. As a child Alice had been fascinated by its deeply ridged bark, which supported limbs that had been arching over the landscape for nearly two centuries.

The brick and limestone house on N. Fremont Street looked exactly the same: a set of six stone stairs leading to the front door, a shade of black as glossy as doors you see in Paris or London with sidelights to the left and right and, dead center, a gold mail slot. When Alice was growing up, letter carriers delivered the mail on foot and knew everyone on their route. Oftentimes they were invited inside to warm up if it was cold or to have a glass of lemonade in the summertime. Alice remembered coming home from junior high school one afternoon to find their postman, who spoke in a thick Irish brogue, talking politics with Babe at the kitchen table. Being Irish Catholic himself, Thomas "Red" O'Sullivan was a staunch supporter of John F. Kennedy's campaign for president.

There was a vacant parking space in front of the house, and Alice pulled over. She let the car idle while she imagined that if she climbed those stairs, lifted the brass knocker and let it fall, she'd hear her father calling, "Babe, look who's here. It's Alice."

It was late afternoon when she decided to make another stop. If she were going to take a trip down memory lane she might as well visit the University of Chicago in Hyde Park where she'd met Lily's father during the Summer of Love when she felt like the last virgin in Chicago. On the radio Scott McKenzie was reminding girls bound for California to wear some flowers in their hair, but Alice couldn't imagine her parents letting her go that far away from home even if she wanted to, and she would never have gone without telling them. From what she'd read in *Time* magazine, Alice knew that thousands of kids her age were in Haight-Ashbury that summer, dropping acid and making love to people they'd just met and might never see again.

So, with her virginity weighing her down like a sodden overcoat, Alice began searching for someone to give it to, though she was unwilling to simply hand it over to one of the jocks or frat boys who got drunk at parties, unhooking your bra without asking, touching and groping when you'd made it perfectly clear that you were a "nice girl." Well, if she did manage to lose her virginity, the coin of the realm for nice girls everywhere, she wouldn't be a nice girl anymore, would she? Or maybe she'd still be a nice girl, just not a "good" girl. That was the prevailing notion, at least among girls Alice's age, who had yet to discover that such mandates about purity had nothing to do with goodness and everything to do with the exploitation and control of women.

Alice was working at the library on campus that summer, checking books in and out, organizing files and answering phones. That's how she met Zeke, short for Ezekiel.

"My mother had a thing for Biblical names," he informed her much later when she asked if he had any brothers or sisters and he told her about Gabriel, Ezra and Naomi.

Zeke was repeating an economics course he failed that winter and was working on a paper he'd put off until the last minute.

"That's not really what I do here," Alice told him when he showed her a list of materials he needed, "but I can tell you where to look."

Alice preferred lanky blondes with blue eyes, and Zeke was neither of those things, but when he fixed her with a boyish smile, a kind of non-verbal pretty please, she snatched the paper from his hand.

"You can't take this stuff out of the library," she said when she returned with a stack of books and scholarly journals, "so you're going to have to take notes or Xerox what you need."

He came back every afternoon for the next couple of days, his brow furrowed in concentration as he took notes. That Friday he found Alice re-shelving books from a metal cart. "Do you know anyone who could type my paper for me?" After fishing through his backpack, he produced a composition book.

"How much are you paying?"

"I don't know." He narrowed his eyes as if divining a figure. "What's the going rate?"

"Depends on how long the paper is," said Alice, forcing a book whose binding was in tatters into a too-small space. "Ten dollars?"

"So, do you know someone?"

"I'll do it."

"I hope you can read my handwriting."

Alice flipped through a few pages and decided that she'd seen worse. "What's your deadline?"

Alice had taken typing as an elective in high school so she could have finished Zeke's paper in less than an hour, but the English major in her was compelled to fix grammatical errors, correct misspelled words and tighten up the syntax, which took a bit longer.

"Wow, I should give you another ten bucks," he said after he'd read a couple of paragraphs.

"It's okay," said Alice with a shrug. "You didn't ask me to."

"Hey, my roommates and I are having a party next Saturday. Want to come?"

"Maybe," said Alice, who had already decided to go but didn't want to seem too anxious.

"Any time after eight," he said, tearing a page out of his notebook and scribbling an address. "I live on South Kenwood."

The house was in a rundown neighborhood, and she had to park a couple of blocks away. Lights blazed in every room, and people drinking from plastic cups or smoking cigarettes spilled out onto the front porch. Zeke was in the kitchen, and he gave Alice an awkward hug before handing her a cup of some high-octane wine with a cloying citrus taste. Music blasted from the stereo: *I can't get no satisfaction.*

Alice followed Zeke into the living room where a complex drinking game was in progress.

"That's Dallas," said Zeke, cocking his head toward the person in the center of the circle, who had been designated Prince. "He lives here."

"Wales tails, Prince of Wales, somebody stole my tails, I accuse number—" Dallas glanced at his inebriated subjects. The whole group seemed to heel to one side, a ship tilting port or starboard. "Three."

Everyone stared at a pretty girl whose hair fell nearly to her waist.

"What, me?" She giggled, and they all yelled, "Drink."

"Hey, I got an A on that paper you helped me with," Zeke told Alice. "I think that's the first A I ever got."

"Ever?"

Zeke closed one eye in a squint. "Yeah, ever," he said after some reflection.

Alice had hoped her first time would be with another English major, someone who wrote lyrical poetry like Pablo Neruda: *A long time I have loved the sunned mother-of-pearl of your body until I even believe that you own the universe.* So far, she hadn't met anyone like that, but she had come to this party with the sole purpose of losing her virginity and Zeke had a certain rakish charm. Besides, it wasn't like she was going to marry him, so when he draped one arm around her shoulder and asked, "You want to go outside?" she said, "Sure."

Zeke took a bottle of Thunderbird with him and held the screen door open for her. Someone had dragged a beat-up old sofa to the front porch, and Zeke collapsed against the floral cushions.

"You're really pretty," he said, pulling Alice onto his lap. "You kind of remind me of that actress in that Alfred Hitchcock flick with Jimmy Stewart."

"*Rear Window*?"

He shook his head. "The one where he's a cop who's afraid of heights."

"*Vertigo*?" said Alice, and Zeke nodded. "You mean Kim Novak?"

"Yeah, the blonde."

"They're all blondes."

"Who?"

"Hitchcock's leading ladies. They're all blondes: Grace Kelly, Tippi Hedren, Janet Leigh."

"The one from *Psycho!* Man, that movie freaked me out."

Music from the stereo wafted onto the porch through the open window: *I'm pickin' up some good vibrations.*

"You like the Beach Boys?" asked Zeke, taking a pull from the bottle before offering it to Alice, who took a swig and grimaced.

"Rot gut," said Zeke with a laugh, "but it gets you where you want to go."

"The Beach Boys are okay," said Alice, slipping off his lap. "I guess I'm more of a Dylan fan."

Zeke pulled a face. "Strike one."

"What? Have you even listened to *Mr. Tambourine Man?*"

"Why would I?"

"To dance beneath a diamond sky with one hand waving free, silhouetted by the sea, circled by the circus sands," said Alice, who knew every word by heart. "That's poetry."

"Okay, I'll give you another chance. Stones or Beatles?"

"Stones," said Alice without hesitation.

Zeke leaned in to kiss her. "Maybe there's hope for you yet," he said before kissing her again.

By the time Zeke suggested that they go upstairs, the party was winding down. Dallas was passed out on a leather couch in the living room, and two stoners were sitting cross-legged in front of the stereo, passing a joint and listening to The Dead: "Viola Lee Blues." Zeke slept in the top bunk, which was disconcerting at first. After all, who wants to lose her virginity in a bunk bed? Still, Alice had made up her mind, and after Zeke assured her that his roommate was staying at his girlfriend's apartment that night, she resolutely climbed the ladder.

"I'm a virgin," she told him, though she was unsure if that was important or he even needed to know.

Zeke shucked his jeans and jockey shorts. "Okay, that's a lot of pressure."

"Look, if you don't want to—"

"I didn't say that." He nuzzled her neck, and Alice giggled. "Sorry, that tickles."

He helped her out of her jeans. "You on the pill?"

Alice shook her head. "You've got something, right?"

"Don't worry, I'll pull out in time," he said, and Alice believed him.

The whole business took less than a few minutes. Alice was still wearing her T-shirt, though Zeke had managed to unhook her bra and fondle her breasts in a lackluster attempt at foreplay. After being raised on pop songs and movies that promised pyrotechnics on the scale of fireworks over the Capitol on the Fourth of July, sex had been kind of a letdown.

"So, how was it?" Zeke asked.

Alice hesitated. He didn't really want to know, did he? "I guess I thought the ceiling would come crashing in on us."

"Why?"

"Catholic guilt."

"I'm Methodist, so—" He vaulted over the side of the bed and climbed back up the ladder with a pack of Marlboros. "Want one?"

She did, but it felt like a cliché and she declined the offer.

He struck a match, briefly illuminating the scene of the crime as it were: a tangle of sheets, their jeans and his T-shirt balled up at the foot of the bed. "You can stay over if you want."

"I can't."

"Why not?" Smoke from his cigarette spiraled toward the ceiling.

"I live with my parents," Alice told him.

"So."

"My mother will be waiting up for me."

Zeke choked back a laugh. "How old *are* you?"

"They're strict, that's all," said Alice defensively. "You're a guy, so you wouldn't understand. Guys get away with everything."

As expected, her mother was in the living room when Alice got home.

"It's about time," was all she said before turning off the lamp and going upstairs.

Later, lying in bed under a thin sheet, Alice closed her eyes and allowed the events that had just transpired to unfold in slow motion, romanticizing the entire incident the way people romanticize trains or pirates. She had lost her virginity. No, that wasn't right. She hadn't misplaced it like a favorite book she'd loved since childhood; she had willingly given it away, and now she wondered what all the fuss had been about.

When she missed her period the next month, she tried not to panic. What were the chances of getting pregnant the first time you had sex? Okay, so it was statistically possible, but Alice was convinced that those things only happened on the soap operas her mother watched each afternoon.

There was a girl on campus who, it had been reported, knew a lot of things about a lot of things, like how to buy pot or procure a fake ID. She recommended Humphrey's 11, a homeopathic remedy for delayed menses that could be purchased at any drugstore without a prescription.

"They'll bring on your period right away," she promised.

Alice thought of it like jump-starting a car, though years later she learned that women had been taking the little white pills to induce abortions since the Victorian era. How effective they were was anyone's guess. They certainly did nothing to bring on Alice's menses.

After a few more weeks, Alice went to Zeke's house late in the afternoon, hoping he'd be there.

"Alice, hey," he said when he answered the door.

"We need to talk," she told him. "It's important."

"You mean now?"

"Yes, now."

He held the screen door open for her.

She decided to get right to the point. "I think I'm pregnant."

"Whoa, what?" He followed her into the living room. "You serious?"

"Believe me, I wouldn't be here if I wasn't."

He lowered his voice to a whisper. "Are you sure?"

"I have to see a doctor, obviously, but I thought you should know."

Unmarried women like Alice who found themselves in the family way could be expelled from college, and she wasn't taking any chances. After finding the name of an ob-gyn in the phone book, she made an appointment for later that week as Mrs. Robert Zimmerman, an in-joke for a serious Dylan fan like her who knew that was his real name. To be on the safe side (she didn't need someone becoming suspicious because she wasn't wearing a wedding ring), she bought a cheap gold band at Woolworth's and wore it on her ring finger that day.

The nurse handed her a specimen cup and pointed her to the bathroom.

"We should have the results in a few days," she told Alice when she handed over the urine sample.

Alice paid in cash and gave them Zeke's phone number. That Thursday they sat in his living room, still as statues, waiting for a callback from the doctor's office. When the phone rang, Alice answered it. "Yes, this is Mrs. Zimmerman."

"I'm calling to give you the results of your pregnancy test," said the receptionist, who paused dramatically, a game show host trying to generate excitement before revealing what's behind door number two.

Alice closed her eyes and offered a silent prayer to St. Jude, the patron saint of hopeless situations. All she heard before slamming down the receiver was, "Congratulations!" as if Alice would be driving a new Pontiac home later that day.

She and Zeke exchanged looks. "What are we going to do?" she said.

"You're not going to have it, are you?"

"What's that mean?"

"Don't you want an abortion?"

"No, that's not what I want," said Alice, who didn't necessarily want to marry someone she wasn't in love with either. "Besides, they're illegal, remember?"

"There are doctors who'll do them anyway if you've got enough money," he said. "I could ask around, you know, find someone."

"I could bleed to death," she reminded him, "or die from an infection."

"Well, I'm too young to be a father," Zeke said, "and besides, we hardly know each other."

Alice glared at him. "So, what? This is my problem?"

Zeke let out a long breath. "I've got a girlfriend." He flinched as if to deflect the blow he was sure was coming. "She lives in Wheaton. We've been going out since high school."

Alice got to her feet. "You're an asshole, you know that?"

"I thought we were just having fun that night."

"And a liar." She grabbed her purse.

He caught her by the wrist. "I didn't know this was going to happen."

Alice wrenched her hand away. "Well, it did."

She pushed through the screen door and let it slam behind her.

"Wait up," he hollered, but she was already down the stairs.

Alice crossed the street, and Zeke followed her, nearly colliding with a battered Chevy Caprice.

The driver slammed on the brakes and rolled down the window. "Asshole," he shouted, corroborating Alice's assessment.

A week after Alice broke the news to her parents, Zeke was summoned to Lincoln Park. His father had already offered assurances to Alice's father that his son would do the right thing. Alice's mother called the priest at St. Mary of the Angels, the church built by Polish immigrants, including Alice's great-grandfather Andrzej Kowalczyk. He put the wedding on his calendar for the following Friday afternoon, and Alice went to Marshall Field's to buy a dress.

Zeke drove to Wheaton to break the news to his girl-friend, Virginia, who demanded her day in court so to speak. She wanted to talk to Alice, and Zeke, who was both guilty and remorseful, acquiesced.

"She's really upset," he told Alice a few days later when he got back from Wheaton.

"Well, what did you expect?"

The phone rang sharply, and Zeke answered it. After his initial "hello," he didn't say much of anything, and from his pained expression Alice deduced that the caller must be Virginia.

"Yeah, okay," he said. Then, fixing Alice with a pitiful look, he pushed the phone in her direction. "Just talk to her, please."

Alice held the receiver to her ear. "Hello."

"You know what you are?" Virginia shrieked. "You're nothing but a slut. I hope you rot in hell." When she was finished with her tirade, she hung up on Alice, who listened to the dial tone for a few seconds before handing the phone back to Zeke.

Alice walked down the aisle in a white voile mini-dress and a headband festooned with fresh daisies. Zeke's parents and siblings, except for Gabriel who was in college on the West Coast, attended the brief ceremony. In lieu of a reception, their little party, which included Alice's younger sister Audrey, walked to an Italian restaurant in the neighborhood.

Zeke's sister Naomi, who was twelve, completely ignored Alice at dinner and scowled when Ezra offered a toast, Zeke's cue to kiss his new bride. Later, Zeke's mother took Alice aside and explained that Naomi had been rather fond of Virginia and that it might take some time for things to sort themselves out and that she hoped Alice would understand.

As a wedding present, Zeke's father paid for a room at a fancy hotel downtown. As they rode the elevator in nervous silence to the ninth floor, Alice glanced at the brushed-gold wedding band on her left hand and felt a sense of giddy optimism. The bedspread had been turned down, and there was a piece of foil-wrapped chocolate on the center of each pillow.

Zeke checked out the bathroom with its marble shower enclosure. "This must have cost my old man a fortune."

Alice went to the window, which overlooked the square where the water changed colors as it rose and fell in the enormous stone fountain. On impulse she suggested that they go outside, imagining them splashing in the fountain, letting the water soak them to the skin before walking back to the hotel arm in arm. It was her *Barefoot in the Park* moment, and Zeke blew it.

"We're not going anywhere," he said, stripping off his shirt and tie. He stepped out of his pants and kicked them to the corner before climbing into bed. "We're going to stay here and get our money's worth."

Alice went to the bathroom to change into the *peignoir* her mother had insisted on buying just a few days ago. Mercifully, she'd skipped the what-to-expect-on-your-wedding-night lecture, given the circumstances. When she played with paper dolls as a little girl, the groom had been superfluous. For Alice it was all about folding the tabs back on the bride's voluminous white gown, pretend-walking her down the aisle and dressing her up in items from her *trousseau*: kid gloves, a saucy hat, matching shoes and handbags. As for what happened after the pretend honeymoon, well, Alice wasn't sure; she was eight. Now she had a real-life husband, who looked nothing like the handsome cardboard groom she'd based all of her childhood fantasies about marriage upon. He looked like a kid, which, of course, he was. Stepping out of her strappy sandals and unzipping her dress, she caught her reflection in the mirror over the marble vanity and knew with absolute certainty that she had made a terrible mistake.

Lily was barely a year old when Zeke announced that he was going backpacking across Europe with Dallas, leaving Alice to hold down the fort. The fort was a cramped one-bedroom apartment near Grant Park. There were a few postcards: one from Amsterdam and another from Zurich where he and Dallas were washing dishes at a ski resort in exchange for room and board. The postcards stopped coming after that, and when it became clear that Zeke had left Alice for good, her father hired an attorney to start divorce proceedings. Later, Alice wrote a letter telling Zeke that he was free to start a new life but not to contact her or Lily again. She mailed it to the house in Wheaton where he grew up and never heard from him again.

Chapter 31

———◦———

In Oklahoma City, Alice stopped for gas at Love's Travel Stop and bought a map, a pack of Twizzlers, a bottle of Coca-Cola and a hotdog from the roller grill, which she ate in three bites leaning against the checkout counter. She paid with her credit card and asked the girl working the register how to get to Sears where she charged enough clothing, mostly T-shirts and shorts plus a light sweater, to make it to the West Coast.

Outside of Amarillo, she stopped to see a public art installation in a wheat field on Route 66. Ten Cadillacs, covered with graffiti, were buried nose-first in the ground. A teenage boy was tagging a tail fin.

"Want to try it?" he said when he was finished.

Alice glanced around furtively. "Aren't you worried you'll get caught?"

"Go on. They want you to. It's art." He handed her a can of spray paint: Krylon Color Master in Blue Ocean Breeze.

"What's your name?" she asked him.

"Miguel."

Alice shook the can until the ball bearing rattled inside and pointed the nozzle at the door of a '62 Caddy like the one her father had way back when. When she was done, she stood back to admire her handiwork: ALICE WAS HERE in all caps.

"Thanks," she said, handing the can back to Miguel. "Whose idea was this anyway?"

"Some hippies," he said. "Guess they were sorry to see tail fins go."

It was almost dinnertime when Alice got back on the road, so she drove into Amarillo to find a restaurant. Henk's Bar-B-Que had a drive-up window, but she decided to go inside. On one wall was a poster called Cowboy Commandments. 1. *Just one God.* 2. *Honor yer Ma & Pa.* Alice looked at the menu. Henk's Favorites included something called Frito pie.

"Is it good?" she asked the boy behind the counter.

He gave her a sour look. "It's Frito pie," he said as if she was the stupidest person he'd ever met.

Alice placed her order and found a table.

"Howdy," said a man in a Western shirt, who was working his way through a plate of ribs.

"Hi," said Alice, and then just to make conversation, said, "That looks good."

He used his napkin to mop up some barbeque sauce that dripped down his chin. "You're not from around here, are you? The accent. I don't recognize it."

"Pennsylvania."

"Whereabouts?"

"Near the Poconos."

"Just driving through, are you?" he asked, selecting another rib from his plate and tearing off a chunk of meat.

Alice nodded.

"Where you headed?"

"Not sure."

"Nothing like a road trip with no destination in mind to clear the cobwebs, am I right?"

She heard her name called. "My order's ready," she told him.

He tipped his hat, a black Stetson that threw shade across his full, florid face, and scraped back his chair. "Well, safe travels, Ma'am."

Alice carried the Frito pie—layers of homemade chili, ranch style beans, cheese and enchilada sauce with crispy Fritos on top—to the table and went back for her side of slaw and a Coke.

She'd put almost fifteen hundred miles on her car in the past four days. Except for a trip to Las Vegas with Bill five years ago, she'd never been this far from home, which was beginning to feel as small and insignificant as if she were looking at it through the wrong end of a pair of binoculars. When she and Bill went to Vegas, they boarded a plane in Pittsburgh and landed four hours later. It had taken her that long just to make it through Ohio.

In Alto Pass, Illinois, she saw a cross made of concrete, its exterior metal panels covered in white porcelain, rising more than one hundred feet into the night sky. Along I-40 billboards battled for her soul: REPENT! JESUS IS COMING SOON; GOD SAYS NO TO HOMOSEXUALITY AND ABORTION! One, with a toll-free number, inquired, "Pregnant? Baby's heart beats in 18 days."

The animosity between Chicago and the rest of the state was legendary. While technically in Illinois, Chicago might as well have been on Pluto, which appeared as a dim speck in even the largest telescopes. Her father had dismissed downstaters as a "bunch of farmers, Baptists and gun owners."

Alice took a bite of her Frito pie, letting the gooey cheese ooze through the crust. Tomorrow she would be in New Mexico. She had already decided to get off I-40 in Tucumcari for no other reason than that she remembered a song by Little Feat called "Willin'" about a truck driver traveling from Tucson to Tucumcari: *And out on the road late last night, I'd see my pretty Alice in every headlight.* Growing up, Alice had heard lots of songs about girls named Cathy or Diana or Susie, but this was the first time anyone had ever written a love song about her, and it filled her with a sense of pride as if she'd been singled out.

There was a vacancy sign in front of The Blue Swallow Motel with its stepped parapet and pink façade decorated with shell designs. The owner, Lillian Redman, checked her in and was happy to tell Alice how she had arrived in New Mexico by covered wagon with her family in 1915.

"My husband Floyd—he died in '73—bought this place for me as an engagement present in 1958," she said. "We operated this motel back before the new highway came in and Route 66 was closed to most traffic." Lillian ran Alice's credit card. "I just felt like I lost an old friend, but some of us stuck it out and are still here."

Lillian handed Alice the key to her room. "There's lots to do here," she told her. "Go see the Historical Museum if you want to learn about local history."

Alice wondered what made Lillian Redman stick it out when she could have sold the motel and moved somewhere else. She must have been lonely living out here in the middle of nowhere. Alice believed that loneliness was just as lethal as smoking and must be assiduously avoided. She was almost certain that it was Anaïs Nin who'd said, "Man can never know the loneliness a woman knows," but now she wondered if the novelist had been mistaken and that Bill had known that kind of loneliness as well.

The next morning Alice checked out of the motel and had breakfast at a café in town. There was a pay phone out front, and she thought about calling Bill but was afraid that hearing his voice would break the spell she had been under for the past few days. The sky was a brilliant shade of blue with low moving clouds. With its grand sandstone cliffs and alpenglow skies at sunset, the landscape felt expansive as if suggesting that anything was possible here where nature had adapted so that common yarrow grew wild in dry soil and desert marigold, impervious to drought, flowered in bright yellow profusion.

That afternoon, after consulting her map, she drove west for an hour before detouring north toward Santa Fe. Alice had introduced Nina to Mary Cassatt, but Nina had told Alice about Georgia O'Keeffe, who had described Ghost Ranch, a retreat in Northern New Mexico where she had a studio, as a "beautiful, untouched lonely feeling place, such a fine part of what I call the faraway." Somehow those words had resonated with Alice, who felt compelled to see Ghost Ranch for herself.

She stopped for a late lunch in Santa Fe where she visited Loretto Chapel, designed in the Gothic Revival style by renowned French architect Antoine Mouly, who did not live to see its completion. A docent explained that it was left to the nuns, who had made the arduous journey to Santa Fe in 1852, to have a staircase built to connect the chapel to the choir loft. After praying to St. Joseph, the patron saint of carpenters, a stranger arrived at their door, offering to build the staircase for them. Using simple tools and wooden pegs, the carpenter built a spiral helix-shaped staircase (the entire weight rested on the bottom stair) out of rare wood not native to the American Southwest before disappearing without asking for thanks or payment. Naturally, the nuns decided that the carpenter was St. Joseph himself and named his creation the Miraculous Staircase. Since then, thousands of the faithful had flocked to see the miracle for themselves.

The mystery of faith: something that transcends reason. That's how Theresa had explained the concept to Alice, who desperately wanted to believe, as Theresa did, that Lily was in heaven, or at least that she still existed somewhere. On her way out of the chapel, she stopped at the gift shop and bought a sterling silver pendant engraved with a picture of the Blessed Mother, Our Lady of Loretto, a talisman perhaps.

Since it was too late to visit Ghost Ranch, Alice got a room in town and ate dinner at the bar where she struck up a conversation with an older woman who had come to New Mexico on a pilgrimage. Her grandson was gravely ill, and she hoped for a miracle.

"People come to El Santuario de Chimayo every year," she told Alice, "because of the holy dirt, which has curative powers."

Alice regarded her curiously, and she explained that the chapel outside of Santa Fe had been built over a hole where a crucifix bearing the image of a black Christ marked the grave of a Guatemalan priest. Visitors were encouraged to take some of the restorative clay from a well (*el pocito*) to use as poultices.

"Of course, belief in the curative powers of the holy dirt are purely faith-based," she said, "but my faith is pretty strong."

Alice had prayed for a miracle after Lily's accident, but those prayers had gone unanswered. *Had she just not prayed hard enough? Or was her faith too weak to move mountains?*

Alice identified with the apostle Peter, who had walked on water with Jesus until he became afraid and sank beneath the waves. Filled with the same doubt and fear ever since Lily's death, Alice felt herself sinking a little more each day.

El Santuario de Chimayo was in the foothills of the Sangre de Cristo and Jemez Mountains, and Alice decided to go there the next morning before visiting Ghost Ranch. Built of adobe with a bell tower on each side, it was an unimposing structure, nothing like the Loretto Chapel with its Gothic altar and ornate stained-glass windows. In a small prayer room to the left of the nave, crutches and baby shoes had been discarded, testimonials from people claiming to have experienced miraculous healings. Alice followed a procession of the faithful into the sacristy, and when her turn came she knelt down and reached into *el pocito* to remove a handful of the restorative clay, which she placed in her pocket (a good luck token?).

Outside the sky was wide open, a dazzling shade of blue. Dozens of people were waiting to enter the church. A few pushed old people in wheelchairs, and a young mother consoled her crying baby. Two women in black leather jackets posed for a photo in front of a rough-hewn wooden cross. Alice overheard a Hispanic man tell a woman in line with him that he had come from Albuquerque to collect a bag of holy dirt, which he intended to spread across the grave of his five-year-old son.

"I come here once a year," he said. "It helps me cope."

Alice imagined scattering the red earth in her pocket across Lily's grave and wondered if it would provide any comfort.

After driving north to Abiquiú that afternoon, Alice took a walking tour of the property that had inspired Georgia O'Keeffe. In the shifting light, surrounded by colorful sandstone cliffs, red hills and mesas, Alice felt closer to God than she had on the entire trip. There amid the acres of towering rock walls, she understood why this place called to O'Keeffe, who moved there after the loss of her husband. On impulse Alice bought one of her prints: the flat-topped mountain to the south of Ghost Ranch called Pedernal. The artist, whose ashes were scattered on that narrow mesa, believed that if she painted Pedernal often enough, God would give it to her.

Alice stopped for something to eat on Highway 84, which O'Keeffe would have taken to Okhkay Owingeh on the San Juan Indian Reservation to purchase the antlers she painted in *Deer's Skull with Pedernal*. Alice had no idea whether or not the artist was Catholic or even religious, but she imagined that she might have turned off 84 in Española to see El Santuario for herself. Or perhaps she had visited the Monastery of Christ in the Desert on a winding dirt road off 84. Designed by a Japanese monk, the Benedictine monastery was built of rock and adobe and offered a place of quiet contemplation. It was a complicated landscape full of ghosts: tranquil and serene, yet also mysterious, otherworldly, haunted.

Late the next afternoon, Alice crossed the border into California and got a room at a hotel in Needles on the western bank of the Colorado River. Alice had read *The Grapes of Wrath* in college, and now she remembered that the Joad family had stopped here for gas and supplies before crossing the Mojave Desert. Having fallen in love with the cool, clear water, Noah, the oldest son, had decided to stay instead of heading further west with his family. Now Alice sensed that she, too, had a decision to make. Maybe it was time to call her husband.

Frigid air blasted from an air conditioning unit on the wall. Bill answered on the first ring.

"It's me."

"Where the hell are you?"

"Literally in hell." It was well over a hundred degrees outside. When the joke fell flat, she told him she was in California.

"So, you're not on your way home."

"No."

"Do you even plan on coming home?"

She could hear the television in the background, some kind of sporting event by the sound of it. Baseball? "I'm not sure," she told him because she wasn't.

"I don't understand you, Alice," he said. "I've tried to be a good husband."

She scooted to the edge of the bed. "I'm sorry."

"What does that even mean? Are you sorry you left or sorry you married me?"

That was tricky, and Alice equivocated. "It's just that I haven't been the same since Lily died." She stopped short of adding, "It has nothing to do with you," fearing perhaps that it had everything to do with him and that Bill would see right through the deception. "I'm lost, Bill," she told him, which was closer to the truth than anything else.

He lowered the volume on the television. "Sometimes I wonder if you even love me anymore. Maybe you never did."

"That's not true," said Alice, though she had admitted as much to Nina over the years. Why hadn't she left Bill when Noah was in high school, she wondered, though since Lily's death she had felt like she was slogging through quicksand, unable to move forward or backward for fear of sinking even deeper into despair. Now that she'd run away from home, and that was what this trip was beginning to feel like, Alice realized that she had just been postponing the inevitable.

"Are you even going to ask about Noah?" said Bill. "He's called a couple of times, and I've had to make up excuses about why you can't come to the phone. He's a smart kid, and he's going to start asking questions."

"How's school? Does he like it there?" she asked, and Bill seemed to set aside his anger.

"His roommate is some whiz kid from Seattle, who likes Dungeons & Dragons as much as our son does, so, yeah, I guess he likes it there."

Alice winced. *Our son.* No matter what she decided to do, Noah would always be the common denominator. She remembered that when her fictional doppelganger came to a fork in the road and asked the Cheshire Cat which direction to take, he had replied, "That depends a good deal on where you want to get to."

Alice wasn't completely sure how she wanted her journey to end or which road she should take to get there, but she sensed that it was time to stop running away and figure it out. But first, she'd see the ocean. After all, she'd come this far.

Chapter 32

T he drive from Needles to Santa Monica took Alice less
than five hours, much of it through the arid Mojave
Desert, the driest in North America. Needles was so geo-
graphically isolated that the nearest city, Barstow, was one
hundred forty miles away through high desert. The heat
was extreme, the sky a piercing, almost jubilant shade of
blue. Every so often a red-tailed hawk would glide over the
harsh landscape, its wingbeats heavy and substantial. The
sense of isolation, of being cut off from civilization, was not
entirely unpleasant. It gave her time to think.

In Barstow, Alice stopped for gas and something cold
to drink before heading south past Victorville and through
the Cajon Pass, which snaked for twenty miles between the
San Bernardino and San Gabriel mountain ranges before
giving way to the fast-food restaurants and strip malls in
San Bernardino.

Traffic was crawling, and it took nearly two hours to
reach Santa Monica where she found a place to park and
walked to the ocean. When she was thirteen Alice had seen
photographs in *Life* magazine of three teenage boys on

surfboards gliding over the waves at Malibu. The vaguely self-indulgent promise of all that sun and sand, even in winter, had seemed idyllic to her, and she wondered if this would be a good place to start over if it came to that.

The drive home was bittersweet, and Alice had mixed emotions about what to expect when she got there. Joshua Tree was technically a detour, but she decided to take I-10 East past Palm Springs anyway, reasoning that if she decided to stay with Bill that she might never get this far west again. In the summer months it was possible to watch monsoons build over the park, and Alice was sorry she'd missed that.

With its rugged rock formations and stark desert landscapes, Joshua Tree was actually two distinct ecosystems, and she was surprised to learn that Joshua trees weren't trees at all but members of the agave family (*yucca brevifolia*). The Spanish called them *izote de desierto* (desert dagger) because of their spiky leaves, but it was Mormon settlers who thought their unique shape resembled Joshua lifting his hands to the sky in prayer.

It was late in the day when Alice got back on the road, heading north toward Las Vegas, avoiding Arizona and New Mexico entirely this time to take the northern route through Nevada and Colorado, across the central plains of Nebraska and deep into the Midwest through Iowa, Illinois and Indiana. Driving across Ohio and into Pennsylvania, she experienced an acute sense of loss. It was not unlike how she felt when she married Bill and left Chicago for a new life in Pennsylvania all those years ago. Where was home exactly? Alice wasn't sure she knew anymore.

It was late morning when she arrived in Pittsburgh where she had lunch with Noah at a Mediterranean restaurant in Oakland. His hair was darker than it had been in childhood, and he pushed it out of his eyes, which in contrast seemed bluer than usual. Dipping a piece of pita bread into a bowl of hummus, he asked Alice if she was leaving his father.

"I don't know," she said because she hadn't made up her mind yet.

"You and Dad should have gotten a divorce years ago," he said, wiping his fingers on a napkin. "If the only reason you didn't was because of me, I'm letting you off the hook, not that you need my permission."

Alice lowered her eyes.

"Look at me, Mom," said Noah, forcing her to meet his gaze. "You're not the only one whose life changed when Lily died, but we never talked about it. Why is that?"

Alice put her fork down. "I guess I wanted to protect you."

"From what? From missing my sister? I miss her every day." He pushed his plate away. "Dad and I used to talk about Lily all the time. I'll bet you didn't know that."

Alice shook her head.

"It was like you were the only one whose grief counted for anything after Lily died." He reached across the table to take one of her hands in his. "I'm not trying to make you feel bad, Mom. I want you to be happy, and you haven't been happy for a long time."

Alice looked at her son, so grown up now with his broad shoulders, hands twice the size of hers, the hint of a mustache on his upper lip. When had that happened? Sometimes Alice still thought of Noah as that little boy with the flaxen hair that Lily used to tickle until he begged her to stop.

He poked at his Greek salad. "I want Dad to be happy too. I just don't think you two can be happy together."

"I'm the one at fault here," said Alice. "Your father is a good man. He deserved better, but that's not something I should be discussing with you."

"You can talk to me about anything, Mom," said Noah, leaning forward on his elbows so their faces were inches apart. "If you want to."

While she had no intention of taking him up on his offer, she wondered if it might be different with Lily. Did mothers and daughters share intimacies that mothers would never think of sharing with their sons? Alice had no way of knowing.

The waitress appeared with their check, and Alice pushed her credit card across the table. Noah had a class at two, and Alice dropped him off at Smith Hall. Leaning across the seat, he pulled her into a tight embrace.

"What was that for?" asked Alice, and Noah gave her a cryptic smile before snatching his backpack and getting out of the car.

She watched him lope across campus, taking long strides and nearly colliding with two girls who weren't paying attention to where they were going. The pretty dark-haired girl, watchful and attentive, lingered to talk to Noah while her friend kept walking. It felt like a private moment, and Alice looked away, but she hoped that someone would always look at Noah that way. *How long had it been since she'd paid Bill that same kind of attention? Had she ever?* She called him from a pay phone on I-80 to tell him she was on her way home.

It was nearly sunset when Alice pulled into the garage next to Bill's staid Volvo 840 GL, an automobile chosen specifically for its record of safety and reliability. She turned off the car and listened to the engine cool down: tick, tick,

tick. Her overnight bag was in the trunk, and she brought it in through the kitchen, taking in the collection of vintage bottles on the windowsill, the dishes stacked neatly in the drainer next to the sink, the drop leaf table with a single placemat and Sunday's paper open to the sports section.

She found Bill upstairs. He'd just taken a shower and was blow-drying his hair, a towel wrapped around his waist. "Hey, sorry," he said when he saw her in the doorway. "I just finished mowing the lawn. Give me a minute, okay?"

She nodded, briefly wondering if she should make some kind of physical contact. It had been almost two weeks after all. Bill regarded her curiously before going back to the task at hand. Alice turned and walked down the hall, passing Lily's old room and then Noah's: the empty nest. Light filtered in through the sheer curtains at her bedroom window, falling in shadows across the duvet. A novel by Joyce Carol Oates (*What I Lived For*) was on the bedside table. She hadn't bothered packing it before she left since she'd only planned to stay overnight in Pittsburgh and come home the next afternoon. That all seemed so long ago now, that life a distant memory.

She sat down on the edge of the bed, a mail-order bride waiting for a groom she barely knew. *Had she ever really known Bill? Had she ever really known herself?*

When he came out of the bathroom, he seemed surprised to see her waiting for him. Letting the towel fall to the floor, he approached the bed, and Alice wondered if this was some kind of test. He leaned down to kiss her, and she let him. After more than twenty years, she knew every inch of his body: the chest, hairless except for a furrow of downy hair on his abdomen, the sinewy arms and back, the faint scar from a childhood appendectomy. When he lifted her T-shirt, hesitant at first and then, when she didn't resist, more assertive, it all felt so familiar. He helped her undress, taking his time before straddling her the way he had the morning Noah was conceived and all those times since then too numerous to remember. He came quickly and apologized. The last light of day was fading now to a musky shade of indigo, and when he rolled on his side, away from her, Alice sensed that it was finally over between them.

Chapter 33

Nina planned her first trip to Paris to coincide with her fiftieth birthday in April when the entire city would be in bloom, the first cherry blossoms appearing at the Hotel de Ville and in Square Rene Viviana across the river from Notre Dame. She had lost touch with Alice a few years ago, but she still remembered her phone number. When she booked her trip, she called to see if Alice might want to tag along so they could celebrate the Big 5-0 together (Alice's birthday was in May), but the number had been disconnected.

Nina still had the book of pastel portraits by Mary Cassatt that Alice had given her years ago, and she planned a visit the artist's home in Le Mesnil-Theribus. One of her professors in art school had told Nina that art is more powerful if people feel they can connect to the subject matter.

"Art is just a way of telling a story without using words," he said, and Nina had understood right away what kinds of stories she needed to tell. Since then, she'd done dozens of paintings from photographs of Grace. In one she is practicing scales at the piano, her toes barely touching the pedals.

In another she is wearing a red velvet dress with a white satin petal collar, dwarfed by the enormous Christmas tree in Eleanor's living room.

Ordinarily Nina preferred not to live in the land of what-might-have-been, but facts were facts. If Grace had lived, she would have turned thirty in March, a milestone birthday just like Nina's, and they might have gone to Paris together to mark the occasion. Art historians agreed that Cassatt's paintings of mother and child in domestic settings had allowed her to sublimate her desire to have children, and Nina was astute enough to realize that by choosing similar material, she had been able her sublimate her grief over the loss of her daughter.

Nina booked a hotel on the Rue Mouffetard, the oldest street in Paris. Checking in, she felt Alice's presence as surely as if she were haunting these streets where her favorite writers (F. Scott Fitzgerald and Edith Wharton) had been members of the great artistic community at Montparnasse.

Nina hadn't been to church in years, but she was determined to light a candle for Grace at the Basilica of Sacre-Coeur, which presided over the city from the summit of Montmartre, a sketchy neighborhood where the great Impressionists had lived and worked. The streets were lined with stalls where vendors sold linens, sheets, towels and other household items for next to nothing, and she bought cotton dish towels with images of the Paris skyline or the Eiffel Tower made of macarons to take home as souvenirs. Sacre-Coeur was accessible by funicular, a kind of cable car that climbed the steep hill, and from there Nina took in the sweeping view of Paris before following other tourists into the church. A mosaic of Christ in glory—arms extended, his golden heart revealed—loomed overhead. Surrounding him were the Virgin Mary, Saint Michael and Saint Joan of Arc, who were believed to protect France.

She had to admire the resilience of the French people, who had restored the stained-glass windows two years after they were destroyed during the Liberation of Paris in 1944. For a few years after Grace died, Nina had seen a therapist, who suggested that adversity, as Nietzsche believed, made us stronger precisely because it provided the opportunity to develop resilience. She thought about that as she wandered into an alcove and discovered a bank of candles. After lighting one for Grace, she lit another for Lily and, on impulse, one for Alice before exiting from a side door to emerge into bright sunshine from the dim recesses of Sacre-Coeur.

Her plan was to spend the entire afternoon at the *Musée d'Orsay. All* of the paintings she had admired in art school were there: *The Ballet Class* by Edgar Degas in which he created the illusion that the room was receding; *The Magpie,* Monet's oil-on-canvas landscape that seemed lit from within and evoked the muffled silence that comes after a heavy snowfall; and Van Gogh's *Starry Night Over the Rhone,* one of his paintings of Arles, which allowed him to experiment with the effects of light at night.

She was examining Courbet's masterwork, *A Burial at Ornans,* when she heard an announcement on the public address system. Nina knew enough French to understand that she was being ordered to evacuate the building immediately. Apparently, someone had called in a bomb threat, a common enough occurrence in Paris that the gendarmes would quickly confiscate and destroy luggage left unattended at Gare du Nord.

Nina followed the crowd moving toward the exit— Parisians ambling slowly as if strolling past the shops on the

Champs-Élysées, indifferent to the tourists chattering in English and German and Italian, who elbowed each other out of the way in their rush to escape. She had only walked a few blocks when she was caught in a sudden shower on Rue de Bellechasse. Ducking into a small shop for shelter, Nina noticed bottles of expensive looking perfume displayed on glass shelving or bunched together on a table in the center of the store. Each ribbed-glass bottle bore the gold Annick Goutal insignia.

"That is one of our oldest fragrances," said the sales person in heavily accented though perfect English when Nina removed the gold cap from a bottle of Eau D'hadrien.

Nina inhaled the lush citrus scent.

The woman produced a bottle of Eau de Camille. "Do you know the actress Isabelle Adjani? This was her favorite fragrance."

There had been something in the tabloids a couple of years ago about Daniel Day Lewis leaving the actress for someone else before the birth of their son. Nina relayed what she knew to the sales woman, who leaned in and whispered conspiratorially, "He married Rebecca Miller, the playwright Arthur Miller's daughter? Do you know how he told Mademoiselle Adjani?"

Nina shook her head.

"By fax." She delivered the news with an outraged shake of her head. "She used to come in here a lot then, always in dark sunglasses. You could tell she'd been crying. She seemed so lost, so sad. *Très triste*. Such a beautiful, intelligent woman, and she is discarded like day-old bread from the boulangerie." She spritzed some Eau de Camille on Nina's wrist, describing it as a mix of ivy, cut grass and honeysuckle.

Nina told the saleswoman to wrap it up, an act that felt impetuous and faintly liberating.

Marianne Dougherty

"Madame Goutal was a *divorcée* selling beauty products when she was diagnosed with breast cancer." She ran Nina's credit card and asked for her signature. "Then she met a perfumer in Grasse and discovered her true gift. She opened this shop in 1982." She handed Nina a gift bag. "She created this fragrance for her daughter, Camille. Women are remarkably resilient creatures, are we not?"

Nina smiled. "Sometimes we have no choice."

"How long are you in Paris?"

"A few more days. I want to visit Mary Cassatt's house. Years ago, a good friend gave me a book of her paintings," said Nina. "She was the only woman to exhibit her works among the Impressionists."

"Ah," the Frenchwoman said knowingly. "Like Berthe Morisot. She was also a woman in a man's world."

Nina remembered a painting called *Girl with Greyhound* from art school. The model was Morisot's daughter, Julie, which is why Nina had loved it. "Wasn't she Manet's muse?"

"*Oui.* She married his younger brother, Eugene, also a painter. Her work has been undervalued for far too long, but then she was a woman after all."

Nina was reminded of Camille Claudel, Rodin's muse and mistress, a gifted sculptor in her own right, whose work was overlooked in her lifetime. She mentioned this to the sales woman, who nodded solemnly.

"She died penniless in an asylum, a woman who had tried being an artist in a time when women weren't taken seriously as artists," she said. "You have seen the film starring Mademoiselle Adjani?"

"Of course," said Nina, who remembered that the actress had been nominated for an Academy Award for that performance.

"You must visit the *Musée Rodin* while you are here." She leaned across the counter. "Some of her pieces are on display there, but you have to look for them."

That evening Nina had dinner at a bistro near her hotel. Hemingway had lived just steps away from Place Contrescarpe. Nina tried to imagine his wife Hadley buying pastries or *fromage*, perhaps a moist, creamy Camembert at one of the stalls on the southern end of the cobblestoned street.

At the next table a slim young man in a dark suit and white shirt was smoking an unfiltered Gauloises. He loosened his tie and signaled the waiter. "*Une autre bierre,*" he said, pushing an empty bottle of Kronenbourg across the table.

The waiter returned with his beer and asked Nina if she'd like another glass of wine.

"Café," she said, "with cream and sugar."

"American?" asked the young man, tipping his chair back so it teetered precariously on two legs.

Nina smiled.

He ran his fingers through a thatch of dark hair and put out his cigarette. "Nicholas," he said by way of introduction.

"Nina."

The waiter came back with her coffee and cleared the table.

Nicholas brought his chair into an upright position again. "May I?" he asked, though he didn't wait for an answer. Instead, he scooped up his beer and pulled out the chair across from her.

He had remarkably long eyelashes, which Nina found faintly disconcerting. She took a sip of her coffee. How old was he anyway?

"Is this your first time in Paris?"

"First time."

"What have you seen so far?"

"The typical tourist spots: Notre Dame, Sacre-Coeur, the Louvre," she told him, "although I went to *Musée d'Orsay* this afternoon, but there was a bomb threat and we had to leave."

"We have become a target of Islamic terrorists. Last December four people were killed in a bombing at the Port Royal station." He lit another cigarette, which he held between two long, slender fingers. "The explosion ripped apart one whole car at the height of rush hour."

"Aren't you afraid to live here?"

"You get used to it."

He was watching her with a provocative look that made her uncomfortable. "You are very beautiful, Nina," he said. *"Très belle."*

She felt the heat rise in her face. No one had called her beautiful for a very long time. She ran through a list of reasons why she needed to shut this down, whatever this was, as quickly as possible. She was too old for him, she hadn't been with anyone since Paul, he could be a sociopath for all she knew.

She dropped a cube of sugar into her coffee. "It's my birthday," she told him because, well, because it was and the day had been a disappointment so far.

"We must have a toast." He flagged down their waiter. *"Deux coupes de champagne. Veuve Clicquot, s'il vous plait."*

He was staring at her now, his eyes dark and brooding, and Nina looked away, though she seemed to recall that French men revered older women, who embraced their age. She'd seen Parisian women older than her in cafes or walking along Avenue Montaigne in their chic haircuts and understated jewelry and ballet flats, everything carefully curated (a leather jacket, a trench coat) to seem effortless.

The waiter returned with their drinks.

Nicholas touched the rim of his glass to hers. "*Bon anniversaire.*"

In the spirit of reinvention, Nina decided not to tell him anything about her life before they met. What was the point of dredging up her tragic past? Instead, she told him about art school and that she had promised herself a trip to Paris when she graduated. What else did he need to know? When she asked what he did, Nicholas told her that he worked in finance near Place Victor Hugo. She had no idea what working in finance entailed; he could be a teller in a bank for all she knew.

The waiter returned with their checks, and Nicholas snatched them up. "Allow me," he said. "It's your birthday." When he settled the bill, he shoved the crumpled pale blue packet of cigarettes into the inside pocket of his jacket. Leaning across the table, he told her, "I live nearby."

Nina hesitated for a moment, unsure whether to be flattered or insulted. Was he asking her to go home with him? She had never been an impulsive person like Alice, but she was in Paris after all where Edith Piaf famously claimed to regret nothing (*Je ne regrette rien*) and she didn't want to find herself filled with remorse someday about the things she might have done if she'd just had the courage.

Nicholas got to his feet, and Nina did too, surprising them both when she kissed him, all that pent-up yearning unfettered after years of suppression. He hailed a taxi (so, no bank teller, she thought) and held the door for her. "So, maybe I should show you my Paris first."

"*Places des Vosges,*" he told the driver, and Nina settled back against his shoulder as they eased into traffic. He rolled down the window to point out the Pantheon, which had been designed to resemble a Greek temple. "The paintings in the Southern and Northern naves celebrate the Christian heroes of France: Charlemagne, Joan of Arc," he told her. "The physicist Leon Foucault demonstrated the rotation of the earth by constructing the Focault pendulum beneath the central dome."

"I read the book," Nina told him. "Umberto Eco."

"Yes, very famous." He removed his cigarettes from his jacket and offered one to Nina. She had never been much of a smoker, but she had been acting on impulse all evening so she allowed him to light one and pass it over to her. Nicholas watched with amusement as she took a long pull.

"How can you smoke these things?" she said, choking and coughing.

He took the cigarette from her. "You know Serge Gainsbourg?"

"The singer?"

"He chain-smoked five packs of these a day."

"Ten to one he died of lung cancer."

"Heart attack," said Nicholas with a wry smile.

Nina seemed to recall that Gainsbourg had a hit song in the '60s, a scandalous duet with some English singer, or maybe she was an actress.

"*Je t'aime...moi non plus*," said Nicholas when she asked him if he remembered it. "Some people found the lyrics to be offensive, a dialogue between two lovers during sex."

As they neared Place des Vosges, a perfect symmetrical square bordered by thirty-six buildings of red brick with rows of stone wedges and dormer windows set into steep slate roofs, Nicholas asked the driver to slow down. "This is the oldest planned square in Paris. King Henry IV commissioned the construction in 1605, but he was assassinated by a lunatic before it was completed," he told her, and Nina wondered if France's violent history— the assassinations, all those beheadings during the French Revolution, rioters storming the Bastille—had prepared the French to take the recent spate of terrorist attacks in stride.

Tapping on the glass partition, he asked the driver to take them to Place de la Concorde so he could point out the Obelisk of Luxor rising from the center of the public square. "It was brought here in 1836 to mark the place where the guillotine stood during the French Revolution. This is where Louis XVI, Marie Antoinette and forty thousand members of the upper class were executed."

They lingered long enough to reflect upon the grave events that had taken place here on what Nina imagined the French people regarded as hallowed ground in the same way she had been raised to think about Gettysburg and other Civil War battlefields.

Nicholas tapped on the glass again to indicate that the driver should go on. "*Place du Trocadero*," he said, flipping his cigarette out the window and telling Nina, "I have another surprise for you."

He paid the driver and assured Nina that Place du Trocadero was the best vantage point from which to view the Eiffel Tower at night, though he insisted that she keep her eyes closed until he told her to open them.

"How will I know where I'm going?" she asked as they entered the gardens.

"You'll just have to trust me," he said, taking her hand. When they'd gone no more than a few hundred feet, he told her, "Okay, now look," and there was the Eiffel Tower bathed in a warm orange glow against an ultramarine sky. He glanced over to gauge her reaction, but Nina was speechless.

"The look on your face is priceless," he said, and Nina slipped one arm inside his jacket and around his waist, taking in the scent of some citrusy French cologne and the strong, distinctive aroma of his cigarettes. After a while they meandered down the hill to the base of the Tower where they bought crepes topped with Nutella, another first for Nina, and this time when he asked her to go home with him, it felt right.

Nicholas had an apartment on the second floor of a charming building in the 3rd arrondissement. Nina followed him up the stairs and waited while he turned the key in the lock. The door swung open to reveal a large, open space with burnished wood floors and a marble fireplace. Nina took in the plush velvet sofa upholstered in a rich shade of aubergine and the glass coffee table with stacks of books on French architecture and several heavy glass paperweights. A sterling silver cigarette box and a Limoges ashtray were arranged on an enameled tray. Black-and-white photographs in silver frames (a man in uniform, three small children with pails and shovels at the seashore, a bride and groom from some bygone era) were displayed on a drum table covered with tooled leather. Nina went to the window, which overlooked a narrow street lined with Linden trees.

"Would you like something to drink?" Nicholas asked her. "Brandy?"

Nina nodded and took a seat on the sofa.

He went to the kitchen and returned with a bottle of Armagnac and two snifters, poured a little of the amber liquid into each glass and handed one to Nina. She took a sip and let the complex flavor of butterscotch and licorice dissolve on her tongue.

"It's good, *non*?"

Nina sank back against the cushions. "Very good," she agreed.

Nicholas removed a vinyl record from its sleeve and placed it on the turntable. "Juliette Gréco," he said, lowering the needle into the groove. "'*La Javanaise*.' Serge Gainsbourg wrote this song for her."

"Who is she?"

"Very famous *chanteuse*. She started singing in cafes after the war and became friends with the French existentialists." He lit a cigarette. "Sartre said that her voice carried millions of poems that haven't been written yet."

Nina closed her eyes and let the ravaged, world-weary voice wash over her.

Nicholas peeled off his jacket and draped it over the back of a chair before taking a seat next to Nina. "He is telling his lover that life is not worth living without love," he whispered, "and that in dancing the Javanaise they loved each other for the length of the song."

They finished their brandy, and Nicholas put his cigarette out in the porcelain ashtray. He kissed her then, a lock of dark hair falling across his forehead. Nina took her time unbuttoning his shirt, and he covered her mouth with warm, deep kisses, French kisses, she thought, before following him wordlessly across the room and down a narrow hallway, dropping articles of clothing along the way (her blouse and skirt, the lacy underwire bra she'd bought a few days ago at a lingerie shop on St-Germain-des-Prés).

A lamp on a side table next to the bed, which occupied most of the small space, cast a warm glow across the ochre-colored walls and ceiling. They fell onto the duvet, a tangle of limbs, and Nicholas took his time, his hands moving slowly and deliberately across those parts of her body that she had forgotten could bring such pure physical pleasure, pleasure that had been denied to her when she was with Paul and that she had denied herself since Grace's death.

When she woke up, Nicholas was still asleep—his face smooth and unlined, one arm thrown across his forehead to block out the early morning light that seeped through the window blinds. Slipping out of bed, Nina went to the bathroom where she ran a comb through her hair and rinsed her mouth. When she was dressed, she walked through the apartment, pocketing the empty pack of cigarettes he left on the coffee table, flipping through books and magazines stacked on the floor, running a finger along the edge of a table or the back of a chair as if leaving her mark. Something significant had happened to her, and she didn't want to forget any of it.

Years later Nina remembered that night as an awakening, a line of demarcation—the end of one life and the start of another.

On her last day in Paris, Nina boarded a train for Château de Beaufresne at Le Mesnil-Théribus. Nicholas had asked her to spend her last night in Paris with him, and now, infused with an unfamiliar sense of purpose, she visited the country home where Mary Cassatt lived and worked in her final years. Nina believed that Cassatt had been marginalized because of her subject matter, and one of her professors in art school agreed with her. He argued that Cassatt's portraits depicting the social and private lives of women were important precisely because they suggested that women had rich, meaningful inner lives, an unpopular notion in the nineteenth century.

A stream cut across the lower part of the estate. Sunshine poured through the windows at the rear of the chateau where Cassatt had spent the last years of her life in relative darkness, her eyesight failing just as it had for her longtime friend and collaborator, Edgar Degas. Nina couldn't imagine a fate worse than blindness for an artist.

Before she left, Nina followed the footpath from the chateau to the village cemetery where Cassatt was interred in the family tomb along with her mother and father as well as two of her siblings. She'd outlived Degas and most of the Impressionist artists she'd known except for Claude Monet by almost a decade.

There had been rumors, which were never substantiated, that Cassatt and Degas were lovers, though most historians agreed that theirs was an artistic friendship at best. Still, neither of them ever married, though Cassatt's decision was likely to avoid an unwanted pregnancy, which would have curtailed her career. Fortunately, thought Nina, women didn't have to make those kinds of choices anymore.

She boarded the train back to Paris and found a window seat where she watched the French countryside pass by in a blur of rolling hills and trees (spruce and fir and horse chestnut), the occasional steeple rising from a village church, everything appearing to move faster like time lapse photography, and she was overcome by a feeling of deep melancholy as if her life were slipping away.

How much time did she have left? There was no way of knowing, of course, but she knew instinctively that she couldn't afford to waste any more of it. Maybe it wasn't too late to pursue a career as a serious artist. All she knew for certain was that she had to try, and even if she never sold a single painting, what of it? Most of the great artists she admired died in relative obscurity: Toulouse-Lautrec, Cezanne, Van Gogh, Vermeer. What she had to do was push past her fear and paint. Just paint.

Chapter 34

While their divorce had been a *fait accompli*, it took Bill and Alice another year or so to end their marriage. The housing market had taken a dive in 1994 so selling their house took longer than they expected, but when it did, Bill moved into an apartment complex with amenities like a pool and a fitness center. Determined to make a fresh start, Alice moved to Los Angeles.

It had been more than a decade since she and Nina had seen *American Gigolo*, but Alice had never forgotten the opening credits: Richard Gere, decked out in Armani, driving along the Pacific Coast Highway in a black Mercedes convertible with the top down, the wind in his hair, Blondie's "Call Me" blasting from the radio. When they left the movie theater that day, Alice had turned to Nina and asked her what they were doing in a place like this where the weather was unforgiving and people were set in their ways when they could be living on the West Coast surrounded by all that natural beauty and promise.

Now there was nothing holding her back, and Alice found an apartment in Laurel Canyon and a job at a small publishing company in Brentwood. She had missed the whole O.J. media circus presided over by Judge Lance Ito, who became a minor celebrity for those fifteen minutes Andy Warhol used to talk about. Frankly, she was sick of celebrity culture, but there was no escaping it here.

A blonde bombshell named Angelyne had become famous for being famous just by appearing in suggestive poses on billboards all over the city. Alice's take on the whole phenomenon was that the country seemed to be heading toward some seismic societal shift fueled by popular culture that trivialized the intellect and celebrated the fatuous and idiotic.

There was a bar and restaurant on the Sunset Strip called the Rainbow where, rumor had it, John Belushi had eaten his last meal (lentil soup) at table 16. Before it became a hangout for rock musicians like Robert Plant and Keith Moon, the Rainbow had been a restaurant owned by Judy Garland's husband, the film director Vincente Minelli. Joe DiMaggio and Marilyn Monroe met there on a blind date in 1952.

By the time Alice discovered it, the Rainbow was attracting a different kind of crowd, mostly Nikki Sixx lookalikes in Mötley Crüe T-shirts and studded wristbands, who got wasted at one of the bars upstairs. Sometimes, if she had enough to drink, Alice took one of the Mötleys home with her.

She came to think of those vodka-infused one-night stands as a temporary respite from the crippling fear that she'd made a mistake moving to a place where she knew absolutely no one. Every so often she had to remind herself that she had felt the same sense of fear and isolation when she left everyone she knew and loved in Chicago all those years ago.

On weekends if she was feeling restless and uneasy, she'd drive to Zuma Beach and watch the surfers paddle out, wait for the perfect wave (the face vertical, the lip feathering out) and ride it into shore. A boy about Noah's age in board shorts and a rash guard emerged from the surf one day and sat down next to her on the wet sand. When she asked him what it felt like out there, he described it as an addiction (part fear, part joy) but over all a spiritual connection with the universe he never experienced in church.

Alice had seen photos of daredevils at Praia do Norte riding barrel waves, what surfers called the green room, and they'd seemed as small and inconsequential as a grain of sand inside a wall of water two to three times higher than a two-story house, which put things in perspective for her as far as her place in a universe too vast to comprehend.

Gazing out at the water, she imagined the Atlantic Ocean just beyond the horizon. She liked to think that in some version of Einstein's space-time continuum, she and Audrey were walking the boardwalk in Ocean City, stopping for custard at Kohr Brothers or for taffy at Shriver's, which had been in business since the turn of the century. If she could meet her fearless ten-year-old self there, she wondered, would she remember what it felt like to be so confident and self-assured?

There were days when Alice missed her friends, especially Nina. The two of them were members of a club nobody wanted to belong to: mothers who had lost children. Then she met Kiki at a pottery class at Hollywood High School. Kiki was unlike anyone Alice had ever known, a free spirit, who had grown up in the San Fernando Valley and saw The Doors at the Whisky and Elton John at the Troubadour. During the Summer of Love when Alice was in Chicago contemplating the loss of her virginity, Kiki and her sister were among those girls who actually went to San Francisco. Long hair parted in the middle, they walked the Haight in paisley-print tunics and faded bell-bottoms embroidered with roses.

Kiki had lived in an ashram in India, eaten peyote in Mexico after reading Carlos Castaneda, and worked as a receptionist at *Rolling Stone* for a few months in 1970 before eloping with the drummer of a switchblade rock band. He had concealed a nasty heroin habit from her and died of an overdose a year later. She'd been married twice since then, first to a record producer with a cocaine problem—"That didn't work out either, but I did get to meet Axl Rose," she told Alice—and then to a "nice guy who worked in drafting and design."

"He wasn't really my type," said Kiki, "but I'd had such bad luck dating guys who were great in the sack but either cheated on me or did a shitload of drugs, and I thought I should do the sensible thing and marry the kind of guy my mother told me to marry in the first place."

"That's what I did, too," said Alice, remembering how happy her mother had been when she and Bill announced their engagement.

After a few months Alice and Kiki fell into a routine. Every Friday after work they'd meet for dinner at some new restaurant Kiki had discovered. At Café Angeli on Melrose where the tables were covered with butcher paper, they had angel hair pasta with fresh tomatoes, basil, olive oil and fresh mozzarella. Later they'd browse through the magazines at Book Soup on Sunset before walking across the street to listen to new music at Tower Records. Alice felt like she was shedding skins, leaving parts of her life behind and embracing something new and unfamiliar.

They were in the world music section at Tower Records one night where Alice had discovered Cesária Évora, a Cape Verdean vocalist whose sorrowful folk songs resonated with her. Removing her headphones, she asked Kiki if she believed in God.

"You mean Yahweh, the dude from the Old Testament? Well, that's just one of his names." Kiki was flipping through a stack of CDs. "Did you know that in the Jewish tradition the divine name was considered too sacred to be uttered aloud and was replaced by the Hebrew word *Adonai,* which means my Lord, or to paraphrase George Harrison, my sweet Lord."

"How do you know all this stuff?" asked Alice, and Kiki shrugged. "My second husband was Jewish."

It had been nearly ten years since Lily's death, and Alice was still struggling with the notion that she had simply ceased to exist, taking all of her joyful exuberance with her. "I want to believe that there's something bigger than us out there," she said, "but sometimes I worry that there isn't."

"You're having a spiritual crisis," Kiki told her. She held a CD up for Alice's approval: something by a Hawaiian singer named IZ. "Ever hear of him?"

"I don't think so," said Alice, examining the cover.

"He has the most beautiful voice. I like his version of 'Somewhere Over the Rainbow' better than Judy Garland's." She replaced the CD in the rack. "Let's get out of here. I want to take you somewhere that might have the answers you're looking for."

Alice followed Kiki to the Bodhi Tree, a bookstore on Melrose that attracted astrologers, psychics, Buddhists, yogis, and anyone seeking enlightenment. The owners had been aerospace engineers at Douglas Aircraft in Santa

Monica where they worked on weapons of mass destruction before they decided that they'd had enough and walked away to pursue a contemplative life. The shelves were crammed with books by enlightened masters, and Kiki found one on death and the afterlife by a Persian mystic and Sufi named Abu Hamid Al-Ghazali. She handed it to Alice, who found a chair in the corner and sat down to read.

Disappearing into a warren of bookshelves, Kiki returned every now and then with a few more books she insisted Alice had to buy: *You Can Heal Your Life* by Louise Hay, *A Return to Love* by Marianne Williamson and *Think on These Things* by an Indian philosopher named Jiddu Krisnamurti.

"You need to read Krisnamurti if you wonder if there's something beyond the framework of time as we know it," she told Alice. "That's what you want to know, right? That there's something more than just this physical existence, that the soul is indestructible?"

"I want to know if Lily is—" Alice closed her eyes for a moment. "I want to know where she is."

"Krishnamurti had a lot to say about immortality," Kiki said, "and he found the idea that consciousness simply ceases to exist when we die to be false."

"So, he believed in an afterlife?"

"It's complicated," said Kiki. "I know he believed that our need to know what happens to us is born of longing and confusion and that immortality exists only when we free ourselves from that conflict."

Alice let out a long, exasperated breath.

"It's a lot, I know." Kiki located *A Return to Love* in the stack of books on the floor. "Why don't you start with this one for now? It's based on *A Course in Miracles*."

"I'm not sure I believe in miracles," said Alice, remembering how she'd prayed for one when Lily was on life support.

"Miracles are merely a shift in perception," Kiki explained. "What we're asking for is a return to inner peace."

Alice shrugged, but she took the book from Kiki and placed it in her lap with the others.

"The whole idea is to see the world through a filter of love instead of fear," said Kiki, "and that's a choice only you can make."

Chapter 35

That summer Kiki took Alice to visit Krishnamurti's former home in Ojai about ninety miles north of Los Angeles. The writer and speaker had died at his beloved Pine Cottage on February 17, 1986, at ten minutes past midnight, his mind clear until the very last. Visitors were encouraged to explore the grounds or browse his archives and library, which housed all of his books and an extensive selection of talks and interviews in audio and video format.

Kiki had a 1968 candy-apple red Mustang convertible, and they drove with the top down, taking the 101 north to Highway 33, which hugged the coastline, twisting and turning as they drove deep into the Los Padres National Forest. The vegetation was unlike anything Alice had ever seen: large shrubs like toyon, parts of which, Kiki explained, were used medicinally by the Ohlone people; laurel sumac with its scent of green apples; elderberry heavy with bluish-black fruit; and holly-leaf cherry with its spiny toothed leaves.

"There's something magical about Ojai," Kiki told Alice as they descended into the valley. "The Chumash knew about its healing properties, and so did Krishnamurti and his disciples. A lot of people think it's because of the electromagnetic vortexes." Kiki described them as an unseen force that concentrates energy. "Ojai has seven of them."

Alice could see the Topa Mountains in the distance as they took the turn onto a narrow road, which was flanked by orange trees. Krishnamurti had famously walked these hills, mingling with orange pickers working in the East End groves.

"In the 1930s any number of famous people came to hear Krishnamurti speak," said Kiki, slowing down to look for the entrance and rattling off a list of names: Aldous Huxley, Charlie Chaplin, Greta Garbo, Charles Laughton, Jackson Pollack and Ann Morrow Lindbergh. "I wish you could have seen him in person."

"Did you?"

She pulled into the parking lot and cut the engine. "Oh, yes, several times. He was very charismatic, and his English was beautifully elegant. He had the habit of sitting on his hands when he spoke, and he carried a handkerchief, which he'd use to wipe away tears when he became emotional."

"Did that happen often?"

Kiki shrugged. "Often enough, I guess. He had a deep connection to the divine."

They got out of the car, and Kiki motioned for Alice to follow her up a stone pathway surrounded by pepper trees with leaves as fine as Belgian lace. Red and pink peppercorns hung in clusters from the branches.

"Krishnamurti didn't believe in organized religion," said Kiki, crushing a peppercorn between her fingers and inhaling the pungent aroma. "He believed that true religion was free of blind faith and fear."

Alice nodded, remembering how she used to envy Theresa's unwavering faith, her deeply held Catholicism, which offered consolation in the direst of circumstances. Since her first visit to the Bodhi Tree, Alice had chosen a different path, immersing herself in the mysticism of spiritual teachers like Krishnamurti and Ram Dass to find answers to life's existential questions: what's my purpose, does God exist, what happens when we die?

Kiki pointed out a modest white frame house situated among cypress, cedar and eucalyptus trees. "That's Pine Cottage."

Alice tried to imagine what it must have been like to be one of the faithful who gathered here to hear the young Krishnamurti speak in person.

"Did I ever tell you about Meher Baba?" asked Kiki, and Alice shook her head. "I don't think so."

"He was this Indian spiritual master who believed that he was an avatar for Christ come to earth," she explained. "Pete Townsend was a discipline."

"You mean Pete Townsend from The Who?"

"I met him a long time ago when the band played in Los Angeles." She shrugged as if it was no big deal. "He's the one who told me about Meher Baba, who didn't understand why anyone would believe that psychedelics were the key to religious experience. Pete stopped doing acid after he met him."

Alice wasn't sure what that story had to do with anything, but then Kiki often went off on tangents like that and Alice simply went along for the ride.

"My point is that there are no shortcuts to enlightenment."

The late afternoon sun cast long shadows across the lawn, and while Kiki was visiting the library, Alice joined a half dozen people meditating under a pepper tree with pendulous branches. Sitting next to her was a young man whose dark beauty was disarming. His hands were remarkably expressive: index fingers touching thumbs, palms facing down over his knees.

Since meeting Kiki, Alice had not only become a vegetarian but also learned to meditate using a set of prayer beads with 108 sacred malas. Now, closing her eyes, she allowed the teacher's voice to wash over her: *If the mind wanders, just notice it and gently bring it back to the breath.*

Alice wasn't aware of how much time had passed when she felt someone touch her lightly on the shoulder. It was the man who had been sitting next to her, his hair so black that it seemed to absorb the light flickering through the branches of the pepper tree. The rest of the group had dispersed, and Alice felt briefly disoriented.

"You are afraid." It was not a question, just a simple, declarative statement.

Alice looked deeply into his eyes, dark and opaque, and understood that he knew what frightened her was death: her own, certainly, and Lily's (where had she gone?) but also Noah's, which she knew she simply could not bear if she outlived him, too. While such a scenario was unlikely, it was not without precedent. Just recently she'd heard a story about a mother who lost two of her children to a house fire that consumed her single-wide trailer before firemen could rescue them all, and she knew that she could simply not lose anyone else she loved without the absolute certainty that death was not simply a wrecking ball that leveled everything in its path.

Alice remembered that the Greeks believed that at the moment of death the psyche, or spirit of the dead, left the body as a slight exhalation of air, a little puff of wind, though there was some disagreement as to whether or not the soul was immortal. Perhaps to be safe, the Greeks put a coin in the mouth of the dead so they could pay the ferryman who would transport them across the River Styx.

Now, the stranger took her hand, and Alice felt as if her heart, her broken heart, suddenly leapt out of her chest.

"Take out your fear and look at it," he said, gently stroking her palm. "Do not suppress it, but take hold of it. When you are afraid of death, you run away from it. You do everything you can to avoid that thing." His eyes went soft. "You must understand that attempting to escape from fear only creates more conflict and that it is only when you face your fears that you are free."

The man had a kind smile, and Alice held onto his hand, grateful when he did not pull away. They remained under the pepper tree for some time discussing philosophy and consciousness as a concept. After a while, he got to his feet, and Alice had to shade her eyes to see his face, which was backlit in the strong, natural light.

Sensing that he had the answer to her question, Alice asked him, "What happens after we die?"

He took her hand and helped her up. "Would you agree that each of us goes through various forms of hell? Tragedies, misfortunes and the like?"

"I guess so."

"And so, we are one?"

Alice nodded, though she wasn't sure she understood.

He placed a hand gently on her forearm. "If man's consciousness is the consciousness of the world, then we are all part of the vast river which has no beginning, which is still going on."

Krishnamurti had said much the same thing, and Alice wondered if he was quoting the philosopher directly. "So, what you're saying is that we're all part of the same stream?"

"Yes, of all humanity."

Alice sighed deeply.

"Do not be afraid," he told her. "It's really not that complicated."

She glanced away for just a moment, but when she looked up again, he was gone.

Later, on the way home, Alice told Kiki about what happened that afternoon.

"Which tree was it?" Kiki asked.

"The one right by the house."

"That's not just any tree. It's the tree Krishnamurti was sitting under when he had his spiritual awakening. Aldous Huxley called it a mystical apocalypse." Kiki shifted into second gear to negotiate the steep climb out of Ojai. "Wait, what day is it?"

"Sunday."

"No, I mean what's the date?"

"August 16."

Kiki slammed her open palm against the steering wheel. "Wow! This is all starting to make sense now. The anniversary's tomorrow."

"The anniversary of what?"

"His mystical apocalypse, if that's what you want to call it." She stole a quick glance at Alice. "It took three days, but it started on August 17."

"So, you don't think it's a coincidence that we decided to show up here today?"

"There is no such thing as coincidence," said Kiki, "only *hitsuzen*." She explained that it was a Japanese word that loosely translated to mean destiny or fate or inevitability. "I like to think of it as the driving force in the world."

"Kind of like how we met in the first place," said Alice,

reminding Kiki of how she had signed up at the last minute for the same pottery class as Alice. "Maybe that was *hitsuzen*."

"Precisely," said Kiki, who gazed out at the high desert where fir and pine trees dotted the landscape. "He was only twenty-seven when he experienced his enlightenment."

Alice thought about all the rock stars who had died when they were twenty-seven: Janis Joplin, Jimi Hendrix, Jim Morrison, and now Kurt Cobain. "Do you think there's something significant about that number?"

"It's a highly spiritual number that resonates with your soul's higher purpose," said Kiki. "In numerology the number seven relates to mysticism and spiritual aware-ness, and those energies combine to make twenty-seven the number of spiritual insights and unconditional love."

"Tell me more about Krishamurti's enlightenment," said Alice, and Kiki told her that he felt vibrations of the Lord Buddha and saw other spiritual entities and masters of ancient wisdom.

Glancing at Alice, Kiki said, "From what you've told me, I think the man you met under the pepper tree may have been an enlightened master."

Alice thought so too. Trailing her hand out the window, deep in thought, she let the wind rush through her fingers, hoping to hold onto that feeling as Ojai receded into the dis-tance and they merged onto the freeway, clogged with traffic.

Chapter 36

Kiki knew a very famous medium named Susan Bernstein who lived in Sedona, and she wanted Alice to meet her. "I think she can help you contact Lily," she said, as if Lily were a missing person and Susan Bernstein a private investigator.

At first Alice was skeptical. "What kind of name is that for a psychic?"

"I guess Esmeralda was taken," said Kiki, who sounded cross. "She's not a psychic like those charlatans who read our cards in Venice Beach. She's a medium. There's a difference. Believe me, she's the real deal. You'll see when we get there."

"What's so special about Sedona?"

"It's one of the most spiritual places on Earth, like Angkor Wat in Cambodia or the Sanctuary of Apollo in Delphi," said Kiki, who assured Alice that Native Americans considered Sedona a sacred place because of its transformational energy vortexes, which were powerful enough to twist the trunks of juniper trees so the bark spiraled upward.

Kiki made the arrangements. They'd fly from LA to Phoenix, rent a car, stay overnight somewhere and drive to

Sedona the next morning. It was nearly dark by the time they checked into Motel 6, which Kiki promptly nicknamed Motel 666. There was no lobby to speak of, just a man behind what looked like bulletproof glass in a window/drawer/intercom unit. He was arguing with a girl, who appeared to be very drunk and wanted a partial refund since she'd only used the room for an hour.

"Next," he shouted through the intercom, and she staggered off, shouting obscenities.

"Credit card," he said when Alice stepped up to the window.

She dropped her Visa in the tray. It came back with a key to their room where two double beds with shabby polyester spreads flanked a cigarette-scarred nightstand.

"This is not going to touch any part of my body," said Kiki, yanking the bedspread off the mattress and placing a threadbare towel, which she found in the bathroom, across the pillow.

"Are you hungry?" asked Alice, who draped her own bedspread over a chair.

Kiki was lying corpse-like on top of the sheet. "I ate peanuts on the plane. Besides, I'm afraid to go outside in this neighborhood without a firearm of some kind." She reached over and turned off the light. "Let's just get some sleep. We have a two-hour drive in the morning."

They had breakfast at the Waffle House where a sullen waitress appeared with two glasses of water. "What can I get you?"

Kiki kicked Alice's foot and cocked her head toward the waitress, who she recognized from the motel the night before. Alice hid behind her menu, shoulders shaking.

"Real mature," said the waitress, who apparently recognized them, too. "So, I had a lot to drink last night, and the guy I was with couldn't even get it up. You'd have asked for a refund, too."

Alice lowered her menu. "Sorry."

"I'll have an omelet," said Kiki, struggling to regain her composure. "With cheese."

"Me, too, and coffee," said Alice. "Please."

The waitress took their menus and stalked off.

Kiki waggled her eyebrows like Harpo Marx to register total astonishment and disbelief. "First, that motel. Now breakfast at the Awful House. Remind me not to come back here anytime soon."

Earlene (her nametag was clipped to her uniform) was back with their omelets. "Can I get you anything else?" she asked, anchoring their check under a saltshaker.

"No, thank you," said Alice, who felt guilty enough to leave a bigger tip than was absolutely necessary.

Kiki offered to drive, and Alice watched the Arizona landscape open up, remembering her trip across country a few years ago when she fell in love with the red buttes and white sandstone cliffs. She had never been to a medium before and wasn't sure what to expect, but Susan Bernstein was no gypsy in a headscarf. Impeccably dressed in linen slacks with a crisp white shirt, she wore a chunk of turquoise on a silver chain around her neck.

Kiki waited in the living room, which overlooked an expanse of red rock, while Alice followed Susan into her office. The tufted sofa was upholstered in natural linen, and there was a bowl of coral peonies on the glass coffee table.

Susan sat next to Alice. "May I?" she asked, taking Alice's hands and stroking the pads of each finger with her thumb. "You have very unusual energy, both masculine and feminine, and it flows from one hand to the other."

Her voice was soft and mellifluous, slightly hypnotic. "Part of you is very nurturing, but I also sense a very strong, masculine energy that you have not always used to your advantage." She let Alice's hands fall into her lap. Shifting her weight on the sofa, she looked closely at Alice. "You could be a healer if you wanted to, but—" She took Alice's right hand and turned it over in her palm. "I can also see you speaking in front of large groups of people, who have paid a great deal of money to hear you."

Alice withdrew her hand.

"You don't care about any of that, do you?" said Susan, holding Alice's gaze long enough for her to feel uncomfortable. "Tell me why you came here today."

Tears sprung to Alice's eyes, and she brushed them away.

Susan smiled warmly. "Take your time."

It was as if someone had opened a lock in a shipping channel, allowing the river to rise. All of the feelings Alice had been bottling up since Lily's death came rushing to the surface, and she poured out the entire story to this total stranger, who radiated stillness.

When Alice was finished, Susan took both of her hands again. "What do you want to know?"

"I want to know if she still exists somewhere, if she's not just—"

"Gone," said Susan, squeezing Alice's fingers. "I understand." Closing her eyes, she said, "I need to call my spirit guides into the room."

There was a time when Alice would have laughed at such a suggestion, but something was happening here that she couldn't explain. For all Alice knew, the house might have been built right on top of a vortex that was a portal to the afterlife.

After a few moments, Susan opened her eyes. "She told me, 'Tell my mother to stop worrying about how I died.'"

Alice's hand flew to her mouth because that was all she'd thought about since the accident, which had been so violent. Was Lily afraid when she was thrown with such force through the window of Frankie's car? Was she still conscious when the paramedics arrived? Did she suffer?

Susan took Alice firmly by the shoulders. "Your daughter said to tell you that she's alright and that she's with you, always." She gave Alice a minute. "She exists in a state of pure energy now, so when you're thinking about her it's because you're sensing that energy, which is all around you."

What was it the dark-haired man with the soulful eyes had said to her under the pepper tree in Ojai? *We are all part of the vast river, which has no beginning, which is still going on.*

WHEN ALICE GOT back to Los Angeles, she signed up for a workshop at the Bodhi Tree with a professor from USC who taught writing and helped her find her "secret story." As it turned out, that story was universal, which is why *Gardens of Memory* resonated with so many people when it was published.

Alice was working on her second book about the power of female friendship when Noah called to tell her that he was getting married. He and his fiancé, Melissa, worked for the Carnegie Mellon Navigation Laboratory, which built computer-controlled vehicles. Navlab had been building robotic cars, vans and buses since 1984, and Noah insisted that self-driving cars were the way of the future. Alice suspected that he harbored the notion that Lily might still be alive if a computer instead of Frankie had been calling the shots that day.

She still remembered how Noah had reacted to Lily's death, refusing to believe that the mangled body in the ICU even belonged to his sister. Now, after studying the Gnostics, who believed that flesh is nothing more than a leather tunic to be discarded as a suit of old clothes, Alice understood that Noah had been right. Lily's soul was something else entirely.

Alice flew to Pittsburgh a few days before the wedding. Noah made arrangements for them to have dinner at an Italian restaurant he liked in Shadyside. Melissa was nearly as tall as Noah, and her dark hair was cropped short, but it was her smile that won Alice over: warm and friendly and totally without guile. Alice liked her right away.

They were at the bar when Bill and his wife arrived. "I hope you don't mind that I invited them," Noah whispered to Alice, who shook her head. "Of course not."

Judy was the antithesis of Alice in every way (simple and uncomplicated), but that had probably been intentional. Bill's hair was shot through with silver, but he hadn't changed that much.

"I heard about your book," he told her as they followed the hostess to their table. "Congratulations."

"Thanks."

He pulled out a chair for Judy, who fake-punched him in the arm. "You didn't tell me she wrote a book." She glanced over at Alice. "What's it about?"

"Healing after the loss of a loved one or after any life-shattering event for that matter. I lecture now, mostly at conferences or grief support groups," said Alice, remembering that Susan Bernstein had predicted that she'd be paid to address large groups of people one day.

"Mom was on *Oprah*," said Noah with a puckish grin.

"Seriously?" said Judy. "*Oprah*?" She fake-punched her husband again. "Gee, Bill, you didn't tell me that Alice was famous."

"I'm not famous," Alice assured her, "but I am in a much better place than I ever thought I'd be."

When she and Bill exchanged glances, Alice felt her heart expand. Their marriage may not have gone the distance, but they had shared a life, and that was not insignificant. Now they were here to celebrate their son's marriage to someone who was right for him in every way, which seemed remarkable to her.

The Course in Miracles had taught Alice that only love is real: not sin, not guilt, not fear, not anger, not grief, not pain, and in that knowledge, she had found peace.

Chapter 37

━━━━━ ◆ ━━━━━

August, 2016

One by one, Fern found them on Facebook: Alice, Nina and Theresa. Hoping to arrange a reunion on her mother's behalf, she invited them to her summer home in Cape May. The Victorian house was pale yellow and retained much of its original character with porches on both the front and the back and views of the ocean. Black iron railing was mounted on the low stone boundary walls that ringed the property, and symmetrical flowerbeds over-flowed with blue delphinium, purple aster and pale lemon and carmine daylilies.

Fern and her husband Owen worked at a marine research laboratory on the Jersey Shore where they studied coastal and estuarine organisms and the effects of human activity on marine populations. Fern had talked him into buying the house as an investment, convincing him that it would pay for itself if they used it as an Airbnb except for a few months each year. Secretly, she longed to recreate for her own children the experience she'd had that summer when she was a young girl and they'd all come to Cape May:

the clamor of voices at the breakfast table, Grace practicing arpeggios on the old Baldwin piano in the parlor, rainy afternoons playing Hearts with Lily.

Fern met Owen when they were conducting research in ecology and conservation at the Hopkins Marine Station on the Monterey Peninsula while pursuing their PhDs at Stanford, and he had agreed to spend their honeymoon in Cape May. One morning while he was out for a run, Fern had actually gone looking for the old Victorian house that she still remembered in graphic detail: the high ceilings and deep archways, the ornate chandeliers, the library stocked with books, the turrets converted into bedrooms.

Driving through the historic district, she hoped she'd recognize the house if she saw it, and suddenly there it was: a sweet little Queen Anne Victorian with a sharply gabled roof and wraparound veranda. Lace curtains fluttered at the sitting room window as if beckoning her inside where Grace had played Chopin for them on the last night of their vacation, something so melancholy and sorrowful that it had made Fern's adolescent heart ache, though she wasn't exactly sure why.

The ample front porch was unremarkable except for the ceiling, which had been painted an unexpected shade of blue. Nina, who grew up in the South, had explained that in places like Georgia and South Carolina that shade of blue had a very specific name: Haint Blue.

"It's a variation on the word haunt," she told Fern. "The Gullah, who were descended from slaves, believed that ghosts can't traverse water so they painted the ceilings blue, and sometimes the window trim and doors as well, to keep evil spirits away."

Fern was not a superstitious person. She put her faith in science, which sought to understand the physical and natural world through observation and experiment. So, when she and Owen bought their house in Cape May, Fern painted the ceiling a bright shade of vermillion simply because she liked the color.

Now she waited on the porch swing for her mother's friends to arrive. They'd asked about Charlotte, but all she would tell them was that she'd explain everything when they got here.

Chapter 38

Theresa had moved to Philadelphia so she offered to pick Alice and Nina up at the airport. Nina's connecting flight through Denver from Santa Fe where she lived now was early, while Alice's direct flight from Los Angeles was delayed so Theresa circled the airport, texting Nina every ten minutes asking for an update.

Frequent visits to the Georgia O'Keeffe Museum had inspired Nina to paint landscapes. It seemed like a natural transition once she felt that she had nothing more to say on the subject that had compelled her to paint in the first place. Over the years her prints of mothers and children had sold well, while her newer work was being shown in galleries in New York and San Francisco.

Alice's book had not been an easy read for Nina, who felt a stab of recognition when Alice described grief as something you learn to live with, like a constant ringing in your ears or chronic back pain. There'd been an epigraph attributed to the Mad Hatter: *In the gardens of memory, in the palace of dreams, that is where you and I shall meet.*

She and Alice had exchanged Christmas and birthday

cards for a few years after Nina went to Tucson with the girls, but then Alice had simply disappeared, leaving Nina to wonder if she didn't want to be found. Now, here she was after all this time, striding confidently in Nina's direction in jeans cuffed at the ankles and a black leather jacket over a *Hillary for President* T-shirt.

Nina waved, rows of silver bracelets jangling on her sinewy arms, and Alice broke into a broad smile. Wriggling out of her backpack, she pulled Nina into a warm embrace. "You haven't changed one bit."

"Liar," said Nina, inhaling the scent of lilac, or perhaps violet. "You're the one who looks exactly the same."

"Hair dye. That's the secret to looking younger. Nora Ephron thought so anyway."

"I threw in the towel years ago," said Nina, whose own hair, which she wore in a low ponytail, was the color of a Liberty silver dollar.

"It doesn't matter. I'm just so glad to see you." Alice held Nina at arm's length, her expression solemn and reflective. "I never thought I'd see you again."

Nina nodded. "I know."

"Do you know any more than I do about why we're here?" asked Alice, dragging her suitcase off the baggage carousel.

"Not really."

"I hope it's nothing serious." Alice had lost two friends, including Kiki, to ovarian cancer in the last few years.

"I have to text Theresa," said Nina, tapping out a message: *the eagle has landed.*

"Fern told me she has her own catering business now," said Alice, fishing through her backpack and reapplying her lipstick, which was a dramatic shade of crimson. "Apparently she's making a ton of money."

Nina slipped her phone back into her pocket. "I guess it makes sense. She was such a good cook, remember?"

They wheeled their suitcases outside where the heat felt oppressive. Alice removed her jacket. "I forgot how hot it gets here."

A red Range Rover screeched to a stop, and Theresa jumped out. "Oh, my God," she shrieked.

A police officer approached the car. "You can't park here," he said, but Theresa, who outweighed him by at least thirty-five pounds, brushed him off and threw herself at Alice and Nina, pulling both of them into a bear hug.

"Ma'am, if you don't move your car right now, I'll have it towed."

"Okay, okay." Theresa popped the trunk. "I'm going." She took Alice's bag. "Rent-a-cop," she said, lowering her voice.

"Actually, he might be a Federal employee, but it's your funeral." Alice climbed into the backseat. "Nina, you sit up front."

Theresa eased the car into traffic. "I guess you two have noticed that I've put on a lot of weight since the last time you saw me." She turned off the radio: Sirius XM *'60s on 6.* "I almost canceled because I didn't want you to see me looking like this, but Tina said that real friends wouldn't judge me for how I look, and you two are the best friends I ever had."

Nina glanced at Theresa with a reassuring smile.

"I always said that you were too hard on yourself," said Alice. "I remember the first time we met at Cookie's house and you were beating yourself up because you couldn't lose ten measly pounds."

Theresa barked out a laugh. "Frank's the one who told me I was fat."

"And you believed him," said Alice. "That's the problem."

"I wish I was as thin as I was when I thought I was fat," said Theresa, putting on her turn signal and crossing two lanes of traffic.

"Speaking of Frank, is he still with that gold-digger?" asked Alice.

"God, no. She divorced him when he went to jail."

Alice gripped Theresa's headrest with both hands. "Wait, what?"

"Oh, right, you don't know about that. It turns out that Frank's uncle was some low-level mobster and Frank was using Carpet Warehouse to launder money for him. The Feds found out and Frank spent ten years in Lewisburg."

Nina looked over her shoulder at Alice, who seemed as shocked as she was.

Theresa slowed down to allow a Honda Civic to switch lanes. "He lived with me for the first few months after he got out of prison, but I'm not sure what he's doing now."

"Wait a minute," said Alice. "You took Frank in after all he put you through?"

Theresa glanced at Alice in the rearview mirror. "He was my husband and the father of my children. It's water over the dam now. Besides, you should have seen him, Alice. He looked like an old man."

Theresa had driven to Lewisburg when Frank was released, and she had been horrified when she saw him: his skin sallow and pitted, all that thick dark hair leached of color.

Alice decided to change the subject. "So, Fern told me you have a catering business. What's it called?"

"Mangia Bene."

"Translation?"

"He who eats well lives well," she said. "I started small, but things really took off. I've got a whole staff of people who work for me now. That's how I was able to expand. Tina's the one who convinced me to move to Philly. She and her husband have a house here." She consulted the navigation device on her dashboard. "We should be there in about an hour and a half."

"I can't believe you're still using one of those," said Alice. "Don't you have Google Maps on your phone?"

"I like my Garmin. Frankie programmed it to talk to me in an Italian accent. You can't do that with Siri."

Alice wanted to ask how Frankie was doing, but she wasn't sure she was ready to find out. That was one of the advantages of running away from home. She didn't have to watch Frankie grow up and do all of the things Lily would never get to do: marry, have children.

Theresa glanced at Alice in the rearview mirror again. "I saw you on *Oprah*. So, what's she like?"

"She changed my life," said Alice as Theresa merged into traffic on the Walt Whitman Bridge.

They stopped for coffee on the Garden State Parkway where Theresa peppered her conversation with Italian words and phrases: *Prego* when a woman thanked her for holding the door at Starbucks, *Ciao* when greeting the barista at said Starbucks.

"I thought Fern said she had a beach house," said Alice when Theresa pulled up in front of a sprawling Victorian with a concave mansard roof. "This is not at all what I expected."

She and Nina exchanged looks, and Alice knew that they were thinking the same thing.

"Talk about *déjà vu*," said Nina with a wistful expression.

Fern ran down the stairs, and Alice was struck by how much she looked like her mother. It had been years since Alice had seen Charlotte's daughter, who was a grown woman now with children of her own: Jacob, who was six-teen and thus a very late millennial, and Emma, who was, at twelve, part of Generation Z. Alice had lost track of who was who after Generation X, the latchkey kids presumed to be disaffected and directionless, all that existential ennui stemming from broken homes and too much daycare.

Theresa yanked her suitcase out of the trunk. "Where's your mother?" she asked Fern.

"Sleeping."

"So, wake her up. We've got to get this party started."

"We need to talk first."

It looked like Theresa had brought enough food to last a week, and Fern offered to help her get everything into the house.

"Is Charlotte alright?" asked Theresa with a worried expression. "It's not cancer, is it?

Fern shook her head.

"Thank God."

They followed Fern up the steps to the front porch where baskets of mildly fragrant Hosta with waxy, heart-shaped leaves were suspended from hooks under the eaves. Now Theresa had a new theory. "Don't tell me that your father left her after all these years."

"Why don't we all sit down?" Fern gestured to a white wicker loveseat and a couple of chairs with overstuffed cush-ions. "I hope you all drink wine. Owen, that's my husband, and I went to Napa this spring, and we brought a case of it back with us."

"I could use a drink," said Alice, who also wished that Fern would get to the point. The suspense was killing her.

"Name your poison," said Fern, who seemed relieved to be off the hook for a moment. "Chardonnay, pinot noir, sauvignon blanc, zinfandel."

"Chardonnay," said Alice.

"Me, too," said Nina.

"Do you have anything stronger?" asked Theresa, and Alice wondered why she hadn't thought of that.

"I think we have vodka or maybe it's gin. I'll go look." Fern took the groceries with her and disappeared into the house.

"I should have told her just to bring the bottle," said Theresa with a nervous laugh. "Something tells me this is going to be a long night."

"None of us is getting any younger," said Alice. "Maybe Charlotte just wanted to get the whole gang back together one more time."

"Well, if that's the case, I'm glad she did," said Nina, fingering the turquoise squash blossom necklace at her throat. "It's been too long. Why didn't we do this years ago?"

Fern returned with their wine and a gin and tonic for Theresa. "I'll be right back. I picked up a few things at Trader Joe's, nothing fancy." She gave Theresa a rueful look. "I don't cook."

"Me either," said Alice, taking a sip of her chardonnay, which was rich and buttery.

Fern was back with a walnut cutting board on which she had artfully arranged her bounty from Trader Joe's: cheddar, Havarti and gouda cheese from the looks of it, thin slices of pepperoni and prosciutto, plump green grapes, roasted almonds and dark purple Kalamata olives. Nina took a wedge of gouda just to be polite and Theresa helped herself to a few olives, but it was clear that everyone was too keyed up to eat.

"So, I guess you all want to know why you're here," said Fern, setting the tray on a side table.

It seemed to Alice that they were holding their collective breath when Fern glanced at each of them and sighed deeply. "Mom has Alzheimer's."

They all began speaking at once, and Fern fielded their questions one at a time, explaining that Charlotte had some mild cognitive impairment. "You might notice that she'll ask the same question more than once or seem more anxious than usual. She gets confused easily, especially when she's tired." Sensing their apprehension, Fern assured them that Charlotte was still in the early stages. "It was actually her idea to find you. She just needed my help to do it."

Alice wondered how Kip was handling all this. Presumably he and Charlotte were still together or Fern would have said as much. "How's your father taking it?"

Fern drew a deep breath. "He died five years ago."

Theresa gasped. "What?"

"Colon cancer."

"I'm so sorry, Fern," said Nina. "I always liked your father."

Alice closed her eyes and imagined Kip, shit-faced on gin, flirting with someone dressed like Eleanor Rigby at Theresa's pool party, while Charlotte watched from an Adirondack chair, her heart on her sleeve. How was it possible that all that youthful bravado had simply ceased to exist?

Theresa was close to tears. "This is too much for me. First Charlotte and now Kip."

"I'll talk to her," said Fern, following Theresa into the house.

"Alzheimer's," said Alice, who was struggling with her emotions, which ping-ponged between complete incredulity and profound sadness. "That's a death sentence."

"I guess they have drugs now that can slow down the progression of the disease," said Nina, "but there's no cure."

"At least if you have cancer, there's something you can try: chemo, radiation, some clinical trial." Alice took a sip of wine and placed her glass on a side table, thinking of Kiki again, who had faced cancer like Joan of Arc battling English forces to break the siege of Orleans.

Nina stabbed a chunk of cheddar cheese with a toothpick. "How's Noah?"

Alice took an olive and chewed gently around the pit. "He got married about ten years ago. They haven't started a family yet, but they're both forty now and the clock may run out on them if they don't hurry." She placed the stone in the palm of her cupped hand and took another olive. "I think they're married to their jobs. Besides, they have a dog, a Maltese named Lucky. I'll probably end up like one of those people who put magnetic stickers on their cars that say *I Heart My Granddog*." She waved one hand dismissively. "Who am I kidding? That ship has sailed. Last year I bought Lucky a sweater for Christmas."

"Harper was married to a nice guy who worked for Microsoft, but they had fertility issues and the stress got to be too much. You know how it goes." Nina's expression was one of acquiescence. "Hayley's had a lot of boyfriends, but I don't think she'll ever get married. Let's just say that she doesn't suffer fools, unlike her mother." She gave Alice a sidelong glance. "I took a lot of shit from Paul, didn't I?"

"You're not that person anymore," said Alice, helping herself to a handful of almonds. "Where are they living these days?"

"Harper was in Seattle, but she's in New York City now. Hayley's been living there since she graduated from college."

"What do they do?"

"Hayley works for a human rights campaign that combats transgender violence, and Harper works for an organization advocating for gun reform."

"They sound amazing."

"So, are you seeing anyone?" asked Nina.

"Not really," said Alice, who had met a man at one of her readings. His daughter had died of neuroblastoma, and while their chemistry had been off the charts, he was just too broken to sustain a meaningful relationship. Since then, there had been no one else. Noah was always posting pictures on Facebook of Bill and Judy, who, by the looks of things, spent all their time exploring ports of call on one Carnival cruise ship or another. While it wasn't the life Alice would have imagined for herself, she felt a twinge of jealousy that Bill ended up with a plus-one while she ended up alone.

There had been a time when Alice had allowed herself to imagine what would have happened if she and Colin Maguire had run off together all those years ago. Then, when Lily was about twelve or thirteen, she agreed to meet Theresa for happy hour at the Best Western, and there he was, surrounded by speakers and turntables.

"I never thought I'd see you again," he said when she approached him.

"You look exactly the same."

"So do you."

"Still married?" she asked him. Somehow it seemed important to know how his story had ended.

"No."

"What happened?"

"She ran off with our priest."

"The marriage counselor?"

"He left the priesthood for her. Took my wife and kids and moved to Albany."

"I'm really sorry."

"Yeah, well, that's life." He gave her a wry smile and began sorting through a stack of albums.

"I can see you're busy," said Alice, who felt as if some spell had been broken. "I just wanted to say hello."

"Alice?" he said as she turned to go.

"What?"

"Are you still with Bill?"

"It's complicated," she said, sensing that it was a mistake to open up this particular can of worms again after all these years.

"Do you ever wonder what would have happened if—"

"I used to," she told him, "but I don't anymore." That was not strictly the truth, but what was the point of rehashing the past now?

He sighed deeply. "I think about it all the time."

A woman holding a cocktail glass filled with something pink and creamy interrupted them. "Can you play something by Queen?"

"What do you want to hear?" said Colin, and Alice slipped away.

Theresa was at the bar. "Who was that?" she asked, moving the paper umbrella aside to take a sip of her drink.

Alice shrugged. "Just someone I used to know."

When Colin announced that he was slowing things down with an oldie from Bill Withers, couples moved onto the dance floor.

"This one's for all of you who know what it feels like to lose the love of your life," he said in his rich baritone, a voice made for radio. He didn't have to say anything else.

Nina had been watching Alice, who seemed lost in thought. "I read your book," she said, and Alice seemed surprised. "Theresa's not the only one who saw you on *Oprah*."

"So, what did you think?" asked Alice, who had felt Nina's presence as she reworked each draft.

"Every word rang true for me. All the people who have no idea what it's like to lose a child but tell you that they know exactly how you feel because their dog just died." Nina frowned. "Or their ninety-year-old mother." She drew her knees toward her chest. "I'm sorry, that sounded awful."

"It's okay," said Alice, "but I know what you mean. You have no idea how many people told me that Lily's death was God's will. Not helpful."

"I wanted to scream every time someone told me that Grace was in a better place. Grace was at Curtis. *That* was her better place."

"I've missed you," said Alice, wishing that she had not let so much time pass without contacting the women who knew her better than anyone: the memory keepers. "I should have stayed in touch. I'm sorry I didn't call you when I moved to California."

"Well, we're here now," said Nina. "That's something."

———— ◦ ————

BEFORE THEY WENT to bed, Alice and Nina looked in on Theresa. Fern had put her in the guest room on the first floor where she leaned back against a stack of pillows like a sultana.

"Feeling better?" asked Nina.

"A little." Theresa pushed aside a pile of magazines and patted the comforter.

Nina sat on the edge of the bed. "So, what's it like being a grandmother? Fern said Tina has four kids."

"Three boys and a girl, Olivia. She's the youngest," said Theresa. "They keep me busy. Beck just turned twelve. He's into soccer. Obsessed with it. Axel's fourteen, and he's into girls. Thinks he's a real lady's man. Spitting image of his father at that age. Kurt, with a K, not a C, just graduated from high school." Frowning, she added, "His arms are covered in tattoos. I don't even know what half of them mean, but it breaks my heart. I still remember when Tina brought him home from the hospital and we just couldn't get over how perfect he was. Why would he want to disfigure himself like that? Well, anyway, Tina tells me that tattoos are a rite of passage for teenagers now, like piercing our ears was for us, and that I should be glad he doesn't have gauges."

"Gauges?" said Nina.

"You know, those holes the size of quarters that kids put in their earlobes," Theresa told her. "Half the cashiers at Whole Foods have them."

"Oh, those."

"She named him after that singer who killed himself, the one from Seattle."

"Kurt Cobain," said Nina, whose daughters had wept the day Kurt Loder announced his suicide on MTV the way Walter Cronkite had announced Kennedy's assassination on CBS.

"What's her husband like?" said Alice, who recalled that Tina had been a troubled teenager.

"Hank?" said Theresa. "Salt of the earth, that kid. He works for his dad, who owns an autobody shop in South Philly. Tina was into this band called The Black Crowes, and she drove all the way to Philly to see them. That's how they met."

"How long ago was that?" asked Alice.

"They did the long-distance thing for a couple of years and finally tied the knot in 1996. They waited to have kids for a few years, but both of them wanted a big family." Theresa sighed deeply. "I think Tina's trying to create the nuclear family she missed out on."

"And Frankie?" It had taken Alice all day to work up the courage to ask about him.

Theresa cast a sidelong glance at Alice. "He married a nice girl he met in grief support. After all those years of blaming himself for Lily's death, he finally agreed to go to therapy."

Alice leaned against the chest of drawers. "It wasn't his fault. I thought he knew that."

"He did, on some level, but he still blamed himself. Then he found this support group where they talked about blameless guilt." Frankie had explained it to her as feeling guilty for something for which you are not legitimately responsible. "That's how he met his wife. When she was in high school, a little boy ran out between two parked cars, and she couldn't stop in time."

"How awful," said Nina with a troubled expression.

"She was exonerated, but she still couldn't forgive herself for what happened," Theresa said. "After things got serious between them, she told Frankie that she had decided not to have children and that he should find someone else if he wanted a family." Theresa glanced briefly at Alice. "She didn't think she deserved to have a child of her own because she'd taken someone else's child away from them."

Alice thought about what it would take to make that kind of sacrifice. "Has she changed her mind?"

Theresa hesitated. "They have a little girl now. She's twelve."

Alice braced herself. "Do you have a picture?"

Theresa scrolled through her iPhone until she found a recent photo. She was sweet: dark hair like Frankie's, a mischievous smile.

Alice handed the phone back to Theresa. "What's her name?"

Theresa's shoulders slumped, but there was something in Alice's expression that suggested that she already knew the answer and was just waiting for Theresa to say it out loud.

"Lily." The word hung there like a rosary from a rearview mirror. "They named her Lily."

Chapter 39

When her friends arrived in Cape May that evening, Charlotte was not asleep but sitting in an upstairs window in her cotton nightgown listening to the conversation drift up from the front porch. It had not been a good day for Charlotte, who'd had difficulty making herself understood, losing her train of thought and becoming frustrated when Fern asked what she wanted to wear that morning. The sheer number of choices had seemed overwhelming, and she only felt her anxiety subside when Fern laid out a pair of shorts and a cotton T-shirt the way she had laid Fern's clothes out for her when she was a child.

Charlotte didn't want her friends to see her that way and asked her daughter to tell them that she'd gone to bed early and would be down first thing in the morning. She'd only gone to the window when she heard the slam of a car door, the commotion as suitcases were dragged up the stairs to the front porch, and then Alice's unmistakable throaty laugh, which triggered an impulse to rush downstairs to make sure it was really her.

Sometimes Charlotte felt like she was disintegrating, the pounding surf carrying bits and pieces of her away now that the sea wall was no longer able to resist the storm surge. There were days when she became so listless that she couldn't get out of bed and others when she was lucid enough to know that her conscious tomorrows were numbered. It was during one of those moments that Charlotte began thinking about the women who knew her when she was young and full of life, and it seemed important that she see them again before her memory was erased like equations from the chalkboard in her organic chemistry class.

Memory, Charlotte believed, defined us, but what happened when those memories ceased to exist? Did we simply cease to exist as well? Often when she was lying in bed at night, what Proust called remembrances of things past surfaced like bubbles in ginger ale before dissipating just as quickly: her parents playing pinochle with another couple at the kitchen table on Saturday night, games of hopscotch or Red Rover with the army of other children in the neighborhood, watching her older brother Alex change the oil in his Ford F1 pickup.

Determined not to be a pipefitter like his father or work in the mines like his grandfathers, Alex joined the Air Force right out of high school, met his wife Ingrid when he was stationed in Germany and never lived in Hazleton again. Meanwhile, Charlotte had stayed put, as immobile as a piece of coral, as fixed in place as an insect trapped in amber.

Lately she had been thinking a lot about her maternal grandmother, Ava, who had lived with them in the red brick house on N. Church Street where they shared a room. Their single beds were separated by a side table with a small lamp that cast a soft glow on the Westclox alarm clock and a framed photo of Charlotte's grandfather, dead at sixty-eight from black lung. Each night before they went to sleep, Ava told her granddaughter a fable she remembered from her own childhood in Ukraine, morality tales symbolizing the people's struggle against adversity: *The Straw Ox, The Tsar of the Forest.*

Ava was an excellent seamstress, and she made all of Charlotte's clothes: hand-smocked cotton dresses and blouses with jewel necklines, working the cast-iron treadle on her Singer 201 as she fed a bodice or a sleeve across the throat plate. When Charlotte was ten, Ava taught her how to crochet antimacassars from cotton thread, which they draped over the back and arms of her mother's sectional davenport. Every Sunday she baked enough bread to last all week, and she taught Charlotte how to press and knead the dough to form a ball, which they placed into a bowl and covered with a tea towel. After the dough had doubled in size, Charlotte was permitted to roll it out and shape it into a loaf. Later, sitting cross-legged in front of the stove, she switched on the oven light to watch the crust turn a golden shade of brown, and when the loaves were cool enough, her grandmother gave Charlotte the first slice, which was good enough to eat without embellishment.

Ava was in the hospital being treated for pneumonia when, on Charlotte's twelfth birthday, she drew her last breath. At the time, Charlotte's mother was serving cake and ice cream in the backyard to five of Charlotte's childhood friends, and Ava died alone, which had always troubled Charlotte. For years she wondered if it was a sign that her grandmother died on the exact same day that she was born. Did it mean that they were bound throughout eternity, their souls inexorably entwined? For months after Ava's death,

Charlotte felt her grandmother's presence in the room they had shared for so many years. The lamp might flicker for just a second or the radiator splutter or spit, and Charlotte would lie perfectly still, allowing the feeling, as ephemeral as an ice sculpture, to wash over her and quickly disappear.

While she and her mother never talked about Ava's failing health, Charlotte understood that her grandmother had exhibited all the classic signs of dementia in those last few years: confusion, apathy and depression, changes in behavior or personality. A tiny woman who had always been fastidious about her appearance, drawing her long hair into a bun which she fastened with pins at the nape of her neck each morning, she let her hair go wild, a diadem of coarse ashen strands that grew untamed like lichen.

Charlotte remembered one afternoon in particular (she must have been about ten) when she walked into her bedroom to find her grandmother emptying the chest of drawers, tossing one item of lingerie after another—satin briefs with elastic waistbands, rayon slips with adjustable straps and cone-shaped brassieres—out the window, each piece drifting at a languid pace into the backyard where Charlotte's mother was hanging wash.

After that there were no more fairy tales before she fell asleep, though admittedly Charlotte was too old for such stories and preferred books in the *Five Little Peppers* series about five children who are born into poverty but rescued by a wealthy gentleman who takes an interest in their family. Secretly Charlotte wished that someone like Mr. J. Horatio King, Senior, their benefactor, would take interest in her family.

Two years ago when Charlotte was diagnosed, she had become obsessed with the notion of time and began reading everything she could on the subject while she was still able to concentrate: Stephen Hawking's *A Brief History of Time* and Neil DeGrasse Tyson's *Death by Black Hole*, which explained that gravity was so great and the mass so extreme in a black hole that time slowed down to the point that you would observe the entire history of the universe unfolding right before your eyes if you fell into one, but, of course, if you fell into a black hole you could never come back and tell anyone what you saw. Still, Charlotte wished for nothing more than to be able to slow down the passage of time and halt the inevitable progression of her disease.

Now that her own mortality was not just an abstract concept but a very real possibility, Charlotte found herself thinking a lot about life and death. The Buddhist concept of reincarnation made more sense to her than the catechism of her Catholic girlhood (all that talk of souls languishing in Purgatory like drivers stuck in rush-hour traffic). Physicists theorized that as you fell toward the center of a black hole where the mass is concentrated, your body would be stretched like a noodle and pulled apart before disintegrating into its fundamental particles, which would pass through the other side and join the primordial soup of a new beginning. She hadn't been to mass since Kip's funeral, but she wanted very much to believe that there was something greater than us at play in the cosmos, even if it was just a field of energy that produced the particles whose masses and charges were precise enough to allow human life in the first place.

Charlotte's parents were gone now: her father of congestive heart failure, her mother of complications from diabetes, and Alex too, riddled with cancer, most likely caused by exposure to Agent Orange. In 1965 when he was sent to Da Nang, a coastal city in central Vietnam known for its sandy beaches and clear blue waters, he and the men under his command loaded the defoliant onto C-123 aircraft and played golf in their free time, oblivious to the threat the herbicide posed to their health. In letters home to their parents, Alex had described his stint in Da Nang as a country club existence.

Her grandmother had been gone for nearly sixty years now, and while Charlotte thought of her less frequently than she used to, on the occasions that she baked bread from Ava's recipe and the aroma filled the kitchen, she felt her grandmother's presence as surely as she had in those first few months after she died. Charlotte had never passed down any of the domestic skills she learned from her grandmother to her own granddaughter, and now she wondered if perhaps there was still time.

Owen would be arriving with the children in a couple of days. Maybe after her friends went home, Charlotte would ask Fern to take her to the market. Then, when Emma got here, she'd teach her how to dissolve yeast into warm water, how to add flour and a pinch of salt and let the dough rise, scoop it out of the bowl and knead it with the heels of her hands for a good long while before turning the dough and folding it over, making a fist and punching it down. When the bread came out of the oven, she'd offer Emma the first slice, though Emma might insist upon butter and possibly a little honey or homemade jam. Still, Emma would remember that day long after Charlotte was gone, which was, she reasoned, its own kind of immortality.

THAT NIGHT CHARLOTTE dreamed that she was a little girl again. At ten, after reading *Black Beauty* and *My Friend Flicka*, she had beome obsessed with the idea of owning a horse. Since her father had neither the money nor the inclination to buy her one, she pretended to be a horse. Tossing her mane of long blonde hair from side to side, she galloped around her shabby neighborhood, cantering through narrow front yards of patchy grass, trotting past wood frame houses crowded together like a mouthful of crooked teeth.

That was the summer she learned to ride a two-wheeler, threading baseball cards through the spokes so they'd clickety-clack as she pedaled to the five-and-dime to buy penny candy or paper dolls. She liked the accessories they came with: those little handbags or fur stoles you had to be very careful cutting out. Brides and grooms were her favorite, and she made starter homes for them out of shoeboxes decorated with pictures of appliances or sectional sofas from the Sears Catalog.

Wearing her skate key on a ribbon around her neck, Charlotte whizzed past the cars parked on Locust Street, picking up speed as she hurtled downhill, but when she told her mother that she'd outrun the fastest boy in the neighborhood, she looked concerned.

"Don't beat the boys, dear," she said, her iron moving effortlessly along the length of her father's Van Heusen shirt. "They won't like you."

Charlotte had never forgotten that, and by the time she was in high school she began making adjustments in her behavior around anyone with a Y chromosome. If she got an A on a math or biology test, which she often did, she kept that information to herself, and she was careful not to raise her hand too often in class.

Her boyfriend Kip was the star quarterback at Hazleton High School. Wearing his class ring on a chain around her neck, Charlotte cheered him on at home games. By their junior year she let him go to second base, snaking his hand under her mohair sweater while they French kissed in the balcony at the Empire Theater. Kip hadn't pressured her to "go all the way" yet, but Charlotte knew she couldn't put him off indefinitely and agreed to consummate their relationship after prom.

Kip had saved enough money to rent a room at a motel in White Haven, which was far enough away from Hazleton that they were unlikely to be seen by anyone their parents knew, and after dinner they slipped out of the gymnasium, which was decorated to resemble an island in the South Seas. Kip helped Charlotte into his car, a powder-blue 1954 Chevy Bel Air. Her pink satin prom gown billowed out around her narrow waist, and when Kip yanked open the door on the driver's side and slid into the front seat, Charlotte's heart swelled with pride. Kip was what her girlfriends called a catch: handsome, popular and athletic, and he had a good sense of humor. Charlotte kept his photograph on her nightstand: blue eyes beneath heavy, dark brows and a smile that made her blush, imagining his full lips, soft and warm, planting kisses on her own upturned mouth.

Charlotte waited in the car while Kip checked in.

"You go in first," he said, handing her the plastic key fob. "I'll park in the back."

She removed her wrist corsage of roses and pink carnations and placed it on the maple dresser. When he returned, Charlotte was sitting on the edge of the bed. Towering over her, Kip lifted her chin. Kissing her softly, he reached around to slowly unzip her dress, allowing the straps to fall over her shoulders. Charlotte loosened his bow tie, and he

Marianne Dougherty

went through the pockets of his white jacket looking for the pack of Trojans he'd brought at her insistence. Kip was in a hurry, but Charlotte wanted him to take his time. She'd been waiting for this moment her whole life, and she wanted it to last. When he finally entered her, his St. Christopher medal swinging from a gold chain, his chest damp with perspiration, Charlotte gave a little cry of pleasure. Surely life didn't get much better than this.

In their senior year, Kip was offered a football scholarship to Lehigh University and they talked about getting married as soon as he graduated. Charlotte had no idea what she was going to do after high school other than marry Kip and raise the children they hoped to have right away. He wanted a house full of boys, future wide receivers or quarterbacks like him.

Both of Charlotte's grandfathers had mined anthracite coal in the Susquehanna Valley when they arrived in Pennsylvania from Ukraine, and she'd grown up hearing stories about men being killed when the mines became flooded. Her father had only a marginally better job as a pipefitter, and Charlotte had never been encouraged to apply to college, but she was smart and she was good at science so she started giving it a lot of thought.

"Girls in our family don't go to college," her father explained when she broached the subject after dinner one evening. "It's a waste of money. You'll marry that boyfriend of yours and raise a family."

Despite the fact that Charlotte had envisioned just such a future for herself once she married Kip, she bristled when her father refused to entertain the notion that there might be something more she could do with her life.

"My chemistry teacher says I'm the best student he has," she told him.

"What about nursing school?" said her mother, who was clearing the table. "Your Aunt Helen is an RN."

"All she does is empty bedpans," said Charlotte, ignoring a disapproving look from her father (Helen was his sister). "I could get a really good job with a degree in chemistry."

Her mother lowered a stack of plates into a basin of soapy water. "Like what?"

"Analytical chemists can specialize in toxicology or pharmaceuticals or even forensics."

"Don't encourage her, Rose," her father said. "She's not going to college."

"If I went into medical research, I could help develop new drugs," said Charlotte as if she hadn't heard him. "Maybe find a cure for cancer."

"That's no job for a girl," said her father, scowling.

"Why not?"

He looked up from his newspaper. "Why don't you be a secretary like your cousin Donna?"

"Or a science teacher," suggested her mother.

"I don't want to be a secretary or a science teacher," said Charlotte, who was losing her patience.

Her mother removed her apron and draped it over the back of a chair. "You'd have summers off. It's a good job for a woman."

"I don't know why we're even talking about this." Her father folded his newspaper in half. "You'll just get knocked up like all the other women in this family."

Her mother smacked him with a dishtowel. "Viktor, that's a terrible thing to say."

Eventually her father capitulated, but even with scholarships and student loans, there was no way Charlotte could afford to go to a prestigious school like Temple or the

University of Pittsburgh. So, as a concession to her mother, she applied to a small Catholic college in the Allegheny Mountains that offered a bachelor's degree in education.

Her parents dropped her off and stayed long enough to help her get settled before turning around to make the three-hour drive back home. When she unpacked that afternoon, Charlotte found an envelope in her suitcase. Inside was a five-dollar bill and a note in her mother's cramped handwriting: "Buy yourself something nice, *moy dorogoy.*" The endearment meant *dearest one* and brought tears to Charlotte's eyes.

She had dinner in the cafeteria that evening with her roommate, a girl from Pittsburgh named Rosie, who wore a pleated skirt and knee socks with Bass Weejun loafers. She had affixed a circle pin to the Peter Pan collar of her white cotton shirt and seemed fascinated by Charlotte, who didn't own a single item of clothing that she hadn't made for herself.

"Who taught you to sew?" asked Rosie, who wore an enormous topaz ring on one hand and a signet ring with her initials on the other.

"My grandmother," Charlotte explained.

After that Rosie seemed to lose interest and began spending all of her free time with other theater majors like her, who planned to try out for the school play, *The Fantasticks.* That fall, unless he was at an away game, Charlotte took the bus to visit Kip at Lehigh, and during the off-season he came to see her nearly every weekend. By their senior year when they were both student teaching, those visits had become less frequent.

Charlotte had been assigned to teach chemistry at a high school in Ebensburg near Johnstown where the students in her class were only a few years younger than her. For the first few weeks she was nearly paralyzed with fear, her voice barely rising above a whisper when she tried to restore order in the classroom, and she was frequently heckled by some of the rowdier boys. One of them chose to completely disregard her safety instructions about working with Bunsen burners and actually laughed out loud when she told him that a cacodyl explosion had left Robert Bunsen blind in his right eye.

Her supervisor had been observing her quietly from a seat in the last row, but one afternoon he took her aside. "I know how much you love chemistry, but it's your job to inspire the same enthusiasm in your students without frightening them," he told her. "Do you think you can do that?"

Charlotte smiled weakly. She'd already decided that she'd never be a good teacher, but she couldn't tell him that she'd imagined a career in forensics or toxicology instead. No, she'd painted herself into a corner by listening to her mother, and now she was forced to fake-smile her way through an entire semester trying to interest a class of bored or disruptive teenagers in chemistry, a subject that had fascinated her since grade school when she and her mother stayed up late one Saturday night to watch *Madame Curie* with Greer Garson.

Then one morning in late October, a transfer student named Byron Mazur walked into her classroom and slipped into an empty seat. Byron loved chemistry as much as Charlotte did. She didn't have to tell him that it struck the perfect balance between the conceptual sciences like physics and math and the more observable sciences like biology and geology or that the more you knew about chemistry, the more you understood the world around you. He just knew.

One afternoon while Charlotte was in the library working on lesson plans for the following week, Byron asked if he could join her. After that he'd poke his head in the door after her last class and help her wash the blackboard or tidy up while they talked. Byron made her realize how little she and Kip had in common, and after a while their conversations felt like a betrayal.

"My grandfather's a chemist," Byron told her one afternoon. "He came here after World War II. When I was six, he taught me how to combine peroxide and potassium iodide so it would shoot out a column of foam. He called it elephant toothpaste." Byron laughed, remembering. "He's the one who encouraged me to major in chemistry after I graduate."

"So, what do you want to do with your degree?"

"I'm leaning toward medical research, you know, discovering new medicines or vaccines."

"I wanted to be an analytical chemist."

"But now you want to be a teacher instead?"

"Not really. My mother thinks that teaching is a more appropriate job for a girl."

"Didn't she ever hear of Madame Curie?"

Charlotte glanced away, remembering how Pierre Curie had talked his future wife out of returning to Poland to teach instead of dedicating herself to a life of science. Maybe what she needed was a man like Pierre Curie, or Byron Mazur, instead of a mother with old-fashioned ideas about what women could or could not do with their lives.

"What's wrong?" asked Byron, who was straddling one of the chairs in Charlotte's classroom.

"Nothing," she said, stuffing some papers into her tote bag.

Byron got to his feet when the janitor came in to empty the trash, and Charlotte wondered if he was trying to create the illusion that nothing inappropriate was going on. *Was something going on?* She hoped she hadn't given Byron the wrong impression by letting him spend so much time with her outside of the classroom because that had not been her intention.

"Hello, Miss Koval," said the custodian, dumping the contents of the wastebasket into a garbage bag on his cleaning cart. He nodded briefly at Byron on his way out, and Charlotte felt uneasy.

Lately she had allowed herself to imagine a different life, one with a partner whose intellectual curiosity was equal to hers. The irony was that she had dumbed herself down so boys like Kip would like her, and now that she'd met someone who liked her precisely because of how smart she was there was nothing she could do about it.

Ultimately, none of it mattered. When Charlotte found herself in the family way just as her father had predicted, she and Kip were married on a bitterly cold day in February. Charlotte wore a brocade dress and jacket, a penny in her shoe for good luck. Kip wore a dark suit and tie. After the wedding, they spent the night at the Holiday Inn, and Charlotte drove back to school the next morning so she could finish her senior year.

After graduation that June, Kip accepted a job as a history teacher and assistant football coach at a public school near Scranton and Charlotte set up housekeeping. Fern was born in September, and when she began telling everyone that she wanted to be a marine biologist when she grew up, Charlotte took her seriously.

Chapter 40

———◆·◆———

When Charlotte came downstairs the next morning, Fern told her that everyone was on the front porch. Theresa was examining a basket of nasturtiums trailing vivid orange flowers. "Did you know that these are edible?" she said to no one in particular.

"Does that mean I'm going to find them in my salad tonight?" asked Nina from the porch swing.

Theresa touched one of the soft, waxy leaves. "Maybe." She startled when she saw Charlotte in the doorway. "You're awake."

Alice was on the porch steps lacing her pink Chuck Taylors and only now looked up. Charlotte glanced at each of them. "I can't believe you're all here."

Nina crossed the porch and placed one hand on each of Charlotte's shoulders before pulling her into a tight embrace. "Charlotte," she said as if she couldn't believe it either.

"You hungry?" asked Theresa since food was her default setting.

"Not really."

"Not even homemade brioche with jam?" said Theresa in the same tone of voice she had used to coax her children, who were always picky eaters, into trying snow peas or Brussels sprouts.

"No thanks," said Charlotte, who was watching Alice.

Hundreds of migrating songbirds darkened the sky overhead, flying north toward the Cape May Ferry Terminal where they'd find safe places to feed and rest before continuing their journey. Now Alice pushed herself up from the front steps. It had been decades since she had seen Charlotte, who seemed fragile and apprehensive. Her face was deeply lined, and all that long blonde hair had lost its luster, a field lying fallow.

Alice held back, unsure what to do, but after taking a tentative step in Charlotte's direction, the distance between them dissolved like a sugar cube in warm tea.

"Alice," said Charlotte, her tone freighted with regret and longing. "I've missed you." She wrapped her arms around Alice so tightly that when she finally let go Alice felt out of breath.

On the sidewalk a young mother admonished two small children, who were leaving a breadcrumb trail of plastic rakes, sand sifters and shovels behind them. She stooped to retrieve each item, wearily stuffing them into her straw tote.

"That was us forty years ago," said Charlotte, and they all nodded as if remembering their younger selves, too preoccupied to realize how fast it would all go by.

"I'm so sorry about Kip," said Nina, and Charlotte's shoulders slumped as if she had been relieved of a great weight she'd been carrying for a very long time.

"I still can't believe it, and it's been five years." Charlotte glanced at each of them. "I was with him at the end." She cast about for the right words to describe what it had felt like to be there when Kip took his last breath. "To be with someone you love in the end feels—"

"Profound," said Alice, remembering how she'd held Lily's hand when she died. "It changes you."

"Yes," said Charlotte. "It does."

After an awkward silence, Alice asked Charlotte about her grandchildren, which seemed like a safe enough subject.

Charlotte smiled slightly, but her eyes had a faraway look. Then, as if her thoughts were fast-moving storm clouds, she seemed focused and attentive again. "I see a lot of them now that I live with Fern, who didn't want me rattling around in that big house all by myself."

Theresa was deadheading a few faded flowers from a basket of impatiens. "So, none of us live there anymore," she said with a rueful expression. "When we moved to Canterbury Commons, I thought Frank and I would grow old and die there." She pinched another stem and removed the spent flower. "Nothing turned out like we imagined, did it?"

Charlotte walked tentatively to the edge of the porch and looked across the front yard. Hummingbirds raced between lyre leaf sage that bloomed pale blue in meadows and along roadsides in late spring and summer. It was so peaceful here that she wondered if she should let sleeping dogs lie, but she also knew that this might be the last chance she'd have to unburden herself.

"Are you okay?" said Alice, who sensed that Charlotte may have had another reason for inviting them here that had nothing to do with her failing memory.

Charlotte shrugged, though the gesture was almost imperceptible, just a slight lift of her shoulders beneath her flimsy T-shirt. Where to start, she wondered, and then it came to her: start at the beginning.

Later they would all remember that it was a beautiful morning, clouds like meringue scudding across a sky so blue you had to shield your eyes against the glare. Alice had suggested that they go to the beach to talk since Charlotte seemed worried that Fern might overhear their conversation. When they found a relatively secluded spot, Nina unfurled a worn patchwork quilt she found in a basket on the front porch, and it fluttered in the breeze blowing in off the ocean. Charlotte waited until they were all settled before turning a key in a lock on a room that she had not allowed herself to enter for nearly fifty years.

"I did something a long time ago that I've never told anyone about," she said, "but I don't want to die with it on my conscience."

———————

CHARLOTTE HAD NOT thought about Byron Mazur in years. Decades actually. She'd shoved that part of her life down so deep inside that there were times when she could convince herself that she'd imagined everything. Lately though, it felt like the most deeply encoded memories in her subconscious were swimming to the surface, and Byron Mazur was one of them.

Neither of them had meant for it to happen. At least that's what they told themselves at the time, though later Charlotte could see that it was inevitable, that they had ignored the subtext beneath all those seemingly innocent after-school conversations.

She had taught her last class that afternoon and was packing to go home for the long Thanksgiving weekend. Snow had not been predicted, but fat, heavy flakes were falling steadily, drifting over the hoods of cars parked on narrow streets and descending upon boxwood hedges and rhododendrons, whose broad leaves, doleful and dispirited, curled in upon themselves.

She decided to risk the short drive to The Village Inn where she parked in the lot around back.

"We're closing early," said the cashier, who was balancing the register.

Charlotte removed her scarf, which was wet with snow. "Can I just get a small pizza to go?"

The girl frowned.

Byron, who had been taking the trash out, came in through the back door.

"Hey," he said when he saw Charlotte.

"She wants a small pizza to go," said the girl, pushing the cash drawer shut. "You want to make it?"

"Sure," he said. "You can go. I'll close up."

The girl shook a few bills and some change from the tip jar onto the counter and pocketed half of it. "Thanks. I owe you."

When she left, Byron locked the door behind her. Charlotte ate slices of pepperoni pizza shiny with oil at a table near the window while Byron mopped the floor.

"I'll walk you out," he said when she was finished.

Her Chevy was the only car in the parking lot, and Byron used the palm of his hand to clear a circle of glass large enough for her to see through.

Charlotte slipped behind the wheel and rolled down the window. "So, where did you park?"

He shoved his hands deep into the pockets of his coat. "I took a bus."

"Well, it doesn't look like they're running. Come on, I'll give you a lift."

Byron walked around to the passenger side and got in. Cold air poured from the heat vents, and Charlotte let the engine idle for a few moments. The wipers slapped against the windshield, clearing snow away from one side, then the other. On the radio, Creedence Clearwater Revival: "Bad Moon Rising." She turned the volume down and considered her options, but when Byron leaned across the seat and kissed her roughly on the mouth, Charlotte knew there was no turning back. Carried away by some primal instinct (his) and an unresolved need for validation (hers), neither of them was thinking about what would happen if someone found out. Charlotte simply killed the wipers and let the snow pile up, sealing them safely inside the Biscayne where Byron's fingers moved over her body in the dim light as if reading Braille.

⸻ ⬦ ⸻

AFTER CHARLOTTE'S CONFESSION they all turned to Theresa, who had long held the role of moral arbiter, but Theresa's expression was unreadable behind her dark sunglasses.

"Okay, so it was unethical, but you were practically the same age," said Nina after an uncomfortable silence. "It's not the worst thing you could have done."

Charlotte drew her knees toward her chest. "I haven't told you everything."

Alice glanced apprehensively at the others. "What else is there?"

Charlotte let out a long breath, one it seemed like she'd been holding for a very long time, and the words tumbled out. "I got pregnant."

"Oh, my God," said Theresa with a sudden intake of breath. "You had an abortion."

"No."

Nina leaned forward, her voice barely a whisper. "You gave the baby up for adoption?"

"No."

Alice was the first to guess the truth. "Fern isn't Kip's daughter, is she?"

"No."

"And you never told him."

Charlotte shook her head. "I couldn't." Tears pooled in the corners of her eyes, and she blinked once or twice to keep them there. "I made a big mistake, but I didn't want it to ruin our lives."

"Maybe he would have understood," said Alice, but Charlotte shook her head.

"It would have killed him." She knew her husband. He would never have forgiven that kind of betrayal. "What I did was stupid, but it turned out alright in the end, didn't it? Kip loved Fern, and she loved him. He was a good father."

Alice shrugged. It was a twisted kind of logic, but there was no disputing the fact that Kip had adored Fern.

"Why tell us now?" Nina asked, and Alice realized that she had been thinking the same thing. "You're not thinking of telling Fern, are you?"

"Doesn't she deserve to know?" asked Charlotte, and Theresa removed her sunglasses in exasperation. "Why? It might relieve your guilty conscience, but it would kill Fern."

"I have to agree with Theresa," said Nina. "Fern would just feel betrayed, and that's not what you want, is it? After all, she's lost the only father she ever knew, and you don't even know if this Byron is still alive, or where he is for that matter."

"What if she decides to take one of those DNA tests?" said Charlotte, who had given this possibility a lot of thought recently. "Could she find out that Kip wasn't her real father?"

"Kip *was* her real father," said Theresa testily.

Charlotte flinched. "You know what I mean."

"I don't think that's how those kits work," said Alice. "They're not like a paternity test."

Charlotte took a deep, ragged breath. "That's been keeping me up at night, mostly because I don't want her to find out the truth when—" She brought her hands up to cover her face. "When I can't remember anything anymore." She glanced at each of them through splayed fingers. "Or when I'm dead. Either way, she'd have so many questions, and I wouldn't be here to answer them."

"We'll be here," said Alice, "and we'll answer them for her if it comes to that."

"Can I ask you something," said Nina, and Charlotte nodded. "Did you and Kip ever try to have more children?"

"Of course, we did, and I know what you're thinking."

"That Kip was shooting blanks," said Theresa, "and you wouldn't have had children at all if it wasn't for—" Her voice trailed off.

Nina squeezed Charlotte's hand. "Maybe that's your silver lining."

Seagulls wheeled overhead, their distant squeals and caws rising and falling on currents of salty air. Charlotte watched them swoop and soar, flashing white against a cloudless sky. She hadn't been a practicing Catholic for years, but lately she had been thinking a lot about the notion of sin and the need for absolution.

She lowered her voice until it was almost a whisper. "Do you think God will forgive me?"

"Oh, Charlotte," said Nina, her voice filled with sorrow and compassion.

Alice placed one arm protectively around one of

Charlotte's narrow shoulders. "Maybe the real question is, can you forgive yourself?"

In the cloistered silence that settled upon them, creating a sacred space, they gazed out across the vast and mysterious ocean: keeper of secrets, of unexplained sounds, cursed shipwrecks and mythical creatures, lost empires and ancient ruins.

Finally, Alice got to her feet, brushing the sand from her pants and extending her hand toward Charlotte. "You've shared your secret with us," she said. "Now let us keep it for you."

———— ◆ ————

THAT NIGHT AFTER Charlotte was asleep, Alice wandered into the living room where Fern was dozing on the sofa. The regulator clock on the mantle kept time in one-second intervals with each swing of the pendulum: 86,400 a day, more than thirty-one million a year, time that could never be recovered. There was no going back, thought Alice, no changing course, no redo for any of them. She drew the afghan of colorful granny squares over Fern's shoulders and turned off the lamp.

She found Nina and Theresa on the front porch. Nina was wearing yoga pants and a T-shirt that said *ZEN AS F**K*.

"Nice shirt," said Alice. "Scoot over."

"Oh, this," said Nina, making room on the porch swing. "Max gave it to me."

"Max?" said Theresa. "You didn't tell us about him."

"Nothing to tell. I met him at an arts and crafts festival in Santa Fe. He bought one of my landscapes."

Max was a retired crisis counselor who'd helped Vietnam veterans cope with trauma. A voracious reader, he had introduced Nina to Dave Eggers, Cormac McCarthy and the Australian author Evie Wyld, whose debut novel resonated with him on a number of levels. Like the protagonist, Max had not only lost his wife but also served in Vietnam, and when Nina told him about Ethan, he had been a sympathetic listener.

"So, are you two a thing?" asked Alice, who sensed that Nina was holding out on them.

"He's good company." Nina was hesitant to say any more for fear of jinxing what had become a companionable relationship—no fireworks, but no drama either, which suited her just fine.

"Have you met anyone, Alice," asked Theresa.

Alice shook her head. "What about you?"

"Not really," she said before reconsidering. "Okay, there's this man who was an advertising executive for one of the big agencies in Philly. I catered a couple of parties for him, and believe me when I tell you that he likes to eat as much as I do. At least we have that in common. He insists that he likes a woman with a little meat on her bones, so maybe my weight isn't an issue for him."

Alice remembered an expression her mother had used years ago: *There's a lid for every pot.* Maybe Theresa had found her lid at long last. "Has he asked you out yet?"

"He wants me to go to an Eagles game with him next month. He has season tickets."

"Do you even like football?" asked Nina.

Theresa lifted her shoulders in a gesture of resignation. "I'll pretend."

They kept company in silence for a few moments before Theresa finally asked, "So, can we all talk about what happened today?"

Alice closed the front door. "Keep your voice down. The last thing we need is for Fern to overhear us."

"It's hard to believe that Charlotte kept something like that to herself all these years," Nina said. "It must have eaten her up."

"Still waters run deep I guess," said Alice, remembering that her mother had used the same expression to describe Charlotte when they met for the first time all those years ago. Even so, Alice was as surprised as the rest of them that Charlotte of all people had a secret life none of them knew about.

In the leafy trees out front, katydids were making a racket that Alice associated with summers growing up in the Midwest. Like the melodic ding-a-ling of the Bermuda bells mounted on the vintage bicycles for rent in town, the sound transported her to a time and place she would give anything to visit again. Closing her eyes, she imagined her mother in a cotton housedress watching her father trim the boxwood hedge in the front yard. How young they were then: faces unlined, all that thick, dark hair. It seemed like a distant memory now, a place as inaccessible to her as Neptune or Jupiter.

Nina went inside for a bottle of chardonnay and returned with two glasses. "Has Fern said anything else about Charlotte's prognosis?" She poured herself a glass of wine and offered one to Alice. "That sounds so clinical, but I guess that's what it is."

Theresa removed a slice of lime from the lip of her martini glass and placed it in her napkin. "I was up early this morning so I asked Fern a few questions before she went out for a run."

"What did she say?" asked Alice.

"She has good days and bad days. Fern said that last week she became obsessed with finding her high school year book because she couldn't remember the name of the school she went to." Theresa shook her head. "If you ask me, this is worse than cancer. It's like a disappearing act."

"Do we know how long she has?" asked Alice.

"Fern thinks about six to eight years, more or less. I don't think anyone knows for sure."

"So, what's going to happen to her?"

"Most likely a stroke or a heart attack will kill her," said Theresa, and Nina recoiled. "Sorry, that was harsh, but it's the reality of her situation."

Alice pushed herself off the swing and walked the length of the porch to look over the railing where moonflower bloomed iridescent white in the gathering darkness. By sunrise their trumpet-shaped flowers would close in upon themselves, yet somehow the life cycle would begin anew that evening. Alice had always believed that nature held the secret to life's mysteries, and she hoped the night-blooming plant offered the promise of life anew for Grace and Lily and now Charlotte, who was slipping away.

"Let's talk about something else," she said. "Did I ever tell you about the time that Charlotte and I walked into the men's locker room by accident after a game of racquetball?"

"I think we would remember a story like that," said Nina.

Charlotte had talked Alice into playing racquetball despite her insistence that she didn't have an athletic bone in her body. In junior high she had failed to pass the Presidential Physical Fitness Test because she couldn't shimmy up a rope or execute the squat-and-kick move common in Ukrainian folk dancing.

"She said it burned more calories and was a lot more fun than doing jumping jacks at Elaine Powers," said Alice, and Theresa groaned.

"Oh, God, don't mention that place," she said with a grimace.

"She'd taken a few lessons and told me that all I had to do was smash the ball against the front wall as hard as I could," said Alice, remembering the squeal of rubber on the polished hardwood floor when she lunged to return Charlotte's serve. She had felt like an athlete for the first time in her life that day. "So, anyway, they put us on one court and then moved us to another one so we got all turned around. I guess that's why we walked into the wrong locker room after our game." Alice dissolved into laughter just thinking about it. "Some guy, naked as a jaybird with this huge mustache, was blow-drying his hair in front of a mirror. We stood there like we were mired in quicksand for what felt like an eternity but was probably just a few seconds, and then we ran. I don't think there was an actual door, just the word MEN painted on the side of the wall, which we hadn't even noticed when we made our grand entrance."

Alice glanced at Theresa. "Don't take this the wrong way, but I told Charlotte that if you'd been in the locker room with us and saw that guy's dick at half-mast, you would have fainted."

Theresa pulled a face. "I'm not the same person anymore."

"Really?" said Nina.

"For one thing, I'm Episcopalian now," Theresa said. "Did you know that they let women become priests? Gay people, too."

Alice drained her glass. "You're just full of surprises, aren't you?"

Chapter 41

———— ◦ ————

Theresa knew her friends thought she was a prude, and maybe she had been, but there were also a few things they didn't know about her. They might be surprised to learn that she and Tina had been at the Women's March for Reproductive Freedom in Washington, D.C. in 1989. The truth was, Theresa had evolved.

Sometimes she wondered how her friends had put up with her, so holier than thou, so convinced that she knew everything about everything when it came to morality. Now when she remembered her old self, Theresa was shocked by how narrow-minded she had been. There was a time when she affixed pre-printed PRAY TO END ABORTION labels to every piece of mail that left her house: utility bills, credit card payments, the birthday cards she sent to all her nieces and nephews.

"Maybe you should worry about nuclear war or AIDS instead," Frankie told her when he found the phone bill, stamped and ready to mail, on the hall table, the offensive (his words) message in 14-point type on the back.

By the time she and Tina boarded a chartered bus with

a hundred other people bound for the nation's capital that Sunday, Theresa was already questioning her long-held beliefs about a woman's right to choose. The church had taken an increasingly virulent pro-life stance that made her uneasy because it left no room for nuance.

"It doesn't matter if you believe in abortion or not," said Tina. "A woman's right to choose is an inalienable right just like freedom of religion or freedom of expression, and this march is important because the Supreme Court is going to hear a case that could be used to overturn *Roe v. Wade*. Molly Yard has already told President Bush that for women there's no turning back."

"Who's Molly Yard?" asked Theresa.

"You're hopeless," Tina said with an audible sigh. "She's president of NOW." She waited a beat before adding, "National Organization of Women?"

"I know what NOW is," said Theresa. "I wasn't born yesterday."

"Sometimes you act like you were," said Tina, who seemed to think that the right to choose was a matter of life or death. Whose life and whose death were still up for debate, but Theresa decided to keep an open mind. Frankly, she was impressed that her daughter could speak so articulately and with such passion about an issue that seemed important to her.

Theresa brought a lunch of fried chicken, zesty cabbage slaw and potato salad in an insulated tote, which she placed in the overhead bin before taking a seat next to her daughter. To fulfill her obligation, Theresa had gone to mass on Saturday, though she'd slipped out a side door to avoid running into Father Phil. She'd already lied to him (was that a venial sin?) when he asked why she wasn't on the list of people who would be driving to D.C. on Sunday to stage pro-life protests at the Capitol.

Before they crossed over into Maryland, Theresa suggested that she and Tina eat something. When she stood up to retrieve their lunch from the overhead bin, she saw Fernando and his boyfriend Marco, who was dozing against his shoulder, in the last row. Theresa had not been back to the salon since her makeover, partly because looking like Gina Lollobrigida required too much upkeep, but she didn't want to be rude so she gave him a little wave.

In the parking lot Fernando rushed over to say hello. "I didn't know you were coming." He waved Marco over. "Look who I found."

"Long time, no see," said Marco, lighting a cigarette.

"So, how have you been, doll? Are you seeing anyone?" asked Fernando. "Alice told me your ex married that bimbo he was cheating on you with." He fingered a gold stud in his right ear. "Remember that night we all went to the gym and put that bumper sticker on his car?"

Theresa smiled. "My last hurrah."

She had no idea what two gay men were doing at a women's march in Washington, so she asked them why they'd come. Fernando placed one hand on her shoulder. "We figure that if we march for you, maybe you'll march for us someday."

Swept up by the crowd moving down Constitution Avenue, they passed women brandishing wire hangers, chanting, "Keep abortion safe and legal." Some were wearing white, purple and gold, the colors of the women's suffrage movement.

Marco and Fernando veered off when they ran into a group of gay activists: men in leather harnesses, lesbians in graphic tees and Lambda pins. A reporter was interviewing a drag queen dressed as Barbara Bush.

"Maybe we'll catch up with you with you later," said Marco, who stopped to watch.

On the grassy lawn on the west side of the Capitol, a handful of pro-lifers had created what they described as the "Cemetery of the Innocents" with 4,400 white crosses and Stars of David designed to represent the number of abortions performed daily just in the United States. Nearly prostrate, a woman prayed there, and Theresa felt a stab of recognition, but when a jogger ran past, raising her fist and shouting, "Pro-choice," Theresa felt a tug, the undertow tearing her away from shore. Which side was she on, she wondered.

When they got to the Capitol, Tina dragged her mother by the hand and pushed her way closer to the stage where a lesbian activist named Robin Tyler was at the podium.

"There are several groups out there who are anti-choice. One of them call themselves right-to-lifers, and you'd better agree with the right-to-lifers or they'll kill you," she said, raising her voice to be heard. "Another is a group calling themselves Operation Rescue. They're the ones that are blocking the abortion clinics, and their leader is Randall Terry. Randall Terry is a born again." She took a beat before delivering the punch line. "We don't mind Randall Terry being born again, but why the hell did he have to come back as himself?"

The crowd laughed, and Theresa laughed with them because she had to admit that it was funny even though the joke hit a little too close to home.

"The anti-choice people believe that life begins at conception and ends at birth," said Tyler, letting that remark sink in for a few moments. "If they truly cared about babies, they would fight to end nuclear war. Where were their voices last week during the Exxon Oil Spill? Do they not care about the ecology of this planet so their children will have something to live for? If these so-called right-to-lifers are so concerned about life, where were they when the Reagan administration refused to release millions of dollars, which had been allocated to those who are curing AIDS?"

Theresa remembered that Frankie had made the same argument a few months ago.

"Were they out on the streets when thousands and thousands of gays were dying of AIDS?" asked Tyler. "No. Because these same people say that homosexuality is a disease. Well, if homosexuality is a disease, we should all call in sick to work. Sorry, can't come in, still queer." She paused until the laughter died down before delivering the *coup de grace*. "And, of course, Dan Quayle, our Vice President, agrees with these people, but Dan Quayle used to think that *Roe v. Wade* was a debate over how to cross the Potomac."

Theresa glanced around. There were women older than her here, their silver hair bobbed short; middle-aged women in perms and car coats; young women, like Tina, their faces hopeful and determined. Theresa sensed that something significant was taking place and that she was part of it. When Patricia Schroeder was introduced, Theresa asked her daughter if she knew who she was.

"No clue," said Tina, and a woman in front of them turned around to answer Theresa's question. "The first female ever elected to the House in Colorado."

"Why didn't I know that?" Theresa wondered, feeling a bit like Rip Van Winkle waking up to discover that he'd missed the American Revolution.

"This is 1989. We are finally ending the '80s, thank goodness," Schroeder shouted. "You know what happened in the '80s? Ronald Reagan got elected, and he said, put down your picket signs, put on those cute little dress-for-success suits, and not to worry, I'm for little e, little r." She looked out at the crowd, adding, "Yeah, sure" to murmurs of approval. "A lot of people put down their picket signs and put on their little suits and lost their rights."

Theresa had never worn a dress-for-success suit. She had never held a fulltime job. Instead, she had handed all of her power over to Frank. It was a startling realization. Theresa heard a lot of speeches that day, but one of them stayed with her. Wearing a white suit and white hat with a sprig of flowers tucked into the broad brim, Bella Abzug approached the podium, flags flapping in the breeze behind her on the Capitol steps. In a booming Bronx accent, she asserted that a woman's right to choose was as equal a liberty as the "right to think, the right to believe, the right to speak, and the right to pray, without the free exercise of which no woman can be deemed to be fully free and equal."

For Theresa, that moment was a turning point that set her on a path that diverged so completely from the one she had imagined for herself as a young girl that even now she found it hard to believe.

Chapter 42

O n Sunday, their last day together, Theresa made brunch. She put Alice to work frothing cappuccinos in Fern's Nespresso and asked Nina to set the table.

"I wish you lived here," said Fern when she saw the spread Theresa had prepared: scrambled eggs, cranberry scones with homemade jam, fried potatoes, breakfast sausage and fruit compote.

Theresa placed a stoneware plate piled high with pancakes on the Lazy Susan. "Dig in," she said before rushing back to the kitchen and returning with a plate of Fakin' Bacon for Alice.

After dousing her pancakes with maple syrup, Nina passed the bottle to Charlotte, who seemed confused.

"Do I know her?" Charlotte asked Fern, who whispered, "That's Nina. You remember."

Charlotte struck her forehead with the palm of her hand. "Stupid, stupid. I know that," she said, and Nina and Alice exchanged troubled looks.

"She didn't sleep well last night," Fern explained, patting Charlotte's hand. "She might need a nap later."

Charlotte, angry now, pulled away. "I'm not a baby. I don't need a nap."

"Well, I might need one," said Theresa brightly, and they all sensed a slight shift in the fizz of nervous energy zinging around the table.

After breakfast, they went outside to the front porch where Theresa propped her feet in their bright yellow Crocs on the coffee table.

"What?" she asked when Alice gave her the side-eye.

"Nothing," said Alice, who thought Crocs were a fashion blunder on par with shower sandals and tube socks.

"They're my work shoes," said Theresa defensively.

"I didn't say anything."

"You didn't have to." Now Theresa seemed miffed, and Alice apologized.

"Love means never having to say you're sorry," said Nina with a sardonic grin.

"That's the stupidest thing I ever heard," said Theresa, and they all agreed.

"We grew up with a lot of ridiculous ideas about love," said Alice, "and we got most of them from movies."

"My generation had *Say Anything*," Fern reminded them. "Do you know how many girls my age wanted a boyfriend like Lloyd Dobler who would stand in their front yard holding a boom box over his head with Peter Gabriel blasting from the speakers?"

"That's the trouble with movies like that," said Theresa. "They fill our heads with all this romantic nonsense."

"I loved paper dolls, especially brides and grooms," said Charlotte, who seemed pensive.

It was a completely random observation, but Fern was always glad to have her mother back. "What was your favorite set of paper dolls?" she asked just to keep Charlotte talking.

"Heavenly Blue Wedding," said Charlotte with a broad smile. "Everyone in the wedding party was dressed in blue except for the bride, who wore a strapless white gown with a blue sash at the waist."

"Didn't Tina have bride and groom Cabbage Patch dolls," said Fern, glancing at Theresa for confirmation. "I remember that one of them was wearing a white tux."

"They were supposed to be twins," said Theresa. "Brother and sister, not bride and groom."

Fern pushed back her chair and began clearing the table. "Why don't I go inside and give you some time alone?"

"No, wait," said Theresa. "I have something to say." Glancing at Fern, she told her, "I owe you an apology."

"For what?"

"For something I did a long time ago." Theresa drew a deep breath and let it out slowly. "I wasn't very supportive when you made a decision that must have been extremely difficult for you."

Alice and Nina exchanged puzzled looks.

"I want you to know that I'm not that person anymore," she said with a catch in her throat, "and I am so sorry for what I put you through when you and Frankie—" Fern crossed the room before Theresa could finish her thought.

She gave Theresa a hug. "Thank you for telling me that. It means a lot to me."

Theresa glanced briefly at Charlotte, who gave her a slight nod. She hadn't thought about any of this for years and struggled to regain her composure. "I never told any of you, but I went to a woman's march for reproductive freedom with Tina in 1989, and it changed the way I looked at things."

"I was there, too," said Fern, who seemed surprised that her former adversary had become something of an ally. "My college roommate and I drove down from Boston."

"Tina and I took a bus to D.C."

"I don't know if Frankie ever told you, but Operation Rescue was at the clinic that day," said Fern, and by now they all knew what day she was talking about. "He said he'd never eat Domino's pizza again because the owner gave money to them."

"That sounds like him," said Theresa. "I remember how worried I was when he stopped going to mass, but Frankie has a strong moral compass that has nothing to do with organized religion." She glanced at Alice. "You won't believe who was on the bus with us the day we went to Washington."

Alice, who understood that this was a rhetorical question, didn't bother to hazard a guess, though she was surprised to learn that it was Fernando and Marco.

"What were they doing at a women's march?" she asked Theresa, who said, "I asked them the same thing, and they said they were marching for us so that someday we'd march for them." She paused dramatically. "I guess enough of us did because they got married last year."

"Wait, Fernando got married?" said Alice. "Did you go to the wedding?"

"I catered it."

"It's funny how so many people objected to same-sex marriage because they thought of it as a threat to their way of life and the sanctity of marriage," said Nina, "but what about us? I'm divorced, Theresa's divorced and—" She glanced at Alice. "You've been divorced twice. Meanwhile, Fernando and Marco are still together."

"I can't imagine how hard it must have been for them to keep their relationship a secret all those years," said Alice.

"I went to see Oscar Wilde's grave at Père Lachaise when I was in Paris," said Nina. They all knew that story: convicted of gross indecency and sentenced to two years' hard labor. "His gravestone was covered with red lipstick kisses."

"*A kiss may ruin a human life*," said Alice. "It's a line in one of his plays."

"Well, you better hope Hillary gets elected because Mike Pence will make it his mission to see that *Roe* is overturned," said Fern, "and then he'll go after same-sex marriage."

"I don't think we have anything to worry about," said Alice. "She's way ahead in the polls."

———— ◆ ————

EARLY THAT EVENING while everyone else was packing, Alice walked to the cove at the end of the Promenade. She had always loved the golden hour just before sunset when the light was softer than any other time of day. Looking out across the Atlantic Ocean, she imagined a place just beyond the horizon where time was only a construct just as she had once imagined it from her vantage point at Zuma Beach.

Alice had Kiki to thank for her interest in metaphysics. They had spent hours in Alice's apartment in Laurel Canyon discussing the philosophy inherent in Frank Herbert's *Dune* series. "*The mystery of life isn't a problem to solve, but a reality to experience*," was one of Kiki's favorite quotes by the author, who she claimed to have met and become friends with in 1978 when he was a featured speaker at a science fiction convention in Santa Rosa, California. While Alice would have been inclined to dismiss the story as a total fabrication if she'd heard it from anyone else, she took Kiki at her word because, quite simply, Kiki was one of those people who had lived an extraordinary life.

Now Alice recalled something else Kiki had attributed to Herbert: *Deep in the human unconscious is a pervasive need for a logical universe that makes sense. But the real universe is always one step behind logic.* Alice wondered if Kiki would be amused that she was still looking for absolutes in a universe that, according to Herbert, made no logical sense.

A small group of people began gathering at the western end of the promenade for the lowering of the flag. It had been a tradition at Sunset Beach since the late 1950s, attracting veterans from World War II, Korea, Vietnam and now, Alice imagined, Iraq and Afghanistan. Etiquette required that the flag be raised briskly and lowered slowly and ceremoniously. The sky was streaked with orange when the flag began its slow descent. A few volunteers removed it from the flagpole before folding it into its traditional triangular shape, stripes first, a total of thirteen times, while over the loudspeaker Kate Smith sang, "God Bless America." A few men placed their caps back on their heads as the crowd began to disperse.

Alice had never been particularly patriotic (she and her father had argued vehemently about Vietnam), but there was something moving about the ceremony she'd just observed, which was meant to honor duty and sacrifice. She couldn't help but think about Nina's husband, Ethan, who made the ultimate sacrifice in Vietnam. Alice had never met her father's brother Harold who was killed at Omaha Beach. Like so many others of their generation, her parents didn't seem to question everything (organized religion, the government, the inherent unfairness of life in general) the way Alice and her generation did. Now she wondered if perhaps there was something to be said for tradition, the glue that had held cultures and communities together for centuries.

Alice's father had served with distinction in the Pacific Theater, and she remembered that his casket had been draped with a flag donated by the U.S. Department of Veterans Affairs. When a military officer presented the flag to Alice and her sister after the funeral, Audrey's son Jason asked why it was folded thirteen times. The officer explained that the thirteen folds were based on the religious principles upon which the country was founded. He had enumerated each step for her nephew. One: a symbol of life. Two: a symbol of our belief in eternal life. Alice couldn't remember the rest, but she realized that what she had always wanted for Lily was eternal life. Why was it so hard to imagine?

Watching the sun disappear behind the distant lighthouse, Alice experienced a profound sense of wonder and awe. What had Einstein believed? That the past, present and future were only a stubbornly persistent illusion? If that were true, she reasoned, then perhaps nothing was ever really lost. Perhaps just beyond her range of vision where a cloudless sky met the azure sea, Grace and Lily, exactly as she remembered them, were waiting to welcome her and Nina when they finally arrived.

Epilogue

January 21, 2017

Ostensibly, the march was about women's rights with a nod to issues like race, immigration, healthcare, gender and social justice. Not only were women taking to the streets in cities all over the world, they were bringing their daughters with them. So, on a cold day in January, Alice, Nina, Harper and Hayley joined three generations of Moretti women—Theresa, Tina, Olivia and Lily—in the nation's capital. Fern and Emma would be watching the march on television with Charlotte, who didn't feel up to the trip.

Because Harper and Hayley lived in Manhattan, they suggested that everyone meet there so they could all take the Acela Express to Washington. At Penn Station, Alice and Harper agreed to keep an eye on Frankie's daughter while everyone else scattered—Nina to Hudson Booksellers, Theresa to Magnolia Bakery, Hayley to Starbucks, and Tina and Olivia to Vans where Olivia hoped to talk her mother into a new pair of checkerboard slip-ons.

A strand of long, dark hair had gotten snarled in the thin gold chain Harper wore around her neck, and she asked Alice to untangle it. "It was Grace's. I found it in her jewelry box after she died," she said with a wistful smile. "I never take it off."

Alice suggested that it had become a kind of totem, and Harper agreed.

Hayley, juggling a biodegradable cup holder, dispensed the drinks: a hot chocolate for Lily, a cappuccino for Alice and a Flat White for her sister. "Just the way you like it."

The twins had made posters, and Harper asked Alice what she thought of hers: THE GUN LOBBY IS MAKING A KILLING ON GUN SALES.

"Ever since Sandy Hook she's been obsessed with gun reform," Hayley explained.

Harper removed the lid from her coffee. "I wouldn't say I'm obsessed. I just don't think there's any reason why someone should be able to buy an AR-15, which is basically a weapon of mass destruction." She gave her sister a playful shove. "I'm sure you could give Alice an earful about sexual assault in this country."

Hayley shrugged. "It's an epidemic. That's all I'm going to say."

Over the loudspeaker, a garbled voice announced a departure from track ten in fifteen minutes.

"Don't worry, our train doesn't leave for another half hour," said Harper, sensing Alice's apprehension.

Alice stole a glance at Lily, who was engrossed in a book. "What are you reading?" she asked her.

She held up the tattered paperback: *The Wind in the Willows*.

"My daughter loved that book," Alice told her, remembering how she'd read entire chapters to Lily while she hovered between life and death all those years ago.

"I know. My dad told me."

Alice glanced at Lily before quickly turning away. "Did he say anything else about her?"

"Only that she died when she was really, really young and that she was the best person he ever knew." She came to sit next to Alice and placed one hand lightly on her forearm. "I was named after her."

Alice lowered her eyes. "I know."

"What was *her* favorite chapter?"

"The one where Rat and Mole meet the great god Pan," Alice told her, and Lily nodded vigorously. "Mine too!"

Alice smiled.

"Know how Pan blessed them with the gift of forgetfulness?" She glanced at Alice, who nodded. "Sometimes I wish I could do that for my mom and dad." She grew quiet, her expressive brown eyes a well of sadness and compassion. "I used to hear them talking about what happened, and they seemed so sad."

"You know the accidents weren't their fault, right?"

Lily sighed deeply. "I know."

They both saw Theresa approaching. "Who wants one?" she asked, opening a pastry box to reveal a dozen cupcakes in pastel colors.

"I want the pink one," said Lily, "and maybe the blue one, too."

"Wait until we see if we have enough for everyone," Theresa told her.

"She can have mine," said Alice, glancing at Lily.

"Are you sure you don't want one? They're really, really good."

"Lily is the cupcake aficionado," said Theresa, and Lily giggled.

Now Nina was back with a book about the private lives of the Impressionists.

Harper helped herself to a cupcake with yellow frosting.

"I was just telling Alice about how Dad tried to talk us into going to law school like he did," she told her mother.

"But we resisted," said Hayley with a smug smile.

"Wait, remember what he told us a couple of years ago? That it would have been a waste of money because we would have probably gone to work for Neighborhood Legal Services or some other do-gooder organization." Harper put the words do-gooder in air quotes. "He has no soul."

Alice was inclined to agree, but then she had never thought much of Paul.

"So, I have enough of these for everyone," said Tina, reaching into her backpack and removing one pink wool hat after another.

Theresa examined hers closely. "What are these things on top?"

"They're ears, Mother. Pussycat ears."

"I don't get it."

Tina rolled her eyes just like she did as a teenager when Theresa was being obtuse. "Remember how he said women let him grab them by the pussy? This is us reclaiming that word and throwing it back in his face."

"Watch your language," said Theresa, gesturing toward Olivia, who removed her ear buds.

"I've heard the word pussy before, Grandma," she said. "It's no big deal."

"You're ten," Theresa reminded her.

Another eye roll, this one from Olivia.

Gathering up their things, they boarded the nonstop to D.C. Alice took a seat next to Nina, who was examining a portrait by Mary Cassatt: *Little Girl in a Blue Armchair*.

"This picture is in the National Gallery of Art in Washington," she told Alice. "I wish we could see it while we're there."

"Maybe next time," Alice said because she hoped that this reunion would not be their last.

As soon as the train pulled into Union Station, Theresa began issuing instructions. "Let's stay together. I don't want us to lose each other."

Nina squeezed her hand. "Don't worry, we're not going to lose each other again, not after twenty years."

Theresa removed a bottle of water from her bag and took a swig. "I heard Gloria Steinem will be here," she told Alice. "She's eighty-three for Christ's sake. Don't you think she'd rather be at home binge-watching *Grace and Frankie*?"

"She's been an activist forever," said Alice. "It's in her blood."

"Well, maybe it's time to pass the torch."

"To who?"

"America Ferrera," said Harper. "Ashley Judd."

"Janet Mock," said Hayley, glancing over at Alice, who had to know who she was talking about. Alice had been the cool mom when they were growing up, the one who seemed to know everything.

"Who's Janet Mock?" asked Theresa.

"The transgender rights activist," said Alice, and Hayley gave her a high five.

There was a long line of people at the closest metro station so they decided to walk.

"Let me hear it loud and clear," the twins sang out. "Refugees are welcome here." Other young women their age picked up the chant.

The sky was overcast as they marched down Pennsylvania Avenue. Harper, who had been checking her Twitter feed, reported that there were almost half a million people marching up Fifth Avenue in New York and another 750,000 in Los Angeles. "Kind of makes you feel part of something bigger than we are, doesn't it?"

Alice took in the diverse crowd of people. Nearly everyone carried some kind of homemade sign: BLACK GIRLS ROCK, THERE IS NO PLANET B, HATE HAS NO HOME HERE.

If after Lily's death Alice had felt like she'd stepped through the looking glass into a strange and mysterious world where time moved backward, lately she seemed to be moving forward toward something she didn't quite understand, though it felt important. For years she had nursed the notion that marrying Bill and leaving Chicago had been a mistake, yet it was precisely because of that decision that she'd met the women who had become her best friends. Perhaps their friendship had been *hitsuzen*, which Kiki had described all those years ago as a state in which other outcomes are impossible.

Charlotte and Nina and Theresa had included her in their circle, which had widened to include their children and grandchildren. Up ahead, Olivia waved at them from her perch high on Tina's shoulders, and Alice's first thought was that life was unpredictable but that sometimes it surprised you.

Now Lily tugged at Alice's hand, and as they fell in step with thousands of other women, a wave of pink hats and raised fists and homemade banners that rolled all the way to the White House, Alice felt an existential connection to the universe with all its inherent messiness, joy, fear, sadness and surprise. She searched for Theresa and Nina in the crowd of people—young and old, Black and white, gay and straight—and when they turned in unison as if willed to do so, she knew that they felt it, too.

ACKNOWLEDGMENTS

There are a number of people who believed in this book enough to read first and second drafts, offering insightful suggestions. Bonnie Brown came up with the idea of giving Charlotte a secret. After reading several chapters, Monte Schulz's assessment was that they were "vastly underwritten." Nina's solo trip to Paris soared once I followed his advice. Kathy McFarland and Laura Hanifin were careful readers, who caught typos and any number of other errors. My daughter Erin Dougherty, a gifted writer in her own right, offered sage advice, and my longtime friend Renne Barolet shared a few hilarious stories with me that made their way into this novel. Diane Corey, who was a public health nurse for more than thirty years, helped me navigate hospital protocol. I have Walter Claudio to thank for the expression, "The mystery of selection is tragic." Jane St. Clair, whose writing is pure poetry, has provided encouragement and support since we met at the Santa Barbara Writers Conference nearly thirty years ago. Yes, that's how long I've been at this. Through it all, my grandson Evan's faith in me never wavered. "It's your destiny, Grandma," he reminded me when I despaired of even finishing this novel let alone finding a publisher.

I learned so much about the craft of writing from Sid Stebel, the "greatest writing teacher that ever was" to paraphrase Ray Bradbury. Sid invited me to join the Chautauqua Writers Group, which he and Ray had been part of since the 1960s. With Sid at the helm, the group evolved over the years, and after his death his wife Karen Ford became our fearless leader. My heartfelt thanks goes out to Karen Ford, Ted Humphrey, Dyanne Asimow, Gwendolyn Irby, Andrew Loschert, Barbara La Salle, Gaylen Grody and Nancy Klann for listening attentively to each chapter of this novel and offering notes and suggestions that made it better.

Why authors tackle the subjects they do is a bit of a mystery, but often it is to make sense of life's vicissitudes. In 1996, my oldest daughter Rachel survived a traumatic brain injury after a horrific car accident that altered the course of her life. While I was spared the heartbreak of losing her, three of my closest friends were not so fortunate. Who among us would want to know what the future holds in store for us? The novelist Ursula K. Le Guin put it best when she wrote: *The only thing that makes life possible is permanent intolerable uncertainty: not knowing what comes next.*

Lori Zepponi was my Nina. She had three children under the age of five when she moved into the house across the street from me, and we were there for each other through good times and bad. We watched our children grow up, but neither of us could have anticipated that she would lose her daughter Valerie in 2001 and her son Ryan in 2018, a cruel twist of fate for which there is no explanation (*the mystery of selection is tragic*).

I met Linda Bloom in high school. She called her son Matthew her "beautiful boy," and she missed him every day for the rest of her life after he was killed by a drunk driver in 2005. Linda told me about Compassionate Friends, which helped her enormously.

Claudia Clemente was my college roommate and a force of nature. Her children and grandchildren call her Queen

CC and rightly so. Claudia and her husband Frank raised eight children, four of which were adopted. Two years ago, they lost their son Cale, who had been part of their family since he was two years old.

The resilience of these remarkable women in the face of unspeakable loss was the inspiration for this novel. Sadly, two of them will never read this book, which they championed from the beginning. Linda died of pneumonia in 2020, Lori in 2021 of complications from Covid. Linda's daughter Jenny and Lori's daughter Tara are their only surviving children.

Here's the thing about old friends: They are your memory keepers, the people who know you better than anyone. I'd give anything to hear Linda's contagious laugh again or see Lori's name show up on my iPhone as in incoming call. What brings me comfort is imagining that they have been reunited with the children they loved, perhaps in another dimension beyond time and space where nothing is ever truly lost.

Made in the USA
Las Vegas, NV
13 March 2024